Praise for

#1 National Bestselling Regency Romance

"This book is a joy. Loved every page. Keep a fan handy, the sex scenes are some of the best written erotic scenes...hot hot hot!!" -Miriam, *Goodreads*

"This book has easily become one of my favorites....If you love Elizabeth Hoyt, I strongly suggest this book for you!" -Sara, *Goodreads*

"Ambrose and Marianne are complete opposites and they somehow end up being absolutely perfect for each other. Their romance is sexy, heartfelt, and so swoonworthy... Whenever the usually coolheaded Ambrose loses control, the pages of the book are in serious danger of burning up." -*Romance Library*

"Grace Callaway literally captivates me with her deep and complex characters and unique and suspenseful plots. Angst, lust and intrigue all in equal, perfect measure. This story was both a moving and heartwrenching nail-biter and one of the steamiest and most thrilling books I've read." -Dagmar, *Goodreads*

"In my experience of reading hundreds of HR books by hundreds of authors, no one, NOT ONE SINGLE AUTHOR, EVEN MY FAVES LIKE KLEYPAS OR HOYT OR DARE, can write sex scenes like Callaway does." -Sara, *Goodreads*

"Ambrose is one of those perfect romance heroes—strong, intensely passionate and over protective. Totally swoon-worthy." -Nancy, *Goodreads*

"I loved the heroine, she is so strong and determined and smart, and the hero is her perfect equal in every way. The storyline behind her past is truly captivating and there were scenes where I literally had to put the book down because I was sobbing (especially one scene that made me so happy I cried like a baby). I recommend this book with all my heart!" -MTC, *Goodreads*

"*Her Protector's Pleasure* is a must-read for those who like their historical romance with plenty of adventure, humor, and sizzling hot sex." -*The Indie Voice*

"I really enjoy the way Callaway portrays this desperate love between her characters...and the intimate scenes despite being erotic is so romantically written that you can't help but enjoy it." -Gilgamesha, *Goodreads*

"I loved Ambrose. He is one of the best heroes ever and Marianne was a great heroine as well--very strong but nevertheless vulnerable and with some flaws. Their relationship developed slowly; although there was an instant attraction, Mrs. Callaway did not take the easy way and let them develop their feelings." -Claudia, *Goodreads*

"Highly recommend this if you enjoyed books like *Lady Sophia's Lover* or *Marrying Winterbourne* and crave that same fiercely protective/stoic but mostly soft countenance/self-made hero archetype—in this book, you'll get all of that and more." -Shaira, *Goodreads*

Also by Grace Callaway

MAYHEM IN MAYFAIR

Her Husband's Harlot

Her Wanton Wager

Her Protector's Pleasure

Her Prodigal Passion

HEART OF ENQUIRY (The Kents)

The Widow Vanishes (Prequel Novella)

The Duke Who Knew Too Much

M is for Marquess

The Lady Who Came in from the Cold

The Viscount Always Knocks Twice

Never Say Never to an Earl

The Gentleman Who Loved Me

GAME OF DUKES

The Duke Identity

Enter the Duke

Regarding the Duke

The Duke Redemption

The Return of the Duke

Steamy Winter Wishes (A Holiday Short Story)

LADY CHARLOTTE'S SOCIETY OF ANGELS

HER
Protector's
PLEASURE

Mayhem
IN MAYFAIR

BOOK THREE

GRACE
CALLAWAY

USA TODAY BESTSELLING AUTHOR

Cover Art: Chris Coccozza

Typography & Book Design: KM Designs

Formatting: Colchester & Page

Chapter One

Lady Marianne Draven studied the window display. Though she was a widow and had lost her innocence before her marriage, the offering behind the glass caused a wary flutter beneath the bodice of her sea-green sarcenet. She was all for extravagant shopping, but this night's expedition was no traipse down Bond Street. On the other side of the glass, the man lounged on a scarlet daybed like a Roman god. He wore a short toga that left little of his muscular form to the imagination. Tossing his dark curls, he gave her a smoldering, come-hither look.

Marianne suppressed a shudder as the proprietress chuckled beside her.

"Prime quality, ain't he, milady?" Dressed in a pink, beribboned gown and painted as brightly as a doll, Mrs. Wilson ought to have looked silly. Instead, the contrast between the girlish get-up and the madam's hard features served to heighten her aura of ruthlessness. "You said you wanted the best, and 'ere 'e is."

Marianne masked her unease by raising a brow. "I'm afraid this specimen is a bit common for my taste, Mrs. Wilson," she drawled.

"But Ernesto is my most popular stud. 'E's in 'igh demand

with duchesses and countesses alike," the bawd protested. "'Ave another look, dearie, and you'll see what I mean."

Stifling her impatience, Marianne looked to the glass again. Mrs. Wilson gave a nod of her improbable black curls, and in response the gigolo bent one sinewy leg. The white folds of the toga parted, falling open at the groin.

"The *Italian Stallion*, that's what they call 'im," the madam said with satisfaction.

As if to prove that point, the man gripped his erect and undoubtedly horse-like attribute. He stroked from root to tip, lingering at the blood-engorged dome. Marianne swallowed a sudden panicky laugh.

Lud. What in blazes am I doing here?

The *ton*, of course, wouldn't blink an eye to see the notorious Baroness Draven at a male brothel. Indeed, Marianne had cultivated her reputation for debauchery with care: she'd needed the status of a voluptuary to gain access into this exclusive establishment. She alone knew her true purpose.

Ever since Draven's death—God rot his soul—she'd been searching for her heart's one desire. A memory slipped free from the tightly locked box inside her heart. She saw a beautiful babe with shiny corn-silk curls and wide jade eyes. Clinging to a bench in a sun-washed garden, the little cherub stood on wobbly legs, gurgling a sound so close to *Mama*. Marianne felt again the grass beneath her knees, the proud yet anxious flutter of her pulse as she held out her arms and called out words of encouragement.

You can do it, Rosie. Just take one step at a time. Come to Mama.

Marianne's fingers curled inside her satin gloves as talons of longing clawed at her breast. It had been seven years since she'd last seen Primrose. The loss had continued to fester and would never heal until she had her babe back in her arms once more.

Eyes gritty, Marianne told herself she'd *know* if anything had happened to Primrose. Day by day, she could still feel that bond, the connection that had been forged between them from the moment she'd held her child to her breast and felt selfless love for the first time. Love that would see her through any trial, including the one she currently faced: within the walls of this brothel lay her last remaining lead to her precious daughter, and she had to find him. To get the information she needed, at any cost.

I'm coming for you, Rosie. Wait for me.

"So you'll take Ernesto?" Mrs. Wilson said brightly.

Marianne let her lips form a cool smile. During the five hellish years of her marriage, she'd learned to control her emotions. She'd had to. Boxing up sentiment had been a means of survival; now, three years after Draven's death, she rarely examined what had been placed inside. Composure had become her armor.

"He's not what I'm looking for," she said.

"But you've already seen all my stables," the bawd said in a wheedling tone, waving her jewel-crusted fingers to the hallway behind them, "and you still 'aven't made a choice."

Marianne wished she could wash her memory clean of Mrs. Wilson's famed "stables," which consisted of a long row of glass viewing rooms. Within each one, studs like Ernesto showed off their goods in the manner of auction day at Tattersall's. Prime flesh strutted out and sold to the highest bidder. Marianne hid her shudder.

Men in glass houses ... I suppose there is something apropos to that.

With deliberate insouciance, she said, "Not *all* your stables, I believe."

"I don't know what you mean, milady." Mrs. Wilson's gaze sharpened, and coupled with her beaky nose, her expression became hawk-like. Predatory.

Marianne's nape tingled with caution. She had labored too long, too tirelessly, to show her hand now. In the three years she'd spent searching for Rosie in London, she'd discovered that vice looked after its own. Gaining the subscription to Mrs. Wilson's had proved more arduous than obtaining vouchers to Almack's. If she roused the bawd's suspicions now, she'd be tossed out of Covent Garden, any chance of finding her daughter dashed.

You're supposed to be a lascivious widow. Bloody hell act like one.

"I'm told you have a prize mount," she said, "one whose blood runs not only hot, but possibly blue as well. And I've heard you might allow your favored clients a ride on occasion."

"Where'd you 'ear that?" the madam demanded.

"Word gets around, Mrs. Wilson. I want the best your establishment has to offer, and I'm willing to pay for it." Marianne paused. "A *royal* sum, in point of fact."

The bawd's eyes hooded in a considering manner. Marianne had made a bold move, and she prayed it would pay off. It was no small matter, after all, to request the company of the madam's own lover. According to Marianne's sources, Andrew Corbett was an Adonis in his twenties, the bastard son of an actress and, if one was to believe gossip, the current King. Due to his good looks and questionably exalted heritage, Corbett had made a niche for himself as a *cicisbeo* to rich, older women. Currently, he lived under lock and key as Mrs. Wilson's pampered pet.

Emotions played across the older woman's hard, powdered features. Anger, ambivalence ... and ah, yes, the leverage Marianne had been counting on. Greed.

Mrs. Wilson said in brittle tones, "So 'tis my own dear Corby you're after then, eh?"

God, yes, Marianne wanted Andrew Corbett. Not for carnal purposes, but for his possible connection to her daughter's disappearance. After the years of searching, of dead ends and betrayal by those who had promised to help her, Marianne had no other leads left. Corbett was her last hope.

"'Twould be a loan of one night, Mrs. Wilson." She kept her tone calm; it wouldn't help negotiations to seem too eager. Smoothing a wrinkle from her gloves, she said, "I confess I am curious to experience first-hand what all the brouhaha is about."

The other woman sniffed. "The talk ain't exaggeration, if that's what you're gettin' at. My Corby's a cut above the rest. A prince amongst men."

"And the price for an audience with his highness?" Marianne inquired.

"You can't afford 'im."

"Try me."

The bawd's blackened eyelashes lowered. When she raised them, the candlelight glinted like guineas in her pupils. "A thousand pounds."

"Five hundred."

"Won't let 'im go for less than nine."

"Let us split the difference. Seven hundred pounds for one night. My final offer, Mrs. Wilson." Seeing the other's lips tremble, Marianne felt the thrill of victory. In truth, she'd have paid a thousand for Corbett, but had bargained to appear less keen.

"We 'ave a deal." The madam held out a hand.

Marianne withdrew crisp, folded banknotes from her reticule. Predictably, Mrs. Wilson counted the stack. The bundle disappeared into her pink chiffon skirts.

"Come this way," the bawd said.

Marianne followed the proprietress down the plush corridor of scarlet and gilt. Paintings of couples tangled in sexual poses lined the walls, the air heavy with the scent of musk and roses. As they passed a series of doors, Marianne's belly tightened at the sound of muffled moaning, yet she kept her step sedate, her expression indolent. The corridor came to an end at a pair of ebony doors painted with golden stars.

"You'll 'ave the Arabian Suite—nothin' but the best for Corby." Mrs. Wilson dangled a key from her fingers. "Room and food's extra."

No doubt Marianne would be paying through the nose for half-rate caviar and watered champagne. Nonetheless, she inclined her head. "Of course."

"And there's to be no namby-pamby talk of love or any such thing." Mrs. Wilson's lips thinned as she raked a glance over Marianne. "Usually talk o' a lady's looks is exaggerated, but you *are* a stunner. I got eyes to see why the Mayfair lot's fallen elbows o'er arse for you." She paused, the menace in her tone unmistakable. "But my Corby's 'eart's off limits, you 'ear me?"

"I have no interest in that particular organ," Marianne said.

Mrs. Wilson sniffed. "You 'aven't seen 'im as yet."

"Surely you trust your paramour, if not me?"

"*Trust* Corby? Why would I do that?" The bawd snorted. "'E may be a prince, but 'e's still a man."

And men could not be trusted. On this issue, she and the madam were in perfect accord. Experience had repeatedly proven to Marianne that putting faith in any male led to disastrous consequences; she'd never make that mistake again.

"Go on in, then," the other woman grumbled as she unlocked the doors. "I'll 'ave Corby fetched."

Alone in the chamber, Marianne tamed her anticipation by perusing her new surroundings. Mrs. Wilson certainly had a knack for setting the stage. At the center of the room, sheer ivory panels cascaded from the ceiling to create a tent-like effect. Jewel-toned reclining cushions lined the interior of the canopy; at the thought of the activities conducted upon those pillows, Marianne cringed and made note to carry out the night's business standing.

She walked the perimeter of the room, searching for viewing holes in the gold-on-gold damask wallpaper. She found four. From her reticule, she produced small squares of black velvet and a tiny bottle of adhesive, and she proceeded to plug the cavities.

For seven hundred pounds, she expected a modicum of privacy.

She would need it for the subject she planned to discuss. Her palms dampened as she reviewed her options for interrogating Corbett. She planned to begin by luring with honey rather than vinegar. Yet if sweetness and money failed, she had an alternate plan. One that rested, pearl-handled and loaded, in the hidden pocket of her skirts. She was no stranger to the use of weapons; her jaw hardened as she recalled the last discharge of her pistol.

For months, Marianne had paid a Bow Street Runner named Burke Skinner to help her find Rosie. He'd kept her subsisting on crumbs of information—and all the while he'd kept the loaf to himself. He'd bled her for more and more money, and desperate for any news of her daughter, she had paid. But when he'd wanted more than coin for payment, when he'd had the temerity to demand that she perform sexual favors for his services ...

Marianne's fingers curled around the delicate stem of the pistol; gaining Corbett's name had come at no small price. The knock on the door yanked her from her thoughts.

Never mind the past. Focus on Corbett. He's your last hope.

"Come in," she said.

The doors parted, and a tall, bronze-haired gentleman strode in. Marianne could see why Andrew Corbett was considered the stuff of female fantasies. He had the face of Narcissus: high cheekbones, squared jaw, full lips. His blue silk dressing gown was figured with silver dragons and molded to his athletic form. His velvety brown eyes traveled with practiced sensuality over her. Closing the door, he strutted over and issued an elegant leg.

"My lady," he said in accents clearly polished through elocution lessons, "has anyone ever told you how beautiful you are?"

Only about every man I've ever met. The inanity was hardly surprising. From what Marianne had gleaned, Corbett's fame had little to do with his wit.

"How kind of you," she said. "Consider the compliment returned."

"Thank you," he said, preening. "We are a pair, are we not?"

A silence ensued, during which Marianne wondered if she was expected to continue this idiotic game of dousing the butter boat. Surely not. Suddenly, Corbett reached out and ran a finger along her upper arm; beneath her sleeve, her skin crawled. She jerked away.

"Skittish, are we?" he murmured. "Never fear, fair lady. Corby's got a gentle touch."

Corby's going to lose a hand if he touches me again.

"I'd like a drink, if you please," she said, keeping her voice even.

"Whatever the lady wishes." Winking at her, he sauntered on long legs over to the bucket of champagne. He filled two flutes and carried them to the tent. "Shall we make ourselves more comfortable?" he said, nodding toward the cushions.

"I am perfectly comfortable where I am." Seeing the uncertainty ripple across his features, she warned herself to rein it in. In a softer tone, she said, "Could we talk for a few minutes?"

Doubt clouded his gaze. "About what?"

"I'd like to know more about you. 'Tis difficult for a lady to be at ease with a stranger ... even if he is as handsome as sin." Marianne made a moue, a coquettish gesture designed to lay waste to male defenses.

Corbett brightened immediately. He came over and handed her a glass of the champagne. "I'll tell you anything you want to know, my love."

She sipped, pretending to ponder. "Have you been here long?"

"Three years, give or take."

"And you enjoy ... your work?" she said delicately.

Color spread over his perfect cheekbones. *Interesting—so he's not quite as debonair as he appears.* She tucked the information away for later.

"What's not to enjoy when I get to spend time in the company of a lady as lovely as yourself, eh?" he said lightly.

Well turned. Her opinion of Corbett rose—which made her proceed with greater caution. "And before Mrs. Wilson? What were you doing then?" she said innocently.

He blinked. "This and that. Nothing of import." Downing his

champagne, he set the glass aside. "Now why don't you let me show you—"

She stepped out of his reach and made the calculation. No more pretenses; time to hit the nail directly on the head. "But, you see, your time with Kitty Barnes *is* of import to me," she said in a low yet clear voice. "And it is the reason I am here tonight."

The color drained from his face. His eyes darted to the peep holes, his brows shooting up at the sight of the velvet buffers.

"I've ensured our privacy," she said.

"Who are you?" he said. "What do you want?"

"I want to know where Kitty Barnes is," she said.

"I—I don't know what you're talking about."

"You were with her for several years, albeit under a different name. By all the accounts, the two of you shared a connection beyond that of employer and employee. Then Kitty disappeared three years ago—the most infamous and successful bawd of her time *gone*"—Marianne snapped her fingers—"as if she never existed. I want to know where she is."

"Why? Because she owes you blunt?" Some hidden reserve lifted Corbett's chin. "Well, get in queue. But you and the rest of the cutthroats and moneylenders are bound for disappointment. Kitty's not coming back. I don't know where she is, and even if I did, I wouldn't tell you."

"You think this is about a thing as paltry as money?" Fury thrumming in her veins, Marianne removed a folded piece of parchment from her reticule. She held it up to Corbett's face.

"What the devil is that?" he said, trying to push her away.

She did not budge. "A receipt. For my *daughter*."

Corbett stilled. In that instant, a spasm gripped Marianne's heart: hope fiercer than pain. He *knew* something.

"I found this amongst my husband's belongings after he died. The date lines up with when he kidnapped my daughter Primrose —stole her from her nursery where she lay sleeping." Grief and rage made Marianne's hand tremble as she held the receipt higher, reciting the words branded into memory.

"*To Baron Draven: Your package and the five hundred pounds have been received. As discussed, monthly payments of fifty pounds will be required for its ongoing care. Your servant, Kitty Barnes.*" Marianne's breath burned in her lungs. "That *package* was my daughter. And I will have her back."

Corbett stared at her. "But I don't understand. Why would your husband kidnap his own daughter and put her in Kitty's care?"

Because Primrose was not Draven's child. Because though Draven had vowed before marriage to take care of the bastard growing inside Marianne's womb, he had resented every moment Marianne had spent with her newborn girl. He'd resented that and the fact that motherhood had made Marianne strong, resilient in the face of his cruelties. And because of that, he had taken Primrose away and used an innocent's life to keep Marianne a slave to his whims.

Guilt, shame—no time for that now. Later, Marianne would punish herself anew for her recklessness, her stupidity. For now she had to concentrate on getting Primrose back.

"My daughter has paid for my mistakes." The words abraded her throat. "I will do anything to find her. What is it that you want in exchange for information of her whereabouts, Mr. Corbett? Money? I have plenty of it. Name your price."

Corbett continued to stare at her. Lines flickered at the sides of his mouth.

"I can't do this here," he said in a low voice.

Her heart quickened. "Where, then?"

"I'll come to you." With a quick glance around, he raked his hands through his hair, mussing the coiffed curls.

When he began to untie his robe, Marianne narrowed her eyes. "What are you doing?"

"Mrs. Wilson will be inspecting us when we emerge from our

love nest." He parted the brocade, exposing his naked, sculpted form. Cheeks burning, Marianne looked away as he continued in matter-of-fact tones, "She'll expect to find the usual signs of fornication—she likes to examine me *post coitus*. If you don't want your motive exposed, you had best do something about yourself, too." He paused, cocking a brow. "Unless you'd care to exchange a helping hand?"

At that, Marianne cast him a withering look.

"Right-o," he muttered. "I'll keep my hands and my eyes to myself." So saying, he turned his broad shoulders. The jerking of his arm left no doubt as to how he meant to pass his employer's scrutiny.

Her stomach knotting, Marianne retreated a few steps back. She'd do anything to regain Rosie, and for the first time in a very long while, she saw a faint glimmer on the dark horizon. She let out a resigned breath. With a slight tremor to her hand, she reached for her bodice.

Chapter Two

The tavern was noisy, smoky, and to Ambrose Kent's mind, a dismal place to interview for a job. Yet Sir Gerald Coyner had suggested meeting at The White Hart rather than the Bow Street offices, and wanting to get things off on the right foot with the magistrate—and, potentially, his future employer—Ambrose had agreed.

In the decade he'd spent working for the Thames River Police, Ambrose had learned to judge a man's character quickly. When training new recruits, Ambrose emphasized two things: observation and patience. Being a successful waterman, in his view, was less about brute force and more about collecting facts, missing no details, and waiting for the pieces to come together.

For instance, he could tell a lot about Coyner from the quarter hour they'd spent together. Well-nourished and dressed in fashionable clothes, Coyner was obviously a man of means. Without so much as a glance at the menu, he'd ordered the most expensive items the tavern had to offer. His accent was educated, yet not of the highest class, and though his thinning brown hair and lined features put him in his fifth decade, he wore no wedding band. He had the fastidious habits of a man who lived on his own, wiping his mustache after each sip from his foaming tankard.

Ambrose looked down at his own barely touched ale. Though the amber liquid had tasted smooth and delicious and his stomach was growling, he had to stretch the drink to make it last the duration of the meeting. As it was, he'd had to choose between that single beverage and a hackney ride home afterward—he hadn't coin enough for both.

Which focused him on his goal: he needed money. His full-time position with the River Police could not provide what was required, so he had to secure additional employment. He cleared his throat, readying to make his pitch for contract work with Bow Street.

Before he could speak, the serving wench returned to the table.

"'Ere you go, sir." Red-haired and plump-cheeked, the woman's generous bosom jiggled as she set a platter heaped with beef and creamed potatoes in front of the magistrate.

Ambrose swallowed; typically, his stringent self-discipline overrode his impulses, but now 'twas as if all his hungers were spread before him. For food ... and for female companionship. Thinking of Jane—of her dark, laughing eyes and bountiful curves—he experienced a pang.

Did you think I'd wait around forever, Ambrose? I may be a widow, but I'm still young, and I've got a future ahead of me. You had a choice: me or your family—and as you've made your decision, I've made mine. I won't go down with a sinking ship.

Though a year had passed, the loss of Jane still stung. Yet he understood: it had been too much to ask of Jane or any woman to tie herself to a man with his troubles. He *had* put his family first, and given the same scenario, he'd do so again.

The family is counting on you. Buck up, man, and get the job done.

"Rare an' juicy—the way gents like it," the wench said, winking at Coyner.

With a disinterested nod, the magistrate cut into his beef.

She swiveled to Ambrose, her tone losing its friendly sauce. "An' you, sir? Nothin' more than the ale?"

Ambrose felt his cheekbones heat. "No, thank you," he said.

"Up to you." Her plump lips curled with disdain. "Though you could use some meat on those bones, if you ask me."

Ambrose was not unused to such comments. Hovering at six feet and a goodly number of inches besides, he'd been lanky to begin with; now, having made do on a steady diet of bread and cheese for months, he was approaching rawboned. He saw no reason to defend himself against what was fact, however. He took no stock in personal vanity.

Coyner spoke up. "That's enough lip from you, miss. Don't you have customers to see to?"

Flipping her hair over her shoulders, the wench sauntered off.

Coyner's brow furrowed, knife and fork suspended above his plate. "Sure you don't want anything, Kent? Hate to eat alone. My treat, eh?"

"Thank you, but I'm not hungry." Though he might not have two shillings to rub together, Ambrose still had his pride. "Please enjoy your supper. If you don't mind, however, I'd like to discuss an opportunity to work with Bow Street."

The other man swallowed a mouthful. "Your reputation precedes you, Kent. From what I hear, you're a dedicated member of the Thames River Police. Made Principle Surveyor over at Wapping Station—though by my reckoning it took too long for a man of your talent." The magistrate gave him a keen look. "Not much for politics, eh?"

If by politics, Coyner meant toadying up to Ambrose's own magistrate and superior, John Dalrymple, then the answer was no. Several years ago, Dalrymple had approached Ambrose with a suggestion to overlook a certain piece of evidence in exchange for recompense. Dalrymple had called it a favor; Ambrose had seen it as a bribe. He'd refused that and subsequent "favors" as well. In retribution, Dalrymple had stalled Ambrose's promotions and tried to blacken his reputation. Without solid proof of his superior's wrongdoing, Ambrose had borne the attacks in silence, believing that justice would prevail.

Now he drew his shoulders back. "My only concern is justice, sir," he said flatly. "If you've heard anything different—"

"Ease up, Kent. Dalrymple's not my only source," Coyner said. "Your peers speak highly of your ethics and ability."

Some of Ambrose's tension eased. "They are too kind. I merely do my job."

"They said you were overly modest, too." Coyner reached for his tankard. "Take it from me, Kent: if you want to get somewhere in life, you best get used to sounding your own trumpet. Hard work will only get you so far."

"Yes, sir," Ambrose said.

His father Samuel had always claimed that success came from honest, honorable toil. Yet despite a lifetime devoted to educating young minds as the village schoolmaster, Samuel now found himself mired in debt. His future and that of Ambrose's five younger siblings teetered in the balance. Beneath the table, Ambrose's hands balled.

"I don't doubt your abilities or your work ethic," Coyner continued, "but I find myself circling a delicate question. If I may?"

"I have no secrets."

The magistrate's thin eyebrows winged above his faded blue eyes. "Not many a man could claim that. My question, then, is this: why are you in need of additional employ? As a Principle Surveyor, you earn a decent living. And you're not married, are you?"

"I am not." Ambrose faltered; unaccustomed to speaking of his troubles, he didn't know how to go about it. "My father has had health troubles of late. And I have siblings in need of care."

"What about your mother?"

"She passed when I was a young boy. 'Twas my stepmother who raised me and my siblings—or half-siblings, I should say. She was taken from us two summers ago."

Ambrose oft forgot that he did not share a biological mother with his siblings. His stepmother Marjorie had treated him like her own blood. Loving and practical, she had been the family's Rock of Gibraltar; the loss of her had left them all floundering—and his father especially.

"My condolences." The other man cleared his throat. "Don't mean to pry, but between you and me, I've had some problems with past employees I've taken on independent contract. Men with vices, who'd do anything for extra coin." His mouth firmed. "A Bow Street Runner must represent justice. Like Caesar's wife, he must be above suspicion."

Ambrose saw no argument with that. "You have my word that I would uphold my duties."

For a minute, Coyner studied him. "I believe you would, Kent."

"I have the job, then?"

"When I have a fitting assignment, I'll let you know."

Some of Ambrose's hope faded. "How long will that take, sir?" The payment on his family's cottage was due by the end of the month. If he didn't come up with the extra money, the Kents would lose the roof over their heads—and his shrew of a landlady would never allow his family to join him in his Spartan one-room apartment. Nor did he want his young, country-bred brother and sisters introduced to the harsh realities of city life.

"Can't predict. But since the Cato Street Conspiracy last year, there's been plenty of mayhem afoot. Mark my words," the magistrate said darkly, "the anarchists are merely biding their time."

Last year, Bow Street had played an instrumental role in the capture of a group of radicals dedicated to overthrowing the government and instituting social reform. Whilst Ambrose had sympathy with some of their beliefs—the government-sponsored massacre at Peterloo had been an atrocity through and through—he did not agree with their methods. Change must be made through law and order, not chaos. The Cato Street ruffians had planned on assassinating Members of Parliament, including the Prime Minister; thanks to the hard work of the magistrates, the plot had been foiled and the perpetrators punished for their crimes.

"If there's any ongoing investigation in need of an extra pair of hands, I should be glad to—" Ambrose began.

"Everything's under wraps at the moment." Finishing the last of his supper, the magistrate signaled to have his tankard refilled. "Not to worry. You'll be the first to know when a new case comes up."

Ambrose had to content himself with that. After bidding the magistrate farewell, he exited the tavern into the cool summer night. At this hour, Covent Garden's collection of bawdy houses, theatres, and gaming hells threw together people of all classes, and the resulting mishmash overflowed the streets. Beneath a lamppost, a well-dressed cove bartered for the evening's pleasure with a pretty, bored-looking whore. A gang of young swells roared with laughter as one of their own cast up his accounts, splattering his Hessians in the process. Dirt-streaked urchins scampered about with sharp eyes and ready hands.

Weary of vice—he'd spent the first ten hours of his day chasing down river thieves—Ambrose began his journey home. He had a two-mile trek back to his room in Cheapside. On the street corner, he passed a hawker selling paper cones filled with chestnuts. The rich, sugary smell of the browning nuts caused his belly to growl, but he walked on. He'd treat himself to a supper of toast and eggs when he arrived home.

The promise of hot food lengthened his stride. Up ahead, he spotted a disturbance: two carts had collided, spilling produce and goods everywhere. Angry shouts rang through the night, and a mob began to gather, blocking off the street. *Any opportunity to pillage and plunder.* Disgruntled, Ambrose switched his path, cutting right down the next lane.

He found himself on a quiet block lined with well-maintained Palladian buildings. Brothels, he guessed, from the muted red glow emanating from the shuttered windows. The night breeze carried a cloying scent which irritated Ambrose's nose. He had never understood the attractions of paid pleasure. All his life, he'd respected his stepmother and protected his four younger sisters; the idea of using someone else's womenfolk for selfish ends was despicable. For him, there'd be no enjoyment in knowing that his bed partner was selling her favors—and, more likely than not, out of pure desperation.

His mouth twisted with wry humor. *It hardly matters what you think, does it? Because you haven't even the entry fee to such an establishment. So enough of your high-brow views and onto more important concerns.*

Such as how to keep his family afloat.

Devil and damn, if only Father hadn't tried to hide the money troubles. Last year, Samuel Kent had suffered an apoplectic fit; it had cost him his health and his thirty year tenure at the village school. Ever a proud man, he'd reassured Ambrose that he was receiving a pension and that all was well. In reality, the pension had turned out to be a paltry, one-time payment—one that, in a fit of desperation, Samuel had invested recklessly in a mining scheme. In the end, Father had lost everything. And he'd been too proud to say a word until it was nearly too late.

Ambrose had poured all his savings into staving off the family's debts. The money he'd put aside for marriage, for that tidy brick cottage Jane had wanted ... that had been the first to go. And his bride-to-be along with it. Yet that had been only the tip of the proverbial iceberg. As he strode through the shadows, his ever-present worries surfaced: in addition to keeping everyone housed and fed, he had to find a way to keep Harry in school, to pay for his father's and Dorothea's medical bills, to keep Violet and Polly in petticoats, and to provide relief for Emma who was somehow managing it all—

A flash of movement caught Ambrose's eye. His policeman's instincts kicked in. His mind blanked, his senses sharpening. His hand gripping the solid oak truncheon at his hip, he peered steadily into the alleyway to his left. A mouth of darkness ... yet he sensed the presence lurking in the shadows. His muscles bunched, his eyes probing the corridor of pitch—

A scuffling noise. Then, "Bloody bitch bit me!"

A feminine scream rent the night.

The fear in that cry galvanized Ambrose into action. He ran into the alley. His eyes adjusting to the dimness, he could discern hulking figures, two of them, holding a slim captive against the wall. A hood obscured the victim's face, yet her voice was shrill with terror. Ambrose went in low and fast, his truncheon connecting with a satisfying crack against a kneecap. One of the villains groaned in pain, falling to the ground.

"Release her," Ambrose commanded to the other brute.

In response, the cutthroat charged him like a bull.

His shoulder blades jammed against brick, his club slipping from his grasp. His attacker raised a ham-sized fist, and Ambrose dodged it at the last moment, jerking his knee up as he did so. The bastard groaned, doubling over at the strike to the gut. Taking swift aim, Ambrose followed up with a jab-and-hook combination, snapping the other's jaw back. The man crumpled to the ground. Lungs burning, Ambrose stood over his opponent and nudged the fallen figure with his boot. No response; the cull would be out for a while.

A cloak streaked past him—the victim. The instinct to protect and serve made Ambrose go after her. He had to make sure she was unharmed, to get her medical attention if need be and justice as well. In his line of work, he'd seen all too often how the law turned a blind eye to crimes against the disadvantaged, and whores, in particular, received the shoddiest treatment. Well, if he had any say about it, the night's ruffians would be thrown in Newgate for attacking the hapless moll.

With his long stride, he caught up to the fleeing prostitute and reached to tap her on the shoulder. "Beg pardon, miss, are you alright—"

She whirled around. Her hood slid off … and the rest of his words faded. Along with his capacity for thought. For there, before his eyes, was the most stunning female he'd ever seen.

A creature of moonlight and water, too beautiful to be real. From the depths of his memory surfaced a tale told by his step-mother: about a *selkie*, an enchantress born of the ocean and imbued with the power to lure hapless males to their demise. He could almost believe that myth had manifested into reality. Beneath the dim street lamp, waves of silver-blonde hair tumbled around a perfect oval face; sea-green eyes appraised him, the vivid depths swirling with panic. In that same moment, he registered the rich velvet of her cloak and the string of emeralds circling her graceful throat.

No whore … but a lady?

Ambrose blinked. What the devil was the matter with him? He tried to summon his heretofore stalwart common sense. He opened his mouth to tell her that she had nothing to fear, that he wasn't going to hurt her. That he'd protect her and see her home safely.

And that she could lower the delicate pistol she held aimed at his chest.

As he struggled to find his voice, footsteps sounded from the alley behind him. Bloody hell, hadn't he taken care of the bastards? In the instant before he turned to face his foe, he saw the lady's magnificent eyes harden into icy gems. Her gloved fingers tight-ened on her weapon. All the hairs shot up on his skin.

"Don't—" The word left him in a shout.

She pulled the trigger anyway.

Chapter Three

"I can't believe you shot me," the stranger said and not for the first time since they'd boarded her carriage.

"I wasn't aiming for you. You got in the way of my bullet," Marianne said.

Really, the man could show a bit more gratitude seeing as how she'd saved his life. She'd let off the shot to deter the advancing cutthroat; seconds later, her trusted African manservant Lugo had arrived. The sight of Lugo's imposing form and stern profile—not to mention his double-barreled Flintlock—had sent the ruffians scurrying off into the night. She'd waved off Lugo's apologies (a mob in the street had detained his arrival) and asked him to load her would-be rescuer into the conveyance.

Now the vehicle rolled smoothly along, and the big man with the intriguing amber eyes scowled at her from his corner. Somewhere along the way, he'd lost his hat; his mahogany hair—neither curly nor straight, but somewhere in between—gleamed beneath the carriage lamp. Long of limb and dressed in a greatcoat that had seen better days, he looked at odds sitting against the plush lavender squabs. He clasped his injured arm with one large hand; with a twinge, she noted the crimson seeping through his fingers.

"Let's have a look at that." She went over to his side of the carriage. When he backed away from her, she said with a hint of asperity, "Hold still, will you? I've just had the upholstery changed, and you're bleeding all over it."

He gave her a dark glance, but when she gestured for him to remove his greatcoat he obliged. Her heartbeat kicked up at the red splotch on his left sleeve. Yet he said nothing, staring straight ahead as she withdrew a handkerchief from her reticule and wrapped it around the wound. Beneath the rough linen of his shirt, his bicep —an unexpectedly solid ridge of muscle given his lean form—gave a twitch, but other than that he betrayed no sign of pain. Another surprise. In her experience, males became indistinguishable from babes when it came to the loss of blood.

But this fellow ... he was different from other males. She didn't like the fact that she found him difficult to read. His face possessed little in the way of beauty, but she supposed there was a certain character to the ascetic lines. The set of his strong jaw suggested he was a man of perseverance. One who'd weathered hard times—if the gaunt hollows beneath his cheekbones were any indication. Only a full mouth and faint laughter lines at the eyes saved him from complete austerity.

At present moment, his curiously bright gaze was hooded, and she realized that she was not the only one making an assessment. His lips formed a tight seam, as if he found her ... *lacking*? A rare appraisal indeed from a man. She acknowledged this without vanity: she knew the fact of her physical beauty and its effect on males. Her looks had proved both a blessing and a curse. And rarely did anyone bother to look beneath the surface.

If they did, they would encounter something quite the opposite of loveliness.

She secured the handkerchief with a knot and enough pressure to make a muscle leap in the stranger's jaw. "I think we're overdue for introductions," she said. "Who are you?"

"Ambrose Kent, at your service." He inclined his head. A wary motion.

His name rang a bell. "You are acquainted with the Hartefords." Her eyes narrowed. "A constable of some sort, aren't you?"

Something flickered in his gaze. Perhaps he caught the edge of derision in her voice. In her experience, so-called upholders of the law used their power against those whom they were supposed to protect. A case in point: Skinner, the blasted Runner she'd once hired. She wouldn't trust a thief-taker, Charley, policeman—or, for that matter, *any* man—farther than she could toss him.

"I'm a Principle Surveyor with the Thames River Police," he said stiffly. "And with whom do I have the pleasure of speaking?"

"Marianne Sedgwick, Baroness Draven," she said.

At the mention of her title, the tension lines deepened around his mouth. *Interesting. Doesn't like the peerage, does he?* Yet from what she could recollect, her friend Helena, the Marchioness of Harteford, had positively raved about this Mr. Kent. Apparently, Kent had helped to solve several thefts for Helena's husband and had once saved the Marquess of Harteford's life. Harteford—another stoic type—apparently got on with Kent, though heaven only knew what a marquess and a policeman had to talk about.

Intrigued, Marianne continued to peruse her companion. If it wasn't titles he held in contempt, then perhaps it was something particular to her? Perhaps he knew of her reputation; perhaps he shared the pulpit with the priggish, hypocritical types who'd dubbed her "The Merry Widow." Who scorned her for making full use of the freedoms that were hers by right—by virtue of the five years of hell that had been her marriage and the pain she continued to endure to this day.

Anger straightened her spine. "Does my reputation precede me?" she said coolly.

"Your reputation?" His brow furrowed.

So he hasn't heard the rumors about me—well that's not surpris-

ing, is it? We hardly move in the same circles. Either way, 'tis not as if I give a damn what he thinks.

"If you don't mind my asking," he said abruptly, "what were you doing alone in that area of Covent Garden and at this time of night?"

Marianne's jaw slackened. It had been a good long while since anyone had taken her to task to her face. That this rawboned policeman in his shoddy clothes would presume to do so rankled her. After all that she'd survived, she was her own woman; she answered to no one. She responded with icy calm, a weapon she'd honed amongst the *ton*.

"As a matter of fact, I do mind," she said. "My business is my own."

"Not when it endangers your life and those of others who must rescue you from your folly."

The nerve of the man. "I didn't ask for your help," she snapped.

"No, you didn't," he agreed. "As I recall, it was more of a scream for assistance."

For the first time in years, Marianne felt her composure crack a little. "I was not screaming. I was alerting my man Lugo to my whereabouts. At any rate, I had the situation well in hand before you came barging in." With a start, she heard the irritation simmering in her voice. She drew a breath. When she was once again collected, she arched a brow and pointed a glance at his arm. "Do you doubt that I would hesitate to do what was necessary?"

"I doubt your common sense, my lady. And your ability to control your impulses. No pursuit of pleasure could be worth taking the risk you did tonight," he said grimly.

That did it. The judgmental pedant thought to govern her, did he? A memory slipped through before she could stop it: kneeling between Draven's withered thighs, shame and fear making her gag. *Try harder, you useless cunt, or you shall never see your little Primrose again ...*

Chest constricting, she pushed the image aside. Let out a

breath. From the moment of Draven's demise, she'd sworn to be her own mistress. No one—least of all this sanctimonious *nobody* —would ever control her again.

Fury cleared her mind, made it as sharp and crystalline as ice. A plan took shape in her head, and its simplicity nearly made her smile. *Lecture me, will you Mr. Kent? Well, we shall see who learns the lesson this eve.*

"Obviously you haven't been pursuing the right pleasures," she drawled. "As a widow, I can assure you that certain delights are worth any risk."

His dark brows drew together, color spilling over the ridge of his cheekbones. Good—she'd shocked the prig. Before she could enjoy the spark of satisfaction, however, he said in dogged tones, "This isn't about me. It's about you and your disregard for your own safety. Many a constable's work would be lessened if only people practiced common sense—"

"And, you, Mr. Kent, are a fount of *common* wisdom, are you not?"

Her sarcasm did not escape him. Despite his holier-than-thou attitude, Ambrose Kent was apparently no idiot. "I have seen suffering in my line of work," he said, "much of which could have been prevented with a little forethought."

"Indeed," she said in a bored voice.

"I do not wish to preach, my lady, only to be of service." The muscle along his jaw ticked again; Kent was not quite as unflappable as he wished to be. "If you think yourself above my advice, then don't take it."

"Above, sir? Not at all. In point of fact, I am in need of your services at this very moment."

His eyes—the shade of light filtered through amber— narrowed at her.

"We have arrived at my home," she said. The upward sweep of his long lashes indicated that he'd been so engrossed in his righteous dispensing of advice that he hadn't noticed the carriage stop.

"And after the night's disquieting events,"—she faked a delicate shudder—"I shall require escort inside."

He frowned. "Can't your manservant accompany you?"

"He could. But I am requesting your presence specifically." She bestowed a sultry look upon him, one that typically reduced males to puddles at her slippered feet. The policeman, however, continued to eye her with suspicion. She let her lips take on a seductive curve. "I should like to privately express my gratitude for your intervention tonight."

His color rose. "If you've learned your lesson, then that will be thanks enough."

My, this man *was* a challenge, wasn't he? Her interest piqued further. No male was without his Achilles' heel. And she had a good inkling where the chink in this would-be knight's armor was located.

"Perhaps another time, then," she said in a tone of indifference.

She tapped on the door, and it opened to reveal Lugo's impassive face. Ignoring the steps, Kent sprung easily to the ground and turned to offer her his hand. She took it, and as she alighted, she purposely missed a step.

Kent caught her. "Are you alright?" he demanded.

Crushed against the solid wall of his chest, she felt a strange wave of giddiness. She spoke, perturbed to realize that the breathlessness in her voice was not entirely feigned. "I must be more overset than I realized," she murmured. "Thank you, sir."

In the next instant, Kent swung her up in his arms.

"But your arm," she said in surprise.

"'Tis a scratch," he said dismissively. "I'll see you in."

Chapter Four

Rarely did Ambrose ignore his instincts. They'd saved his hide more than once, and he respected anything that kept him alive. Yet, like a character in some topsy-turvy dream, he found himself carrying a mysterious baroness—who, incidentally, gave meaning to the expression *soft and light as thistledown*—up the steps of a hulking gothic mansion. Inside, he blinked at the brilliant pink marble atrium. If the exterior of the place was all doom and gloom, the interior created the opposite effect, one of elegance and light.

Overhead, a tiered chandelier winked with crystal teardrops, and watered ivory silk flowed over the walls. Eyeing the large glass-fronted cabinet in his path, Ambrose navigated past with care. Even so, a Chinese vase rattled within, and his breath held until the bloody thing stilled. The piece of blue and white porcelain probably cost more than his year's wages.

"Would you mind taking me to my suite, sir?" Lady Draven tipped her head back to meet his eyes. "I'm afraid the steps may be a bit much for me at the moment."

How could he refuse that bewitching gaze? Tucking her closer, he followed the African manservant up the grand curved stairwell to the first floor. Even the hallway whispered of extravagance; his boots sank into cream carpet thick enough to sleep upon, and he lost track of the number of rooms they passed. At the end of the corridor, the servant ushered him into a lavish suite of peach and pale gold.

"Please have a repast and the necessary supplies sent up, Lugo," Lady Draven said.

Lugo bowed and departed, his expression giving away nothing. Perhaps it was nothing out of the ordinary for his mistress to arrive home in a strange man's arms and to entertain said man in her bedchamber. For some reason, the notion made Ambrose's gut clench. He spied the enormous bed upon the dais—hard to miss that enormous confection of feather pillows and blush-colored silk —and he felt another jolt farther south.

Bloody hell. What is the matter with me?

He didn't believe for a moment that his glamorous hostess had any personal interest in him; the notion was laughable. What was she after then?

Whatever it was, he didn't like being dallied with. He set her firmly on her feet.

"If there's nothing else," he said curtly.

"But there is," she said in a husky voice. "I am not yet done with you, sir."

In the dancing candlelight, he experienced the full effect of her lushly fringed gaze. Her eyes tilted slightly up at the corners—not enough to be exotic, but sufficient for English perfection. It seemed nigh impossible that irises could reflect such a vibrant shade of green or that they could mesmerize so with their depths of knowledge and mystery. With a wry flash, he understood why she wore that emerald necklace: not to match her eyes, but to highlight their natural superiority over the most dazzling of jewels.

Aye, he could not argue with her beauty.

But that she was also wicked, he had no doubt. Wicked, clever ... and dangerous. Now that he had her measure, he told himself that her physical attractions did not matter. He had no interest in a *femme fatale* or in sophisticated games. He was a simple man, with simple desires. Though the loss of Jane had dimmed his optimism, it had not altered his vision for the future.

He still wanted a loyal, amiable wife, a companion to ease the solitude of life's journey. Together, he and she would occupy a snug, ivy-covered cottage. In his idyllic musings, his better half would come to care for his family and bring some semblance of stability to the chaotic Kent brood. And if they were so blessed, he and his wife might have a child or children of their own to nurture and watch grow.

In other words, he yearned for normality. Peace.

The very opposite of what Lady Marianne Draven represented.

As if reading his thoughts, she smiled and untied her cloak. His pulse thudded as the velvet skin slid down her body, pooling at her feet. Aye, this sinful temptress would bring no man peace. His blood heated as his eyes traced the slender elegance of her figure. The misty green gown bared her creamy shoulders and clung to her high, rounded breasts. It hinted at her small waist and softly curved hips before frothing at her dainty slippered toes.

She was a woman without physical equal. Yet despite her polished exterior, he glimpsed shadows in the lucid depths of her eyes. Could such a pampered creature know pain or suffering? His thoughts blurred as she came closer to him. Her perfume curled in his nostrils, and the complex scent—exotic yet clean and utterly mouth-watering—roused a primal male response. Desire punched him in the gut, and he became almost light-headed.

No wonder: his blood had been redirected to another organ instead. To his shock, he felt his cock growing hard beneath his smalls.

Inwardly cursing his lack of control, he said, "I must take my leave."

"Nonsense. You've just arrived. And I cannot in good conscience allow you to leave without attending to your injuries."

She placed a hand on his arm, and he flinched at the sudden sting. Glancing down, he saw that blood had soaked through the makeshift bandage. Damn, her shot must have done more damage than he'd realized. His wooziness intensified.

"You'd best sit before you fall down," she added.

Shaking his head and finding that it only made matters worse, he saw no choice but to do as she instructed. He stumbled over to the gilded settee and sprawled onto the snowy velvet. The room spun from the effort.

His hostess peered down at him. "Let's get your clothes off, then," she said. "Can you manage or shall I do it?"

Shock pierced his buffle-headedness. "Beg pardon?" he managed.

"I can't very well examine your arm with your shirt on. Come, you aren't afraid for your virtue, are you?" she said, her brows lifting. "I promise I shan't take advantage."

"Of course I'm not afraid," he muttered. "But it's hardly proper."

She gave a throaty laugh. "And you *are* a proper sort, aren't you, Mr. Kent?"

"I believe in decency, yes," he retorted.

Her gaze thinned just as a knock sounded. At her command, a small army of uniformed servants entered bearing trays, towels, and a steaming copper basin. The one in charge, a sturdy brunette with a scar that extended from her ear down into her starched collar, said curtly, "Where would you like this, milady?"

"The bathing implements by me," Lady Draven said. "And the refreshments can go next to Mr. Kent. Thank you, Tilda."

As the maid set about her duties, she shot a dirty look at Ambrose from beneath her lashes. He frowned, wondering what he'd done to offend her. Was it the mere fact of his presence? The manservant hadn't seemed to mind. Whatever the cause, Lady Draven's servants were an odd bunch, to say the least. They did, however, follow their mistress' orders with well-trained efficiency.

A round table covered with silver-domed plates soon sprung up to his right. As the servants departed, Tilda gave him a last warning scowl.

Thoughts of the maid vanished as the baroness sat down next to him. She was so close that her skirts brushed against his trousers. She shed her satin gloves, and at the sight of the bruise circling one fragile white wrist, his gut twisted.

"You are hurt," he said roughly.

"'Tis nothing." She shrugged, as if being accosted by cutthroats was a commonplace experience for her. She unwound the handkerchief from his arm, revealing the oozing crimson stain upon his sleeve. "Well, Mr. Kent, I haven't got all night. Have you recovered sufficiently from your blushes to remove your shirt?"

Like a pendulum, his emotions swung in a wild arc. From concern for her to ... irritation.

He was beginning to heartily dislike this particular expression of hers: the arched eyebrows and curled lip made him feel like a squalid object dragged in by the cat. She thought him prudish, did she? Lacking in sophistication—and mayhap in general? Though he was not a man given easily to anger, his equanimity began to fray. The truth was his arm now throbbed like the very devil, and if she had no qualms about being alone with a half-naked man, then why should he worry for her reputation?

Grimly, he began to unbutton his waistcoat. Her gaze did not waver as he stripped it off, followed by his leather braces and cravat. Untying the laces on his shirt, he pulled the rough linen over his head, grimacing as the movement set his injured limb afire. He glanced at the wound: gory, but he'd suffered worse. He sat before her, a shirtless, bleeding stranger ... and not so much as a ripple passed over her calm, exquisite visage.

In point of fact, the brazen woman was *appraising* him. He told himself he didn't give a whit about her opinion of his person, yet his body ignored his brain's command. Beneath her languid perusal, his shoulders drew back, his chest muscles flexing as if being caressed. The ridges of his abdomen twitched, and when her gaze dipped below his waistband, heat flooded his face.

Elsewhere, as well.

Her tongue touched her upper lip, and he had to bite back a groan.

An image blazed from the darkest recesses of fantasy: moon-spun tresses spilling like liquid silk into his palms and across his thighs. A breath, a lick ... that soft pink mouth worshipping the hardest part of him. It was the naughtiest of acts that assailed his imagination—one he'd secretly fantasized about but never experienced. After all, he did not purchase his pleasures and wouldn't expect a decent woman to engage in so depraved a deed. Yet the vision took hold of him, of this wicked widow taking him this way, her eyes vivid and knowing as she swallowed him whole—

"Why, Mr. Kent, I do believe there's more to you than meets the eye."

The amused drawl jerked him back to reality. He blinked, mortification burning the back of his neck. Hell's teeth, what was he about? He was acting like some sex-starved debaucher. Clearly it had been too long since he'd been with a woman—not since the couplings with Jane and those had been well over a year ago.

Still, it was no excuse. Jaw clenching, he fought to regain control. He gripped his thighs, willing his erection to subside.

Show some self-discipline, man. And for God's sake, get your mind out of the gutter.

"Hold still for the next part," Lady Draven said.

Before he could respond, she applied a hot, moist towel over his wound. He sucked in a breath as she blotted and dabbed, pausing to rinse out the towel before repeating the process. He told himself the pain was good: it dulled the need gnawing at his belly. Dulled, but did not take it away completely. He kept his gaze fixed on the basin, watching as the water turned red with his blood.

"I think you'll live," she announced, "and I shan't have to put stitches in."

That got his attention. "You have stitched a wound?" he said in disbelief.

"It is no different from stitching anything else. I have a steady hand." As if to prove it, she picked up a glass of clear liquid and dumped it over his lesion. Fire scorched his battered flesh.

"And a steady constitution, apparently." His teeth gritted as she secured the bandage with a firm knot. What kind of woman was this? Did she shoot people as a habit, tidy them up on a regular basis?

Her lips curved. "Now that we've taken care of your injury, I believe you have other needs that require attention, Mr. Kent. What would you like to begin with?"

Sweat glazed his brow, and his lungs suddenly felt short of air. Surely she could not have guessed his carnal thoughts ...

"How do you mean?" he said in a strangled voice.

She leaned closer to him, and his muscles went rigid in anticipation. He dug his fingers into the cushions, afraid of what his hands might do otherwise. His mouth pooled with hunger as her unique scent pervaded his senses. Savage need surged within him to kiss the mocking smile off her lips, to taste every inch of her milky skin, to hear her pant his name in bliss—

His lungs burned as she casually reached for his lap ... and over it. To the table of refreshments, which he'd somehow forgotten about entirely. She lifted a silver cover, revealing a plate of golden brown pastries.

"Ah, excellent. Cook's pheasant pie," she said. "Shall I serve?"

He could not summon a proper response.

She went to inspect the offerings. Even this proved a special kind of torture. She bent over the table, affording him a tantalizing view of her bosom. He could not tear his gaze from the rounded white mounds peeping over the edge of green fabric. Not too big, nor too small, her breasts had a ripe, firm curve that made his palms itch to touch them. To discover what sort of delight tipped their centers. Would her nipples be a shy, blush pink or—God help him, his personal weakness—a rich, berry red ...

"Hungry, Mr. Kent?"

Not for food. Heart hammering, he had to squeeze the words past his cinched throat. "Not particularly."

"Pity. Cook has a way with sausages."

So saying, Lady Marianne forked a plump length of meat.

Devil and damn. Don't watch, turn away—

It was too late. Like a victim of the gorgon Medusa, he remained rooted in place. The analogy extended for when she held the sausage up, the blunt tip nudging her lips, a part of him did indeed turn to stone. Hard as rock, his shaft throbbed as her mouth opened. The meat slid inside with excruciating slowness. She bit down with dainty precision, juice dribbling from the corner of her lips. When her pink tongue appeared, sweeping her lips in a sensuous arc, lust shattered the remnants of his control.

His vision turned black. The beast of need broke free, obliterating all else.

He was on his feet before he knew what he was doing. His hands closed on her waist, and he yanked her against him. Pleasure shocked his system as her softness collided with his own hard edges. His fingers knotted in the fine silk of her tresses. And the animal in him roared as he bent down and claimed the kiss that was more essential than his next breath.

Hot. Carnal. *Take.*

His blood pounded in his ears as he ravaged the softness of her mouth. She tasted sweet and savory, like cinnamon and sage, the flavor addictive beyond description. All he knew was that he needed more. He drove his tongue deeply, penetrating her, groaning as his tongue found hers. At the wet, sinuous tangling, his erection threatened to burst free from his trousers. He clamped his hands on her bottom, urging her closer, dragging her against his raging cockstand—

The slap snapped his head back.

It took a minute for reality to sink in. Lady Draven was glaring at him, her lips red and swollen from his kisses. Tangled by his hands, her hair cascaded in pale streamers to her waist. Her bosom rose and fell in rapid breaths as her gaze clashed with his. Rage glittered in the icy emerald depths. Appalled at his lack of control, he dropped his hands. Took a step back.

"My lady, I ..." He trailed off, not knowing how to continue. Had he misread her intentions? Good God, if he had, he'd acted like the veriest scoundrel. The sort of man he most despised. Self-loathing bubbled through his veins as he racked his brain for a suitable apology.

"Now, Mr. Kent, what *were* you lecturing me about earlier in the carriage?"

Her lingering taste clouded his faculties. His body was still hard and humming from the contact with her lithe form. "I beg your pardon?" he said.

She tapped her chin with one elegant finger. "Yes, I have it. I believe you shared your expertise on the matter of controlling one's impulses." Her brows formed sardonic arches. "Should you care to add anything to your learned discourse?"

The motive for her actions became instantly clear. Humiliation seized him; all of this had been a ploy to put him in his place? This false seduction nothing more than her way of proving a point? In that moment, his anger almost equaled his desire ... almost, but not quite. Which infuriated him further.

"Nothing to add, my lady," he bit out.

Her gaze hardened. "Then I believe you know your way out."

A word formed in his head, one he'd never before used in conjunction with any female. He retained sufficient control to keep his mouth shut. He threw on his clothes, and hands fisted at his sides, issued a stiff bow. As he strode toward the door, he silently cursed himself and made a vow: he would never get entangled in this black widow's web again.

Chapter Five

The sun-drenched meadow brimmed with birdsong and blossoming clover. Overhead, a pair of larks soared across the azure sky, their shadows gliding over Marianne's skin while she lay stretched against the grass, her hair loose and free. Her eyes closed with pleasure as her lover whispered in her ear. His words were as sweet as his berry-flavored kisses, the promises of forever holding her as securely as his arms.

At seventeen, it was so easy to believe in love.

His lips touched her neck. The hesitant yet sweet caress brought a warm flush to her skin. She knew she ought to stop him. But desire had a stronger hold than maidenly modesty, and she abandoned herself to impulse, to the reckless curiosity coursing through her. His mouth found hers, and need shivered through her. Her nerves tingled. No longer uncertain and innocent, this kiss burned with a new intensity.

Not a boy's fledgling ardor ... but a man's hunger.

Every part of her responded. Her lips parted to the thrust of his tongue, and his spicy, male flavor infused her senses. He tasted right, smelled right, *felt* right ... she moaned as his lean length pressed her deeper into the soft grass. Her neck arching to his kisses, she fitted herself shamelessly against his hardness, the bold shape of him fueling her inner fire. Her insides turned liquid, and hot honey trickled between her thighs.

"Oh, Thomas ..." she sighed.

"I'm not Thomas." Her eyelids flew open. Above her was not her lover's handsome, boyish countenance, but a stark face carved by time and experience. Amber eyes pinned her and penetrated her very soul.

Marianne awoke with a gasp. She was clutching the bedclothes, breathing hard. Blackberries, her first taste of desire, lingered upon her tongue as she stared up into the swirls of the damask canopy.

What is the matter with me? Why him, *of all people?*

It was the third night in a row that she'd dreamt of Ambrose Kent.

Pushing a damp tendril off her cheek, she waited for her heart-beat to calm and the wave of arousal to pass. Bodily needs always did—and if they didn't, she knew well enough how to take matters into her own hands. For she did not trust any man to do for her what she could safely and efficiently do for herself. Having been saddled with a hot-blooded nature—she was never one to lie to herself—she tended to her own needs regularly.

And with alarming frequency in the past three days.

For reasons she could not entirely comprehend, the encounter with the blasted policeman had thrown her off-balance. Ambrose Kent did not possess good looks, at least not in the traditional sense. He was her social inferior. While these two facts did not bother her over much, the next one did: he had dared to interfere in her business and to question her judgment. He, who knew nothing about her—about the life-or-death plight of her daughter —had presumed to *judge* her?

Anger welled. She lived by her own rules, and no man would govern her again. Turning onto her side, she yanked a pillow into position beneath her neck.

Kent deserved what I dished out. Let him experience what it is like to lose control. Let him know how it feels to be subject to another's whims.

Yet despite her livid state, she could not stop the image from forming in her head. Of Kent stripping before her, undressing with the ease of a man who didn't use the services of a valet. There could be no other explanation for the rumpled state of Kent's waistcoat and his hopeless excuse for a cravat. Yet she had to admit that those drab, ignominious garments had concealed a bit of a surprise.

Ambrose Kent's physique was ... splendid.

Her pulse quickened at the memory of his lean, sinewy body. Though somewhat undernourished, Kent's shape had been undoubtedly virile: the body of a man whose strength had come from necessity rather than vanity. From chasing criminals and rowing policing lighters rather than a fancy fencing or boxing saloon. Subtle power had emanated from the hard curve of his biceps and the rigid paving of his chest. The only softness had come from the dark hair dusted across his upper torso and narrowing into a line between the taut bands of his belly.

She swallowed, remembering how that line had circled his navel before arrowing south. Her eyes had followed the delicious trail until it disappeared beneath his waistband. And there, between his thighs, had been a prominent bulge that not even the poor cut of his trousers could hide.

Kent had looked to be a large man in *every* respect.

Perturbed, she realized that her musings were fanning rather than dimming her arousal. Her stiffened nipples chafed against her satin chemise. Between her legs, the flesh had grown damp and throbbing, the coil at her core wound tight. She shut her eyes and tried to dispel Kent's image. Instead, he seemed to expand in her mind's eye. Her breath quickened as she pictured the proud policeman losing control. The moment his will lost to desire, his mouth twisting in a sensual smile, his amber eyes blazing as his big hands reached for her ...

Her resolve began to melt. She'd been under so much tension as of late. Surely, a quick release couldn't hurt ... The rap on the door stilled the downward path of her hand. Her eyes opened. Blowing out a breath, she fought off the simmering frustration.

You ought to be glad for the interruption. Because no matter how you rationalize it, fantasizing about Kent just won't do.

She sat up as Tilda bustled into the chamber. As ever, the lady's maid was the image of competence. Tilda's starched cap sat upright upon her tamed brown curls, and nary a wrinkle could be found on the black bombazine that covered her voluptuous figure from neck to ankle. With the exception of the scar below her right ear and her accent (rapidly improving under the tutelage of the elocution master), there was nothing to betray the fact that Tilda Collier had once made her living in the alleyways of St. Giles.

"Good mornin', milady. Brought your breakfast," Tilda said, sliding the tray onto the table next to the bed. "You've got a busy day ahead o' you."

Marianne sat up straighter. "There's news?"

"No, milady." A look of understanding shadowed the other's blue-grey eyes as Marianne's heart plummeted. "But I'm sure there will be soon. That fellow Corbett said 'e'd call, didn't 'e?"

"And I am to trust the word of a male prostitute?" Marianne said bitterly. "To hinge my daughter's future upon his ill-begotten promise?"

"A whore's word is no different than anyone else's." Shoulders hunched, the maid turned and poured the chocolate.

Shame stabbed Marianne at her own carelessness. She was reminded that hers was not the only tragedy that lived in this house. "Forgive me, Tilda," she said quietly. "That is not what I meant."

Tilda handed her a steaming porcelain cup. "I know," she said with such simplicity that Marianne felt even smaller. "After what you've done for me an' my boy, I wouldn't take the words to 'eart."

Three years ago, returning home from a night's futile search for Rosie, Marianne had seen a commotion in the street: a prostitute being brutalized by her pimp. Though such sights were not uncommon in the stews, something in the whore's eyes had made Marianne stop her carriage. She knew that look: had seen it on her own face as she'd stared blindly into the looking glass after Draven's nightly degradations. She'd paid off the pimp and brought Tilda and Tilda's young son home with her.

It was a situation that had ended up benefitting them all. Bereft of her own family, Marianne had come to depend upon Tilda's loyalty and good sense; she trusted this woman who had known as much pain as she had. For Tilda, too, had been abandoned by a young lover only to find herself increasing and alone in the world. With no other option, Tilda had turned to prostitution; Marianne had chosen marriage. In the end, they'd both sold their bodies, and Marianne could not say which of them had suffered more.

"You've a lot on your mind, milady, what with findin' Corbett and ... other events."

Marianne recognized the lines of disapproval etched around Tilda's mouth. "By other events, you are referring to Mr. Kent?"

"I don't trust 'is sort," Tilda said grimly. "'E's a constable, ain't 'e? 'Ad my fair share o' them on my old walk. If they didn't expect a tumble free o' charge, they wanted a cut o' your earnings. Cursed wretches, the lot o' them."

"I don't think Mr. Kent is that sort of man." The words slipped out, and Marianne frowned at herself. Why was she defending him? "That is to say, he did come to my assistance. He fought off those cutthroats."

"What do you know o' 'is intentions? I saw the way 'e was lookin' at you." Tilda shook her head. "Mark my words: a man don't do somethin' for nothin'. Look what 'appened with that bastard Skinner. Warned you not to trust a Runner, didn't I?"

Unease prickled Marianne's nape. She could not argue with

the other's wisdom. "Since I don't plan on seeing Mr. Kent again, it shan't be a problem."

"See that it isn't," Tilda said dourly.

As Tilda laid out the morning ensemble, Marianne sipped her chocolate. The creamy concoction dissolved some of the chill within, and she idly browsed the society pages of *The Times*. She knew the power of information and collected gossip the way a numismatist did rare coins. Her lips curved as she saw the entry concerning the Hartefords' anticipated return from their vacation on the Continent.

Marianne had known Helena, the Marchioness of Harteford, since childhood. They'd lived on neighboring estates and had been inseparable as girls. Though fate had parted them, they had rekindled their friendship three years ago in London, when Helena had arrived as a timid newlywed and Marianne a newly minted widow.

Now Helena had twin boys and a devoted husband. Whilst Marianne was genuinely happy for her friend, she could not help the bittersweet pang in her chest. Envy, yes ... but mostly guilt. For she had a secret she'd yet to share with her friend. And she didn't know if she ever would.

You will—once you get Rosie back. Then you'll tell Helena. About everything.

Pride and shame proved powerful sentinels against the truth. Moreover, Marianne had always kept her own counsel, and the years with Draven had only reinforced that trust should be doled out sparingly, if at all.

Tilda brought over a silk dressing robe. "Ready for your ablutions, then?"

Marianne was about to answer when a familiar scratching sounded on the door.

Tilda went to open it, revealing Lugo's imposing figure. "Why a giant of a fellow scratches like a mouse, I'll never know," the maid said. "Why don't you knock like everyone else?"

Something flashed in Lugo's black eyes, an emotion that Marianne recognized all too well. For years, Lugo had been Draven's manservant; one did not shed Draven's training easily. Though a freed slave, Lugo had been bound by debt to Draven, who'd delighted in abusing the large African. One time, Marianne had witnessed Lugo accidently breaking a glass. Draven had entered the room, and the look of malevolent glee on his face had curdled her stomach.

He'd been ready to horsewhip Lugo; she'd intervened, claiming the accident as her own. For while she, too, had endured Draven's sadistic side, his abuses toward her had been less violent. He'd enjoyed her beauty too much to leave visible scars. Whenever he'd beaten her, he'd taken care not to break her skin; he'd scarred her in invisible places, ones that did not interfere with his pride of ownership. Or with the image of the benevolent husband that he'd projected to the world.

After Draven's death, Lugo had become Marianne's trusted servant, filling the roles of butler, footman, and guard. Unspoken camaraderie existed between them: they were survivors of the same war. In his stoic way, Lugo had pledged himself to helping her find her little girl.

"Good day, my lady," he said. His baritone carried the flavor of his native Africa, and his deeply carved features had a mask-like formality. "You instructed that I inform you of any arriving correspondence." He bowed his closely shorn head and held out a folded note. "This just arrived for you."

Marianne's heart sped up a notch. In an instant, she was on her feet, yanking on her robe. With trembling hands, she took the letter from Lugo and broke open the wax seal. She scanned the brief lines. The words blurred as excitement gripped her.

"What is it, milady?" Tilda asked.

"An invitation," Marianne said breathlessly. "Ready the carriage, Lugo. We are going shopping."

Chapter Six

An hour later, Marianne stepped into the Bond Street salon, one of the most exclusive in London. The tinkling silver bell announced her arrival, and within moments the famed modiste emerged from the back to greet her. As usual, Amelie Rousseau looked chic and severe in unrelieved black. A tight chignon confined her ebony hair, and her dark eyes snapped with energy.

"*Bonjour*, Lady Draven." Amelie kissed the air near Marianne's cheeks. "The day brings such surprises, *non*?"

"For me as well as you. I hope you have not been inconvenienced by this," Marianne said, "and you must allow me to compensate you for the use of your shop."

"Normally, I would not condone such *brouhaha* on my premises, but for you, *chérie*, I shall make an exception. And there must be no talk of compensation between friends."

"*Merci*, Amelie. Once again, I am in your debt." Marianne inclined her head. She had few friends and considered the clever dressmaker one of them.

"*Pas du tout.* 'Twas your patronage, after all, that helped to launch my star. To this day, no one shines as bright as Baroness

Draven." Amelie ran an appraising eye over Marianne's ensemble. "As usual, I was right about the marigold silk. *C'est parfait.*"

Marianne smiled at the satisfaction in the other's voice. "Now, Amelie, if I may conduct my business ...?"

"*Mais oui.* The, ahem, ... gentleman is in the orchid dressing room."

Hearing the subtle contempt in the other's voice, Marianne said, "Though I am not at liberty to say more, this isn't an amorous assignation, Amelie. That I can assure you."

The modiste's narrow forehead smoothed. "I suspected as much. Your taste, my lady, has always been indisputable." She gave a quick nod. "You must attend to whatever intrigue awaits you. I shall remain in front to deter prying eyes."

Thankful that the other did not ask further questions— Amelie was nothing if not discreet—Marianne passed through the curtain to the back of the shop. Like everything in the modiste's domain, the space was spotless and elegant. She passed by two dressing rooms before entering the final room to the right.

She shut the door behind her. Standing in a far corner, Andrew Corbett turned in her direction. His tailored blue cutaway and buff trousers molded to his fit form. He held the spotted petal of an orchid between his manicured fingertips.

"Pretty thing, ain't it?" His eyes assessed her; in the daylight, the brown orbs had depths to them that the darkness of the bawdy house had obscured. A self-deprecating smile edged his chiseled lips. "Had to see for myself if it was real."

"Let us cut to the chase, Mr. Corbett," she replied. "How much?"

"Beg pardon?"

"For the information you bring today," she said impatiently. "Name your sum."

He released the flower. "What makes you think I can be bought for any sum?"

She lifted her brows. "You have gone to no small lengths to

arrange this meeting, so surely you expect a reward for your efforts."

"Perhaps, my lady, doing what is right is reward enough."

Faint color slid along his high cheekbones. His youth suddenly shone through the mask of sophistication; with a jolt, Marianne realized Andrew Corbett could not be more than three-and-twenty at most. For all the rumors of his manly prowess, he had not left boyhood far behind.

"If that is true," she said quietly, "then tell me what you know of Kitty Barnes and my daughter's whereabouts."

For a minute, Corbett said nothing. Then his shoulders drew back. "I don't know the location of Kitty or your daughter. The truth is, I haven't had contact with Kitty for over three years."

Another dead end. The familiar dark undertow dragged at Marianne. She fought the waves of despair closing over her head. *I've failed you, Rosie ...*

"But I have an idea of how you might find them," he said.

His words hooked her, yanked her gasping to the surface. "How?" she managed.

His gaze went to the closed door, as if expecting someone to barge in at any moment. He drew in a breath. "Kitty engineered her disappearance because of debt. She'd overestimated her own success and invested badly besides. In the end, she owed a pile of blunt—and to a man not known for his patience. As a warning, he set one of her bawdy houses aflame. We barely escaped that night with the clothes on our backs."

"But Kitty is alive. She is alive, and she has my daughter." *Please, God, let that be true.*

"Last I knew, Kitty was headed to the country. She wouldn't tell me where—said she had some friends to turn to." Corbett paused. "At the time, she still had your little Primrose."

Hearing her daughter's name battered at Marianne's composure. She shut her eyes against the hot welling of hope. In three years of searching, this was the first real news she'd had of her daughter. Longing seeped through the cracks, the hinges of her self-possession creaking as everything she'd locked away threatened to burst free.

Rosie laughing as Marianne tickled her. Rosie splashing in her bath and soaking Marianne in the process. Rosie snug in her little pink ruffled bed one night—and gone the next morning.

Oh, my darling ... wait for me. Mama's coming.

Drawing a breath, Marianne numbed her heart. She shifted the acuity to her head. Now that she finally had Rosie's trail, she must *focus*.

"Why didn't you go with them?" she said.

"Kitty and I had been at odds for some time. We did not see eye to eye on the matter of your daughter." A muscle quirked along Corbett's smooth jaw. "Unlike her, I do not believe that children should be used in such a manner."

Marianne swallowed over the razors in her throat. "Used?"

"You said your husband was the one who sent Primrose to Kitty?"

Marianne nodded numbly.

Corbett's lips formed a grim line. "He must have been the one paying for her upkeep, then. Kitty said the cove paid fifty pounds a month, with the instruction to care for Primrose like her own child. And Kitty kept her end of the bargain—until the payments suddenly stopped coming three years ago."

"When Draven died," Marianne said through dry lips.

"Without the income and her own dire straits, Kitty's first priority was saving her own hide. Before we parted ways, she had talked about ... about selling Primrose." The stark look in Corbett's eyes thrust the blade deeper into her heart. "I don't know if she did or not. But knowing this possibility—knowing what your daughter may have suffered, what she might have become if indeed she still lives—will you still want her then?"

"I will always want her," Marianne said fiercely, her hands

balling up. "Nothing can change that. And I'll stop at nothing to bring her home."

Raw emotion flashed in Corbett's eyes and vanished before she could know if she'd imagined it or not.

"Then you will want to start with Bartholomew Black," he said.

The hairs rose on Marianne's neck. She'd heard that name before. In her search for Primrose, she'd scoured the stews, and in that hotbed of vice and depravity, only one name consistently roused fear and trembling. A man notorious for his power, temper, and love of killing.

Bartholomew Black: the rookery's most infamous cutthroat.

"What has Black to do with this?" she asked.

"Kitty owed him money. He was the reason she left Town. If he lifts the death warrant off her head, I have no doubt she'll pop up again." Corbett's lips formed a wry curve. "Kitty ain't cut out for rustication."

"So if I pay off her debt to Black, then she can return?"

Corbett shook his head. "'Tis not that easy. Black saw Kitty's flit as an act of cowardice and took personal affront. 'Tis her lack of honor as much as the money that has him up in the boughs."

Marianne thought it over. "You'll help me contact Black?"

"Like hell I will," Corbett said. "I'm a young man with a long life ahead of me—and I plan to keep it that way. Speaking of which, I must head back. Mrs. Wilson hates to be kept waiting; luckily, I have a set of Madame Rousseau's fine handkerchiefs to explain my absence. Paid for by you, of course." He made a leg and headed for the door.

"Wait," Marianne called out.

He stopped and pivoted with brows raised.

"You are a true gentleman, Mr. Corbett," she said steadily, "and I cannot thank you enough."

His face reddened. "Good afternoon, Lady Draven."

A few moments later, Marianne heard the front door opening

and closing. Amelie Rousseau came into the dressing room, her dark eyes filled with curiosity.

"*Comment ça va, ma chère?*"

"*Bien. Tout est bien,*" Marianne said softly.

And all *would* be well—as soon as she paid a visit to Bartholomew Black. Determination lifted her chin. Black might be the stew's most formidable villain, but he hadn't met *her* yet.

Chapter Seven

Ambrose entered the spacious office above the warehouse.
Large windows framed the view of the West India docks,
the water itself hidden beneath the crowded field of
ships. Despite the early hour, lumpers marched along the wharves,
conducting the flow of cargo to and from the vessels with the
single-mindedness of ants. Light filtered through the morning fog
and sparkling glass, gleaming off the dark head of the man who
rose from behind the large desk.

Ambrose bowed. "Good morning, my lord."

Nicholas Morgan, the Marquess of Harteford, gave him a wry
look. "Good might be an exaggeration," he said. "But it is morning, and I must thank you for coming this early, Kent. Especially
after your assistance with Miss Fines last evening."

"'Twas my duty, my lord," Ambrose said.

Which wasn't precisely true. The Thames River Police did not
typically concern itself with the affairs of young misses gone astray.
But when the Marquess of Harteford—noted patron of said
policing force—had requested help in retrieving a close family
friend from a potentially ruinous situation last night, the Chief

Magistrate had been more than willing to send Ambrose and as many Thames River constables as Harteford needed.

Not that Ambrose had minded. He was grateful for Harteford's support of the River Police, and, more than that, he respected the man. Despite his wealth and position, the marquess was no snob—unlike certain other titled personages. Ambrose's jaw clenched as the mocking, beautiful visage flared in his head as it had done so many times in the past three days. With gritty resolve, he pushed aside the lowering memory and focused on the present. The marquess was watching him with sharp grey eyes honed by an unorthodox upbringing in the stews.

"Duty or not, you have done me a favor," Harteford said, "and I plan to show my appreciation to you and the force."

Though Ambrose's shoulders tensed at the mention of money, his ethics would not allow him to take beyond what he'd earned. "I have been amply rewarded through your patronage of the River Police, my lord." Before the other man could argue, he added, "And how is Miss Fines faring?"

Harteford's expression grew stark, grooves deepening around his mouth. "The truth is, Kent, I remain concerned for her safety. Though we intervened before any ... irrevocable damage had been done"—the marquess dragged a hand through his silver-shot hair —"that blackguard Gavin Hunt has her under his spell." In the ensuing silence, ghosts flitted through Harteford's eyes. He went to the window, staring out into the fog. "And I think you and I both know who Hunt is to me."

Three years ago, Harteford had confided a part of his past to Ambrose. The marquess had survived a dark childhood, and not even his current power and position had dispelled its horrors completely. In particular, he remained haunted by the memory of a boy whom he'd wronged; in hopes of making amends, he'd entrusted Ambrose with the task of investigating the fate of that nameless urchin. But Ambrose's best efforts had yielded only dead ends.

Now it seemed Harteford's childhood ghost had suddenly returned—no longer a helpless boy, but a powerful man hell-bent on revenge. It seemed Gavin Hunt meant to hurt the marquess by seducing Miss Persephone Fines, Harteford's sister in heart if not in blood. Last night, Ambrose and Harteford had arrived at Hunt's gaming hell to find Miss Fines; they'd been greeted by a scene of chaos. Hunt had suffered an attack by rival club owners, and Miss Fines had been caught in the thick of things. Luckily, she'd been unhurt—in a physical sense, at least. Her broken heart might prove a different matter. Though Ambrose had not been privy to the exchange that followed between her, Harteford, and Hunt, he could guess that it had been painful.

Betrayal invariably was.

"I see now that any notion of restitution was foolish," Harteford said, his voice bleak. "Hunt has every right to avenge himself against me. But I cannot allow him to do so by hurting Miss Fines." He turned, his hands curled at his sides. "That is why I summoned you today, Kent. I have yet another favor to ask of you."

"Yes, my lord?"

"I need you to keep an eye on Miss Fines. I fear Hunt will try to contact her, and I must have her protected from him until this matter is resolved. If you are willing, I will clear my request with your superiors at Wapping Station."

Ambrose inclined his head. "I am at your service, my lord."

"Thank you, Kent. I am glad for your support." Clasping his hands behind his back, Harteford looked out the window again and into the darkening sky. "I fear a storm brews ahead."

The following morning, Ambrose reflected that his mission might not be as simple as it had first sounded. How difficult could it be to accompany a young heiress on her daily activities? Yet ensconced in

a well-sprung carriage with Harteford's quasi-sister, Miss Persephone Fines, Ambrose quickly realized his error. Behind the pretty
countenance and innocent eyes lay a miss with a strong will and
mind of her own.

He should know: he had four young sisters himself.

In fact, something of Miss Fines' fresh beauty reminded him
of Emma. His throat tightened as he thought of the eldest of his
sisters. At sixteen, Emma had too much on her shoulders. With
their father ill and Ambrose away earning the family's keep, poor
Em was left with the day-to-day running of the Kent household.
Though she'd never once complained and seemed to tackle all
tasks with boundless energy, Ambrose wished a different life for
her. One filled with balls and shopping, whatever a girl would
enjoy.

His chest constricted. Another brick dropped into the sack
upon his shoulders. It was up to *him* to provide for Emma and all
his family, and he was failing in that task.

"Mr. Kent, might I solicit your advice on a matter?" Miss
Fines' cheerful voice distracted him from the downward spiral of
his thoughts.

He gave a curt nod.

"I'm wondering how one might locate the whereabouts of a
criminal," she said.

For a moment, he stared at her heart-shaped face, her guileless
blue eyes. His lips twitched. Firming them, he said, "Are you
indeed?"

Her gaze darted briefly to the side before returning to his. A
telltale sign of deception to any investigator worth his salt.

"It's for my novel," she continued. "One of the characters is,
um ..."—her brief hesitation was another giveaway—"a detective.
And he needs to search out a villain from the past."

As she continued to spin her tale, Ambrose bit back a smile. It
took a spirited girl to try to pump information from an experienced policeman. Entertained by her imagination, he listened as

she rambled on. In this trait, she more resembled his middle sister, Violet, who, too, possessed a flair for drama.

Ultimately, however, he could not allow Miss Fines to believe that she could interfere in the business between Lord Harteford and Gavin Hunt. By the sound of things, she still thought herself head over heels for Hunt, even though the man clearly meant to use her for his own ends. The bastard deserved to be strung up for involving an innocent in his plot for revenge.

So in a gentle yet firm manner, Ambrose informed Miss Fines that she must, in a nutshell, stay clear of the matter. She sighed and turned to face the window, her hand reaching to fiddle with the unusual quill-shaped brooch upon her frock. In silence, they reached their destination. Hatchard's was a popular bookstore on Piccadilly frequented by many members of the upper and middling classes. Ambrose alighted from the carriage first.

"Wait here, if you please, Miss Fines," he said. "I shall return in a moment."

His gaze swept the territory. He saw no trouble, but he posted two of his men at the entrance to be certain. Inside, he did a quick check of the rows of bookshelves and detected nothing suspicious. He found a door hidden at a back corner of the shop; jiggling the lock, he found it secure. Satisfied, he returned to the carriage and escorted his charge inside.

"I am going to browse around," Miss Fines announced, "and there's no use following me through the stacks. Perhaps you'd care to wait for me at an assigned place?"

Seeing the pucker of impatience on her brow, Ambrose debated the best plan. He decided not to push his luck. From his experience with his sisters, he knew that pushing too hard led to the inevitable resistance. Besides, he could survey most of the store from the central point by the fireplace. Posted outside, his men had been given a likeness of Gavin Hunt and would nab the bastard if he tried to step foot into the shop.

"I'll be here if you need me," Ambrose said.

He stifled a snort of amusement as Miss Fines bounded off like a hare released from a trap. He kept a watchful eye on her straw bonnet, seeing the tip of its white plume float over the top of the shelves. Around him, gentlemen sat in overstuffed chairs by the fireplace, their newspapers rustling as they perused the pages. The notion of such leisure was foreign to Ambrose. He enjoyed reading —his father had taught all the children their letters at an early age —but his life left scant time for such luxury.

At the age of sixteen, Ambrose had left school to support his family. Father had protested, of course; whilst a brilliant scholar and philosopher, Samuel had never been a very practical man. There'd been babes to feed, and Ambrose's duty to protect his new siblings far outweighed his personal desires. Between him and his sensible stepmother, Marjorie, they'd managed to keep the Kent brood thriving.

Ambrose continued to track his charge's bobbing white feather through the shop. Miss Fines passed by another lady, and the platinum curls bouncing at the sides of the latter's bonnet snagged his attention. As if she sensed his regard, the lady in question turned; her square countenance creased, and her small eyes formed slits of suspicion.

Ambrose looked away, cursing himself.

Devil and damn, why couldn't he get Lady Marianne Draven out of his head?

She was like some dangerous drug in his blood. Every time he thought himself rid of her poison, something would remind him of her, and a feverish, wicked desire would escalate within him. His rational mind knew this yearning was pointless. And potentially destructive, for she roused a part of him—a lustful, bestial presence —that was at jarring odds with his principles.

Though not a gentleman by class, he was a man of honor, and he believed in treating the fairer sex with respect. At two-and-thirty, he'd had a handful of lovers: experienced women who'd taught him about female pleasure. Jane, a widow, had enticed him into her bed during their engagement—not that it had taken much enticing. He'd always enjoyed a woman's desire, the soft, lush response that let him know he was doing things right. Unlike some men, he'd looked forward to the marital bed. To making love with his wife and exploring intimacies that could only be found with one's gentle lady.

Never, ever had he lost control with Jane or any other woman. He'd never experienced the urge to tear the clothes from Jane's body. To grasp her hair in his palms and back her against a wall. To shove himself so hard and deep inside her that nothing but desire remained in her eyes. He'd never craved to see his own self reflected in her glassy, wanton gaze as he pounded into her, rooted himself in her sweet sex so thoroughly she could only pant his name—

"Beg pardon, sir."

With a start, Ambrose realized a gentleman was attempting to get by him. That, and the fact that his shaft had begun to stiffen in his smalls. With a silent curse, he stepped aside and vowed to banish Marianne Draven from his thoughts once and for all. No good could come of such wickedness. Though he had little to call his own, he could count self-discipline and good sense amongst his holdings.

Resolved, he checked in on his charge. The hairs on his nape prickled when no jaunty white feather came into view. He pushed past the startled man whom he'd just let by and began going through the aisles. He told himself Miss Fines had likely bent to examine a book on some lower shelf.

He raced past shelf after shelf. No sign of her anywhere.

It couldn't have been more than three minutes since you saw her last. Think, man. She has to be here somewhere.

A sudden chill raced up his spine, and he raced to the back corner of the shop. The door—the one he'd believed was locked—swung open on its hinges. He pushed through; the alleyway was shadowed and empty, nothing untoward ...

Except for the single white plume lying in the dirt.

Chapter Eight

"Is everything quite alright, Marianne?"

The gentle voice returned Marianne to the elegant cameo blue drawing room. Helena, Marchioness of Harteford, sat on an adjacent curricle chair, a notch between her chestnut brows. Though she was fond of Helena, Marianne did not like the hint of worry in the other's wide hazel eyes. The last thing she needed was for her friend to pry into her affairs.

She'd written Bartholomew Black and received a scrawled reply this morning: *Her Ladyship will be received by Mr. Black at ten o'clock sharp Friday night.* Thinking of the plan she'd set into action, Marianne felt her pulse quicken. Tomorrow evening, she would be bartering with a cutthroat for Primrose's life.

At the moment, however, she had to get through tea.

"Everything is fine," she said lightly. "You needn't count me amongst your chicks, Mother Hen."

Helena's porcelain cheeks turned pink. "'Tis a habit, I suppose. Not that it seems to do me any good." She cast an exasperated look at her twin boys, who were currently busy taking apart the pianoforte. "I do so hate to disturb their explorations of the world, but at times their energy seems quite limitless. Perhaps I should take a firmer hand."

"You are a fine and loving mother," Marianne said. "Your boys and this new babe are fortunate indeed, dearest."

As Helena's blush grew deeper, her hand settling upon the lilac muslin folds over her belly, Marianne took a sip of the fine Darjeeling. The bitterness of the tea was no match for the emotion that leaked inside her breast. Helena was the finest of parents—which was more than Marianne could say for herself. It reminded her too keenly of her own failures, of how much Rosie had had to endure because of her recklessness. Her stupidity.

And, at times, another form of torment came from looking into Helena's sweet hazel eyes. They were so much like Thomas' ... which was hardly surprising, given that Marianne's first lover— and Primrose's father—was Helena's dead brother. The trite tale might have been ripped from the pages of a gothic novel: poor country miss falls for her rich friend's older brother.

She could still hear Helena's innocent, chatty girl's voice:

Now that Thomas is home, Papa's invited over a legion of eligible misses. I like Lady Louisa myself—she's ever so accomplished and beautiful and a duke's daughter to boot. Mama says she'd make a lovely addition to our family, and I think Thomas is quite smitten with her. Why, he wore a dreamy smile all through tea ...

Helena had never suspected that Marianne had put that expression on Thomas' face. Marianne had been with him in the meadow just a half-hour before the arrival of the Northgates' esteemed visitors. Thomas, heir to the earldom, had whispered promises as he took her amongst the shivering grasses.

We'll talk to Papa soon. Trust me, Marianne, you'll be my bride—

"Heavens, what *is* plaguing you?" Helena's voice snapped Marianne back. "Clearly, something is amiss, and I do wish you would confide in me. As I have so oft done in you. I am no longer a silly innocent, you know—you *can* trust me."

To gather herself, Marianne drank more tea. She did not doubt her friend's assertion. Since meeting up with Helena in London, she'd discovered the other had grown up a great deal. Indeed, Helena's fortitude had won her the devotion of her husband, the brooding Marquess of Harteford.

And therein lay the problem. Not every romance had a happy ending; in comparison, Marianne's own tale was a sordid one indeed. The familiar, uneasy mix of love and envy stirred within her. The truth was that she'd always felt lacking compared to her friend. Though Marianne had undoubtedly been the leader of the two, she'd secretly coveted all that Helena took for granted: wealth, doting parents, a childhood of privileged innocence.

Marianne's own mother had died during childbirth, and her father, a bitter, penniless country squire, had cared more for his hounds than his only child.

A gel, he'd rage when in his cups. *What am I supposed to do with a good-for-nothing chit?*

Marianne did not like to remember the past. What was done was done. And she knew jealousy was small of her. While she did not like herself for it, she at least recognized her own flaws. Sweet, virtuous Helena deserved every happiness; Marianne did not begrudge her for it. It did not, however, make Marianne eager to expose her own failures.

And what would she say?

By the by, Helena, your brother and I were tupping behind your back. We went to ask for your father's blessing; the earl said he'd disown Thomas before he let his heir marry a slut like me. Thomas died while trying to get back to me. Oh, and that old lecher I married? He kidnapped my sweet babe and consigned her to purgatory.

Marianne set her Sèvres cup down upon the coffee table. "Thank you, dearest, but nothing is the matter."

Helena chewed on her lip, and Marianne steeled herself for what was to come next. She was relieved by the change in topic.

"In that case, I wondered if you'd care to join us for a supper party next week. Harteford has made a new acquaintance,"—the briefest of pauses betrayed the marchioness' intention—"a very nice gentleman by the name of Mayberry. He's an earl and quite handsome ..."

As Helena waxed on about the earl's attributes, Marianne wondered when she and her friend had switched roles in their relationship. Not so long ago, it had been Helena who asked *her* for advice in the matters of love and romance; now the happily married marchioness saw fit to do the dispensing. And it nettled Marianne's pride.

"Thank you, but I am capable of finding my own gentlemen," she drawled, cutting the other off. "Trust me, there is no shortage."

"I know that, of course. You are ever so popular, Marianne. 'Tis only ..." Helena flushed, yet her shoulders drew up. "I wonder if you are truly *happy*. And if your reluctance to settle down has something to do with your past. Whenever I ask you about your marriage to Lord Draven, you clam up."

Though Marianne resisted, Draven's nasal, angry tones sliced through her, sharper than any crop: *This is your fault, you worthless bitch! I've never had this problem before. Beneath your beauty, you're nothing more than a dirty cunt. Well, you had best employ your whore's tricks or you shall never see your Primrose again ...*

Her hand trembled slightly as she smoothed her skirts. "Suffice it to say, I have no desire to call any man my lord and master again. Please, Helena," she said icily, "let us move on to a less tedious subject."

The marchioness' shoulders fell, hurt sliding across her soft features.

Stifling a sigh, Marianne said in gentler tones, "In point of fact, we have more pressing matters to discuss. How is our young Miss Percy faring?"

A few days ago, Helena had apprised her of their mutual friend Miss Persephone Fines' entanglement with a scoundrel named Gavin Hunt. Marianne regretted any inadvertent part that she'd played in the fiasco. She'd considered herself a mentor of sorts to the feisty Percy, and when Percy had come to her for advice on love, she'd given it freely. She hadn't known, however, that the object of the spirited miss' affections was Hunt, a notorious gaming hell owner who turned out to be a nemesis of Harteford's.

Lud, could the plot thicken any further?

"The dear girl seems to be doing better now," Helena said, though she sounded far from certain. "Her mama should be arriving at any minute, and I must ask you not to mention the matter. Poor Mrs. Fines has been beside herself with worry. Imagine—Percy getting mixed up with some riffraff from the stews!"

Marianne's brows lifted. "Yes, imagine that. Falling in love with a man from the rookery."

"That's not what I meant," Helena said with a huff. "Besides, Harteford may have been born in that unfortunate place, but he is in every way a gentleman. Unlike this detestable fellow Hunt. Why, I'd like to ... to wring his neck for planning to hurt Percy, not to mention Harteford!"

Amused, Marianne took in the spots of color on her friend's rounded cheeks. "I misspoke earlier. You're no Mother Hen, my dear, but a tigress when it comes to your own."

The arrival of the new guests forestalled further discussion. Mrs. Anna Fines, a kindly bespectacled lady of comfortable years, was escorted by her son Paul, a handsome blond rake near Marianne's own age. Helena's butler arrived with refreshments, and soon polite conversation mingled with the tinkling of silver tongs used to serve the bite-sized pastries and sandwiches. Marianne hid a yawn as Paul Fines did his utmost to flirt with her.

Wearying of the scene, she readied to take her leave. At that moment, however, Helena's husband, the Marquess of Harteford, came barging into the drawing room. Following at his heels was another man, equally large and rather brutal looking due to the scar that ran from cheek to jaw. Marianne's brows climbed.

Clearly, things are about to get interesting.

After introducing the stranger as none other than the infamous Gavin Hunt, Harteford said abruptly, "Percy may be in danger. I'll explain all later. First we must locate her—where is she?"

"Hatchard's," Anna Fines said. "Mr. Kent went with her and planned to bring her here afterward."

At the mention of the policeman, the conversation faded to the rushing of blood in Marianne's ears. *Kent might come here ... today?* Tingles tiptoed up her spine; she chided her own foolishness. She'd already taught Kent a lesson, and matters were settled between them. If she saw him, she would treat him with cold *politesse*. And, if he was as smart as she suspected he was, he'd stay out of her path.

The door swung open—it had been doing that a lot this afternoon—and Kent entered with a rapid stride. His keen gaze took in the room, latched upon her face. The spark of surprise across his features was quickly snuffed by the grimness of his expression. Then he spotted Hunt, and his lean frame went rigid.

"What are you doing here?" Kent demanded.

"Where is Percy?" Hunt shot back.

Marianne gripped the strings of her reticule as a premonitory chill touched her nape.

Raw emotion flashed in Kent's remarkable eyes ... shame?

In a hoarse voice, he said, "She has been taken."

In the hallway outside the drawing room, Helena said, "Heavens, poor Percy at the mercy of kidnappers! Who knows what these enemies of Mr. Hunt are capable of? If anything happens to her—oh, I do wish I could help!"

"Don't overtax yourself, dearest," Marianne said. "In your condition, you'd be more hindrance than help. Harteford would be mad with worry over you—and you know he needs his concentration in this instance."

Helena bit her lip and nodded. Her hazel eyes glimmered with anxiety.

Thinking of Percy's predicament, Marianne couldn't help but share her concern. Gavin Hunt had explained the situation: his rivals had taken Percy with the aim of hurting him. To Marianne's surprise—and everyone else's—it seemed Hunt's enemies had hit the nail on the head. Hunt *had* looked desperate, savage in his need to get Percy back. Though the blackguard might have seduced Percy with revenge in mind, he'd clearly lost his heart to her in the process.

But who wouldn't love a girl as open and warm-hearted as Percy?

Marianne made up her mind.

"I'll go along, shall I?" she said lightly. "That way, we won't have to worry about the males bungling it all up."

Helena's eyes welled, and Marianne felt a twinge of alarm. She'd never enjoyed excessive displays of emotion. In her experience, ladies who were increasing had the tendency to become watering pots.

"Oh, would you?" Reaching out, Helena gripped Marianne's arm. "You are ever so clever! When I think of the danger Percy may be in ..."

"I shall be glad to be of help." Marianne gingerly pried free of the other's fingers. "Now you'd best go sit with Mrs. Fines and keep her calm."

With a watery nod, Helena returned to the drawing room.

Marianne went in the opposite direction. The trio of large males stood in the atrium, organizing the passage to Hunt's club where they would await the kidnappers' ransom note. Despite her anxiety for Percy, Marianne couldn't help but notice Kent. He was the tallest of the three, his shoulders just as wide as the other men's despite his lankier frame. He had his hands shoved in the pockets of his threadbare wool coat—did he own but one?—and his wavy brown-black hair was ruffled, as if he'd dragged a hand through it repeatedly.

For some asinine reason, she found his dishevelment ... attractive. Above the slipshod knot of his cravat, his jaw appeared harder than steel, the muscle there ticking like a clock. It was as if there were two Mr. Kents: the preachy policeman who walked the straight and narrow, and this one—a dangerous male on the edge. She knew which version she preferred.

As if sensing her arrival, he jerked his head up. His mouth pulled tight at the edges.

She ignored him and addressed Harteford. "I shall be joining in the night's mission, my lord," she said. "Kindly provide my driver with the directions to Mr. Hunt's club."

"You?" Kent spoke up, his tone incredulous. "This is a dangerous undertaking. It has no place for a lady."

Attractive ... and with the uncanny ability to set her teeth on edge.

"I make my own place in the world, sir." Flicking him a cool glance, she turned to the gaming hell owner. "Now, Mr. Hunt, the name of your establishment?"

"The Underworld. Covent Garden," Hunt said, his gaze fixed on the exit.

Harteford frowned. "Are you certain this is a good idea, my lady?"

"Your wife suggested it. 'Tis either she or I who comes along this eve."

That shut Harteford up. When it came to Helena, the man had the protective instincts of a bulldog. And apparently there was another guard dog in the midst. Kent's eyes roved over her, and Marianne's belly quivered. Strange, because she didn't like overbearing men. Amongst the *ton*, she was famed for three qualities:

beauty, wealth, and indisputable independence. Gentlemen who pursued her knew better than to gainsay her anything, and her razor-sharp wit gave her a reputation for invulnerability. Coldness.

Yet this river constable seemed to think that she was in need of his protection. It was downright laughable. And oddly ... intriguing.

"The notion is ridiculous. You cannot allow her to be involved," Kent snapped to the other men. Never mind that one was a marquess and the other owned the stews—the policeman in his drab clothes stood his own ground. And dash it if his dignity didn't shine through greater than any title or coin. "We are dealing with *cutthroats* here."

"Men like any other," she interjected in a bored voice designed to drive him mad. It seemed to succeed. If he turned any ruddier, steam might spout from his ears. "Now we cannot afford to dally, can we? I shall meet you all at Hunt's club."

"For God's sake, woman, use your brains for more than mischief this once! 'Tis a gaming hell—you cannot go there unaccompanied," Kent exploded. "Think of your safety."

As Harteford stared at Kent and Hunt's brows climbed, a delicious and utterly diabolical notion took hold of Marianne. She had a moment's pause: why should it please her to push the upright Mr. Kent? Yet the imp of perversion was too much to resist.

"See you there, gentlemen," she said. Heading to the door, she paused to add over her shoulder, "Coming, Mr. Kent?"

The furrows on his forehead deepened. "With you?"

"Well, of course." She settled a cool smile upon him. "You are a policeman, aren't you? Since it seems I must be protected, you may provide the escort."

Chapter Nine

As the carriage clip-clopped toward Covent Garden, Ambrose did not know who infuriated him more: the wicked widow sitting across from him or himself. With her silvery skirts draped elegantly over the lavender squabs, Lady Draven was the epitome of cool and collected. A queen supremely aware of her own power. She'd laid a neat trap, and he'd blundered into it like a fool. The question was why she'd bother to ensnare him at all ... and why he couldn't rid himself of his concern for this maddening female. If she wanted to risk her foolish neck, why did he care?

Because ... from beneath lowered eyelids, he slid a glance at said neck. The elegant column was white and delicate, graceful as a swan's. The thought of anything happening to it—

"'Tis rather *déjà-vu*, isn't it? You and I alone in a carriage. Cutthroats lurking about."

"This is no game, my lady." His jaw clenched at her amused tone. "I beg you to reconsider interfering in this business. You must know it is unwise."

"I know no such thing. Miss Fines is a friend to me, and I must do what is in my power to aid her." Lady Draven tilted her head to the side. The dusk's glow seeped from the edge of the curtain, frosting her upswept curls with icy radiance. "How is your arm, Mr. Kent?"

He blinked. She remembered his injury? "It is fine," he said curtly. "As I was saying, if you truly wish to help Miss Fines, you'd turn this carriage around and wait with the other ladies. I am sure they could use your support."

"Tea and sympathy has never been my forte."

"And apprehending kidnappers and murderers is?" He didn't bother to hide the sarcasm.

She gave a throaty laugh. "You have experienced my prowess with a pistol firsthand, sir. You tell me."

Anger blurred the edges of his vision. He'd never done violence to a woman—in action or in thought. But Lady Marianne Draven was no ordinary female. Suddenly, he could hold his tongue no more. The fact that she was a lady and his social superior be damned.

"Why do you take pleasure in baiting me?" he said.

If his bluntness surprised her, she showed no sign. The corners of her mouth tipped up as she replied, "I don't think I can take the credit for your current state—not entirely, at any rate. You're already wound tighter than a clock, Mr. Kent. I can't help but wonder why."

"The life of an innocent miss is at stake," he said through gritted teeth.

And it is my fault. I let Miss Fines and her family down. The truth knotted his chest. He'd never failed in his duty before; the fact that he had shamed him to his very core. To think of what the young miss might be suffering because of his lapse—

"And you take full responsibility," Lady Draven said, as if reading his mind.

"Because the responsibility is mine. I was supposed to keep an eye on her. It was my job to make sure nothing happened, and instead I was—" He bit off the rest of the words.

Don't go there, man. Do. Not.

"Instead you let your attention ... wander. Is that it?"

The knowing gleam in her verdant eyes made his throat clench. But he would not shirk from the truth. He jerked his head in assent.

"How long?" she said.

"I beg your pardon?"

"How long did you let her out of your sight?"

"Two minutes, mayhap three." Disgrace constricted his insides. "When I realized what I had done, I went searching for her. That is when I found the back door open and Miss Fines gone."

"During the time you were distracted, there was no commotion in the shop? No kidnappers at large, no cries for help?"

"I would have noticed if there had been a hubbub," he said. "When I questioned the patrons at the shop afterward, no one witnessed any sign of a struggle. One customer saw a girl fitting Miss Fines' description walking alone toward the back of the shop."

"Ah," Lady Draven said.

That single sound conveyed a world of significance. He frowned. "What are you getting at?"

"Merely that Miss Fines had it in her head to leave the shop. And to do so unhindered by you." The baroness lifted her fair brows. "My guess? She was lured outside—likely with the false prospect of seeing Mr. Hunt."

Ambrose mulled it over. The hypothesis made perfect sense. With grudging respect, he said, "Your skills of deduction are refined, my lady."

"Clever is as clever does."

A hint of genuine warmth entered her smile, and that infinitesimal softening of her lips made his breath falter. *Too beautiful—for her own good as well as yours.*

"It doesn't change the fact that I should have been there every step of the way," he said doggedly. "I could have prevented Miss Fines from making so egregious a decision."

"Oh, I doubt that very much."

"I apprehend criminals for a living. I trust I can handle a young lady," he said stiffly.

Lady Draven laughed again. Despite his simmering anger, that husky sound reached straight to his groin. His bollocks tautened; his member stiffened as if being caressed. The notion of those perfectly shaped pink lips parting to pleasure rather than taunt ...

"Goes to show," she said, "how much you know about young ladies."

Hah. He had her there.

"I have four younger sisters. Trust me, I know the minds of misses." Guilt prodded him to add in gruff tones, "Indeed, I ought to have predicted Miss Fines' behavior from the way she was questioning me about the business between Hunt and Lord Harteford."

"Sisters. Ah, that explains it," Lady Draven murmured.

"Explains what?" Devil and damn, the lady's mind had more twists and turns than the streets of the rookery.

"The sense of duty that hangs upon you like a rusty suit of armor. It's rather passé, you know." She adjusted her smooth gloves. "No one likes a dull Johnny."

"What the devil is that supposed to mean?"

"Simply put? You, sir, are a snob."

For a second, he was rendered speechless. "*I'm* the snob? Of all the hypocritical—"

"Oh, you're not an elitist in a social sense," she said with a thin smile. "You're the other kind. A moralistic snob. You expect perfection of yourself and others. And you take responsibility for everything—even what is not yours to take."

"I don't expect others to be perfect. And I damn well *was* responsible for Miss Fines!"

Her creamy shoulders made an indifferent movement. "Be

that as it may, you cannot control everything, Mr. Kent, no matter how scrupulous you are." While he wrestled with anger and that unpalatable observation, she went on, "If I were to hazard a further guess ... you believe the weight of your entire family, four siblings and all, rests upon your shoulders. Am I right?"

"Five siblings," he shot back. "I have a younger brother as well. And it's not a mere belief—it is a *fact*. They depend upon me for their livelihood."

"No parents?"

How did they get into a conversation about his family? Bewildered, Ambrose raked his hands through his hair. "My stepmother died two years ago. My father has not been well since."

"I am sorry to hear that." Something ghosted through her eyes. Empathy, a flash of ... pain? "It is difficult to lose someone you care about," she said quietly.

He stared at her, befuddled.

Without a doubt, Lady Marianne Draven was the most infuriating, provoking female he'd ever met. At the same time, a disconcerting realization struck him. He'd never talked so much about himself before, not even with his past lovers. And that perceptive gaze of hers? It pushed him to the jagged edge of his restraint. Made him feel exposed. Off balance.

He made an attempt to even the score. "Have you any family, my lady?"

Her eyes shuttered. "No."

A glacial silence descended, during which he wondered why she was lying to him. Because he had observed the flare in her gaze, the way the clear celadon depths churned with a dark emotion. His policeman's instincts told him that she was hiding something ... what?

"No parents or siblings?" he pressed.

"My parents are dead." She gave him a derisive smile. "Isn't it obvious that I am an only child?"

He tried a different tactic. "It must have been difficult being widowed at so young an age."

Her mouth took on a harder edge. "Not really."

"Being left alone in the world cannot have been easy."

Did he imagine the subtle bobbing of her throat?

"My inquisitive sir, I was left with ten thousand pounds per annum and the freedom to do with it what I choose. Nothing could be *easier*. Draven's money has given me the power to purchase my heart's desires."

She flicked a languid gaze over his person, and just like that his temperature shot up again, blood rushing beneath his skin. At the same time, the mention of her "heart's desires" warped his gut. How many men had she consorted with? A strange, crazed possessiveness gripped him. Other males, touching that white skin, kissing those petal-soft lips—

"Who knows?" Her eyes rested on his, cool and deliberate. "If the mood strikes, I might even offer you an arrangement some day."

Shock quelled his words. *Bloody hell.* This shameless woman thought she could *purchase* him, like he was a ... a *male whore*? Heat razed his insides. Rage. Lust. A potent combination of the two.

"You'll apologize for that," he bit out.

"Why? 'Tis the truth. You want me." Her brows formed those damnable arches. "And we've already established that you need the money."

Her words slashed into him with the delicate accuracy of a rapier. Scenting blood, the beast within him growled low in its throat, straining against its chains. The next moment, his hands crushed the cushions on either side of her head. His body crowded hers. He could feel a heartbeat—his, hers—pulsing in the sliver of space between them.

"Apologize," he repeated.

Her bosom rose and fell. Her chin angled in challenge. "Make me."

His control snapped. Blood roaring, he bent his head and smothered that mocking mouth with his own. The kiss was savage, like no kiss he'd ever given a woman before. Her lips yielded, and he thrust his tongue home. She moaned as she did in his darkest fantasies. Her spicy cinnamon flavor fueled his hunger. The kiss turned ravenous, greedy, and when her tongue slid against his, he was lost.

Pushing her back onto the seat, he tasted the smooth slope of her throat. Her exotic, flowery scent made him heady as he licked his way up to her delicate jaw and then her earlobe. The gasp that left her told him all that he needed to know; he suckled, curling his tongue around the sweet curve of her ear until she began to writhe against him. His cock strained, stiff and chafing at the barriers between them. Groaning, he thrust into the cradle of her thighs, his hands moving to cup her breasts.

Soft yet firm. Heaven. He found the hard peaks, rubbed them through the thin layer of silk. She was panting now, her eyes closed, her hands gripping his sleeves. With a growl of pure want, he lowered his head, licked the crevice between her heaving mounds. Somehow, he managed to tug down one shoulder of her gown, and his next breath hissed through his teeth.

A rosy nipple, flushed with color and ripe as a berry.

He cupped her breast, his cock leaping at the sight of his worn leather glove against the pale perfection of her skin. The bounce of the carriage jiggled her flesh as he palmed her. He drew his thumb across the puckered peak, and she jerked, her eyes flying open.

Their gazes clashed.

Another craving took hold of him, foreign yet as potent as the lust beating in his veins. He strummed her nipple again, and her trembling response further incited him. Never before had he experienced this burning desire to assert his dominance—to establish his manhood to this maddening female.

"Say you're sorry," he said.

Her eyes widened.

"Say it." This time he tweaked her nipple lightly.

Her lips parted. "I will not," she said, and the breathiness of her tone almost undid him. Almost. "One cannot be sorry for the truth."

"The truth?" Even as his cock throbbed, something settled within him. Solid and grounding, a sense of power such as he'd never felt. Because every male instinct told him that he could pleasure this *selkie* seductress. Make her moan and lose herself to his touch. To experiment, he thumbed her nipple once more, and her gaze grew cloudy, her spine arching for his caress in spite of her obstinate words.

Wanton and wicked, this one. In need of a firm, steady hand. Whoever took on this woman would have his work cut out for him. And, damn, if he didn't want to interview for the job.

Job ... duty. Rescuing Miss Fines.

Christ, what in blazes was he doing?

The memory of the other encounter with Lady Draven slapped him to his senses. Through the haze of lust, he eyed the beauty panting beneath him. Was she leading him on again? Why did she delight in driving him to the edge of sanity? He might be poor and a policeman, but he was no puppet on a string. No toy to be trifled with.

Somehow, he summoned the willpower to release her. He pulled up her sleeve. "The *truth* is that you're a reckless woman. You need someone to protect you from yourself."

Her gaze sharpened. The next instant she shoved at his shoulders, her cheeks flooded with color. "Get off of me, *you lout.*"

"Steady now. I'm just trying to help," he said, scowling.

"I don't need your help! I dictate my own life," she hissed as she sat up. "What I do is no business of yours."

"You've shot me and propositioned me. The latter twice." Now it was his turn to lift a brow, and devil and damn if that didn't feel good. "I'd say you've invited me into your business, my lady."

Her features smoothed. A *selkie* with her magical, impenetrable skin in place.

"I hope you haven't the wrong idea, Mr. Kent. You're not even the first man I've shot, let alone made advances upon," she drawled. "So let us be clear: I was considering one night with you —two if your performance exceeded my expectations." She gave her skirts a flick. "Trust me when I say no man has held my attention for more than a night or two."

"I could be the first." Why the devil did he say that?

"I doubt it. Come to think of it," she said, tapping a finger to her chin, "I should shop around first. Sample a few wares before I make my decision."

Scarlet flashed across his vision. He was not jealous by nature, and yet the thought of any other man sharing her bed made him want to growl with rage. His fists clenched.

"One of these days, my lady, you'll push me too far," he bit out.

"Is that a threat?" she said with a scornful curve to her lips.

"Not a threat. A promise."

They stared at each other, the air taut with challenge. As if they tugged an invisible rope between them, neither gave any ground. His muscles bunched with the instinct to haul her back into his arms and settle this matter in a more primitive fashion. His mouth on hers, his cock buried in her silken heat ...

Her gaze narrowed. Without breaking eye contact, she reached out and rapped sharply on the carriage door. He'd been so far gone that he hadn't realized that the vehicle had come to a stop. The door opened, revealing Lugo's unreadable features and a looming gaming club behind him.

Taking her manservant's arm, Lady Draven descended with haughty grace.

"Try to keep up, will you Mr. Kent?" she tossed over her shoulder.

Ambrose waited a moment to collect himself. To reestablish his self-discipline and good sense ... and to let his bloody cockstand subside. Only then did he blow out a breath and follow her into the hell.

Chapter Ten

Despite the urgency of the night's mission, Marianne found that it required a surprising amount of willpower to stay focused. She and the three men were seated around a coffee table in Gavin Hunt's office. The ransom note had arrived, and now they were debating the strategy for rescuing Percy from the villains. Marianne kept her gaze firmly away from Kent, who was sitting beside her on the divan. Under no circumstances would she give him the satisfaction of seeing her ruffled.

Awareness of his proximity tingled over her skin. Surely she imagined the heat that seemed to emanate from him, the corresponding melting sensation low in her belly. To think that he'd had the temerity to touch her so boldly ... beneath her bodice, her nipples pebbled, her intimate muscles fluttering.

Cease this foolishness immediately. You're no longer a foolish girl subject to her impulses. Master yourself—for Rosie's sake, if not your own.

She took a steadying breath. Then fate intervened, demanding her full attention.

Hunt tossed a bundle of letters upon the coffee table,

describing them as ammunition. Apparently the missives held proof that Hunt's enemy—who had captured Percy—had also wronged someone else. And that someone was none other than *Bartholomew Black.*

"If Black learns of the betrayal, he may intervene," Hunt said. "But to contact him will be to stir up a hornet's nest. Black is dangerous, unpredictable—and he's as like as not to shoot the messenger."

"I'll deliver the letters."

Marianne's gaze swung to Kent at his calm assertion. The proud jut of his chin conveyed his determination as did the tight line of his lips. Firm and sensual, those lips had suckled her so sweetly ...

"Black smells a Charley, and you'll be dead before you reach twenty paces of his place." Hunt's blunt words jerked her back; she could not agree with his assessment more. "It has to be me."

"Risky. If you get detained, then Percy ..." Harteford's grey eyes turned hard as flint.

The ransom note had demanded that Hunt be the one to meet the captors. The exchange was to take place at midnight, at an old blacking factory on the outskirts of the city. Like the others in the room, Marianne knew it was a suicide mission, with little hope of Hunt or Percy getting out alive.

Marianne's throat tightened. Sometimes, destiny had a way of making one's decisions. She'd already prepared herself to walk into the lion's den; what difference would it make to go to Black a day earlier?

"I'll do it," she said. Rising, she picked up the letters.

"The *hell* you will." Kent was on his feet the next instant. His gaze pinned her, the darkness of his pupils edging out the amber; above the crumpled mess of his cravat, his neck muscles corded, and she saw a vein pulse beneath his jaw. The possessiveness in his tone was unmistakable.

Ignoring the ridiculous shiver that chased over her nape, she said calmly, "I don't require your permission, Mr. Kent." She tucked the packet into her reticule, and Kent's jaw grew even tighter. Really, if the man was not careful he might crack a tooth.

"This is far too dangerous—" Harteford began.

Oh, for heaven's sake. Why do men persist in believing that we're the weaker sex?

Resisting the upward impulse of her eyes, she said, "Black may be dangerous, but he is just a man. We all have our expertise, and mine happens to be the opposite sex. Do you doubt that I am well equipped to deal with Black—or any male for that matter?"

She didn't have to say more. It wasn't an issue of vanity, but of fact. She knew her own attractions, and for once they might prove of use.

"Lady Draven has a point." This came from Hunt—apparently the only one of the fellows with an iota of common sense. "She has a better chance of getting an audience with Black than any of us. If nothing else, he'll see her out of curiosity."

"*Out of the question.*" Kent spoke through his teeth.

He looked ready to throttle someone—perhaps her, though for some reason her instincts told her he wouldn't harm her. Unlike Draven, Kent hadn't the guile to disguise his true desires, and she could read his wish to protect her in the rigid lines of muscle, the grooves flickering around his mouth. Wryly, she acknowledged her own perverse nature: though she needed and wanted no man's protection, the idea that she could rattle this proud policeman's self-control almost ... charmed her.

Though, of course, she would not allow him to sway her decision or actions in any way.

"I ask you to reconsider, my lady. Helena would have my head if anything happened to you," Harteford said.

Marianne squelched a bubble of amusement. The large, imperious marquess looked genuinely concerned about the reaction that might greet him at home. Perhaps he had more brains than she credited him for.

"You do your part, I'll do mine," she told him. "See you at midnight."

Kent planted himself in her path, blocking her from the door. Flames lit his eyes, and his large hand clamped around her arm. "This has gone far enough," he snapped.

Her eyes thinned, her amusement fleeing. It was one thing for Kent to try to dissuade her—quite another for him to manhandle her. Heat rose in her cheeks.

"No man touches me without my permission. Release me this instant," she said coldly.

"Not until you give up this asinine plan."

Asinine? She was many things: stupid was not one of them. Though it was no business of this interfering policeman, she had a plan to deal with Bartholomew Black.

"I said release me," she repeated in a voice of unmistakable warning.

Kent did not budge. As if he had every right to dictate her actions, he glowered at her, his hold unyielding. Her temper escalated when she found herself unable to escape from his strong grasp. He left her no choice, really.

Slipping her free hand into her skirt's hidden pocket—her modiste was a genius in so many ways—Marianne pulled out her pistol. She trained it upon Kent. Just left of his heart.

Still, the stubborn man refused to let her go. She cocked the pistol to show him she meant business. Their gazes locked; her fingers trembled against the smooth metal.

"Stand down, Kent. You cannot stop her, and obviously she can take care of herself."

Harteford's warning seemed to finally pierce Kent's thick skull. The latter's dark lashes veiled his bright gaze, his grip tightening for an instant. Then whatever internal battle he was fighting ended. With obvious reluctance, he let go of her arm—good thing, really, because she didn't wish to shoot him again.

Not unless he made her do it.

"Perhaps Lady Draven would agree to take a few men as escorts?" Harteford said with a worried frown.

"Men are the last thing I need." She said the words whilst looking at Kent. His expression grew even starker. "I can take care of myself."

With that excellent parting line, she exited.

Though situated in the heart of the rookery, Bartholomew Black's fortress was every bit as imposing as any grand Mayfair residence. The foggy night and the tall, spiked iron gate hid the building from the street; Marianne's carriage was let through only after her identity was verified by the guards. A shiver passed through Marianne when she descended the carriage and saw the looming brick edifice. Like Draven, Black had a propensity for the gothic style.

Moonlight dappled the stone gargoyles perched on the rooftop; they peered down with gimlet eyes and mischievous smiles. An eerie orange light flickered behind the mullioned windows. Recessed beneath a pointed arch, the front entrance lay in shadow.

"I don't have a good feeling about this," Lugo said.

Rarely did her stalwart manservant express doubt about her plans; the fact that he was now doing so increased her own sense of unease. Her gaze flitted to the dark-coated guard who stood waiting to escort her inside.

"We'll get this over with as quickly as possible," she said in a low voice. "Stay close."

They started forward.

"Only 'er ladyship comes in." The guard jabbed a finger at Lugo. "You wait 'ere."

"He is my footman—" Marianne began.

"Don't care if 'e's the Archbishop o' Canterbury. I got my orders. Mr. Black says you come in alone or not at all."

In for a penny.

Marianne gave Lugo a nod. "Wait here, then."

"But my lady—"

"I'll be fine." She *had* to be, for Percy's sake and Rosie's. Addressing the guard, she said briskly, "Lead the way."

The man took her into the shadows. He knocked on the door, a complicated sequence of raps that might have been a code of some sort. The door creaked open, and he ushered Marianne inside. Her brows climbed. The light of a hundred candles blazed in the brass chandelier; the marble atrium could have graced a townhouse on Grosvenor Square. She was led down a hallway where priceless landscapes adorned burgundy silk walls.

"Mr. Black will meet with you in 'ere," the guard said, opening a door.

She walked in, and her estimation of Black's taste rose even further. The man might be a villainous cutthroat, but he lived like a king. Richly outfitted in mahogany and leather, the high-ceilinged library put many a lord's to shame. Tall windows fitted with forest green drapery lined one wall, and costly antiques littered the room. At the sight of the collection hanging next to the fireplace, her blood went cold.

Like a sleepwalker, she found herself moving toward the gleaming objects mounted on the wall. There were perhaps a dozen riding crops in all: antiques made of Malacca cane and exotic woods, some fitted with leather thongs, others without. The handles ranged from carved ivory to molded brass. Panic rose in her throat, the memory of degradation crawling over her skin.

Draven had had a similar collection.

"Like my toys, do you, my lady? The set belonged to a French King—one o' 'em Louies."

Marianne spun to face the owner of the deep, booming voice. Her palms clammy beneath her gloves, she forced herself to calm, to tamp down the past. The future was at stake. Draven had tried to break her, but he hadn't. He'd only hardened her, taught her the skills of survival. And she *would* survive this—if only to get Rosie back.

Her eyes narrowed at Black. He stood a few feet away, posed as regally as a Gainsborough portrait. Though short of stature, he held his barrel chest high, and one hand grasped a jewel-knobbed walking stick as if it were a scepter. His grey periwig and knee britches displayed his preference for the fashion of the past century; a man as powerful as Black could dress as he pleased.

Regaining her composure, she said, "Good evening, sir."

As she dipped into a graceful curtsy, she reviewed her three-tier strategy. *The first line of attack: appeal to Black's self-interest. The second—and riskier—line: find his weakness and use it. If necessary, the third: do whatever it takes to get Rosie back and ensure Percy's safety.*

He returned her courtesy with a flourished bow. "Please be seated," he said.

She chose one of the studded wingchairs by the fire, and he took the adjacent seat. His piercing black gaze roved over her. Fair enough, since she was assessing him in return.

"'Tis a pleasure to make your acquaintance, my lady. Though I wasn't expectin' you this evenin'." A note of censure edged his tone.

"My apologies, Mr. Black. You see, a rather urgent situation has come up." She paused. "One that I believe you would care to know about."

"Urgent, eh? Let's 'ear it then."

She drew a breath. "The matter concerns your daughter."

"Mavis? What's this got to do with 'er?"

Black's bushy brows lowered in menace. Apparently paternal feelings had naught to do with class; cutthroats could have them whereas country squires might not. Marianne tucked the information away for later. For now, she withdrew the packet of letters and held them out. Snatching them from her, Black broke the string and unfolded the first note. His face turned florid. The paper crumpled in his fist. He repeated the process with the remaining letters until balls of parchment piled over the buckles of his shoes.

"I'm goin' to gut the bastard. My dogs will 'ave 'is innards for supper."

The calmness of Black's declaration sent a shiver down Marianne's spine. But she said only, "The villain will be at Watson's Blacking factory at midnight."

"'E'll rue the day 'e crossed me. I never forget a wrong," Black growled as he rose. "Now if you'll excuse me, I 'ave to go attend to the business."

Marianne exhaled. She'd secured Percy's safety. Now onto Rosie.

"I am not yet finished, Mr. Black," she said in dulcet tones.

His eyes thinned at her. "What do you want, then?"

"You said you never forget a wrong. Can I assume that you also never forget a favor?"

Black looked at her a minute. Then he let out a guffaw. "Nice try, my lady. No doubt you're a clever one. But I don't owe you nothin'."

She forced a smile. "But I came all the way to deliver those letters."

"For your own benefit as much as mine. A man doesn't get to the top by bein' a fool. Gavin Hunt set you up to this—'e wants me to 'elp defeat our common enemy so 'e can get 'is little chit back."

Marianne swallowed. "You know about Percy?"

"I know about everything that 'appens in the rookery," Black said flatly. "So don't go tryin' to pull the wool over my eyes, my lady."

So much for appealing to his self-interest. On to the second line of attack. Now what is his Achilles' heel?

She rose and curtsied again. "You are not only powerful, but intelligent, Mr. Black. I should never presume to deceive you in any way."

He snorted, but she could tell her flattery pleased him. "Best that you don't."

"And it is precisely because you are so wise and influential that I wish to ask a boon of you," she said, keeping her eyes wide and guileless.

"Spit it out, then."

She drew another breath. "It concerns Kitty Barnes." Seeing the bushy brows lower again, she plunged on. "I understand that Mrs. Barnes owes you a vast debt and that she fled Town because of it. I would like to request that you allow her to return so that I may speak with her."

"What do you want with that blowsy bunter, eh?"

"'Tis a private matter."

"Private my arse. You're askin' me a favor, my lady—an' a big one at that." Black pointed the sparkling knob of his walking stick first at her, then at the door. "You'll tell me the nature o' your business, or you can take your leave."

He had her cornered; there was no place to run. Her only escape would be through the truth.

Through a constricted throat, she said, "Seven years ago, my husband stole my bastard daughter from me and sold her to Mrs. Barnes. Ever since his death, I've been searching for my little girl. Kitty Barnes was the last person seen with her."

Black's eyes widened. "Blimey. Your lord was a sick bastard, weren't 'e?"

"Indeed." Marianne released a breath. "Will you help me?"

"Why should I? Ain't none o' my business, is it."

Her heart plummeted. "You're a father, Mr. Black. You understand what it is to love a daughter. To do anything within your power to see her safe from harm."

Something flickered in his obsidian gaze. "Anything, you say?"

Marianne's mouth went dry. The third defense. No more lines left to cross. Her gaze flitted to the riding crops, and her insides quivered. She told herself that she could endure any depravity, no matter how despicable. She had survived years of Draven's abuse; what difference would it make to barter what remained of her tattered soul?

She was a woman with nothing left to lose ... and a child to regain.

"Anything," she said.

Black nodded. "Alright, then."

"Alright? Then you'll ... help me?"

"I'll let that bitch Barnes drag 'er arse back. And I'll 'ave 'er brought to you."

"Thank you, Mr. Black." Inhaling back the tears of relief, Marianne forced herself to ask, "And what shall I offer in return?"

His black gaze did not waver. "Don't know as yet. But one day soon I'll come lookin' for my due, an' I'll 'ave your word that you'll fulfill your end o' the bargain."

A deal with the devil. Though her stomach churned, she didn't hesitate.

"You have it," she said.

Chapter Eleven

The gentleman waited in the shadows as the door swung open on creaky hinges. The cutthroat, who went by the name of Murdoch, staggered into the filthy hovel, bringing with him a malodorous mix of gin, urine, and God only knew what else. The gentleman fought the urge to bring a handkerchief to his nostrils. Instead, he struck a match and lit the tallow stub upon the table.

"What the bloody 'ell?" Murdoch squinted at the sudden light. "What're you doin' 'ere?"

The gentlemen rose, stretching his lips into a smile. "I came to check in on your progress. Haven't heard from you for days now, Murdoch. You took my gold but you've yet to produce results."

The cutthroat blinked bloodshot eyes. "It ain't like I 'aven't tried," he said, "but that Draven bitch is bloody 'ard to kill. She shot me—right in the arm!"

The big brute held up his left arm, which did indeed have a dirty-looking bandage wrapped around the jacket sleeve. A nasty crust had formed along the edges of the crude dressing. A shudder ran through the gentleman. Not so much at the other's festering wound but at the failure.

You'll never amount to anything. You're just like your papa—a disappointment through and through!

Though his pulse skittered, the gentleman shut out his mother's voice. The harridan was dead, Praise God. Now he answered to no one but himself.

"How unfortunate," he said. "When will you try again?"

With a sudden show of bravado, Murdoch slammed his bottle of blue ruin on the table. "When I get paid eno' for the job, that's when. I ain't riskin' my neck for naught, your lordship."

"I paid you fifty pounds."

"Ain't nothin' compared to what I suffered."

Seeing the greed in Murdoch's beady gaze, the gentleman stifled a sigh. He'd suspected it would come to this. He'd had to deal with a similar situation with Murdoch's predecessor; cutthroats were an unreliable bunch.

From his leather satchel, he removed a bottle of whiskey. He placed it upon the table along with two glasses he'd had the foresight to bring along. Murdoch's eyes widened, and the disgusting fellow actually licked his lips.

"What would be adequate recompense then?" the gentleman inquired as he poured out the fine spirits.

Murdoch's gaze remained glued to the stream of liquor. "One 'undred quid."

"Done. Shall we drink to it?" the gentlemen held out a glass.

A feral expression sharpened the cutthroat's face. "Answered that a might quickly, didn't you, guv? Know what that tells me?"

"I haven't the faintest idea."

"That you'd be willin' to pay a whole lot more. That maybe you've been sellin' me short all this time," Murdoch sneered. "Well, I'll 'ave my due."

"Fine. How much do you want?"

The cutthroat's forehead lined in concentration. Likely the brute had difficulty counting as high as his greed demanded. "A thousand quid," Murdoch said triumphantly.

"That's ridiculous," the gentleman snapped. "I'd never pay you such a sum."

"You will if you don't want it bandied 'bout that you 'ired me to kill Lady Draven," Murdoch said, chortling.

The gentleman's teeth ground together. He told himself to relax, that such strain was not good for his delicate stomach. Exhaling, he said, "So you mean to blackmail me?"

"Not if you pay as you should. A thousand quid an' not a penny less."

The gentleman considered his options. Sighing, he said, "Alright, you win. I'll have the money to you on the morrow."

A leering grin spread across Murdoch's face, and he reached for the glass. "I'll drink to that."

The gentleman raised his own cup. He had to wait less than a minute before Murdoch gasped, the latter's empty glass falling to the ground and shattering. The cutthroat's body followed, accompanied by gasps and gurgles. When all was silent, the gentleman crossed over to peer down at Murdoch's unseeing eyes. He nudged the body with the toe of his boot.

No movement—not ever again.

As the gentleman collected the whiskey and the remaining glass, he sighed again. Why was good help so difficult to find? In the end, one could trust no one but oneself, and he could only be grateful that the Lord had blessed him with an abundance of problem-solving abilities. He'd already worked out a new solution. To protect what was his, he would have to rid himself of Lady Marianne Draven once and for all ... and the blade was not the only answer.

To the contrary, there were weapons far more deadly.

Smiling with relief, he closed the door behind him and strolled out into the night.

Chapter Twelve

"God's blood, those thievin' buggers 'ad more brains than I gave 'em credit for." Standing on the dock, the captain shook his head in disbelief at the pile of stolen goods that Ambrose's team of watermen had unloaded from the rowboat. "They fit all that on the bleedin' dinghy?"

Crouching, Ambrose showed him the boat's false bottom.

"Damnation, two or three grown men could fit in there!" the captain said.

"The thieves have a fleet of these lighters," Ambrose said. "They rob ships like yours, fill the hidden compartments with loot, then sail down the Thames in broad daylight."

The other man whistled. "The river's a safer place with you and your men surveying it." Reaching into his pocket, he withdrew a coin purse. "My thanks, Mr. Kent."

"'Tis my duty to keep law and order on the Thames," Ambrose said. "No reward is necessary."

Though God knew he could use the coin. The rent on his family's cottage was coming due next week, and he was still short. Left with no choice, he'd have to sell his last possession: the volumes of philosophy that his father had given him when he'd joined the River Police. Samuel Kent had never quite approved of Ambrose's career choice.

Never forget that the pen is mightier than the sword, my boy, he'd said with mild reproof.

But the sword paid the rent. At least it had, until Samuel's debt had come along.

"Go on, take it." The purse dangled from the captain's fingers. "I insist."

Ambrose shook his head firmly—as much to himself as to the other man.

Grunting, the captain re-pocketed the money.

After ensuring that the recovered goods were in order, Ambrose took his leave of the grateful seaman. Mid-morning was his favorite time along the water, and on impulse he stopped at an empty spot along the pier and allowed himself to look out over the sparkling waves. For a few moments, the salt-tinged breeze and warmth of the sun chased away his worries and responsibilities. Overhead, gulls soared, their cries mournful and beautiful.

The memory of fire and violence blazed in his mind's eye. Two nights ago, they'd defeated the villains in a fierce battle and rescued Miss Fines from harm. The evening's most unexpected triumph, however, had been that of love over revenge: Gavin Hunt, the most ruthless hell owner in the stews, had declared his feelings for Miss Fines, proposing to her before all.

Now the two were engaged to be married.

Love was a mysterious thing. Ambrose shook his head in bemusement. All's well that ended well, except ... His mood darkened as his thoughts returned yet again to Lady Marianne Draven.

That night, he'd been appalled that she meant to approach Bartholomew Black on her own. Worse yet, he'd been powerless to stop or protect her. If he'd tried to follow, his presence would have endangered her further—Black's dislike of those who enforced the law was well known. After her departure, Ambrose had convinced

Hunt to send a pair of the latter's rookery-bred guards to discreetly follow her and defend her if need be.

With concern still gnawing at him, Ambrose had gone to assist in the rescue of Miss Fines. Black had showed up to save the day, and the cutthroat's assertion that Lady Draven had been safely deposited back at home did little to dispel Ambrose's disquiet. So he'd gone to her townhouse. With the aftermath of the fight still thrumming in his veins, the scent of blood and smoke saturating his senses, he hadn't trusted himself to be in her presence. At the best of times, she provoked him; God only knew what he would have been capable of at that moment.

Nonetheless, he'd had to see for himself that she was safe. From the shadows of an elm tree, he'd watched her first floor window. His vigil had been rewarded when her curtains parted. With her hair falling in pale, gleaming waves to her waist, she'd looked so young. She'd turned her flawless face up to the moon, and the silvery glow had revealed the sparkle of tears upon her smiling cheeks.

An expression of happiness enhanced anyone's beauty. On a woman already beautiful beyond measure, the effect had caused Ambrose's heart to stumble in his chest. For the first time, he'd seen Lady Marianne Draven stripped of her armor. Who knew that beneath that sophisticated skin lived such a poignant mix of joy and sorrow, such fragility? No wonder she'd roused his deepest male instincts, made him yearn to protect her from all ills.

What had triggered her bittersweet tears? What secrets was she hiding ... and why?

What the bloody hell business is it of yours?

She'd pulled a pistol on him twice. Propositioned him as many times. All of it, he suspected, had been her way of putting him in his place. And she'd called *him* the snob! She'd enticed and infuriated him in equal turn. Standing beneath that blasted tree, he'd come to a decision: he must wash his hands of her before she distracted him further. Before she clouded his reason, his judgment. He had his family's troubles to contend with, and he could not waste his energy on selfish desires.

In the end, he'd waited until the light from her bedchamber extinguished. Then he'd made his way back to his room in Cheapside to toss and turn on his lumpy pallet. He hadn't been able to escape the memory of her panting beneath him, her sweet, spicy taste, the way her rosy nipple had puckered for his touch ... and not even his conscience could prevent the inevitable conclusion then. Like an unschooled lad, he'd had to frig himself, his seed soaking the sheets whilst green eyes taunted him ...

"Thought I'd find you here, Kent."

The hearty voice drew Ambrose from his thoughts. Flushing, he looked up to see Sir Coyner striding down the dock, the links of a pocket fob swaying and glinting in the sunlight. He observed the Bow Street magistrate's jolly expression and felt a sudden lift of hope.

He has good news. By God, let it be a job.

"You were looking for me, Sir Coyner?" he said.

"The magistrate at Wapping Station said you'd be here. Said you'd apprehended a gang of thieving lumpers and returned the goods to the rightful owners."

"With the help of my crew, sir."

"Modest as ever. Well, Kent, I have come to you with an offer."

Pausing, Coyner cast a glance around. The nearest boat was at least a dozen yards away, and with the hustle and bustle of dockside activity, Ambrose was certain no one could overhear their conversation. Nonetheless, sensing the other's hesitation, he said, "Shall I make an appointment at Bow Street, sir?"

"No, this place is better. Sometimes there is more privacy to be had in public than in the most guarded of offices. This is a sensitive case, and I trust I can depend upon your discretion." The magistrate gave him a stern look. "Your career and mine rely upon it."

"Yes, sir."

Coyner scrutinized him. "This isn't an easy assignment, Kent, but the remuneration is significant. Your share, should you accept, would be five hundred pounds."

Ambrose's breath stuttered. *Five hundred pounds* ... a veritable *fortune*. Enough to save his family from ruin and to see them settled comfortably for the years ahead.

"The case comes with specific conditions set by the client. These conditions are non-negotiable. Any violation will see you off the assignment,"—Coyner's pale blue eyes bored into him—"and I'll personally see to it that you never work for Bow Street or any other force again."

The threat made Ambrose's gut clench. He knew Coyner had the power to back those words. The risk was enormous ... yet the reward even greater. Here, finally, was a way to give his family what they so desperately deserved. Security. A future.

"What are the conditions?" Ambrose said. "Can you tell me who the client is?"

Coyner shook his head. "Even I do not know the identity of our employer. All communications have been directed through his solicitor. In fact, the client specifically asked for a contract investigator—one with no ties to other Runners or the Bow Street office. Only you and I know about this case, Kent."

"Why the need for secrecy?"

"Fear of scandal, most likely. From what I know, the client is a member of the House of Lords. The threat is one involving national security."

The hairs rose upon Ambrose's neck. "Sir?"

"Anarchists, Kent," Coyner said grimly. "I always knew we hadn't heard the last of them. Like poisonous weeds, they're not easily eradicated; they remain dormant, waiting for the moment to take seed and pollute our good English soil. I can say no more without compromising the case; you now have sufficient information to make your decision. Will you accept this mission?"

A chance to save his family and defend his country. He couldn't ask for a more honorable, worthwhile endeavor—and surely he would regain his focus then. Surely this would put all the nonsense with Lady Draven out of his mind and behind him. In truth, his prayers had been answered.

"Count me in," Ambrose said without hesitation.

The men shook hands, sealing the bargain.

"I'll need you on full-time, and I'll work that out with your magistrate at Wapping Station. He owes me a favor," Coyner said. "When this is over, you'll return to your position with none the wiser."

Ambrose hoped Coyner had the leverage to ensure Dalrymple's cooperation.

"What are my specific tasks, sir?" he asked.

"The client provided the name of a suspected anarchist. Your job is to monitor said suspect and provide reports on all her movements."

"*Her*?" Ambrose said in surprise. "The suspect is a female?"

Sir Coyner gave a grim nod. "Not only that, but a baroness no less."

Ambrose's gut turned to ice. *No, it can't be—*

"Your assignment, Mr. Kent, is to track Lady Marianne Draven."

Chapter Thirteen

I t didn't take more than a sennight for Kitty Barnes to crop up in London. With Black's assistance, Marianne secured a meeting with the former bawd. The appointed location was the backroom of a scents shop, and as Marianne waited for Kitty to arrive, her eyes swept over the shelves of glass bottles that lined the windowless room. Mingled notes of musk and florals clung to her nostrils as she tapped her foot impatiently against the leg of the wooden chair.

Kitty Barnes came through the door minutes later, and Marianne found herself surprised by the other's appearance. In her mid-thirties, Mrs. Barnes was a handsome woman with smooth russet hair and light grey eyes. Her tastefully trimmed gown of dove grey showcased a well-kept figure. If one didn't know better, Mrs. Barnes might be mistaken for a gentlewoman and not the cold-hearted whoremonger she truly was.

"Lady Draven," Mrs. Barnes said in a cultured voice as she curtsied.

"Mrs. Barnes." Marianne inclined her head. She did not rise from the chair. In this exchange, she must retain the position of power. She'd dressed accordingly in a bold navy and ecru walking dress styled à la militaire. "Thank you for coming."

Mrs. Barnes' lips bent in a wry curve. "It seems I did not have much choice in the matter. You have powerful friends, my lady."

"You know why I summoned you," Marianne said. "Where is my daughter?"

In response, a muscle twitched alongside the other woman's mouth. Ice percolated through Marianne's veins, numbing her already cold hands.

Mrs. Barnes cleared her throat. "Lord Draven and I had a deal. He promised me fifty pounds a month to care for the girl. And I held up my end of the bargain. I looked after her like she was my own—"

"Where is she, Mrs. Barnes?"

"Out of the blue, the payments stopped coming. I tried to contact Lord Draven, but never heard back."

"He died," Marianne said flatly. "The only evidence that the blighter had a heart was when it failed him. Now where is my child?"

Mrs. Barnes' throat bobbed. "I had my own troubles. For reasons you already know, I couldn't afford to dally in Town." She licked her lips. "And I couldn't afford to keep the girl with me."

"You sold Primrose." Marianne said the words without inflection, though inside, oh inside ... After Corbett's warning, she'd thought herself prepared for this eventuality. For one of the worst nightmares a mother could know. Yet fear eviscerated—and the grief made her wild.

The bawd took an instinctive step backward at what she must have seen in Marianne's gaze.

"To whom?" Marianne said in a frigid voice.

"I don't know his name—"

"*To whom, you bloody bitch.*"

Marianne was on her feet in the next instant, her pistol aimed between the other's shocked eyes. Bottles of scent rattled as Mrs.

Barnes cowered against a shelf. "I n-never met the gentleman," she whimpered. "The transaction was completed through his solicitor —Leach was his name. Reginald Leach."

Marianne's breath burned in her lungs. "Where can I find Leach?"

"H-he has offices near the Inns of Court." The bawd's voice wobbled. "He said his client meant to take good care of Primrose. That she would have a good home."

"What kind of depraved lecher would *purchase* a child? Did you have any doubt as to what the pervert intended?" Bile rose in Marianne's throat. "Not that you gave a damn, did you? Because you got what you wanted. A handful of coins for selling my daughter to the highest bidder."

"I-I had no choice. I couldn't keep her. My debts—"

Rage splintered Marianne's vision. For one blazing moment, she considered putting a hole through the madam. To make Kitty Barnes suffer for what she'd done.

But that would not help Rosie. Last night, Marianne had dreamed of her daughter in the garden again. Only this time, Rosie had been playing a game of hide-and-seek, her laughter merry, her corn-silk ringlets bobbing just out of Marianne's reach. Then Marianne had seen the stormy skies ahead, and helpless fear had climbed in her as she'd watched her daughter skip heedlessly toward the descending darkness.

Come back, Rosie! she'd shouted. *Don't go! Wait for Mama ...*

Marianne's finger trembled on the trigger of the pistol. She told herself not to do anything foolish. She needed Barnes alive; the bawd was the last known link to Rosie.

"Did you inform your buyer of my daughter's true identity?" she demanded.

Barnes shook her head. "I said Primrose was an orphan. An opera singer's bastard."

"You had better pray that I find my girl alive and well. Because if I don't, I will come to you again," Marianne vowed. She lowered her weapon. "And whatever Black had planned for you is nothing compared to what I will do."

Mrs. Barnes paled, her chest rising and falling in shallow waves.

Turning on her heels, Marianne left the shop. Lugo jumped from his perch.

"Success, my lady?" he said as he opened the carriage door.

Marianne's fingernails bit into her palms. "We will be making a visit to the offices of Reginald Leach this evening."

She had no illusions regarding the likelihood of Leach's cooperation. Solicitors made their fortunes from discretion; Leach would no more offer up his client's name than he would shower his gold upon the streets. Besides, what man would admit to being an accomplice in the illegal purchase of a child? No, her best option was to search his office herself.

"You are engaged with the Hartefords tonight," Lugo reminded her.

Dash it. She'd forgotten the supper party to celebrate Percy's safe return and unexpected engagement to Gavin Hunt. Marianne did want to ascertain that the chit was doing well, and her absence at this late hour would be remarked upon.

It mattered naught. She could accomplish both tasks this eve.

She stepped into the carriage. "We'll stop by the Hartefords first and depart before midnight. So you know, our mission afterward will require discretion." Tucking her skirts around her, she gave her manservant a meaningful look. "I trust you will make the necessary preparations."

"I make it a habit to always be prepared," Lugo said.

That night, Ambrose climbed the steps to the grand Palladian residence, his sense of foreboding deepening. *What the devil am I doing?* The refrain had played in his head ever since he'd accepted the assignment from Coyner.

The conflict in him burgeoned, and when he reached the door, his hand hesitated at the bell. He told himself that the reasons for accepting the case were clear. He had to think of his family; by taking on this case, he could uphold his responsibilities and the deathbed promise he'd made to his stepmother.

Take care of your brother and sisters, Ambrose, Marjorie had whispered. *They'll need you now more than ever.*

He had a duty to his country as well. Whatever small part he could play in protecting the welfare of its citizens must be done. In sum, he could not allow whatever personal feelings he might have toward Lady Marianne Draven to get in the way of doing what was right. His ethics had, however, prodded him to inform Sir Coyner that he was acquainted with the subject.

The Bow Street magistrate had frowned. "What is the nature of your association?"

"We have met on two occasions." Being a gentleman, Ambrose couldn't say more—and what more was there to say, really? He and Lady Draven had no relationship, no ties; last night, he'd vowed to himself to steer clear of any future involvement. "She is a friend of the Marchioness of Harteford, with whom I am acquainted."

"Will this compromise your ability to carry out your duties?" Sir Coyner had asked.

Ambrose would not allow it to. He was a man without much in the way of money, looks, or power; the one thing he could pride himself on was his sound judgment. His logic had always held sway over his desires.

"No, sir," he'd said firmly. "Upon my honor, I will do my utmost to uncover the truth."

"I see no problem, then," the other man had replied. "In fact, your acquaintance with the suspect and the Hartefords may prove a boon. It may offer you opportunities to get closer to her."

Which was why Ambrose had accepted the Hartefords' unorthodox invitation to supper. Under normal circumstances, he'd rather undertake a visit to the tooth-drawer than mingle with a class so different from his own. Yet after a futile few days of trailing Lady Draven—which had yielded nothing more telling than visits to several elite shops on Bond Street—he knew he needed to step up his strategy.

If he'd felt relieved at the lack of suspicious behavior on her part, he tucked that feeling away. His job was to remain neutral, to collect evidence with an objective eye. Coyner's facts ran through his head: Lady Draven kept company with bawds and cutthroats, people who thrived on anarchy and violence. Her constant companion was an African manservant; William Davidson, one of the Cato Street conspirators, had hailed from Jamaica. She eschewed society's rules and lived by her own.

To Ambrose, all of this was circumstantial evidence and no proof of any wrongdoing. Yet he could not deny that in his own dealings with Lady Draven she'd shown herself to be clever, unscrupulous—and capable of shooting a man. His arm still bore the mark. And, in his gut, he knew she harbored a secret; he prayed that it did not involve anti-establishment activities.

Having dallied long enough, Ambrose pressed the bell. The door swung open to reveal the butler, whose brows inched up a fraction at the sight of him. Ambrose wondered if he was going to be directed to the entrance at the back of the building.

Before he could open his mouth to explain that he'd been invited, the butler ushered him inside. "Good evening, Mr. Kent. Lord and Lady Harteford are expecting you," the head servant intoned. "May I take your coat, sir?"

"Thank you," Ambrose said.

He handed over his worn great-coat, and surprise rippled across the butler's features. Ambrose felt a twinge of alarm. When he'd received the Hartefords' invitation for supper earlier that week, the card had been accompanied by a suit of evening clothes.

We wish to express our gratitude, and we'll take no excuses, the card had read. *See you Friday evening at nine o'clock.*

Lady Harteford's doing, no doubt. She was nothing if not a thoughtful, gracious lady. In his whole life, Ambrose had never owned any clothing as fine as the black and whites, and when he'd donned the outfit earlier, he'd thought that he looked almost acceptable. Certainly better than he usually did. For once, the clothes did not stretch too tightly across the shoulders or hang loosely from his rangy frame. Though the trousers were still a tad short, they at least accommodated his stride.

But seeing the butler's expression, he wondered if he'd bungled the cravat. Or misbuttoned the charcoal silk waistcoat. For the first time in his life, he wished for a looking glass.

"This way, sir," the butler said.

Ambrose had no choice but to follow. The butler announced his name, and then he was walking into the Hartefords' drawing room. There were many present, but his eyes went directly to Lady Draven. She sat on the bench of the pianoforte next to Mr. Paul Fines, turning the pages of the music. Fines was performing a soulful ballad about a lovelorn lad. Their heads—his bright gold, hers a platinum shade—were close together. They complemented each other like the sun and the moon. Ambrose's hands curled at his sides.

"Mr. Kent, how splendid to see you!"

He tore his gaze from Lady Draven—who hadn't bothered to look up at him—to his approaching hostess. As usual, the marchioness looked lovely; she wore a ruffled sapphire gown, and her hazel eyes reflected her genuine warmth. Harteford was a lucky man, no doubt about it.

"My lady," Ambrose said, bowing.

Harteford joined his wife, circling a proprietary arm around her waist. "Glad you could join us, Kent. We owe you much for your bravery last week."

"I was glad to be of service, my lord," Ambrose said. "And may I say how relieved I am to see Miss Fines safely returned to the bosom of her family."

"No more relieved than I." The heartfelt words came from Gavin Hunt, who hobbled forward with the help of a cane. He'd sustained a temporary injury during the rescue of Miss Fines, who now ambled along at his side. "Never thought I'd say this to a Charley, but I'm in your debt, Kent," the fierce-looking fellow said.

"Happy to have me back, are you?" Miss Fines grinned up at her fiancé.

"Having you in danger took years off my life and well you know it, minx," Hunt said.

Seeing the expression that softened the man's scarred face, Ambrose felt an odd jolt of envy. Certainly he was glad for the beaming couple. And for the Hartefords, who looked on with affection and approval. Yet out of the blue, yearning struck him: what would it be like to know that joy for himself? He'd been fond of his ex-betrothed, had thought he could grow to love her—but her lack of fidelity had made that impossible.

Of their own accord, his eyes returned to the pianoforte. His jaw tautened as Fines leaned over to whisper something in Lady Draven's ear. Her husky laugh drifted over, stirring Ambrose's loins.

Does she possess no shame whatsoever? Not even a week ago, she propositioned me—and now she is flirting with that damned Fines! By Jove, the least she can do is acknowledge me.

Before he knew it, Ambrose was making his way toward the instrument.

"Good evening, Lady Draven. Mr. Fines," he said curtly.

Fines rose languidly to his feet. "Hello, Kent. Didn't recognize you for a moment there. Found a new tailor, have you?"

Ambrose refused to be embarrassed over the truth. "The Hartefords kindly lent me the appropriate garb for the evening. As a policeman, I have little use for such finery. Nor can I afford it."

"Well, that's straight talking, ain't it?" Fines' smooth visage creased with a rueful grin. "Always liked that about you. And even more the fact that you saved my sister's life. No offense meant, eh?"

Ambrose shook the offered hand. "None taken."

"I wouldn't worry over it, Mr. Fines. Our Mr. Kent does not take offense easily." The drawled tones stiffened Ambrose's neck. "In fact, he is a man utterly in control of his impulses, aren't you, sir?"

Devil take it, why was she always baiting him?

"No man is always in control. Nor is any woman," he shot back.

Lady Draven only smiled as she rose from the bench. Her deep purple gown gathered beneath her faultless bosom, flowing in a sleek column to her dark jeweled slippers. Diamonds glittered at her ears and throat, but they were no match for the radiance of her upswept curls.

"It can be amusing to indulge oneself on occasion," she said. "For instance, I must confess to being a creature of impulse when it comes to shopping. For clothing, fripperies ... and anything else that catches my fancy."

A foreign emotion ripped at Ambrose's chest. "Gone shopping lately, have you, my lady?"

"Now what business would that be of yours, Mr. Kent?" she said.

"Er, am I missing something?" Brows lifted, Fines looked back and forth between them. "Why do I feel as if I ought to make myself scarce?"

Because you bloody well should, Ambrose almost snapped.

He was saved from that *faux pas* by Lady Harteford. "Supper is served," their hostess announced gaily. "Since you are already conversing with Lady Draven, Mr. Kent, would you take her in? Mr. Fines, you must accompany dear Miss Sparkler."

Paul Fines shot one longing look at Lady Draven, then strode good-naturedly over to the divan. Ambrose hadn't even noticed the young woman sitting there. Her quiet demeanor and plain frock had made her blend into the cushions.

"If I may have the pleasure?" Fines offered his arm with a flourish.

Flushing to the roots of her brown hair, Miss Sparkler put down her embroidery hoop. Ambrose noticed how the chit's thin fingers trembled against the rake's jacket. Their hostess had paired a lion with a lamb.

"Well, Kent, is it to be your pleasure to take me in?" Lady Draven inquired.

Turning to his own supper partner, Ambrose's lips compressed. No lamb, this one. Best he keep his wits about him and remember his purpose: he was here to monitor Lady Draven. To gather objective evidence about her behavior. Thus far, his main observation was that she was a woman fully capable of eating a man alive.

"Shall we continue our discourse over supper?" he said, jaw clenched.

Her elegant fingers skimmed his sleeve. "By all means, let us have *discourse* together."

Her words shot heat through his veins. His bollocks drew taut; his member stirred. With a silent curse, he prepared himself for the long evening ahead.

Chapter Fourteen

S eated across from Kent at the lavishly set table, Marianne
slid him a surreptitious glance over the elaborate floral
arrangement. He was engaged in conversation with Miss
Charity Sparkler, who sat to his left. Not only had he managed to
draw words from the retiring chit, but whatever he was saying
made roses bloom in her thin cheeks. Marianne's hands curled in
her lap.

Something about Kent brought out the oddest instincts in her.
No man could be as earnest and upstanding—as bloody *good*—as
the policeman appeared to be. She'd behaved outrageously toward
him last week, yet he was sitting there, the picture of polite equanimity. In fact, he didn't even seem to register her presence. For
some reason, this compelled her to test the limits of his restraint.
To force this paragon to show his true colors.

Every man she'd ever known had had weaknesses and ulterior
motives. Her father, for instance, had posed as a respectable
country squire; beneath, he'd been a man obsessed with gaming, to
the point where he'd happily sold his only offspring to his old
friend Baron Draven for a hefty marriage settlement. Draven, of
course, only proved the point further: he'd pretended to be a

kindly rescuer, prepared to forgive her disgraced condition and offer her the protection of his name.

She'd fallen for his act—been so pathetically grateful. She'd sworn to be the kind of wife he deserved. Soon after the marriage, however, the cruelties had begun, and she'd found herself trapped in a hell beyond anything she could have imagined.

All because she'd trusted—stupidly and blindly. Well, once burned, as they said. She'd never make the same error again. Best she forget the business of males altogether and concentrate instead on her plans for after supper. At present, Lugo was conducting surveillance of Leach's office and would return for her at the meal's conclusion. Together, they would search the solicitor's premises to discover the identity of Primrose's captor.

Yet Marianne found herself distracted. Her eyes wandered back to Kent, who was *still* talking with Miss Sparkler. Piqued, Marianne catalogued his deficiencies. He wasn't handsome ... although she had to admit that he looked disturbingly masculine in evening clothes. For once, his garments had a decent fit, molding to the breadth of his shoulders and showcasing his whipcord-lean frame. The casual disarray of his unruly hair lent him a raffish air. Miss Sparkler said something, and he smiled.

Her pulse skipped as his entire countenance transformed. With his eyes crinkling at the corners and that sensual mouth of his curved and relaxed, Ambrose Kent was unexpectedly, undeniably attractive. Not in the usual manner, but one far more compelling. Remembering the flames in his eyes and the possessive way he'd touched her, she felt her breasts tingle, the tips puckering beneath the violet satin.

"Asparagus soup, my lady?"

Chagrined at the direction of her thoughts, she gave an absent nod to the footman. Lud, she was supposed to be listing Kent's faults, not waxing on about his charms. The problem was that what she would typically consider shortcomings in other men seemed oddly favorable in Kent. He was poor and a member of the working class, and yet he had more dignity and pride than men who were his supposed betters. He was righteous, had tried on multiple occasions to govern her behavior; at the same time, if she was honest, he'd protected her from harm—even taking a bullet because of her.

The footman came to Kent and ladled the creamy green concoction into the shallow bowl. As she watched, a line deepened between Kent's dark brows as he studied the array of silverware at his disposal. A daunting selection, no doubt, for a man who looked like he might eat cheese off the knife with which he'd sliced it. At the baffled expression in his amber eyes, something in her chest went soft.

"Mr. Kent, you have yet to regale us with tales of your exploits with the Thames River Police." Gaining his attention, she selected the proper soup spoon from her own setting with deliberate care.

His brow cleared as he mirrored her choice of silverware. And, lud, if she didn't find it endearing that he actually counted his way to the correct spoon. She dipped her utensil into the soup in the proper direction, hiding a smile as he did the same.

"I do not wish to bore the present company," he said.

"Oh no, Mr. Kent," Miss Sparkler piped up in an annoyingly eager manner. "I should love to hear about your work. It must be so exciting."

His cheekbones turned ruddy. "'Tis not as exciting as it seems, I'm afraid. Most days, I deal with disquieted lumpers and petty thefts."

"You are too modest, Kent." Harteford spoke from the far end of the table. Addressing the other guests, he said, "Over the years, Mr. Kent has helped Fines & Company to recover a substantial amount of stolen cargo. His work is highly esteemed by all of us at the West India Docks."

"Not to mention all Mr. Kent has done for us personally," his wife added. Helena was seated at the closer end of the table, and Marianne could see the gratitude in her friend's eyes. "You, sir, have kept those I love safe from harm, and for that I cannot thank you enough. Harteford, would you lead a toast?"

"Of course, my love." Harteford stood and raised his glass. "To Mr. Kent, who is a boon to his profession and our guest of honor. We salute you."

"Hear, hear," the rest of the guests echoed.

Silently, Marianne sipped her wine, her eyes on Kent's flushed face.

"You do me a great honor, my lord," he said, clearly discomfited.

Taking pity on him, Marianne redirected the flow of conversation to Percy, who was seated next to Miss Sparkler. "So, my dear, how are the plans for the wedding coming along?"

Percy's blue eyes danced at her fiancé across the table. "Um, too slowly?"

Marianne stifled a smile. The hungry look on Hunt's face clearly had nothing to do with the delectable quail in truffle sauce placed in front of him. Goodness, but the fellow looked ready to leap across the silverware and gobble Percy up in one bite.

"Nonsense." This came from Percy's mama, whose eyes glinted behind her steel spectacles. "Three months is the absolute minimum required to properly prepare for a wedding. Why, we have invitations to send out, a banquet to prepare for, not to mention your trousseau."

"I don't think Mr. Hunt cares too much about what I wear, do you, sir?" Percy said playfully.

Hunt gulped his wine. "You look beautiful in anything, Miss Fines," he said, shooting an uneasy glance at his future mama-in-law. "Anything at all."

Or better yet, in nothing *at all*. Amused, Marianne interpreted the expression on the man's face. Despite his fierce and rough-around-the-edges appearance, Gavin Hunt was a man hopelessly besotted with his intended. And Percy deserved no less.

Satisfied that her protégée was well settled, Marianne cut into the succulent bird.

Kent cleared his throat. "If I may," he said, "I think we must not overlook Lady Draven's role in all of this."

She froze, her fork inches from her lips. "My role? Whatever do you mean?"

"It was thanks to you that Black came to our assistance. Without your intervention, our task would have been a great deal more difficult," he said, his expression inscrutable.

"Yes, Marianne, you are a heroine," Helena said, smiling.

"And the very best of mentors," Percy chimed in.

Surrounded by beaming faces, Marianne squirmed at being put on the spot. After Draven's death, she'd entered the *ton* with the sole goal of finding Rosie. Her looks, wealth, and cutting wit had quickly made her a favorite of the fast set—jaded sophisticates who made a sport of insults and verbal sparring. Then Marianne had met up with Helena again, and her childhood friend had introduced her to a different circle. One filled with people who were impossibly ... *sincere*, brimming with goodwill. The very opposite of her own nature.

Though they welcomed her, she oft felt like an imposter within this group. Like a shiny apple rotted at the core, hiding amongst a pile of perfect fruit. To her mortification, her cheeks grew warm in response to the other guests' admiration.

Setting down her utensil, she said lightly, "As I said, everyone has their strengths. I was happy to make use of mine."

"By the by, how did you convince Black to listen to our case, my lady?" Kent inquired.

The question seemed innocuous enough, yet the penetrating quality to the policeman's gaze put her on guard. His pupils darkened, his amber irises bright as lanterns in comparison. The hairs rose on her neck as she—one who prided herself on self-possession —felt suddenly as transparent as glass.

She could ill afford disclosing her bargain with Black. If Kent began digging around in her affairs, he could bring all that she'd worked for tumbling down around her. He'd compromise Rosie's safety—and that Marianne would never allow.

"I have my methods," she said with drawling insouciance. "I believe you may be acquainted with some of them."

As Kent turned red, Marianne could almost hear the simultaneous swish of eyebrows going up around the table. She could imagine the questions popping into the other guests' heads. Well, better that they wonder about a peccadillo between her and the policeman than about her true secrets.

"This is no laughing matter, my lady. Though you were lucky enough to escape unscathed, your actions could have led to unthinkable consequences," Kent said stiffly. He paused, his countenance keen despite its high color. "I doubt a woman as clever as you would take such a risk ... unless you had confidence in your ability to negotiate the situation. I wonder, Lady Draven, what gives you such self-assurance in dealing with cutthroats?"

Because my husband was one. Because I've dealt with cutthroats all my life, though they might be disguised as gentlemen. And because one of them has my daughter.

Beneath her diamond necklace, Marianne's skin slickened with perspiration. Kent saw too much—was getting too close. Fear and anticipation pulsed in her blood as she tried to summon a pithy response. She was saved from doing so by their hostess.

"I commend you, Mr. Kent, for your concern over Lady Draven's well-being," Helena said gently. "As a policeman, you must see tragedies happen every day. We can only be grateful that Lady Draven's brave actions did not result in injury to her person."

Kent looked as though he might say something else—likely argue with the use of the word *brave*—but he gave a brusque nod instead. His gaze remained fixed on Marianne. Feeling the thrum of panic, she reacted with venom. The surest way to shake him off.

"As you say, Lady Helena, Mr. Kent is a policeman," she said, infusing the last word with amused disdain. "One can clean up a man and put him in a new set of clothes, but beneath he'll always be who he is, won't he?"

Silence fell upon the table. In other circles, her *hauteur* would have won her points; here, her barb was greeted with shock ... and disapproval. Harteford was frowning, and even Percy was giving her a puzzled look.

"I'm sure Lady Draven does not mean—" Helena began.

"It's quite alright," Kent said quietly. "She said nothing that is untrue."

His calm acceptance of her attack made Marianne feel smaller than an insect.

She lifted her chin. "If you'll excuse me, I have another engagement this evening." She rose, and chairs scraped as the men followed suit politely. "Thank you for supper. I shall see myself out."

Though shamed by the heat of curious stares, she departed the dining room with her head held high.

Fog rolled off the nearby Thames, saturating the summer night with a wet chill. Looking up at the building that housed the offices of Mr. Reginald Leach, Esquire, Marianne shivered in spite of her black velvet cloak. The place was part of a brick terrace off Fleet Street, and from the back lane, she could see that Leach's building stood taller than the rest; the addition of a third floor created a crooked peak in the otherwise flat roofline.

Lugo inserted a tool into the gate's lock, and the iron fence swung open.

"Let us make haste, my lady," he said in a low voice. "I've got a bad feeling in my bones."

"Is anyone inside?" she whispered as she followed him to the back door.

"Leach's clerks left hours ago. Didn't see anyone go in or out before I went to fetch you at the Hartefords'." Forehead creased, Lugo made quick work of this lock as well. The click sounded as loud as a gunshot to Marianne's ears; casting a sharp glance around and seeing nothing, she followed her servant into the house.

Leach was apparently a skinflint for the interior of the building was as cool as the outside. A narrow corridor led them toward the front of the building. The first chamber they entered looked to be the domain of the clerks. Windowless and lined with cracked paint, the room's centerpiece was a long table covered with ledgers and books. Stools lined the table, and Marianne could picture Leach's apprentices hunched over, scribbling in the smoking light of the tallow candles.

"Where are Leach's suites?" she asked.

Lugo jerked his head toward a pair of doors.

Passing through, they found themselves in an atrium outfitted as a waiting area. Here, the furniture gleamed with polish and fresh flowers sprouted from vases. Seeing yet another set of doors, Marianne headed through them.

This third chamber, obviously Leach's inner sanctum, was warm and scented with beeswax and tobacco. Dark drapery covered windows that faced the street. Handsome leather furniture and tall bookshelves contributed to the ambience of authority and affluence. Marianne lit one of the lamps and methodically searched through the cabinets; her search yielded nothing of import. Going over to the large desk, she jiggled the drawers. Locked.

"Let's have a look inside," she said to Lugo.

While he went to work on the lock, she thought of Kent, and shame again crept over her. Which was rich, really. Because here she was presently engaged in an illegal break and entry, and she did not experience an ounce of guilt. Yet she felt remorse over a snub she'd given to a policeman?

Besides, Kent had left her little choice. He'd crowded her with those intrusive questions, that penetrating gaze. It was as if he suspected her secrets and meant to find out everything about her, to bare the darkness of her soul—

"Here you go, my lady."

Marianne exhaled and drew her focus back to the task. Crouching down, she examined the first of the four drawers, all filled with leather portfolios. Flipping open the top file, she leafed through the documents: bills of service from the last year. Ever the discreet solicitor, Leach had only included the name of the client and the amount of his fees. There was no notation concerning the nature of the legal transaction.

She snapped the file shut; she'd have to dig back three years to find the transaction Leach had conducted with Kitty Barnes.

"While I go through these," she said to Lugo, "check the rest of the place. See if there are other files stored elsewhere."

As Lugo strode off, Marianne sorted through the portfolios, looking for the right date. The answer *had* to be here. If she couldn't ascertain the identity of Rosie's captor tonight, then she'd have to question the solicitor personally. She'd have to threaten Leach, a man of the law—and potentially alert his iniquitous client to her quest.

Will that put Rosie in greater jeopardy? What choice do I have?

She was on the last drawer now. She opened the first portfolio and found documents from the wrong year. She reached for the next one. 1817. The year Draven had died and Primrose had been sold. With trembling hands, Marianne riffled through the thick stack of parchment. Her breath stuck in her throat when she found what she'd been looking for.

A bill for services rendered in the month that Mrs. Barnes had sold Rosie. The fees noted on the receipt were astronomical—but Leach's client could afford them. The Earl of Pendleton had untold wealth at his disposal, after all.

Pendleton. Excitement coursed in her veins. *A lead at last.*

She withdrew the parchment, and she spied the paper beneath it. Bloody hell, another receipt for the same month. Same ungodly fees. Only in this instance, Leach had provided legal services to Viscount Ashcroft.

Ashcroft or Pendleton? Which of the bounders had purchased her girl?

Confounded, Marianne continued sifting through the papers. She found one other bill dated for the same month. This one was addressed to Marquess Boyer.

She let out a quivering breath. Damn Leach's eyes. The rotter had been busy. A marquess, an earl, and a viscount: which of the blackguards had her babe?

"*My lady.*" The panicked whisper dragged her attention to the door, where Lugo stood. Even from the distance, she could see his tense features. "We must go. Now."

She shoved the three receipts into her reticule. "Why?"

"Leach is dead," Lugo said tersely. "Murdered. Next door in the sitting room."

Instantaneously, she heard the voices in the distance, footsteps approaching outside. Loud banging sounded on the front door. *Mr. Leach, we're here from Bow Street. We'd like to have a word with you.*

Marianne shot to her feet, her pulse a fierce staccato. Without another word, she raced out of the office behind Lugo. They sprinted through the waiting area and back the way they'd come. Marianne's mind spun with frantic thoughts as she followed Lugo's broad back through the doorway of the clerks' chamber.

Have they surrounded the back entrance? Good God, they'll think we killed Leach—

Her mind went blank as an arm appeared from nowhere, grabbed her by the waist. A large hand muffled her scream. Heart thundering in her ears, she fought, biting and kicking to get away from her captor.

Chapter Fifteen

"It's me, Kent," Ambrose growled. "Stop bloody struggling, or we'll both end up in Newgate."

Even in the dimness, he could see the glassy panic in Marianne's eyes.

"There are constables outside. If you want to get out of here, you'll follow my instructions. Understand?" When she nodded, Ambrose jerked his chin at the looming Lugo. "That goes for your man, too."

The African's eyes narrowed, but he indicated his assent. Ambrose released Marianne, who stumbled away from him.

"Why are you here?" she said in a choked voice.

"No time for that now. They've got the place surrounded."

The voices outside grew in volume. Gut twisting, Ambrose raced through the options. If they caught Marianne breaking into a man's office—whatever the reason—the magistrates would toss her in a cell. Combined with the other circumstantial evidence Coyner had, she might be tried for crimes against the establishment.

Ambrose had convinced himself that he was capable of objectivity—of carrying out his duty, no matter the outcome. He'd believed that his logic ruled his emotions.

At this instant, his error in judgment *stunned* him: how could he have been in such denial?

Then his instincts kicked in, overriding his thoughts. Every muscle tensed, readying to get Marianne out of this mess. He'd save her now and get his answers later.

"We'll have to go up top. Follow me," he growled.

He led the way to the stairwell he'd seen just past the clerks' room. With the other two close behind, he took the steps to the uppermost floor. They entered an attic room, the gloom relieved by a silvery luminescence. He followed the light to the window, which he wrenched open, swiftly looking left and right. No constables were within visual range, although he could hear their voices coming from the front of the building: the men were planning to break down the door.

He looked down at the neighboring rooftop. The fog and darkness obscured his vision, but he estimated a drop of maybe ten feet. A risk they'd have to take.

"I'll go first," he said. "Lady Draven follows. And Lugo, shut the window behind you—we don't want anyone tailing us."

Ambrose climbed onto the outside ledge of the window. He jumped, landing lightly on the shingles. He dropped low, tensing, waiting for any sign that he'd been seen. But no alarm sounded; in fact, the voices had quieted. The constables must have already gotten into the house. Looking up, he saw Marianne's pale face at the open window.

"Go on, I'll catch you," he said as loudly as he dared.

She gave a quick nod and, after an instant's hesitation, came hurtling toward him. He caught her easily. He gestured to Lugo, who took the leap, landing solidly beside them. With no time to waste, Ambrose grabbed Marianne's hand. She grasped on to him tightly as they ran. He kept close to the stacks, stopping now and again to make sure they hadn't been detected.

When they reached the end of the terrace, Ambrose pulled her behind the shelter of the chimney. Breathing hard, he peered around at Leach's building, now six or seven houses away. Fog swirled in the distance they'd crossed, covering their tracks; there was no sign that their rooftop escape had been discovered.

"Our best chance is to wait here," he said, panting, his back flat against the brick. "Once the constables leave, we'll find a way to get down."

Marianne bit her lip, her eyes inscrutable in the moonlight.

"Mayhap this will help, Mr. Kent?" This came from Lugo, who reached into the satchel on his shoulder and pulled out a thick coil of rope.

Incredulity swamped Ambrose, followed by a blast of relief.

"Bloody hell, I should say so," he said, grinning.

It may have been a trick of light, but for an instant the manservant seemed to grin back.

The ride back to Marianne's was too short to address the questions roiling in Ambrose's head. So he bided his time, focused on getting a rein on his temper. Now that the immediate danger had passed, he grew edgy, his blood simmering close to a boil. *What the devil was she up to in that office? What kind of mischief is she mixed up in?* He'd followed her there from supper, arriving in time to hear her shuffling around in the solicitor's study. Then the magistrates had started banging on the door, and he'd acted on instinct.

Marianne—in the heat of the moment, he'd begun thinking of her that way and now couldn't stop—sat with uncharacteristic quietness in her corner of the carriage. He felt a pang at her pallor, the tight grip of her hands upon one another. Hands, he reminded himself, capable of breaking into a man's office.

His anger surged at her—at himself. How could he have allowed himself to get entangled in this mess? He'd betrayed his ethics, his obligation to the assignment. And why? The truth astounded him. Because he couldn't stand to see Marianne come to harm. Because a primal, irrational part of him insisted on protecting a woman who refused to be protected. And because, despite all evidence to the contrary, his gut told him that she was no anarchist.

That she harbored a secret, he did not doubt. He'd have his reckoning with the reckless widow before the night was out.

The carriage stopped. The door opened, and Lugo let down the steps.

Marianne cleared her throat. "It's rather late," she began.

"You're not getting off that easily," Ambrose said, daring her to disagree. "After the events of the evening, I daresay you owe me the courtesy of an explanation."

Her lips clamped shut. She alighted, saying gracelessly over her shoulder, "Very well. Come along if you must."

Once inside, she did not lead him to the drawing room as he'd expected, but upstairs to her chambers. His belly tautened at the sight of her luxurious bed. He heard a snort, and his gaze shot to the sitting area by the fire. He recalled the brown-haired abigail from his last visit, and she appeared no friendlier this time around. Finishing with her task of laying out a collation—the scent of coffee and spiced fruit curled warmly in his nostrils—she scowled at him and said to her mistress, "Are you certain you don't need me to stay, milady?"

"Go to bed, Tilda. I'll be fine," Marianne replied.

"But you'll need 'elp changin' your clothes—"

"I can manage. Besides," her mistress drawled, "I'm sure I can locate an extra pair of hands if I need them."

The innuendo sent heat creeping up Ambrose's neck. And to other portions of his person. All of a sudden, he became aware of the tension in his body—how rigidly he was holding himself in check. God help him if she pushed him tonight ...

The door closed behind the maid, and they were left alone.

"It's been a long evening, hasn't it?" With a languid motion, Marianne stripped off her gloves.

"Enough games," he said curtly. "What the devil were you doing in that place?"

"I could ask you the same."

Proceed with care. Do not give the mission away. His insides knotted. After all he'd already compromised this eve, he must not betray Coyner and the client further. If nothing else, he'd keep his word to safeguard the confidentiality of the case.

"I followed you from the Hartefords. You seemed upset, and I wanted to make sure you were alright." He did not wish to lie to her; what he said was at least part of the truth. "I did not expect you to go from supper to burglarizing a man's office. I repeat, what were you after, my lady?"

Her brows lifted. "Is this an official police interrogation? If so, I shall make myself more comfortable."

Before he could reply, she sauntered off to the dressing screen by the bed. She shed her cloak along the way, the velvet skin fluttering to the carpet. Ambrose swallowed as her silhouette appeared behind the silk panels. The flickering candlelight revealed every perfect line of her figure. As he watched, mesmerized, she undressed, her hands roaming over her curves, undoing, unfastening ...

Focus, man. She's accused of being an anarchist. You have to find out the truth—have to find a way to protect her if the allegations are false.

Frowning at himself, he forced himself to turn around. He stared into the roaring flames of the fire, his thoughts in chaos. Sweat broke upon his forehead, and he yanked off his greatcoat, tossing it onto one of the chairs.

Why did he persist in believing in her innocence when the evidence suggested otherwise? He prided himself on his logical mind, yet around her his judgment took a backseat to other instincts. Ones he found, to his great frustration, that he could not override.

"You owe me an explanation, Lady Draven," he ground out.

"I should think we're past formalities at this point." Her wry voice floated from behind him. "You have permission to use my given name."

"Fine. *Marianne,* then," he said, his jaw clenched, "what the devil were you up to in that solicitor's office?"

A hush fell, broken only by the soft swish of fabric. The tension pulled at his nerves, and, despite knowing better, he turned back toward the screen. His mouth went dry, his manhood rising in an immediate salute. Behind the screen, Marianne's silhouette revealed her flawless figure in what had to be the skimpiest of undergarments. His blood pounded as her hands smoothed upward along the slim curve of her hips, the sharp indentation of her waist. When she reached her breasts—for an instant cupping those beauties—he bit back a groan.

But he couldn't hold back the animal sound that left him when she stepped from behind the dressing partition. Sweat glazed his brow.

Devil and damn. Bloody hell. This cannot be happening.

Like a figment from some feverish erotic fantasy, Lady Marianne Draven stood before him, wearing nothing but a sheer petticoat and corset. He'd never imagined—let alone seen—garments so scandalous. Thin lacy straps held up a bodice with a plunging neckline; the short corset pushed up her breasts so that the smooth, rounded tops nearly burst from the bodice. Below the corset, the sheer skirt of the petticoat revealed her shapely calves and ankles. Lace frothed at the hem, brushing against her pretty bare toes.

"Do you think to distract me with your seductive wiles?" he said hoarsely.

Her lips quirked, her gaze roaming over him. "I'm not certain. Can it be done?"

Bloody hell, yes.

"No," he said firmly and dragged his gaze to her face. Told himself to keep it there.

"What did you witness tonight at Leach's office?" she asked.

"I know you were searching for something." Ambrose swallowed as she walked past him, her hair a rippling platinum river to her waist. "What were you after?" he persisted. "Are you in some kind of trouble? Because if you are, I will find a way to help—"

Her husky laugh sizzled down his spine. Heat flooded his groin, his stones throbbing with pressure close to pain. "You wish to help me, Ambrose?"

God, even his sturdy name sounded like a siren's song from her lips.

"First you must trust me with the truth." His brain raced through the theories he'd been contemplating. Explanations other than her being involved with a band of anti-establishment lunatics. "This Leach—does he have some information that you're after? Or mayhap this is about extortion. Is he trying to blackmail you?"

Something flickered in her eyes; he knew he'd hit a nerve. *The solicitor knows something: either she wants that knowledge or he's holding it against her. What secret is she hiding?*

His frustration mounted when, instead of replying, Marianne selected a plump strawberry and slipped the fruit between even riper lips. "Are you always this persistent when it comes to matters that do not concern you?"

"It concerns me when you put yourself in jeopardy. It concerns me when I have to save your bloody neck time and again." He raked his hands through his hair. "Goddamnit, woman, I am a policeman, and yet tonight I helped you evade the law. And I will have an explanation of your actions or so help me God—"

"Or you'll what? Report me to the magistrate?" She came toward him, her eyes wild as a summer storm. "Does that make you different from any other man who has tried to manipulate me?"

"I'm not trying to manipulate you," he bit out. "I'm trying to protect you."

"I don't want your protection." Her chin angled upward, and her gaze was hard and glittering. "If you're wise, you'll stay out of my way from now on. Or you will regret it."

"Are you *threatening* me?" he said incredulously.

"Not a threat. A promise." As if it wasn't enough that she slapped him with his own words, she said, "And let us not forget the differences between us. Let's face it, Kent,"—her brows rose— "you haven't got what it takes to stop me."

The reins of self-discipline snapped. His vision darkened. He hardly recognized the voice that growled, *"Haven't got what it takes?"* Before he knew what he intended, his hands hauled her against him, his lips descending to show the maddening wench how wrong she was.

Chapter Sixteen

Marianne knew her ploy to seduce Kent was a risky one. She'd gone about it in the most expedient manner possible: by pushing him past his limits. At the instant of contact between his lips and her own, the sparking attraction between them exploded into flames. As she'd known it would. She'd banked on the fact because she needed to throw him off the scent. Obviously, Kent did not yet know that Leach was dead. The last thing she needed was for him to start asking questions and pin her as the culprit.

Her gambit to distract Kent, however, now raged into a conflagration that threatened her own self-control. His male heat melted her resolve, turned her insides molten. Hunger unfurled as his tongue thrust against hers. She gave in a little, winding her arms around his neck to get closer to his virile length. So strong. Solid. Even as pleasure buzzed through her blood, she told herself that this was just all part of her stratagem ...

Don't be a fool. You've never lied to yourself, so why start now? You want Kent—you've wanted him since that first time he saved you.

With the triumphs and horrors of the night still buzzing in her veins, she experienced a sharp need to give into mindlessness. Just this once. To have respite from her demons for just one night. The ever-present anguish surged, yet Marianne knew she could do nothing for her daughter at this moment. Not with her mind and body dulled with fatigue. Not with long-suppressed needs battering her will ...

Her mind grew hazier as the kiss deepened. Kent had a way with kissing—a man who truly seemed to enjoy a woman's mouth. His lips were firm, delicious as they roved over her jaw, her ear.

"This is madness, but I don't give a damn. Tell me you want this." His husky growl sent a quiver through her knees. "By God, tell me you want me as much as I want you."

She found she hadn't the wherewithal to lie any longer—to him or herself.

Tomorrow, I'll begin anew, she vowed. *I'll investigate Boyer, Ashcroft, Pendleton—and I won't stop until Rosie is safe in my arms once more.*

"I want you," she whispered.

"Good girl." Her neck arched at the hot praise uttered against her throat. "Now tell me what you were doing in Leach's office."

She stiffened. Pushed him away. "I can't."

"Can't or won't?" The rim around his irises darkened, making his gaze even more penetrating.

Despite the desire pounding in her blood, she lifted her chin. "It's my private business, Kent. If that's the point of this seduction, you might as well stop now."

"Who's seducing whom?" he said, making her flush. Before she could turn away, he grasped her jaw in one big hand. "If you won't tell me the specifics, then at least give me this: do you have a personal reason for searching Leach's office?"

What good would it do to deny what he'd already guessed? "Yes," she said.

"What does he have that you want?"

She struggled to find some part of the truth to give. "Information."

"Does this information involve crown and country?"

She blinked at the odd question. "No," she said, frowning. "It's of a personal nature."

He stared at her intently, his bright eyes inscrutable.

She shivered. Could he guess her secret? Unfulfilled passion and the night's excitement battered at her self-possession, and she clung to her last shred of good sense.

"It's late," she managed. "It's best you leave—"

The next instant, Kent swung her off her feet, his mouth so hot and hungry that she could have wept with relief. Instead, she kissed him back with all the desperate need climbing inside her. Her senses spun as he carried her over to the bed, his hard body pressing her into the silken coverlet. He caressed her neck, her shoulders, the rasp of his calluses strangely exciting.

"So beautiful," he murmured. "*Selkie*, too beautiful to be real."

Her neck arched as he traced her collarbones. "What's a silky?" she said breathlessly.

"*Selkie*. An enchanted creature from the sea. She enthralls men in the form of a beautiful woman,"—he bent to taste the path he'd traced—"then flees into the sea in the magical skin of a seal."

"A woman with options. I like that," she said, her lips curving. "I believe that is the best compliment I have ever received."

Kent drew a fingertip beneath the edge of her bodice, and her breathing quickened. An inch further and he could reach her nipples, which stood stiff and aching for his touch. As if he knew her desire, his lips quirked, and perversely he withdrew his finger, running it instead over the strings of her front-lacing stays.

"There are ways of keeping a *selkie*, you know," he said, testing one of the knots.

Quelle surprise. When it came to subjugating women, men always had their ways.

"Let me guess," she said derisively. "You steal her skin. Keep it hidden, locked away."

"That is one method," he agreed. "Not the one I would use, however."

"Oh? Pray tell what your scheme would be."

He withdrew, bending to reach for something ... in his boot? Her breath halted at the sight of the blade in his hand. His eyes steady on hers, he lifted a corset string and slid the blade gently beneath. One cut and the laces unraveled. Her breath returned in a heady, unrestricted rush.

"I say if you want a wild thing, you must set it free." Beneath his penetrating gaze, she once again felt laid bare, vulnerable—only it didn't elicit fear this time, but yearning and arousal.

Could it be? A man who might actually understand me ...

"What if she doesn't come back?" she said.

He tossed aside the corset. Grasping the straps at her shoulders, he lowered them down her arms, and her bodice followed. Her spine arched as the fine muslin raked over her nipples, baring the taut peaks to his heated gaze.

"I'd give her a reason to," he said and lowered his head.

She gasped when he drew one sensitive bud into his mouth. When his tongue curled, the sensation shot all the way between her thighs. During her searches through brothels, she'd seen men suckle women—seen much more than that—yet she'd not known the pleasure herself. Indeed, her understanding of sexual matters far outweighed her actual experience. Thomas had been a virgin; the three times they'd made love, they'd only begun to discover what their bodies could do.

Clearly, Kent had a man's knowledge. A moan tore from her throat as he titillated her nipple with wet flicks. He kept an accompanying rhythm on her other breast, his fingers circling, pinching with just enough pressure to drive her mad. Her spine bowed, her hands clenching in his thick hair as desire swamped her. Years of pent-up longing washed away the remaining vestiges of her self-restraint.

"Don't stop." The words emerged from nowhere, in a panting voice she did not recognize. "Just ... don't stop."

"Easy, sweeting. I'm not going anywhere." Even his voice aroused her, the shape of his words pressed against her taut, throbbing peak. "One day, you're going to trust me, to know that I'd never leave you wanting."

She would have argued, but his lips fixed onto her other nipple, and the wildness in her grew to a feverish pitch. Her skin seemed afire, wet heat blazing from her core as he kissed his way down the path between her ribcage. His tongue dipped into her navel, and her hands fisted in the coverlet at the intense, unfamiliar sensation. A tug dragged her petticoat past her hips, baring her most intimate place. Her lungs struggled for air. She told herself to be calm, to just lie back and ... His lips touched the inside of her thigh, and the branding kiss drove a gasp from her lips.

"Don't like that?" he said, raising his head to look at her.

"I don't know. It feels a bit strange," she managed.

That line deepened between his brows. "Haven't you been kissed there before?"

She wanted to lie; for some dashed reason, her head shook of its own accord. Confusion clouded his gaze, and she knew what he was thinking. *The wicked Baroness Draven has never had a man's mouth between her legs?* He'd probably laugh if he knew the truth —or worse yet think that she was an innocent just because she'd not tried the things she knew so much about.

"The fancy has never struck me." Her tone came out as lofty as she could manage given that his thumbs were making mind-melting circles on either side of her quivering sex. "If you wish, however, I give you leave to ... gamahuche me."

His eyes flared at her use of the naughty word. Excellent. Let him know she was no naïf.

Then his lips quirked.

"By your leave, then," he said.

She bit back a sound as he parted her aching flesh. Her cheeks burned when he did nothing but study her for long moments. The look of dark hunger on his features titillated her beyond bearing, and her sex grew even wetter.

"Well, are you or aren't you?" she said when she couldn't take the anticipation any longer.

Kent's hooded eyes met hers. In that bright, erotic gaze, there was a hint of ... laughter? She began to struggle, but his hands clamped her thighs. Held her open.

His husky words stirred her dampened curls, feeding the fire in her blood. "A man likes to look his fill before he feasts," he said. "Especially when the offering is so decadent."

"You best hurry before the feast gets cold," she said.

"Cold?" His eyes crinkled at the edges. "I don't think so, sweeting. You are all heat ..."

The first swipe of his tongue made her gasp with shock. The second had her spine arching off the mattress. Dear God, she'd never felt anything like ... Her mind blanked as pure sensation swamped her. She became nothing but the tides of pleasure rolling over her senses. His plain-spoken praise and wicked caresses lifted her higher and higher.

"I love the way you taste. Salty and sweet. You whet my appetite."

As if to prove his assertion, he tongued her slit, thrusting deeply inside her throbbing folds. Her hips bucked, bliss stealing her breath. Her vision wavered as the sensations mounted. She was close, so close ...

"Kent," she gasped, "I'm going to ... to ..."

"Yes, you are." His savage look pushed her right to the precipice. "Spend for me. Right now, with your sweet quim against my mouth—let me taste your pleasure."

His tongue angled upward, to the little knot that throbbed with her heartbeat. His lips fastened, sucking gently. Her head flung back as the crisis hit. Pulse after pulse of pure delight, like nothing she'd known before. Before she could recover, she felt a shocking stretch ... his finger. He pushed gently past the initial resistance of her entrance. They both groaned as her muscles softened, then clutched the exciting penetration.

"You're so tight," he rasped. His forehead had a sheen of sweat. "Devil and damn, you're pulling me in deeper. So sweet." His chest heaved, the primal look in his eyes inciting her more, making her passage slicker. "You can take more, can't you?"

"Yes, *more* ..."

She moaned as he began to pump with a firm, steady motion. Her pelvis lifted to greet each thrust. He went deeper and deeper with each pass, his rhythm and pressure driving her frantic with need. As his fingers played inside her, his palm slapped wetly against the sensitive peak of her mound, sending sparks across her vision. Just when she thought she could endure no more, he lowered his head once more.

"Again," he said.

She screamed as waves of shocking heat passed over her, through her. *Too much, never like this* ... Tides of bone-melting sweetness carried her away.

Heart thundering, Ambrose wiped a damp tendril from Marianne's love-flushed cheek. She drowsed, worn out by the climaxes he'd given her. His chest inflated with pride. By God, her pleasure had been magnificent ... and he had the damp smalls to prove it. Damn, that had never happened to him before, but the way her passage had squeezed his fingers, her juices raining so sweetly upon his tongue ... he exhaled as his cock hardened once more.

Her passion had been mind-blowing in more ways than one.

He could scarcely credit what he'd discovered. What she'd kept carefully hidden beneath that jaded facade of hers.

The infamous Baroness Draven was a relative novice to lovemaking.

Her past lovers had done a shoddy job of things. In retrospect, Ambrose didn't think there could have been all that many, given her dazed response to her own pleasure as well as the tightness of her heat around his fingers. Even as his blood thickened with arousal, his jaw tautened at the thought of other men touching Marianne. She deserved better than careless intercourse. She deserved a man who would take care of her needs, who had the patience to chip through those layers of ice to reach the hot-blooded and vulnerable woman within.

What Marianne needed was a lover she could trust.

His breath came harshly into his lungs as she mumbled in her sleep, her lips burrowing into his open collar. Lust climbed in his veins, and he couldn't keep his hand from cupping the sweet curve of her breast. Even in sleep, she responded to him, her rosy nipple puckering, her soft sigh heating his skin. The instinct to take her, to free his erection from his trousers and bury himself in her lush pussy was nearly overwhelming.

But he didn't. Because as of this moment, he wasn't deserving of her trust.

Her earlier words rang in his head. *Does that make you different from any other man who has tried to manipulate me?* Who had tried to hurt her? What travails had she suffered? Despite all he didn't know about her, he knew this: Marianne Draven was not the scandalous, heartless sophisticate she appeared to be. She had secrets for certain, but she was no bloody anarchist. When Ambrose had asked her about her involvement in matters of crown and country, he'd seen the honest confusion in her eyes. She hadn't been lying when she said her interest in Leach was personal.

Early on, he'd sensed her hidden pain. It had called to him, and now he could no longer deny his desire to protect her. He would help her with her troubles—which meant he must take care of another matter first.

With self-control he didn't know he possessed, he extricated himself from her silken limbs. He tucked the coverlet over her glorious form. After one last look, he gathered his things and left.

Chapter Seventeen

Marianne awakened, blinking groggily as the peach walls of her bedchamber came into focus. Lud, she must have had a deep slumber for she felt better rested than she had for years. Yawning, she stretched, and the movement elicited an unfamiliar twinge between her thighs. Memory jolted through her, her lungs emptying in a whoosh as several facts hit her at once.

Good God. Leach is dead, and I have three suspects for Rosie's kidnapping.

And last night I let Kent ...

The intimacies that she'd allowed brought a rush of heat to her cheeks and her belly. She'd never done such things with Thomas. Yet Kent had a way of laying waste to her defenses, culling forth her deepest desires. She ought to know better than to trust any man, and yet there was something so damnably *trustworthy* about him. He'd saved her twice. Took a bullet the first time and risked his neck hauling her over the rooftops the second.

Why had he protected her time and again?

Her face grew hotter as another fact struck her: after Kent had pleasured her, he hadn't ... taken anything in return. She believed in even exchanges, and given the sum of what had passed between them, he'd had every right to demand some form of *quid pro quo*. Yet after his heroics—not to mention the two mind-melting climaxes he'd given her—he'd disappeared ... without so much as a *by your leave*?

What in blazes was the matter with the man?

Frowning, she tossed aside the covers and pulled on a silk wrapper. She went to examine herself in the Cheval looking glass. She looked the same as ever—perhaps better, with a new glow upon her cheekbones and her eyes bright and rested. All her adult life, she'd never questioned her physical desirability to the male sex. Surely Kent was no different from other men in this respect. Surely he had *wanted* to make love to her. Surely he had found her desirable ... hadn't he?

Dash it all, I'm feeling insecure over Ambrose Kent?

Ridiculous. Jaw tight, she told herself it was only because she didn't like unpredictability. Kent acted unlike any man she'd known. No male could truly be as earnest and upstanding as this one appeared to be. With a sudden shiver, she wondered if he would have acted so chivalrously if he had seen Leach's dead body. When he heard news of the solicitor's death—and she had no doubt he soon would—would he assume that she had something to do with it? Would he go to the authorities? Or would he hold his silence?

Anxiety buzzed; she calmed herself with the fact that Kent could not report his presence to the magistrates without incriminating himself. How would it look for a Principle Surveyor of the Thames River Police to be lurking at the victim's property? And then to aid the escape of two suspects ... and to make love to one of them afterward?

At this point, Kent's hands would appear as dirty as her own.

Her breathing grew more even. In the best scenario, he would keep her secret—yet that would only place her deeper in his debt. Under his power. She *hated* being beholden to any man. Swallowing, she recalled her bargain with Bartholomew Black, goose pimples dotting her skin at the memory of his foul collection of riding crops.

What's done is done. You had no choice. For Rosie's sake, you must endure anything.

She straightened her spine. The matter with Black might be out of her hands, but she could damn well manage Ambrose Kent. The notion of sitting by, wringing her hands and waiting for Kent to name his terms was unthinkable ... An idea struck her then: perverse and deliciously so.

A way to see to her obligations. To solidify her position as one of power and not passivity. And to pay Kent back in kind for leaving her like a thief in the night.

At her secretaire, she dashed off a note, sealed its contents, and rang for Tilda.

"Have this sent to Mr. Kent," Marianne said.

Tilda took the letter with obvious reluctance. "Yes, milady."

Seeing the disapproval etched on the other's face, Marianne suppressed a sigh. "Do you have something you wish to say to me? I warn you now, Tilda, I'm in no mood for a lecture."

"If you know what I'm thinking, I don't have to say it, do I?"

As Tilda went to draw open the curtains, Marianne reflected wryly that even the maid was getting the best of her. For once, she regretted not going a more conventional route with the hiring of her servants. Surrounding oneself with sharp-witted honesty had its drawbacks.

"Enough of your tongue, Tilda," she said. "Have you seen Lugo yet this morning?"

"He left on an errand at the crack of dawn." Tilda brought over the morning's ensemble and began to help Marianne dress in front of the mirror. "Said to tell you he doesn't believe in coincidences and wants to get to the bottom of what happened last night."

"He and I are of the same mind then," Marianne said grimly.

As the maid fastened her corset strings, Marianne reviewed the many concurrences. She'd gone to search Leach's office, only to find him dead. Then the constables had arrived minutes later—too bloody convenient. Not to mention the matter of the attack by cutthroats in Covent Garden less than a fortnight ago.

Coincidences? She thought not.

The facts pointed to a logical and chilling conclusion: someone knew of her search for Rosie. Someone was monitoring her movements and meant to stop her. If Kent hadn't aided her twice, she might have been killed or framed for Leach's murder.

Mrs. Barnes had claimed that the man who'd purchased Primrose did not know that the girl was Marianne's daughter. Could he have discovered the truth nonetheless? Was one of the three suspects—Boyer, Ashcroft, or Pendleton—Marianne's hidden nemesis? Having met all of them on some occasion or another, she summoned the facts on each.

Marcus Tilson, Marquess Boyer, was widowed and in his forties. Though plain of face, he was considered a handsome catch —although now she remembered something odd about his eyes. Not their precise color, but the fact that something was missing in them. A sense of genuine feeling. Nonetheless, Boyer was a respected peer and an active member of the House of Lords.

In contrast, Devlin St. James, Viscount Ashcroft, was as handsome as the devil and a rake through and through. Heir to a dukedom, Ashcroft had been embroiled in several scandals that had been quickly hushed due to his papa's influence. Marianne's throat tightened as she recalled that one of the indiscretions had involved a rather young vicar's daughter.

Eugene Patten-Jones, the Earl of Pendleton, was the oldest of the three and arguably the most powerful. In his fifties, he cut a robust figure; when Parliament was not in session, he stayed at his country estate, which was renowned for its hunting grounds. He had a sterling reputation and was a notorious snob. On the one occasion she'd been introduced to him, he'd flicked a glance over her, his mouth curling with contempt.

"What do you plan to do next?" Tilda said, smoothing out the emerald gauze skirts.

"I have narrowed the search to three leads. One of them has my daughter, of that I am certain," Marianne said.

Why else would the bastard be trying to stop her at any cost? On an instinctual level, she knew she was getting closer to Rosie. Despite the long years of separation, the maternal bond persisted, vital as ever. It was as if part of her—the *best* part—had gone to her babe at birth. Her breast tingled with a bittersweet memory. For a few weeks, she'd had the joy of nourishing her daughter with her own milk ... until Draven had put an end to it.

You're a baroness, not a cow, he'd said coldly. *Your bastard will use a wet nurse or she'll starve. The choice is yours.*

Marianne's throat clenched. Even that had been taken from her.

"We'll get Miss Primrose back, milady." Tilda squeezed her shoulder, bringing her back. "I know what it's like to worry for your babe. If it weren't for you, my Arthur would be fightin' for his life in the stews with a whore for a ma. I owe you his life and mine; whatever you need, you've only to ask."

Marianne released a breath. "There's to be no talk of debt between us. You and Arthur have brightened my household with your presence. Speaking of which,"—she crossed over to the vanity and removed a brightly-wrapped box from the bottom drawer— "Arthur's birthday is tomorrow, is it not?"

Tilda made a clucking noise. "You'll spoil him, milady."

"'Tis nothing much. I'm told toy soldiers are the rage amongst boys his age." Marianne smiled wistfully. "He's a good lad, Tilda, and you should be proud."

"Aye, that I am." The maid set the package aside. Picking up a hairbrush, she directed Marianne to the vanity. "You'll be a proud mama too, milady, when you have Miss Primrose back. Now what plan do you have for her rescue?"

"I shall be attending Lady Auberville's annual ball at week's end. All the *crème de la crème* will be present,"—Marianne winced as Tilda worked through a snarl—"including the blackguards in question. I plan to interrogate them when they least expect it."

"Will that be safe, milady? Lugo will have to wait with the carriage. You'll be alone."

What choice did she have? It was not as if she could depend on anyone else ... Kent's intent features flashed in her head. *One day, you're going to trust me, to know I'll never leave you wanting.* Longing sparked, but she snuffed it. Those words had been spoken in the heat of passion—and by a man.

Thus, nothing to place her trust in.

"What could possibly happen to me at a Mayfair soiree?" she said.

Snorting, Tilda pinned the final curls in place. Marianne looked this way and that, approving the sleek part down the middle and twists of loose curls that brushed her jaw on either side. The promenade dress brought out the shade of her eyes. Despite the tiresome comparisons to Aphrodite that came her way, she saw herself as Athena preparing for battle. Beauty was a weapon; being a cautious sort, she always thought it wise to bring sufficient reinforcements.

"We'll visit Madame Rousseau's," she said, "so send word ahead, if you please. Tell Madame I wish to book the entire afternoon, and I shall make it worth her while."

Tilda left to do her bidding, and Marianne completed her toilette with lotions and potions from the various jewel-colored bottles on the vanity. Looking at her polished appearance, she remembered what Kent had called her. *Selkie.* A woman who could don and shed her magical skin at will—and who called no man master.

Her lips curved with grim humor. Kent didn't know the half

of it. This *selkie* would stop at nothing to claim what was rightfully hers and woe to any blighter who stood in her way.

Ambrose entered Sir Coyner's Bow Street office with the enthusiasm of a man facing a firing squad. Yet he saw no way around the visit: he'd come to resign from the case. Through one serious error in judgment, he'd placed himself in an impossible situation. Bloody hell, Marianne had been right in calling him a snob: he *had* expected moral perfection from himself. And look where that arrogance had landed him.

Everything in him needed to defend Marianne, yet his honor demanded that he uphold his responsibilities to the client. His gut snarled. Devil take it, how was he going to extricate himself from this minefield without something blowing up in his face?

"Good day, Kent." Coyner rose from behind the desk. "'Tis a coincidence indeed that you came by. I had planned to summon you myself."

Ambrose mentally reviewed his speech. *I have come today to resign, Sir Coyner. Due to unforeseen circumstances, I am no longer the man for the job.* It wasn't entirely a lie. But it wasn't the full truth either, damn his own eyes. He could not bring himself to throw Marianne to the wolves, and he couldn't afford to draw the magistrate's ire, either: to do so would risk his livelihood and thus his family's future.

Shoulders bunched, Ambrose drew breath to speak.

The magistrate beat him to it. "I've bad news, I'm afraid, and no use beating around the bush about it. As of now, the investigation is suspended."

Ambrose blinked as the words trickled into his comprehension. "Beg pardon, Sir Coyner?"

"The case is over for now. Hate to break it to you in this fashion, especially since I just hired you on." Clasping his hands behind his back, the magistrate gave Ambrose a dark look. "I'm going to tell you something, Kent; normally, I wouldn't divulge this information, but I feel I owe it to you. This must be kept confidential."

"Yes, sir."

"The truth is ... the client's solicitor was found dead last night."

Ambrose's insides gave a sudden, premonitory lurch.

"His name was Reginald Leach. He counted more than a few members of the peerage amongst his clients, so we cannot know whom he was representing when he sought our services. Unless that lord chooses to come forward, we have, at this point, no client." Scowling, Coyner rubbed his lined forehead. "No client, no fee, and no proof of any wrongdoing."

Ambrose forced the words through his cinched throat. "How did Leach die?"

"Poison," Coyner said grimly.

A woman's weapon. Dread percolated through disbelief. No, Marianne was no murderess. After last night, Ambrose could not believe it of her. She might put up a frosty exterior, but he'd discovered the warm, vulnerable woman within. The way she'd trembled when he'd showed her pleasures she'd never known before ... But had she seen Leach's dead body? If so, why hadn't she mentioned anything?

"Unfortunately, the constables arrived too late. No suspects were found. Unless ..." Coyner's sharp gaze pierced Ambrose's daze. "Where was Lady Draven last evening?"

The tug-of-war raged within him. His duty, his conscience pitted against some primal instinct that insisted Marianne was innocent. It told him to protect her, keep her safe ... The knot in his chest tightened to the point where he could hardly get the words out.

"She was at a dinner at the Hartefords," he said.

"And afterward?"

His insides pitched. "She went home."

A furrow appeared between Coyner's brows. "You're certain of this?"

Ambrose gave a terse nod, his heart pounding.

"And you've no other suspicious activity to report on?"

"No, sir."

Coyner's gaze flickered, his expression unreadable. "As I said, less than nothing to go on. Unless the client decides to come forward, I'm afraid the case is closed. I'm sorry to have wasted your time, Kent. If anything else comes up, you'll be the first to know."

As much as Ambrose wanted to leave it at that, he knew he could not. He could not be involved with both Marianne and this investigation. And he'd come today because he couldn't fool himself any longer about where his loyalties had inexplicably fallen.

"Sir, about that." He cleared his throat. "Should circumstances merit the continuation of this case, I'm afraid I would no longer be available for the job."

"And why not?"

The truth burned on his tongue. Yet to tell of his involvement with Marianne would compromise her safety; it did not escape him that, as of now, he was her sole alibi. His word stood between her and condemnation for a crime he did not believe her capable of committing. But why *had* she been at Leach's? The timing of her visit and the solicitor's murder was too damned coincidental.

"I shall be committing my time to other work," he said.

"That so?" The other man's jaw tightened, his features lining with disapproval. "Can't say I'm happy to hear it. I must hasten to remind you of our agreement, Kent."

"Sir?"

"When I hire a man on, I expect that he will value Bow Street's commitment to confidentiality no matter the length of his employ. The fact that you're withdrawing your services doesn't negate your promise to me."

Ambrose's throat tightened. Given his dishonorable actions, his discretion was the least he could offer. "Yes. Of course."

The magistrate's moustache bristled, his eyes suspicious slits. "I mean it, Kent. You breathe word of this case to anyone, and you'll never work for Bow Street—or any other agency—again." He paused, no doubt to let his threat sink in. "As you know, Magistrate Dalrymple and I are cronies."

Ambrose gave a bleak nod.

"Well. I'll let your superiors know you'll be returning to duty on the morrow." Returning to his desk, Coyner began shuffling papers, a clear sign of dismissal.

Ambrose left the office and started the trek back to his room in Cheapside. As he walked along the street, he took scarce notice of the hawkers' raucous calls. His chest throbbed with shame. For the first time in his life, he'd knowingly dishonored his duty. He'd kept Marianne's visit to Leach a secret when his oath as a policeman demanded that he tell the truth.

Your emotions are getting in the way. You cannot let yourself be swayed by your attraction to her. Go back, tell Coyner—

But he ... could not. Because the devil in him protested her innocence, would do anything to safeguard her from accusations that could result in her swinging from the gallows. His gut knotted. He had only one option: he had to discover her secrets for himself. What information had she been after at Leach's? If she hadn't killed Leach, who had?

He climbed the steep steps of his tenement. He'd wash his face, change his clothes, then search out Marianne and get the truth. As he approached his room, he saw a footman leaning negligently against the peeling door. Ambrose recognized the blue and silver livery immediately.

"Mr. Kent?" the footman said.

"Yes?"

"My lady sends you this." Bowing, the servant handed over a note.

Pulse thudding, Ambrose brushed his thumb against the silky lavender wax seal that bore the initial "M". He broke it open. At the sight of its contents, disbelief surged ... with fury swift on its heels.

Goddamn her. The note crumpled in his fist.

Chapter Eighteen

"Thank you for seeing me on such short notice, Amelie," Marianne said as she entered the orchid dressing room. With interest, she eyed the colorful bolts piled upon the large work table. "New shipment?"

"*Mais oui.* One must stay abreast of the trends. Now I gather there is an element of urgency?"

"Of the utmost. I am to attend Lady Auberville's soiree in two days, and I must be dressed to the nines. Indeed, I find myself in need of a new wardrobe—the latest fashions for the remainder of the Season."

Marianne saw the emotions flutter across Amelie Rousseau's thin features: an *artiste*'s rapture, a businesswoman's delight. As expected, clever Amelie did not mention the fact that Marianne had purchased a good many gowns at the beginning of the Season.

"The order, it will have to be rushed," the modiste said, with just the right touch of doubt.

"I am happy to pay for the inconvenience," Marianne said.

"Then, *chérie*, time is not to be wasted." Excitement danced in the Frenchwoman's black eyes, and her hands clapped together. "Let us make art."

As the assistant helped Marianne to disrobe to her chemise, Amelie went to sort through the fabric on the table. She picked up one beautiful roll after another, muttering to herself, "*Non, ça ne suffit pas ...*" Finally, she said, "*Bien.* I have found it. Let us have a look in front of the glass."

With capable hands, Amelie draped the material over Marianne. She pinned here, tucked there, muttering in French as she worked. Finally, she stepped back. "What do you think?"

Iridescent shades of blue and green glimmered like mysterious and alluring waves. Even without a finished shape, the chiffon flowed with natural grace, clinging to Marianne's curves. Its beauty infused her with a feeling of power—her armor to protect her from harm.

Marianne sighed with bliss. "A *tour de force* as usual, Amelie."

"*C'est parfait,*" Amelie agreed. "Paired with a sheer underskirt and cut à la Grecque, the gown will be unparalleled."

A bell sounded from the front of the boutique. Amelie nodded at her assistant, who scurried off to attend to the new customer. The modiste continued to play with the fabric at Marianne's neckline, twisting it this way and that. "The exact design, it will depend on your purpose, *non?*"

"I shall be hunting," Marianne said succinctly.

"*Ah.*" Amelie lowered the décolletage an inch. Seductive yet still tasteful. "A particular gentleman of interest?"

Kent's face leapt into Marianne's head. His eyes heavy-lidded with passion, his face stark as his touch drove her higher and higher ... Her throat flexed in the reflection, color creeping up her cheeks.

Stay focused. You are after Ashcroft, Boyer, or Pendleton—they *are your targets.*

"Not in the manner which you are implying," she said.

"*Non?* Then why the blush, *chérie?*"

Marianne thought to deny it. Instead, she said ruefully, "There's no hiding anything from you, is there, Amelie?"

"A dressmaker understands her client's form. A modiste, she must comprehend her client's heart."

"You, of course, are a modiste," Marianne said with fondness.

"And a friend, I hope. Like you, I am a woman of the world ... and French besides. You may speak freely without fear here, my lady."

Marianne believed the modiste. With her philosopher's mind and independent spirit, Amelie had proved a confidante over the years. Though Marianne had not gone so far as to speak of Rosie, she had once mentioned her marriage to Draven. Amelie had listened without judgment or pity. In the end, she'd said simply, "He is dead, and you are rich, *ma chère*. If not kind, the universe is at least, on occasion, just."

Marianne experienced the urge to confide her sexual experience with Kent. There was no one else she could speak to about such matters: Tilda distrusted him, and Helena, well ... Marianne shuddered. The last thing she wanted was for the marchioness to know about her dalliance. Knowing Helena, she'd likely start pestering Marianne. About claptrap like romance and relationships. *Feelings*, God help her.

"There is a man," Marianne said.

"A lover?" Amelie said.

Marianne gave a slow nod.

"I, myself, have had a few. Some better than others," the modiste said with continental candor. "This one, he is good?"

"Very," Marianne admitted. The best she'd ever had in fact, though she'd only known one other. And she hadn't even *known* Kent, at least not in the strictly biblical sense. With just his hands, his mouth, he'd brought her such shattering pleasure ...

Even as her sex quivered, she recognized the danger. With Kent, she'd given into her impulses, something she had not done since Thomas and for good cause: those reckless couplings had resulted in a child. Though she now possessed the knowledge to prevent conception—methods including *coitus interruptus* followed by a special vinegar rinse—could she have trusted Kent to obey her wishes? More to the point, could she trust him at all? He'd already nosed into her business twice, and she still didn't know his true motives.

Men cannot be trusted. If you haven't learned that lesson, you're a fool indeed.

"You do not seem happy about this lover," the modiste observed.

Marianne heaved a sigh. "It's complicated, and I have other more pressing concerns. Besides, he is not someone I ought to get involved with. We fight whenever we meet—and we come from different worlds."

The other woman shrugged as she unpinned the chiffon. "*C'est l'amour.*"

Marianne blinked. "This isn't about love."

"An irrational and inconvenient attraction, a star-crossed relationship, and *very* good lovemaking." Amelie counted off her fingertips. "If not *l'amour*, then what would you call it?"

The possibility struck Marianne like a blade in the chest. She could not possibly be developing feelings for Kent. Could. Not. If she felt anything, it was mere ... obligation. Yes, because he'd saved her twice. Because she'd never met anyone like him. Because ... he'd given her the greatest pleasure she'd ever experienced?

That's physical attraction. Nothing more.

Shoulders tensed, she said, "I cannot afford sentiment. It has never served me well."

"*L'amour* isn't meant to serve. It simply *is*—to our delight and our despair. *Alors*, if we must suffer the aftermath of our foolish hearts, should we not also enjoy the sweetness of their abandon?"

"You advocate for a broken heart?" Marianne said, brows arching.

"Better broken than unused. *Le coeur va guérir*—it is only a matter of time."

Perhaps time healed some hearts, but the pain in Marianne's

organ had not subsided one whit since the fateful morning she'd walked into Primrose's nursery. She'd stayed up late the night before, stitching a ball for her active poppet to play with. But Rosie's bed had been empty, the cupboards bare of all the little dresses Marianne had sewn, and the ball had dropped from Marianne's icy hands ...

Seven years later and the wound still felt as fresh and raw as it had when Draven had informed her that he'd taken away her daughter:

Now you'll do my bidding. You'll breathe when I tell you to, stop when I say so. This is the fate you earned by being a trollop.

A touch on the arm brought her back. "Love takes courage," Amelie said softly, "a quality you possess in spades. Why deny yourself a taste of happiness?"

Because I don't deserve it. Not after all the mistakes I've made.

Throat dry, Marianne said, "The risk is too great."

"Risk, *ma chère? Ah, je comprends.*" The Frenchwoman's eyes gleamed. "As it happens, I can be of assistance—wait here."

The modiste left the room, leaving Marianne alone with her reflection. Clad in only her chemise, she looked less like a sophisticated widow and more like a version of her younger self. Miss Marianne Blunt, wayward daughter of a dusty squire ... A memory unfurled of that first time she'd gone to meet Thomas in the meadow adjoining their fathers' estates. When Helena's brother had returned from Oxford that summer, Marianne had known he was the one she would marry. Sweet Thomas, with his chestnut hair and hazel eyes and the son of an earl to boot.

Had that been love? she wondered. Not a mature vintage, certainly, but the youthful infatuation had been intoxicating nonetheless. Excitement had bubbled through her, heady as champagne, propelling her across the swaying fields toward her dreams. She hadn't known fear then. Or bitterness or guilt. She'd simply reveled in the sun's warmth, the breeze's soft caress.

How long had it been since she'd felt that vitality, that freedom of spirit?

The answer popped into her head with stunning clarity: *last night with Kent.*

"I have returned." Amelie's voice cut through Marianne's thoughts. Shutting the door, the modiste approached, holding out a small flat box. "For you, my lady."

"What is it?" Bemused, Marianne lifted the lid.

"French letters, as you English insist upon calling them." Amelie's eyes flitted heavenward. "A friend of mine owns a shop in Covent Garden, and these are her finest stock. They have been kept in a solution of rosewater for suppleness, and consequently a most delicious scent accompanies them. The red ribbons, they add a pretty touch, *non?*"

"Er, indeed." Marianne fought down her blush. "*Merci,* Amelie."

"You are welcome." The Frenchwoman nodded, smiling. "*Maintenant,* I have a few other ideas for your new gowns ..."

A commotion outside the room cut off the modiste's words. The next instant, the door flung open; Marianne's pulse spiked as Kent stood there, his eyes burning into hers.

Lud. Her bloody note. Obviously he'd gotten it.

The assistant flung herself in his path with valiant effort. "I tried to stop this man, *madame*! He would not listen—"

"Who do you think you are, *monsieur*? Remove yourself this instant, or I shall summon the magistrates," Amelie hissed, moving to stand in front of Marianne.

"I am a friend of Lady Draven's," Kent said in calm tones that sent a thrill of warning up Marianne's spine. "I rather think she is expecting me."

Amelie swung to look at Marianne. "You know this person?"

Marianne licked her suddenly dry lips. "How did you find me here?"

"I'm an investigator, remember?" he said. "Now unless you'd

like to air our laundry in front of all and sundry, I suggest you ask *madame* to give us a few moments."

"*Merde.* I certainly will *not* leave my client—"

"'Tis alright, Amelie. If it is not an inconvenience, I'd like to speak to Mr. Kent." Though her knees were wobbly, Marianne drew up her shoulders. "In private."

Sudden comprehension flashed in Amelie's dark eyes. "Of course, my lady. Er, take your time. Bernadette," she said briskly to her assistant, "*allons-y.*"

The door closed once more. As the tension in the room thickened, Marianne became aware of several things at once. She wore only her chemise, and from the flaring hunger in Kent's eyes, the fact had not escaped his notice. Yet he was angry, his rigid frame quivering like that of a bull about to charge. The box of French letters burned in her hand; as casually as she could, she walked over to the work table and set it down, using those moments to collect herself.

Swiveling, she leaned against the table and crossed her arms, her stance one of cool indifference. "We have a few things to settle between us, don't we?" she said.

Chapter Nineteen

A mbrose gritted his teeth. The woman was bloody impossible, the response she provoked in him savage and bewildering. He didn't know whether he wanted to throttle her or toss her onto the table and have his way with her. He did neither. Instead, he yanked her letter from his pocket. He tossed it—and the five hundred pounds she'd enclosed—onto the table.

"What is the meaning of that?" he bit out.

"Was it not clear?" Her eyes widened in the shoddiest mimicry of innocence he'd ever seen. With a nonchalance that belied the fact that she was almost naked—despite himself, his mouth pooled at the hint of her cheery nipples beneath the shift—she picked up the note and read it aloud. "*Thank you for services rendered.* Hmm. Which part left you confused, I wonder?"

"I am not confused, my lady. I am angry," he said, his jaw ticking.

"Angry? Whatever for?"

"I am not a bloody gigolo. Money has no place in what happened between us, and well you know it." His eyes narrowed as her lips gave a suspicious twitch. "You *do* know it. Devil take it, you sent the note to deliberately goad me, didn't you? Why?"

"We need to talk," she said.

He braced his hands on his hips. "Why didn't you simply invite me over to tea, you infuriating woman?"

"Conventionality has never been my way." She tipped her head to the side. "Although, come to think of it, there would be something deliciously ironic about discussing what happened over a civilized ritual like tea. *Will you take cream and sugar, Mr. Kent?*" she said in a light, mocking voice. "*And, by the by, what a daring rooftop escape we made from Mr. Leach's.*"

"Leach is dead," he said, waiting for her reaction.

Her thick lashes veiled her gaze for an instant. "Indeed."

"Did you kill him?" he said tersely.

Her brilliant emerald gaze locked with his. "Do you think I did?"

"Enough games," he growled. "For once, I want the truth from your lips. Did you kill Reginald Leach?"

Silence pulled between them. Her will was a palpable force, churning the tides of tension. His resolve was no less, a steadfast buttress against her squall.

"No." Her chin lifted. "I did not kill him."

Ambrose fought the wave of relief. Although his gut told him this was the truth—and he could see it in her eyes—he deserved an explanation. She'd been running roughshod over him since the day they'd met. No more.

"Tell me what happened," he demanded.

"Leach was dead when we arrived. Lugo found him in the sitting room," she said in cool, flat tones. "I do not expect you to believe me, and before you waste your breath, no, I have no proof."

"I believe you," Ambrose snapped.

Her lashes fluttered, her lips parting. "You ... you do?" The barest crack in her voice pierced his anger. Despite his irritation, protectiveness surged. What the devil had happened to Marianne to make her a stranger to trust?

"It's a bloody coincidence that you happened to be in his office the night he was killed," Ambrose said grimly. "What did Leach know about you, Marianne? What is this *information* you wanted back?"

Her gaze shuttered, but not before he saw fear flare in her eyes. "That is none of your business."

"The hell it isn't." He advanced upon her, and the stubborn thing did not move or yield any ground even when he stopped mere inches away. Close enough to smell her jasmine-scented skin, to sense the tremor of awareness that passed through her. "I have participated in a crime to help you. I have compromised my principles because I cannot stand the notion of you being hurt." *I've endangered my family's future because I can't believe you're as wicked as you pretend to be.* His hand shot out, cupping the back of her head, holding her steady to his gaze. "Now you will give me the courtesy of the truth."

"Or what?"

The challenge brought his simmering blood to a boil. His rationality dissolved in a molten wave of anger and lust. "Or this," he rasped and yanked her to him.

His lips claimed hers in a kiss that was anything but gentle. His fingers dug into her silken scalp, and her lips softened on a moan, welcoming him inside. He slanted his mouth across hers, his tongue driving into her heat. Spicy and sweet, a woman to feast upon. By God, he would have his fill—and his answers. He was done with being treated like some accommodating lackey. Clamping his hands on her hips, he lifted her onto the table and stepped between her dangling legs, spreading them wider. He grasped the neckline of her shift, and with one savage movement ripped the flimsy material from her body.

She gasped—not from fear, but arousal. He could see it in the swirling depths of her eyes. For a moment, she made a token effort to stop him.

"You're a brute," she said breathlessly, her hands splaying across his chest.

"I begin to think it's what you want from me." With ruthless precision, he reached for her sex. Primal satisfaction tightened his balls to find her slick and ready for him. "Why else would you be this wet, this hot?"

An unrecognizable sound left her as he continued to play with her lush folds. And she allowed it. Nay, welcomed it. Her hands planted upon the table, she arched herself against his touch, her eyes dazed and heavy-lidded as he petted her. His breathing grew harsh as her dew coated his fingers, flowed into his palm.

"That's my girl. Work yourself against my hand. Show me how badly you want this," he commanded.

A strangled noise left her. Her hips moved, and her wanton obedience sent another blast of heat to his groin. His cockstand strained, pushing against the thin wool of his trousers, eager to feel the pussy rubbing so sweetly against his hand. She was drenched, and he knew from her desperate wriggling exactly what she wanted. But he wouldn't oblige her that easily. Not without some give and take.

"Kent, I can't stand it," she gasped. "Lud, touch me ..."

"Where?"

Her pelvis titled in answer, nudging his finger toward her straining peak. Toward that lovely bud beneath her silky floss. He circled the hood, but did not touch her where she wanted.

"Damn you, Kent. Stop teasing me," she said through panted breaths.

"You'll have your satisfaction when I have mine," he said. "What information did you want from Leach?"

Her lashes flew upward. Anger and arousal glittered in her gaze. "How dare you?"

He was quicker than she. He caught the hand that came flying toward his face. In the next heartbeat, he shoved aside the table's contents, pushing her flat onto her back. With one hand, he pinned both her wrists above her head. With the other, he continued to stroke her quim.

"Now tell me what I want to know," he said.

Her hair spread like a moon burst, she glared up at him. "Go to hell."

He pressed his thumb lightly to her pearl, and a whimper escaped her. Her breasts rose and fell with heaving breaths. "Tell me," he repeated.

When she shot him a mutinous look, he bent his head and captured one ruby nipple in his lips. He suckled hard. She moaned, her pussy pleading against his hand as he used his lips and teeth to torment her. He drew away the instant she teetered on the brink.

"I'll let you come when you tell me what you wanted from Leach."

Her eyes were glossy, her cheeks flushed. "I hate you."

"Perhaps. But you still owe me the truth, sweeting." He circled her pearl again and felt the shudder run through her body.

"The information is private." The words were filtered through her teeth.

He flicked his finger. Did it again and again, keeping her on the razor's edge.

"Something was taken from me," she gasped out, writhing against his hand. "Damn you, Kent, I'm owed, and I want what's mine."

God, she'd gotten so slick ... he couldn't help but slide a finger inside, her tight, pulsing heat almost robbing him of his senses. "Tell me. Let me help you."

"I can't. I won't." She let out a keening cry as he thrust his finger deep. "Ambrose, please don't ask it of me ..."

It was then that he saw the wet glimmer upon her lashes, even as she wriggled in helpless pleasure to his touch. Something in his chest went soft, his anger subsiding. She was so vulnerable, his *selkie*. So afraid despite her perfect skin. In place of fury, his determination grew to gain her trust, a thing too delicate to be taken by force and locked away.

He released her wrists, but continued to play with her with slow, easy strokes. "Tell me this one thing," he coaxed, "and I'll give you what you want."

"Wh-what?"

"Have you been involved in illegal activities?" It was the furthest he could go without betraying Coyner's confidence and that of the case.

Her brow furrowed. "I'll do anything to get back what belongs to me, I won't lie. I did break into Leach's office. But I am no criminal, if that's what you're asking."

He knew this. She had secrets aplenty, and he vowed silently to discover them soon. For now, his chest swelled with the progress they'd made—and his cock with the need to reward her for her trust. Because whether or not she acknowledged it, Marianne was beginning to let him inside ... and not just her delectable body, though God knew that was a priority. He added another finger, stretching her gently. By Jove, she was tight. Tight and wonderfully lush. Her muscles gripped his plunging fingers as her silky juices eased the way.

Her lips opened on a sigh. "Dear God, like that ..."

"You're so responsive. So beautiful," he muttered. "Are you ready for me?"

"Yes," she said, her spine arching. "Oh, yes."

"Good. Because I'll explode if I don't get inside you," he said.

He unfastened his trousers—no time to attend to his boots. He shoved the wool past his hips, freeing his throbbing manhood. At the sight of his erection, her eyes widened.

"Kent, wait. We have to be ... careful," she said in a trembling voice.

Her meaning penetrated his lust. "I won't finish inside you," he said hoarsely. To test his willpower, he gripped the base of his cock, ran the bulging head along her slit. They both groaned as her sex slid against his, coating his cockhead with her juices. Her tight channel clamped the tip of his shaft, and sweat beaded on his brow. "I swear I'll pull out if it kills me." He thought it might.

"There's an alternative. Here." Groping the surface of the table, she found a box and shoved the contents at him. "Put this on."

Despite his state of high arousal, his brows shot up at the sight of the white tube with red strings dangling at one end. "Are you always this prepared, sweet?"

"Madame gave it—oh never mind," she said. "You know how to use it?"

In truth, he'd never worn a French letter before. He was no whoremonger, and the women he'd been with had employed other means of contraception. Consequently, he fumbled a little as he attempted to sheath his turgid shaft. The scent of roses mingled with his frustration.

"It doesn't fit," he growled.

"Mayhap it is not big enough for you." The sultry note of laughter in her voice didn't help matters. His cock swelled further. "Perhaps I can lend a hand?"

Leveraging up on her elbows, she reached for his cock. The boldness of her action, the way her tongue touched her lips as she stretched the sheep-gut over his thick, veined rod caused him to spurt a little. The lubrication helped to ease the French letter into place. By the time she tightened the red strings, her cheeks were rosy.

"You're ready," she whispered.

Was he. Kissing into her open mouth, he guided her onto her back. He positioned his cock at her entrance and pressed forward. Despite her dampness, her intimate muscles resisted him. Her passage was small, remarkably snug. He went slow, not wanting to hurt her.

"Alright?" he rasped, holding himself in check as fire enveloped the head of his cock.

Her bottom lip caught beneath her teeth. "I think so. Just go slow ..."

Sweat prickled his forehead as he eased forward another inch. Devil and damn, it was like stepping into an inferno, flames engulfing his shaft, the heat spreading to his balls, his groin, his entire self. Gritting his teeth, he pushed a little farther, and just when he thought he might die from the excruciating torture, her passage gave way. Moans left them both as he suddenly slid all the way home.

"Bloody hell, that's good," he breathed. He drew a stray lock from her cheek. "Sweetheart?"

Her lashes swept back to reveal eyes more vivid than spring. "Yes. Oh, Ambrose, *yes*."

He needed no further urging. He began to move, withdrawing and returning in slow strokes, watching her face the whole while. He wanted to see her pleasure, to know everything about her. As he made love to her, he stored away the signs of her desire: the flush sweeping over her bobbing breasts, the graceful arch of her neck as she met his thrusts. When her legs circled his hips, however, his control wavered. The dark need to possess her swept over him. He plunged with greater force, harder, deeper, wanting everything she had.

"Mmm, yes. Oh *Ambrose* ..."

Hearing his name, the wobble in her voice, turned something loose inside him. He thrust to the hilt, embedding himself so fully that her nest feathered his stones. "Like that, do you?" he growled. "Hard and deep? Will you come with my cock inside you?"

"I'm almost there," she gasped. "Make me come, *please*."

Groaning, he shoved in and out of her lush, tight hole. His thumb found her pearl, diddled it in time with his thrusts, and she went mad, thrashing beneath him. Faster and faster he rubbed her, fucking her harder and harder. Just when the heat threatened to consume him, she went rigid, her back bowing off the table. He covered her mouth, swallowing her scream and feeding her his own guttural shout as her pussy squeezed him. Hard contractions that demanded his seed, that made him shoot hotly over and again in a release that seemed to have no end.

He didn't know how much time had passed before he had the strength to rise on his elbows. Breathing heavily, he looked upon the face of his lover. Her hair lay in tangled skeins over the table; her lips were red and swollen from his kisses. Her eyes glowed with satisfaction and wonder, an expression he'd never seen from her before. His chest puffed with pride as did—astonishingly—his cock. Her gaze widened for he'd not yet parted from her.

He twisted his hips gently, and a purr escaped from her lips. He brushed his knuckles against her silken jaw. In that moment, with their bodies tucked so perfectly together, it didn't matter that he was a policeman and she a baroness, and they were entangled in an affair that could lead nowhere.

"Trust me, Marianne?" he said, giving a lazy thrust.

Her gaze grew dazed, a peachy flush spreading over her skin.

"I'll ... I'll think about it," she whispered.

He told himself not to push his luck. He'd satisfy himself with that answer for the time being. Because in that moment, there was a wealth of satisfaction to be had, and he set about demonstrating that—for these stolen moments at least—he was the man to give it to her.

Chapter Twenty

"Time to get home to the missus. You leaving soon, Mr. Kent?"

Ambrose looked up from the report he was writing. John Oldman—known universally as Johnno—had poked his head through the doorway of Ambrose's cramped office at Wapping Street headquarters. One of the four of Ambrose's crew, the waterman had a cap crammed atop his curly auburn hair and a grin on his freckled face.

"Be a while for me yet, Johnno. Sir Dalrymple wants this report on his desk by morning," Ambrose said.

"Overstuffed goat's still breathing down your neck, eh?" Johnno said with sympathy.

To say the least. Since Ambrose's return, Dalrymple's behavior had grown increasingly malicious. A big case that Ambrose's team should have handled had been given to another Principle Surveyor. In lieu of chasing down criminals, Ambrose had been assigned to making spurious revisions to reports. But two wrongs did not make a right; Ambrose was not one to encourage insubordination.

"Enjoy your evening, Johnno," he said simply.

"Plan to. Lizzie's ma has the bairns for the night, so we've the house to ourselves." Winking, the waterman hitched his satchel higher onto his shoulder. "If you got yourself a wife, sir, you'd have a reason to go home."

Not so long ago Ambrose would have agreed. His vision of contentment had involved a cozy cottage and his better half waiting for him inside with a hot meal and a smile. What spurred him to finish up his work now, however, was a burning impatience to investigate a solicitor's murder. All so he could protect the enigmatic, aristocratic woman whom he desired beyond all reason ... and who refused to trust him.

After their scorching encounter at the dressmaker's—he still couldn't believe that he'd made love to her in a *shop*, for God's sake —he'd escorted Marianne home. During the carriage ride, he'd attempted to learn more about her troubles. He'd asked point-blank if she was in danger: did she know of anyone who might try to frame her for the solicitor's murder? Tight-lipped, she'd given him nothing. When he'd persevered, she'd said sharply, "Don't push me, Ambrose."

At the townhouse, she hadn't invited him in.

Though he'd been frustrated, he'd understood her well enough to know that she needed time and space to come to a decision about him. Given the tenuous truce between them, he'd decided not to push her further. In the meanwhile, however, he was not a man to sit idly upon his thumbs. He'd already learned the names of Leach's clerks and the places most likely to find them. Tonight, he'd begin his own inquiry.

"Stop bragging, Johnno, else I'll find a reason to keep you here," Kent said mildly.

"Good night to you, then, sir." Tipping his cap, the waterman strode off, whistling.

Ambrose finished up his accounting of his crew's activities and placed the ledger atop the neat pile on his desk. He glanced at the clock. It was nearing eight in the evening: time to seek the answers to his questions. Pulling on his greatcoat, he departed the office and hailed a ride from one of the boat men. The craft glided west-ward toward the City, the stars glittering pinpricks in the velvet sky. With the cool night air against his face and the dark water running beneath him, Ambrose let his thoughts unfurl.

Something was taken from me, Marianne had said. *I'm owed, Kent. And I want what's mine.*

In the past two days, Ambrose had dug up information on Reginald Leach; what he'd discovered reinforced his belief that the solicitor had been blackmailing Marianne. Leach had made his name on discretion and flexible ethics: if you had enough money and needed a messy situation taken care of, Leach was your man. Bastard children, duels gone wrong, murders done in a fit of drink or rage ... for the right price, Leach could sweep anything under a carpet of legal protection.

Ambrose wouldn't put it past the unscrupulous bastard to hold a woman ransom with some ill-begotten piece of knowledge. Nor did he think it surprising that Leach had wound up dead. Marianne wasn't the only one Leach might have been extorting. The solicitor had collected a great deal of dirt on London's most powerful men—any of whom might be willing to kill to keep a secret silent. What information had Leach held over Marianne?

As the boat slipped beneath London Bridge, Ambrose puzzled over the coincidence which bothered him most. Why had the client who'd hired Bow Street to watch Marianne—who'd suspected her of being an anarchist—used *Leach* as the intermedi-ary? Who was this supposed lord of the realm, and why had he wanted Marianne monitored?

Even Coyner had admitted that there was no solid proof of Marianne's involvement in an anarchist group. The evidence against her was purely circumstantial. Though her behavior could admittedly be outrageous, Ambrose was beginning to see it was by design: it wasn't anarchy she was after, but something specific. Something precious had been taken from her; why else her desperate actions, the pain in her eyes?

More importantly, why had this anonymous client targeted her? Ambrose considered multiple hypotheses. In the best case scenario, the client had simply been mistaken, erroneously vilifying Marianne based on circumstantial evidence. Another possibility: there had been no client at all, and all of it had been Leach's doing. Perhaps Leach had known that Marianne was after him. Perhaps he'd taken the precautionary measure of having her monitored, of blackening her name. If Leach had been responsible, then his death would have nullified any threat to Marianne.

Ambrose wasn't taking any chances. Logic circled him back to the dead solicitor. He'd start his investigation by finding out everything he could about Reginald Leach and Leach's clientele. If he followed all the threads, he was certain one would lead him to Marianne's secret.

The boat bumped against the dock. Tipping the driver, Ambrose took the stairs up to the road. He headed north until he hit Fleet Street. Halfway down a smoke-clogged alley, he found an entrance with the emblem of three crowns painted over the doorway. Inside, the tavern was a warren of narrow corridors and cozy nooks, and Ambrose had to duck his head more than once to avoid the low-hanging beams. The smell of hops and savory pub cooking filled the air.

Scanning the half-filled room, Ambrose approached the bar.

"What's your fancy, sir?" the barkeep asked.

"I'm looking for someone," Ambrose said, placing a coin on the counter. "Tom Milford. Used to work for a solicitor named Leach."

The barkeep jerked his head toward a table in a secluded corner. "Carrot-pated cove sittin' alone. The one wot looks like 'e lost 'is mother, though I reckon it can't be o'er that skinflint Leach. No loss to the world, that one." The barkeep snorted. "Reckon it's the loss o' pay wot 'as Tom down—'e's been nursin' the same ale all night."

"I'll take two of the same," Ambrose said.

As he fished for another coin, he recalled with a pang the books he'd sold yesterday. His legacy from his father now sat in the dusty corner of a pawnbroker's shop near Drury Lane. He'd sent the bulk of the money to Emma. The funds would keep his family in the cottage until month's end, when Ambrose could make the trip to Chudleigh Crest. He'd look into other housing options in the village and give Emma some much-deserved respite as well.

The barkeep returned with the drinks. Taking the two foaming tankards, Ambrose crossed over to Leach's clerk. "Mr. Milford?"

A bloodshot gaze veered upward. Though Tom Milford looked no more than five-and-twenty, he had dark circles under his eyes and lines of worry etched around his mouth.

"Who's asking?" Milford said.

"Ambrose Kent. I work for the Thames River Police. Would you mind if I join you?" Ambrose held up the two tankards.

Either Milford was desperate for the drink or for relief from his own company because he shrugged. "Suit yourself, Mr. Kent."

Ambrose sat and pushed one of the drinks across the table.

"Hard day?" he said. In questioning witnesses, he'd found it effective to first establish rapport. People spoke more freely and truthfully with those they liked and trusted.

"I'll say." Milford took a long gulp of his new drink; foam formed a moustache above his upper lip. "God Almighty, I needed that. I assume you're here about Mr. Leach? I've already told the constables everything I know."

From what Ambrose had heard, Milford's testimony had amounted to little. Which was why he wanted to speak to the clerk on his own.

"Sometimes new information comes up after a few nights' rest. I imagine it was a shock to learn of your employer's passing," Ambrose said.

"Shock ain't the half of it. Try bloody despair." Milford took another swig of his drink, his tone morose. "For three years of my life, I slaved for that penny-pinching codger. Now I've nothing to show for it—neither money nor the qualifications to strike out on my own. I'm sunk."

"Surely it can't be as bad as all that."

"It's worse. Got a girl waiting on me." The apprentice slanted Ambrose a glum look. "With my current prospects, she ain't likely to wait much longer."

Ambrose felt a spark of empathy; he knew that situation all too well. His ex-fiancée hadn't been the sort to wait either.

"Things have a way of working out as they should," he said.

He was surprised by how much he meant it. Despite the frustration of his dealings with Marianne, the alternative of never meeting her struck a hollow chord in his chest. Though it made him feel somehow disloyal to admit it, he hadn't experienced feelings half as intense when Jane had broken things off—and he'd been with her for three years.

"Sometimes," he added, "a disappointment can turn out to be an opportunity."

"When one door closes, eh? You sound like my ma." Milford sent him a wry smile. "Now what was it you wanted to know, Mr. Kent?"

"Did Leach have any enemies? Anyone who wished him harm?"

Milford rolled his eyes. "Does a dog have fleas? Don't mean to speak ill of the dead, but Reginald Leach was a bastard through and through, and the people who hired him on weren't much better. But Leach kept the meat of his cases to himself and assigned us clerks the banal tasks. Instead of teaching us the practice of the law, he had us making his tea and tidying up after him like sodding servants. Only, like idiots, we worked for free."

"Did you ever witness any altercations in the office? Incensed clients, that sort of thing?"

"Every day raised voices came from Leach's office." Milford's forehead furrowed. "Come to think of it, there was that row just last week. Slipped my mind until you asked. Aye, bloody ripper that one was."

Ambrose's instincts perked. "What and whom did the row involve?"

"Can't say what it was over exactly. But they were shouting something fierce. 'Twas none other than the Earl of Pendleton who came storming out of Leach's office."

Ambrose gripped his tankard. Pendleton was a member of the House of Lords, a wealthy peer. Could he be the mystery client who'd retained Bow Street's services via Leach?

"Did you catch any of the conversation between the earl and your employer?"

Milford shook his head. "Leach's office has thick walls. But before he left, Lord Pendleton said something along the lines of ... *If I go down, I'll find a way to take you with me.*" The clerk's eyes widened. "Good God, you don't think he meant it literally?"

Ambrose had no idea. But he'd definitely be looking into Pendleton. "Any other disgruntled clients stick out in your mind?"

"Certainly none as disgruntled as the earl," Milford said, "though you didn't hear it—or any of this—from me."

Ambrose rose and offered his hand. "You've been very helpful, Mr. Milford. Thank you."

The clerk raised his tankard in a mock salute. "Consider it my departing contribution to the legal profession."

"You never know what's around the corner, Mr. Milford. Another apprenticeship or another career ... or another young lady." With a faint smile, Ambrose said, "Take it from me, lad: life is full of surprises."

Chapter Twenty-One

L ady Auberville's ball was one of the annual crushes of the Season, and this year's fete was proving no exception. Descending the steps to the massive ballroom, Marianne surveyed the glittering scene. Lady Auberville had cleverly taken inspiration from her own backyard: the hostess had done up the place so that it flowed seamlessly into the very English garden just beyond the terrace doors. Instead of the usual towering palms, pots of lavender and trained ivy formed hedges around the dance floor, and blooming lily-of-the valley perfumed the air.

Charming as the setting was, Marianne's attention turned immediately to locating her targets. She found Ashcroft first. The viscount stood next to buffet tables overflowing with picnic foods. As usual, he was surrounded by a circle of females—married ladies and widows mostly—who no doubt wished to end the night in his bed. Sandy-haired, handsome, and possessed of dissolute charm, Ashcroft had a reputation as a gifted lover.

A gifted lover ... beautiful golden eyes flashed in her head. A face stark with desire and intent. The memory of Kent's clever hands, his restrained male strength as he brought her to the peak of pleasure again and again—

Her breathing quickened. The tips of her breasts hardened, warmth blossoming at her core.

Keep your mind on the task, she admonished herself.

As Marianne watched, Ashcroft dipped a glass into a miniature champagne lake complete with tiny floating marzipan swans; he held the dripping glass to a lady's lips. She obediently took a sip. He repeated the motion with the next female in line, who giggled as she followed suit. No doubt he planned to have them all drinking out of his hand before the night was out. Truth be told, he appeared a trifle bored. Suddenly, Ashcroft's gaze lifted.

Marianne forced her lips into a sultry curve as his eyes raked over her with cool interest. She allowed the exchange to continue for a few seconds more before she looked away. Her heart thumped. She'd baited the first trap of the evening. On to the next.

Circling the dance floor, she identified the Earl of Pendleton. He stood with a group of his lofty peers, attempting to converse with the young daughter of one of his cronies. From the way the debutante's gaze flitted toward the dance floor, it was clear she wished to be elsewhere.

Marianne decided she'd tackle Pendleton later. She looked for the third and final suspect on her list; Marquess Boyer, however, was nowhere to be found.

"Marianne, there you are. We have been waiting ages for you to arrive."

Marianne turned to see Helena's approach. Her friend looked resplendent in a gown of amethyst silk ornamented with gold trefoils. The marchioness' most flattering accessory, however, took the form of the very large and obviously possessive husband at her side.

"Lady Draven," the marquess said, bowing.

Helena was looking at her with a slightly anxious expression. Recalling her abrupt exit from the Hartefords' dinner party, Marianne felt a prickle of embarrassment.

In a light tone, she said, "It appears Madame Rousseau has been saving her best work for you. That dress is divine, Helena."

"As is yours," her friend replied. "I've never seen such brilliant shades of blue and green. You look like a beautiful mermaid."

Or another enchanted creature of the sea.

Smiling faintly, Marianne said, "Your bodice is superb. Baring the shoulders is all the rage in Paris, and you shall be setting the trend on English shores."

"Considering what she charges, I do not see why Madame Rousseau needs to economize on fabric," the marquess muttered. He slanted a dark glance at his wife's décolletage. "I shall have to have a word with her."

Helena gave her lord an exasperated look. "You'll do no such thing. Soon I shall be as big as one of those Vauxhall hot air balloons, and all the fabric in the world won't hide it. Until then, I mean to dress as fashionably as I please, and there's nothing you can do to—"

Bending his dark head, Harteford deposited words in his wife's ear; whatever he said stopped Helena mid-sentence. Her mouth fell open, a rosy flush staining her cheeks. With a satisfied gleam in his eye, Harteford straightened.

"I'll make myself useful and fetch you some lemonade, my dear. Lady Draven?"

"None for me, thank you."

Staring off at her departing spouse, Helena said in bemused tones, "One day that man will drive me mad."

"You married him. And did a good deal besides to secure his affection," Marianne said. "I hope it was worth it."

If possible, Helena's color grew higher. "Of course it was—a thousand times over. You know I adore Harteford. It is only that sometimes he can be a bit overbearing."

"A predictably masculine trait."

A pause, and then Helena cleared her throat. "Speaking on

that, as your long-time friend and one who is concerned about your well-being, I have something to ask you."

Marianne stiffened. She knew what was coming. "Indeed."

"What is going on between you and Mr. Kent?" Tipping her head to one side, Helena studied Marianne with concerned hazel eyes. "After the fireworks at our dinner party, Harteford was reminded of a similar interaction between you and Mr. Kent during Percy's rescue. He said Mr. Kent seemed rather *protective* of you."

"Is that so unusual with the male sex? Really, they're not far removed from dogs, the way they growl at the slightest provocation," Marianne drawled.

Inside, panic thudded with each breath. She had not yet come to a decision about Kent. Whether to trust him. Whether to give into her impulses, which had led to nothing but trouble in the past. If she did not fully know herself, how could she explain the situation to Helena?

"'Tis true that males do tend to fall all over you. You've never seemed discomfited by it before." Though gentle, Helena's words were also perceptive. "Yet both Harteford and I have observed that you seem to enjoy baiting Mr. Kent."

Marianne despised indecision—particularly her own. Having no desire to air her laundry in this time and place, she opted for the classic subterfuge.

"Surely you are not accusing me of having interest in a *policeman*, Helena?" she said in haughty tones.

Nothing like snobbery and the schisms of social class to curtail a conversation.

"If I were saying that, it would be no accusation. Mr. Kent is a good, honorable man who has done much for my family." Helena's brow furrowed. "I like him, and Harteford trusts him. As far as I am concerned, you could do a lot worse."

A quiver of old resentment broke through. "Because of my

own lowly origins, you mean? Because my father was a drunken, ill-bred squire?"

"Of course not." Helena blinked at her. "Why would you even think that? What I meant was that Mr. Kent is intelligent and handsome, and he has a kind heart. You deserve a man who would care for you truly."

"Oh." Marianne swallowed, feeling small and foolish for misjudging her friend. Her next words did not improve her assessment of herself. "You think Mr. Kent is handsome?" she blurted.

Helena's chestnut curls bobbed with enthusiasm. "He looked very fine in his evening clothes, wouldn't you agree? More importantly, he is unaffected and honest—a man who knows himself. Do you not find such self-assurance attractive, Marianne?"

Helena didn't know the half of it. Or—judging by the glint in the marchioness' eyes—perhaps she knew too well.

"Yes," Marianne heard herself admit. "I do."

"Then there's no harm in getting to know Mr. Kent better, is there?" Helena said brightly. "If you'll allow, I shall arrange a small get together. A cozy supper perhaps ..."

As Helena chattered on about her plans, Marianne allowed herself to envision that fantasy of a normal life. She and Kent would court like any couple, spending time with her closest friends. In this imaginary reality, she would have never lost Rosie, so her daughter would be there too, playing with Helena's brood ...

For so long, Marianne had been alone, and a lump rose in her throat at the notion of somehow joining the world around her. Of being free to seek out love and true companionship. Of inhabiting her own skin.

Yet she was *not* free. She had suspects to hunt down and a beloved daughter to regain. Could any man support her through such dark travails? Understand and accept the flawed, damaged creature she truly was?

Could Kent?

The thought shot across her mind like a bright star, dazzling in its possibility. She had to admit that Kent had proved himself rather stalwart thus far. He'd put up with being shot, cock-teased, insulted, and propositioned by her; he'd dragged her across the rooftops of London in order to rescue her. Not to mention the fact that he'd shown her time and again pleasure she'd never known existed. He'd done all of this and demanded nothing in return.

"I shall send an invitation to Mr. Kent, then?" Helena inquired.

Marianne's throat tightened. Could she share the truth with Kent? Surely, he wouldn't betray her like other men had—or would he? He had promised to help her: if she told him about Rosie, would he help her find her little girl? She looked at Helena's expectant expression, and guilt punctured her hopes. She'd kept secrets for so long; was she even capable of letting down those walls of fear and shame?

"Let me think on it." At the other's crestfallen countenance, she said quietly, "I appreciate your concern. You are too good to me, dearest."

"Just try not to think too long," Helena sighed, her hand fluttering to the amethyst silk over her belly. "Soon I shan't be fit for company, and you know how Harteford gets when I am increasing."

As if on cue, the marquess came striding through the crowd bearing a glass of lemonade. His eyes flashed with concern as they honed in on the position of Helena's hand. "Tired, my love? Would you like me to find you a seat?"

"No, thank you. What I should like to do is dance," Helena said.

"Dance?" Harteford's dark brows came together. "But are you certain—"

"They're playing a waltz, and you are my favorite partner. You know the physician has cleared me for my normal activities."

When her husband looked as if he meant to argue, the

marchioness stood on tiptoe and whispered something in his ear. She must have delivered her tit-for-tat because his jaw turned quite ruddy.

He cleared his throat, his smoldering gaze fixed on his wife. "If you'll excuse us, Lady Draven?"

"Of course," Marianne said.

The pair headed off—not in the direction of the dance floor, she noted with a mixture of amusement and envy—but toward the exit. When Helena turned back to mouth, "*Let me know,*" Marianne gave a quick nod.

Alone, she was left to deal with the encroaching gentlemen. Turning down offers of champagne, dancing, and other activities best left unrepeated, she made her escape to the periphery of the ballroom. She took momentary shelter behind a small white gazebo the hostess had fancifully erected indoors. Peering around the wood frame, she saw the looks of consternation on the men's faces—thank heavens her pursuers hadn't the brains to match their libidos.

"Tiresome, isn't it?"

Her head whipped in the direction of the smooth accents. She recovered in the next instant.

"What is, pray tell?" she said, arching her brows.

"Being pursued. I, myself, prefer being on the other end of the hunt." The tawny-haired rake flashed her a white smile. "Devlin St. James, Viscount Ashcroft, at your service Lady Draven."

"I know who you are," she said. *Now I mean to discover what you're hiding. What did Leach have on you, you blighter—did he buy Rosie on your behalf?*

"My reputation precedes me, then. In a good way, I hope."

Clenching the sticks of her fan, she shaped her lips into a flirtatious curve. "If your reputation is as large as they say, my lord, then I should say it is in a *very* good way."

Ashcroft laughed. Up close, she saw he had a weak chin—one

made soft by easy living and dissipation. "Touché, my lady. Then, again, you have quite the reputation yourself."

"It takes one to know one," she said in a coquettish tone.

"In that case, I suggest we avail ourselves of Auberville's fine champagne and get to know one another's *reputations* better." Winking, Ashcroft held out an arm.

Though her stomach recoiled, her fingers went to rest lightly on the black superfine. "By all means, my lord, I'd like nothing more than to know you better."

Chapter Twenty-Two

An hour later, Marianne found herself rolling along in Ashcroft's well-sprung carriage. It was a position no doubt envied by some, but it was all she could do to suppress a shudder as he ran a gloved finger down her arm. Though her cloak covered her, his touch raised the hairs on her skin. His pale gaze was bloodshot, his expression more leering than suave. This was likely due to the fact that she'd plied him with drink at the Aubervilles' assembly while scarcely partaking of her own. She wanted him three seas over; it would make him easier to interrogate.

"You have the most beautiful eyes. Like big, shiny emeralds," he said in slurred accents.

"You *are* original, aren't you?" she said.

He grinned, apparently beyond the reach of sarcasm. "That's what all the ladies say. I'll show you things in bed that you've never even heard of. I've got a few tricks up my sleeve to tickle your fancy —and elsewhere."

Be still my beating heart.

"How, er, delightful. As it happens, I was hoping we could put your cleverness to another use first. I find myself in a tight spot, and I thought you might help me."

"Feeling a bit tight myself." Though squiffy, he was quick; he grabbed her hand and pressed it to his groin. She forced herself to stay calm, to keep her mask in place even as her stomach lurched. "Hard as a rock, too. Wager I'm the hardest and biggest you've ever had, eh?"

As a matter of fact ... no.

"How impressive, my lord. Yet I've heard that your manhood is not the only thing about you that is so generous." She squeezed lightly.

He groaned, his head falling back against the cushions. "What is it that you want, you saucy wench? Money? Jewels? Thought that dead husband of yours left you plenty of both."

"I have no need of either. Only a bit of advice."

Ashcroft's eyes closed as he ground his erection against her palm. Dear God, she would need to scrub her hands with lye after this. "What advice?"

"Rumor has it you were acquainted with a certain Reginald Leach," she said.

His eyes slit open. "Who told you that?"

His sharp tone belied his drunkenness. She'd hit a nerve. Through the uncovered windows, she saw that they had arrived back at her townhouse. The street was shadowed, devoid of activity. She inhaled, bolstering her courage to proceed with her plan. If worse came to worse, she'd make a run for it. Her house was steps away; though she could not see Lugo, she knew he was monitoring the goings-on.

Pasting on a smile, she said, "One hears things. I, too, knew Mr. Leach, you see." The rehearsed lie rolled over her tongue with the smoothness of morning chocolate. "And I am concerned about what will happen to certain information he possessed now that he is gone."

Ashcroft stared at her. She judged his expression as surprised ...
yet not worried. He betrayed no sign of guilt, no concern that she
knew the solicitor he might have used to procure a child. The solicitor he might have murdered.

Instead, he barked out a laugh. "It seems we truly are birds of a
feather, dove. Wouldn't worry your pretty head over it, though.
Leach was a bastard, but his lips were locked tighter than a virgin's
thighs. By the by, what nefarious deed was the old goat helping you
keep under wraps?"

If Ashcroft did indeed have Rosie, his behavior concerning the
solicitor was incredibly blasé, even for a jaded scoundrel. Doubt
about his culpability crept in, yet she had to make certain. In for a
penny ...

Leaning close to his ear, she murmured in suggestive tones,
"I'll show you my secret if you show me yours. I think it would be
quite stimulating to whisper our naughty misdeeds to one another,
don't you?"

"Subversive little minx, ain't you? Demme, if that doesn't
make me want to fuck you more," he panted. "On the count of
three, then ..."

At the cue, she whispered a fabricated and lurid indiscretion.
Simultaneously, Ashcroft deposited his transgression into her ear;
though it did not involve her daughter, Marianne's heart nonetheless thudded with disgust.

"I know I haven't shocked you." His hot, moist breath made
her shudder. "In fact, I think you'll like my brand of fun. More
than that squealing provincial bitch did at any rate ..."

Marianne dodged his lips. When she tried to move, he grabbed
her arms.

"Let me go," she hissed.

"Not until I get what you've been flaunting at me all night. Go
ahead and struggle,"—Ashcroft yanked off her cloak, his expression hard, sneering—"the fight only heats the blood."

Fear gave her sudden strength. She twisted away, reaching for the door. The handle did not budge. In the next instant, Ashcroft was upon her, forcing her to the cushions. She clawed at his face, and his curses filled the carriage the moment before he backhanded her. Her cheek exploded with pain, the metallic taste flooding her mouth as she fought a wave of darkness. The colliding of past and present.

You dirty whore. You deserve this. You like this.

Screaming, she continued to struggle, but he overpowered her. His hand clamped over her mouth, and he pinned her in place. Panic suffocated her as he shoved up her skirts. Her moors loosening, she felt herself detach from her skin and begin to float up to that place where nothing could hurt her. Where words and violence could not reach.

Where only numbness existed.

She heard a shout. A door slamming. Ashcroft's weight lifted off her.

Reality came roaring back. She bolted upright. Through the open door, she saw Ashcroft's body fly onto the pavement, a dark figure advancing upon him.

"Get up," Ambrose growled. Bloodlust flowed through his veins as he closed in on the nob sniveling in the street. His hands fisted in readiness to swing again. "Get up and face me like a man."

"You broke my nose, you blackguard! Do you know who I am?" The fop glared up at him, blood trickling from one refined nostril. "I am Viscount Ashcroft, and I'll have you thrown in Newgate for this!"

Ignoring the whiny accents, Ambrose hauled the gent up by the collar and slammed him against the side of the carriage. The bastard groaned. "Driver! Help me—"

"Don't think he's in any shape to." Lugo's deep voice came

from the front of the equipage where the driver lay unconscious by the wheels. The African had arrived at the same time as Ambrose, and wordlessly they'd split the offensive.

Ashcroft paled. "My father is the Duke of—"

"I don't give a damn who he is or who you are," Ambrose said with quiet menace. "You were attacking a lady. And you will pay for it."

"I wasn't attacking anyone. We were just having a bit of a t-tickle." Ashcroft's eyes bulged as Ambrose's grip tightened on his throat. "For God's sake, you silly trollop, tell the man!"

Marianne stood a few steps beyond the carriage door. In the moonlight, her skin had the translucent gleam of porcelain. An animal sound emerged from Ambrose's throat when he saw the bruise darkening on her left cheek.

"Go to hell, Ashcroft," she said.

Though her eyes flashed, Ambrose heard the tremor in her voice. His muscles grew taut. His fingers squeezed instinctively.

The viscount made a choking sound. "Don't let her looks fool you, man! She may look like a lady, but she's a whore through and through. She was asking for it," he pleaded. "Ask anyone, she spreads her thighs for any man—"

Ambrose's fist plowed into the other's face. With nary a sound, the bugger crumpled, sliding into a heap next to the carriage wheels. Breathing hard, Ambrose turned to face Marianne. Blood pounded in his ears; he didn't trust himself to speak.

"Lugo, see that this mess is cleaned up," she said in shaky tones.

"Yes, my lady." The manservant went to inspect the viscount. He nudged the fallen lord none too gently with his boot, eliciting a moan. Meeting Ambrose's gaze, Lugo gave him a nod that might have passed for approval. "I'll get these two where they belong," the African said. "In the meantime, my lady, Mr. Kent looks like he could use some attention. Shall I alert the housekeeper?"

"I'll see to that. You take care of Ashford," Marianne said.

Lugo bowed; when he raised his dark head, Ambrose could have sworn the man's eyelid drooped in a slight wink.

"Coming, Mr. Kent?" Marianne arched a brow at him.

Muscles bunched, he followed her inside.

Chapter Twenty-Three

Marianne sat upon the divan in her bedchamber, holding an herbal compress to her throbbing cheek. She comforted herself with the fact that she could cross Ashcroft off her list. Tonight's events put her one step closer to finding Rosie's captor; everything was going according to plan.

Then why did she feel like a bundle of nerves?

The answer, of course, was Ambrose Kent. He stood at the window in his shirtsleeves, his long, lean silhouette turned from her as he looked out the curtains to the street down below. Vigilance sharpened his profile, his keen eyes sweeping back and forth. A queer pang seized her chest; even with the danger over, he remained on alert. Protecting her. Her gaze drew to his large hands, and the pang deepened into an exquisite ache.

The knuckles of his right hand were swollen and red. In places, the skin had broken.

Clearing her throat, she set down her poultice. "We should attend to your hand. Tilda brought some salve and ice."

He swung to look at her, and her breath stuttered at the emotion darkening his eyes. A muscle ticked on his granite-hard jaw. He looked dangerous: a man on the edge, gripping on to his last vestiges of self-control.

She ought to have feared him. Yet she did not. The realization caught her off guard, scrambled her wits as badly as Ashcroft's blow had. Deep in her marrow, she believed Kent would not hurt her.

"Devil take my hand. You owe me an explanation." Kent's low, quiet voice sent thrills up her spine. "Why were you with Ashford tonight?"

"Come sit first." Though her pulse beat a rapid staccato, she smiled and patted the cushion next to hers. "We can't have you bleeding over the Aubusson."

He crossed over to her. He did not sit; instead, he towered over her, more than six feet of bridling male. His hands planted on his narrow hips. Tension vibrated in the space between them.

"Are you having an affair with Ashcroft?" Kent bit out.

Explanations flitted through her mind. Countless lies. They clung like ashes to her tongue.

So easy to let him think it. Let him believe what everyone else does, that you're a lascivious jade. He'll leave you alone then.

"No," she blurted.

She didn't expect him to believe her. Given their encounters to date, he had plenty of reason to think her a heartless trollop. To believe what Ashcroft had said of her. The notion thickened her throat.

"Why were you alone with the viscount, then? I won't be put off this time, Marianne. First Leach and now this. What is this damned secret of yours—what could possibly move an otherwise intelligent woman to recklessly endanger herself time and again?"

Emotions closed in on her, propelling her to her feet. To her surprise, Kent allowed her to pass, and she went to the fireplace, buying herself time to think. What would Kent think of the fact that she had a bastard? Would he blame her for her indiscretion? Would he still care to involve himself in her affairs if he knew the sins she'd committed—about her little girl who suffered to this day because of her failings?

Licking her lips, Marianne watched the flames leap in the grate. "I've told you I'm not having an affair with Ashcroft. That should suffice—"

"That doesn't begin to suffice."

She spun around as Kent came toward her. He kept advancing, his pace steady, leaving her no option but to retreat. Heartbeats later, he had her backed against the wall next to the mantel. His arms caged her. She should have been angry, afraid. Instead, she ... yearned. He touched her wounded cheek, and she trembled from head to toe.

"What are you afraid of? Tell me, Marianne." Though his touch was gentle, his features were intent, harshly controlled. She understood why criminals would want to confess all their sins in the wake of those bright, piercing eyes. "I won't hurt you. I want only to help. Trust me."

"I ... can't," she said helplessly. Wanting.

"You can," he said and lowered his mouth to hers.

His warmth flowed into her, melting away her resistance. Dear God, how she had missed this—craved his kiss since the moment the last one had ended. He drew her in with his taste, the sustenance of his strength. His wiry length crushed her against the wall, and nothing had ever felt more right. Sighing, she pulled at his cravat, the buttons of his waistcoat. She needed to be closer, needed his heat to banish the chill of the past and to fuel the fire of the moment.

Wordlessly, he stepped back and stripped off his waistcoat. Yanked the shirt over his head. The smooth, sleek muscles of his shoulders gleamed like polished bronze in the candlelight. She touched his chest, delighting in the contrasting textures of coarse hair and hard sinew. His heart beat strong and steadfast beneath her palm. Her gaze dipped to the ridges of his abdomen, following the tantalizing line of hair to where it disappeared into the waistband of his trousers. At the sight of the straining bulge beneath, syrupy warmth flooded her sex.

"Your turn." Though his voice was stern, faint lines fanned from his eyes. "Face the wall, Marianne, and let me undress you."

His command sent a delicious ripple through her blood. She'd never been one to follow orders and yet ... after an instant's hesitation, she obeyed. She could allow herself the luxury of this one small surrender. She turned her head, her cheek brushing against the silk-covered wall. Each breath pushed her breasts outward, skimming her stiff nipples against the hard surface. She stood there, aroused, in an agony of anticipation.

The hot mouth upon her nape made her start. A moan flew from her lips as he licked and sucked the sensitive patch of skin, gnawing gently on the delicate tendon of her shoulder. Her eyes closed as his fingers worked nimbly along her spine, undoing her. Layer after layer whispered to the floor. She shivered, clad in only her stockings and garters.

"Beautiful *selkie*, will you let me pleasure you?" he murmured.

"Yes," she sighed. "Just hurry."

His husky laugh rasped over her senses. "There's no need to rush. We have all night." His hands closed over hers and brought them over her head; he placed her palms against the wall. "Keep your hands there, sweeting."

In this position, her nerves seemed stretched to a new sensitivity. Sensation amplified: the air wafted in a sensual caress against her back, the wallpaper scraping gently against her taut nipples. A feeling of freedom washed over her. Strangely, she felt more powerful than she ever had. There was nothing to keep her here. No bonds, no threats, nothing to stop her from removing her hands and ending the interlude. Yet she was making the choice to yield to this man—to take what she herself wanted.

He kissed her shoulder blades one by one, his hands finding her breasts. He played with the buds, pinching and rolling them until she arched back against him, gasping his name.

"Enough with games. Kent, I need you *now*—"

"Keep your hands on the wall," he reminded her.

She pouted when his hands left her aching bosoms. But her pique dissolved into molten arousal when he wedged his thigh between her legs, widening her stance. A wicked beat took hold of her pulse, echoed by the insistent throb of her flesh as she rode the masculine ridge. She rubbed herself against him, a sinuous friction that only fed her fires. She needed more pressure, an angle that she couldn't quite get to on her own.

"Want more?" His gravelly voice scraped against her ear. His hands held her hips, supporting her as she wriggled against his leg in helpless pleasure. "Tell me, Marianne. I'll give you whatever you need."

"Touch me," she breathed.

He removed his leg, leaving her bereft. Then his lips touched the top of her spine, following the curve with tender persistence. Her lungs strained as he lowered to his knees behind her, his thumbs caressing the sensitive inside of her thighs, spreading her further. When he nipped her on the buttock, her breath stopped altogether.

"You're pretty here. White and tender as a cake."

He soothed the bite with kisses that turned her knees to water. Then his mouth was everywhere, tasting, sucking, driving her wild. Shamelessly, she thrust her bottom out, giving him access to anything he wanted. He licked her, plumbing her intimate folds, making her fingers curl against the wall. Then his tongue dragged upward, sliding along her crease to circle a place too wicked to name. The sizzling flicks around that sensitive rim startled a moan from her throat.

"Too much?" he said hoarsely.

"I can't take anymore," she gasped. "Please, enough playing. Just ... do it."

He was behind her immediately, his cloth-covered manhood a burning weight against the base of her spine. His hot words poured into her ear. "I will. But you'll have to ask for what you want. Tell me your desires, love, and I'll give them to you."

"Your cock. I want your cock inside me," she sighed.

She heard the faint rustle of material and then he was there, his blunt head nudging her swollen lips. "You're so wet for me," he murmured, rubbing against her in exquisite torment. "You make me hard, Marianne—make me want to bury myself in your lovely pussy. Where are the letters?"

Bliss spun her senses. "In the drawer ... by my bed."

"Wait here. Don't move."

Anticipation jangled her nerves as she stood there, shivering and exposed. Empty and aching, living for the instant when he would return to her. Her breath puffed against the wall as her imagination soared with each sound. The drawer opening and closing. Heavy footsteps. The soft crinkling as he sheathed his cock ...

Her eyes shut in ecstasy as he penetrated her. His pace was maddeningly slow. He made her feel every unyielding inch—his thick girth stretching her, filling her, making her crave more and more of him. At this angle, it seemed his manhood had no end, nudging ever closer to her deepest secrets. He kept his rhythm steady, giving her cadence after cadence of pleasure ... but he did not allow her crescendo to build to that critical peak. Moisture gathered on her brow as she strained against him, silently asking for more.

"Aye, love, I'll give you what you want. But you have to trust me," he muttered at her ear.

"I do. I do," she whispered, her palms slick against silk. "God, just make me come."

In the next instant, he left her. Before she could protest, he spun her to face him, lifted her against the wall. He brought her down hard onto his shaft, and she moaned at the devastating impact. She clutched his flexing shoulders as he took all her weight, her shoulders rising and falling against the wall with his steady thrusts. Her control began to unravel as the whirling tension built, gathering in the wanton peak that throbbed for his touch.

"Give me everything. Don't hold back any longer." His eyes burned into her, his guttural command and fierce rhythm brooking no refusal. "Trust me."

Her scalp rocked against the wall as the maelstrom raged higher. As the need for relief grew and grew until there was no holding back. No resisting his intent eyes, his plunging cock, the way he kept her teetering on the precipice of release. *So close.*

"Kent, *please.*" The plea scraped from her throat.

"Everything, Marianne," he said, and she knew what he wanted even as his hips twisted, making her groan. "Let go. Let me help you."

"I ... I ... *oh God.*" The words broke from her as he searched out her pearl. He plucked and stroked in concert with his pistoning shaft, giving her everything she wanted. Everything she needed. *A man I can trust.* The last of her defenses gave way.

"My daughter. I want my Rosie back," she sobbed.

The next instant, the storm shattered within her. She flew apart, rent asunder by pleasure, by relief too potent to bear. Kent pounded into her a final time, his muscles bunching, his guttural shout filling her with euphoria. With a sigh, she let herself float gently away on the tide, warm and safe in her lover's arms.

Chapter Twenty-Four

Ambrose cradled his lover close in the bed, stroking her hair as she slept. Her breathing had the deep, even quality of a babe's. His arms tightened protectively around her, his chest aching with the knowledge that the woman dozing in his arms had suffered entirely too much.

Marianne has a daughter.

She'd guarded her secret well. From this, he surmised that her little girl had not been the product of her union with the much older Lord Draven. Had Marianne had an extramarital affair? The knot in Ambrose's chest tightened as he recalled her anguished words.

I want my Rosie back.

What kind of blackguard would be so cruel as to separate mother and daughter?

Long silken locks slid against his arm, and Marianne's thick lashes fluttered as she came awake. Her gaze wandered about the room, the drowsy quality fleeing when it encountered him. Her lips parted; roses bloomed in her cheeks.

"How are you feeling?" he said tenderly.

He knew the moment everything returned to her. Her body tensed against his, panic darkening her eyes. She struggled to get up, to flee; he kept her in place by rolling atop her, taking care to leverage his weight on his arms.

"Don't go," he said quietly. "Not yet. Talk to me, sweetheart."

"I've already said too much." Her voice was thick, her breathing quick and fitful as she shoved at his shoulders. "Let me go."

"Not until you tell me about your daughter."

Her tresses spilled across the pillow as she shook her head vehemently. "You don't know what you're asking. Please, just get off me ..."

"You've been carrying this on your own for too long. You need to share your secrets with me." He saw his words hit their mark. She bit down on her trembling lower lip, her chin wobbling. "You know I'll help you, Marianne. Once you tell me everything."

Her chest rose and fell in labored surges. Her eyes slid away. "Let me up first," she said in a small voice. He did, and she sat up, her arms circling her raised knees. With her hair tumbling down her back, she looked young, so very vulnerable. "I—I don't know how to begin."

"Start from the beginning. Who is Rosie's father?" he said gently.

She kept her gaze focused on the coverlet. "A young lad I fancied myself in love with. I'd known him for years, and the summer I turned seventeen, we ... acted on our feelings. He and I had planned to marry. But he died." She sighed. "In a carriage accident. Leaving me heartbroken and in an unfortunate condition."

Ambrose's heart squeezed for the girl's pain. Yet he knew the woman well enough to keep any pity from his voice. "Did you have anyone to turn to?" he asked.

"There was no one. Mama died shortly after I was born, and Papa ..." She laughed, a scornful sound. "The squire had more interest in cards and horses than his daughter. Out of desperation, I told him about my pregnancy, and he threatened to disown me. To throw me out of the house unless ..."

Ambrose took one of her hands, linking her elegant fingers with his own callused digits. He willed her the strength to continue on.

"Papa had a friend. A rich and powerful man," she said.

"Baron Draven."

"Yes," she said hollowly. "He'd offered for me, you see. He'd been willing to overlook my lack of dowry and had promised to pay off Papa's debts in return for my hand. Papa told me to keep my mouth shut, to marry Draven by special license and present an heir eight months hence. Papa said Draven would never know—babes were born prematurely all the time. But I couldn't ... I couldn't marry any man under false pretenses."

"Of course you couldn't," Ambrose said, wondering what the hell kind of father would suggest such a deception. "You're a principled little thing."

"You think *I'm* principled?" Her eyes searched his.

"Not in a conventional sense. I won't deny that you're clever and capable of trickery when the occasion merits. But you have your own ethics, including a sense of honor and fierce loyalty to those you care about," he said firmly. "I cannot see you deceiving a man about a matter as vital as his offspring."

"Thank you." He was surprised to see the soft sheen in her eyes. "That is the nicest compliment I've ever received."

"Yes. Well." He cleared his throat. "What happened with Draven?"

The softness in her eyes disappeared. "He listened to my story. At the end, he told me nothing had changed for him. He meant to have me one way or another. He vowed to look after my child as his own; if that child turned out to be a male, Draven said he'd name him his heir. I was stunned, too relieved and grateful to even question his promises.

"We married by special license, and Draven took me to his estate in Yorkshire. Seven months later, I gave birth to a girl. I named her Primrose. She took after me, you see." With a sad smile, Marianne fingered a strand of her blond hair. "For that first year, Rosie was my world. Motherhood brought me joy, a sense of purpose that I had never known before. I would wake excited to see Rosie's sweet face and go to bed dreaming of the adventures we would have together the next day. And then ..." Her voice faltered.

"What happened?" Ambrose said softly.

Silence tautened before she replied, "During my pregnancy, Draven hadn't made husbandly demands of me. He'd explained that he wouldn't touch me while I carried another man's bastard, while I was ... dirty. Tainted." Her voice quivered with shame. "I didn't blame him, and, in truth, I was relieved. But after the birth, things changed. He pressed for his marital rights."

Rage simmered in Ambrose's veins. "He forced you?"

"No." Marianne shook her head. "He would not have needed to. After what he had done for me and Rosie, I fully intended to be a good wife in exchange. To do whatever he asked of me. As it turned out, however, he was the one who could not rise to the occasion." She gave a dry, brittle laugh. "He blamed me for his problem. Said I had unmanned him. And from that moment on, my life became a living hell."

Holding his anger in rigid check, Ambrose said, "What did he do to you, Marianne?"

"The name calling, the accusations about my character got worse. I had no defense against any of it." She shrugged, a casual movement that made Ambrose want to punch the wall. Only because the first option—beating Draven to a pulp—was no longer possible. "He was right. I *had* fornicated outside the marriage bed. I *had* given birth to a bastard. In truth, I *was* no better than a whore—"

"Stop it." His sharp tone cut her off, made her blink as if escaping a trance. "Stop repeating the bugger's words. You were seventeen, no more than a girl. You believed yourself in love. Yes, you acted impulsively, unwisely. But you're no whore, and I won't hear you call yourself that again. Is that understood?"

She said nothing, her gaze uncertain.

"Go on, then." Steeling himself, he asked, "Did the abuse go beyond words?"

"On occasion," she whispered.

Red flashed in Ambrose's vision. His muscles trembled in his effort to contain his fury.

Let her finish. The poison needs to bleed out.

"Physical cruelty was not Draven's preferred method, however. Whenever he whipped me, he took care not to break the skin. He wanted his possession to appear perfect on the outside." Her pained laugh pierced Ambrose's chest. "In truth, I preferred the beatings to ..."

"What did he do?" Ambrose said tersely.

She hugged her knees to her chest. "Because he blamed me for unmanning him, he said it was up to me to fix the problem. He made me ... do things. Humiliating things. Night after night, he made me wear tawdry garments and pose myself, as if I were the lowliest of trollops. With a crop in hand, he made me kneel before him and try to stimulate him by ..." Her voice broke.

Ambrose gathered her close. "It was no fault of yours, whatever he made you do. You know that, don't you?" he said roughly against her hair. "You were never to blame for his impotence. The bastard took pleasure in degrading you because he could not face his own failings as a man."

"It never worked, what he made me do," she said tremulously, "and that only enraged him further. He blamed me for dulling his desires, for being distracted and not applying myself to my wifely duties. So finally one day, as punishment, he ... he took Rosie away from me."

Tears tracked silently down Marianne's face. Ambrose could

do nothing but hold her more tightly, his own eyes stinging with helpless rage.

"He threatened to have Rosie harmed unless I did exactly as he said. For four years, he kept me a prisoner to his whims. I did everything he asked, and in return all I received was the occasional lock of Rosie's hair. A report that she was healthy and, oh God,"— her throat worked—"I never knew if he was lying. But I told myself I'd *know* if ... if ..." She scrubbed her eyes with her fists. "I'd know if anything happened to my little girl. A mother's heart would know," she said fiercely, "and I vowed that I would never give up on finding her. No matter where my search leads or compels me to do, I *will* get her back."

"That is what brought you to London," Ambrose said.

In his mind, the pieces fell into place. By Jove, Marianne's visits to the stews, her much gossiped about lascivious behavior—had all of that been smoke and mirrors? A cover she'd created to hide her search for her little girl? It made sense now. The juxtaposition between her jaded exterior and the desperate fragility he'd discovered beneath ...

"After Draven's death, I discovered that he'd placed Rosie with a bawd named Kitty Barnes. It has taken me three years to hunt the madam down, only to discover that she'd sold my daughter"— Marianne's voice cracked—"to a gentleman."

Ambrose's hands balled. As a policeman, he'd developed calluses against human evil; one had to in order to survive the job. Yet crimes against children always cut to the core. What good was justice if it failed to protect the innocent and the weak?

"Barnes claimed she'd never met the client herself," Marianne said, "because he'd conducted the transaction via the services of a solicitor."

The hairs rose on Ambrose's neck. "Leach."

She nodded, her lips tightening. "In his office that night, I found three bills of service. Though the receipts did not specify the nature of the transactions, Leach provided those services during the month Rosie was sold. One of those three clients must have my daughter."

"Ashcroft is one of your suspects?"

She shuddered. "He was. But I can take him off the list. Tonight I discovered the nature of his sins; repugnant though they are, they have naught to do with Rosie." She paused. "Which leaves me with two possible culprits: Marquess Boyer and—"

"The Earl of Pendleton," Ambrose said grimly.

She stared at him. "How ... how did you know?"

How had things gotten so complicated? Ambrose wished to hell he'd never taken Coyner up on the case; knowing Marianne's secret now, he felt sick with guilt for those handful of days he'd spent tracking her. Monitoring her, for devil's sake, when *she'd* been the victim—when she'd so desperately needed his help.

How would Marianne react to his betrayal?

Self-loathing scorched his insides as he realized the full extent of his dilemma. Upon his honor, he'd sworn confidentiality to Coyner. If he told Marianne about the assignment, he'd be breaking his oath to the magistrate, and Coyner would destroy Ambrose's career if he found out. If it were just him, Ambrose might somehow find a way to deal with those consequences, but what about his family? Where would they live? How would they eat ... survive?

"How did you know?" Marianne repeated sharply.

Ambrose exhaled, hating the position he'd put himself in. "I found one of Leach's clerks and questioned him. He mentioned that Leach had had a recent altercation with Pendleton."

Silence met his words—and he hadn't even got to the confession yet. The next minute, she left the bed, reaching for a robe. When she turned to look at him, her face was a mask of anger.

"What gave you the right to nose into my business?"

Despite his guilt, the accusation stung.

"You wouldn't tell me what was going on between you and the

solicitor, so I had to find out for myself. For God's sake, a man was murdered," he bit out. "You were in a precarious situation. I was only trying to help."

"I didn't ask for your help."

"Just like you didn't ask for my help with the cutthroats in the alley or Ashcroft tonight. Christ, Marianne, do you expect me to stand by and watch you risk your neck time and again?"

"I expect you not to do things behind my back. I expect to be able to trust you," she said, her voice frigid. "I expect you not to act like that bloody treacherous Runner!"

Ambrose's brow furrowed. "What Runner?"

"The one I hired to help me find Primrose. Burke Skinner claimed he did contract work for Bow Street, but I engaged him privately—I wanted as much discretion as possible." She gave a scornful laugh, but Ambrose could see the agitated cadence of her breath. "How could I have been such a fool?"

Ambrose went to her, took her chin in his hand. Though her eyes flashed at him, he saw beneath the anger to the fear. The glittering facets of helplessness.

"What did Skinner do, Marianne?" he said.

"He kept me dangling for months. Though I later learned he'd discovered clues to Primrose's disappearance early on, he doled out the information, made me pay through the nose for it. Then one day," she said bitterly, "he wanted more than money."

Skinner had saw fit to make sexual advances upon a desperate, grieving mother? Skinner was going to *pay*. Ambrose vowed to see to it.

"What happened?" he rasped.

"He wouldn't take no for an answer. So I shot him." Her chin lifted. "I didn't kill him, but scared him into revealing all that he had discovered. Those facts led me to Kitty Barnes."

A faint memory resonated. *You're not even the first man I've shot ...* Despite the dire situation, Ambrose's chest warmed with pride. Though she struggled, he wrapped his arms around his brave girl and held on. How had one woman survived so much?

"You did exactly the right thing, sweetheart," he murmured against her ear. "He deserved to be shot. I wish I could have done it myself."

He could hear her uneven breaths. After a few moments, she stopped trying to get away. Her voice emerged muffled against his chest.

"You won't let me down, will you, Ambrose?" She tipped her head to look at him, and the sheen in her eyes devastated him. Ratcheted up his guilt. "I swore I'd never depend on anyone again. But I think with you ... I could make an exception."

The muscles of his chest stretched as if he were upon the rack. Only his instrument of torture was made not of steel and wood, but of conscience and desire. As much as he wanted to confess the truth to her, he knew the result if he did: she'd shut him out for good. Hadn't she nearly done so because he'd investigated Leach's clerk without informing her first? Her trust was a fragile thing. After all she'd suffered at the hands of men, he couldn't blame her.

But he also couldn't allow her to continue this perilous quest on her own. She *needed* his help, his protection—she was facing a powerful enemy. Conflict tore at him.

"Will you help me get my daughter back, Ambrose?" Her gaze searched his face.

And his decision was made.

"I vow to you, I won't rest until Primrose is safe in your arms once more," he said.

He'd do whatever it took to help her—his guilt and honor be damned.

She smiled through her tears, looking so angelic that his breath dammed in his throat. She tugged his head down for a kiss, and the hot, open sweetness of her mouth made his blood pound, drowning out his thoughts. She fitted her body to his, her eyes heavy-lidded with want, and her surrender made him hunger to give her everything he could. His kiss, his cock ... mayhap even a piece of his soul.

As he tumbled her back onto the bed, he made a silent vow.

I'll find a way to make this work. I'll prove worthy of her trust. I won't let her down.

Chapter Twenty-Five

The smoke rising from the stacks cast a purplish haze over the night sky. As Ambrose strode along Cheapside, his way lit by the candlelight spilling from windows, he drank in the familiar sights and sounds of his neighborhood. The smells of hops and roasting meat filled the air. The bells of St. Mary-Le-Bow church clanged with timeless insistence, signaling the nine o'clock curfew which saw the release of the apprentices from the toils of the day. Young men garbed in ubiquitous brown thronged toward the taverns, more than ready to make use of the night's freedom.

Despite the day's labors—which had included the search of several vessels and the eventual apprehension of a trio of smugglers—Ambrose moved with energy. He turned off Throgmorton Street toward his apartment, his steps quick and impatient. Before bed tonight, he planned to review the profiles he'd put together on Pendleton and Boyer. He and Marianne would be meeting tomorrow to discuss the progress of the investigation. Whilst she was finding out all she could about the peers through discreet queries in the *ton*'s drawing rooms, Ambrose was doing the same in less rarefied realms.

As the first order of business, he'd tapped a man named Willy Trout to look into the suspects' financials. He'd met Trout a while back when he and his crew had put a stop to an extortion racket that had targeted boatmen on the Thames, including Trout's brother. Since then, Trout had proved a staunch ally. A discreet and free-thinking individual, the man could get information on most anything—for the right price.

For once, Ambrose was not limited by the Thames River Police's budgetary constraints; Marianne had made it clear that he had *carte blanche* when it came to conducting the search for Rosie. Ambrose had drawn the line, however, at her offer to pay *him*.

He'd compromised many things, but he'd be damned if he took money from the woman he was sleeping with. The woman for whom he had feelings. Feelings that bewildered him, shook the very tenets of his beliefs about himself and the world. And that made him feel more alive than he'd ever felt before. He blew out a breath. Told himself it was just a combination of powerful physical attraction and a primal need to protect her, to give her the justice she deserved.

On his own coin—he'd managed to add to his meager supply by securing a few extra hours at Wapping and had sent most of the money to his family—he'd also asked Trout to be on the lookout for Burke Skinner, the Runner who had betrayed Marianne. Despite Marianne's expedient handling of the bastard, Ambrose didn't trust that she'd heard the last from Skinner. He wanted to make certain that the blighter would never step foot near her again.

Tomorrow night, Ambrose thought that he and Marianne might make love again. Mayhap even fall asleep in each other's arms. Such was his optimism that he'd made a discreet stop at a Covent Garden shop to purchase more means of contraception; 'twas as much his responsibility as hers, after all. As he turned the corner toward his tenement, his loins tightened in anticipation—at the same time that his conscience picked up its berating refrain.

You can't go on deceiving her. A lie is a lie, even if it only lasted

five days. You have to find a way to tell her about your stint with Bow
Street.

But how? Once he'd made the decision to omit the truth, it became more and more difficult to bring it into the open. He knew she'd never trust him again, and the thought of her continuing her mission on her own ... He quelled his scruples with iron resolve. He had to stay close, to watch over her and help her reunite with her girl. Until he could figure out a better solution, Marianne's welfare took precedence over his honor.

Reaching the landing, he froze. A figure sat huddled in front of his apartment. Her head rested against the doorframe, disheveled raven locks obscuring her visage, but he would know her anywhere.

"Emma?" he said incredulously.

She came awake with a start, pushing the hair from her face. His gut lurched at the sight of her swollen, reddened eyes, the dirt smudging her delicate cheekbones. She swayed to her feet.

"Ambrose?" she whispered.

Concern flooded him as he opened his arms. "What has happened, Em? Why are you here?"

His sister hurtled toward him, a sob breaking from her lips.

Marianne peered out the carriage door at the tenements. Despite the late hour, raggedy bits hung neglected on the clothing lines that crisscrossed the dreary buildings. A few scruffy ruffians loitered at the entryways, swigging from bottles and clearly headed for oblivion. The din of squalling babes and arguing adults was nearly as loud as the clanging church bells had been. Life in Cheapside was not quiet.

"You are sure this is the correct address?" she said.

Standing by the carriage door, Lugo pointed to a door on the second floor. "Mr. Kent lives at number eight. Do you want me to fetch him, my lady?"

"No, thank you," she said. "I'll go myself."

She felt Lugo's watchful gaze as she made her way toward Ambrose's apartment. The drunks she passed were too far gone to do more than leer. The odor of cooking onions turned her stomach as she ascended the creaking steps. Her pulse quickened, not from the physical exertion, but from the uncertainty that had plagued her ever since she'd shared her secret with Ambrose.

Stop worrying and being so dashed suspicious. You can trust him.

Old habits died hard. She knew she'd overreacted when Ambrose had told her about questioning Leach's clerk. It had been a knee-jerk response: suspicion and paranoia left over from her past. All that *was* in the past, she told herself. Ambrose had done nothing to rouse her anxiety. He'd protected her, believed her. And he'd vowed to help her get Rosie back.

Ambrose was like no man she'd ever met. He made her feel *herself* in ways that sparked opposing *frissons* of delight and alarm. For so long, she had mastered her emotions; she hadn't recognized the price of that self-control until he had come along and showed her the thrill of letting go. Of just being. With his persistence and tenderness, he was teaching her to trust bit by bit.

She could see herself changing in ways that both excited and frightened her. The impulsive nature she'd kept buried had come charging to the fore, brought her here to Ambrose's residence because she didn't want to wait until tomorrow night to see him. She wanted to see him *now*. She approached his door, her heart thudding with the giddiness of a debutante waiting for her first dance.

Has he missed me these past two days? Has he longed to make love again as I have?

She raised her gloved fist, rapped on the door.

No response came. She fought the disappointment. Perhaps he had not yet returned from work. Or perhaps he'd gone out with

...iends, to unwind as men were wont to do over drink ... and wenches? She frowned—no, Ambrose wasn't the whoring type. Mayhap he was simply inside asleep in his own bed ... The notion of Ambrose's bed made her heart pump faster. Not expecting success, she reached for the door handle. It turned in her grasp.

Anticipation quickening her breath, she went in. Her gaze skimmed over the dingy space with its sparse furnishings—and honed in on Ambrose. He was not alone. He occupied a chair next to a young woman, their dark heads bent together. Needles prickled in Marianne's chest as he cupped his guest's cheek, the gesture imbued with infinite tenderness. The two were so engrossed in their intimate conversation that neither looked up at her approach.

Marianne heard herself say in a strangely calm voice, "I *am* sorry to interrupt."

Ambrose jumped to his feet. He blinked, as if trying to register Marianne's presence, the bloody bastard. Marianne got a good look at the other woman for the first time, and a hot, foreign feeling swelled beneath her breastbone. With inky hair and large, doe-brown eyes, the female was younger than she'd first thought— young and quite pretty, with a smooth countenance that exuded freshness and innocence, qualities Marianne herself had lost years ago.

"Who are you?" the cheeky miss said.

"Emma, let me explain ..." Kent began.

"Emma, is it?" The acid in Marianne's tone cut Kent off. The line she'd once found charming deepened between his brows. Her heart twisted painfully, but pride came to her rescue. "I am Lady Draven. Kent's lover," she said with absolute hauteur. "Who are you?"

The blasted creature's eyes got even bigger. Her cheeks turned crimson, and Marianne had the cold satisfaction of knowing that she had not been the only one duped. Her gaze shot accusingly to Kent.

He was watching her, the corner of his mouth twitching oddly. He cleared his throat.

"Lady Draven, may I present to you my sister, Miss Emma Kent?" he said.

Despite the grim situation that had necessitated Emma's visit, Ambrose experienced an odd, buoyant feeling in his chest. He chalked it up to the fact that it wasn't every day that gorgeous widows showed up at his rooms and gave a spectacular display of feminine jealousy. Jealousy—*over him*. 'Twas novel and rather delightful. As if tuning into his thoughts, Marianne's eyes flashed at him, brighter than the fireworks at Vauxhall.

Emma brought over what passed for a tea tray and took the chair adjacent to Marianne. Sitting on a wooden crate that served as a third chair, Kent faced the both of them.

"Thank you, Miss Kent," Marianne said.

The jet beads on her crimson frock glimmered as she accepted the chipped cup. An expensive-looking gold pendant rested above the swell of her breasts. Despite the contrast between her finery and the humble setting, she appeared unruffled.

"Please call me Emma, my lady. Most everyone does and since you are ..."—his sister reddened, bit her lip—"er ... friends with Ambrose, you must too."

A delicate shade of peach tinged the crest of Marianne's cheeks at Emma's tactful words. Though Ambrose would have to clarify the situation with his sister later on—and he did not relish the prospect, given his younger sister's youth and innocence—it heartened him to know that his shameless *selkie* could enjoy a moment or two of human embarrassment.

"Then you must return the favor and call me Marianne." His *selkie*, however, was never one to be discomfited for long. "So tell me, Emma, what brings you to London? Your brother did not

...ention he was expecting a family visit." Marianne cast him a narrow-eyed look.

Emma sighed, and before Kent could stop her, she launched into the tale she'd tearfully told him earlier. The situation she described did not improve with the second telling. His neck corded as he wondered what the hell he was going to do. Thanks to his father's absent-mindedness—he prayed to God it was only that and not a more insidious problem—the family was to be thrown out of their home. On the morrow, the Kents would have nowhere to go.

His temples began to throb as he contemplated the options. Unless he could find another roof for them in the village—which he doubted, as news traveled quicker than wildfire in Chudleigh Crest—he would have to bring them to London. Perhaps he could get away with having his family here for a few days without his landlady finding out ...

"Father didn't mean to set the fire," Emma was telling Marianne earnestly. "It was only that he fell asleep reading. It was dratted bad luck that Tabitha knocked over the candle."

"Tabitha?" Marianne said.

"Our cat. She's a tabby," Emma explained. "Most of the time, she is very well-behaved, but of late she's been quite desperate for attention." She slumped, as if the weight of the world were perched on her slim shoulders. "Between father and my brother and sisters, I just haven't had the time to devote to her."

Ambrose's hands balled. Poor Em—*he* should have been there, helping her. She was too young to have such a burden. Before he could speak, however, Marianne surprised him by putting an arm around his sister. Emma stiffened—and then she let out a quivery sigh. Slowly, her head came to rest on Marianne's shoulder. With a pang, Ambrose was reminded of his stepmother Marjorie's comforting hugs.

"'Tis impossible to be everywhere at once," Marianne said. "You are far too young to shoulder such responsibilities."

"I am sixteen," Emma said in a muffled voice. "Old enough to know that I oughtn't have left Father alone for so long. But Thea wasn't feeling well, and Violet and Polly needed help sewing up new petticoats—they've both sprouted like weeds since spring— and Harry nearly set the woodshed afire with his latest experiment ..."

"Goodness, how many Kents *are* there?" Marianne said.

Emma lifted her head, her curious gaze shifting to him. "Hasn't Ambrose told you about us?"

"His description was lacking sufficient detail. Besides," Marianne said, slanting a glance at him, "I do believe your brother is used to keeping things to himself."

"Oh. Well, there's six of us in all, including Ambrose," Emma supplied with the helpfulness that was her nature. "He's the eldest by sixteen years."

"That is quite the gap."

"That is because his mother was father's first wife. After she died, father did not remarry for many years until he met our mother, Marjorie. They had me first, then Dorothea, Harry, Violet, and Polly—she's eight and the babe of the lot."

"And you're in charge of them all? My poor dear," Marianne murmured.

"I had things well in hand until this latest incident. Now there's the damage to the cottage to pay for, *and* the landlord will toss us out by the morrow. I didn't know what to do." To hear his practical, industrious sister confess her helplessness wrenched Ambrose's gut. "So that is why I had to leave Harry in charge and come today. Because Ambrose will have a solution. He always does."

Think of something, you sot.

"We'll go fetch everyone and bring them here," he said. "Do not worry about it further, Em. Everything will be fine."

His sister gave him a smile of relief. "See? Ambrose can make any problem go away."

"Indeed." Marianne gave him an enigmatic look. "A magician are you, Kent?"

"I never said I was," he said curtly.

"It *will* require magic if you plan to fit your entire family in here." Marianne cast a pointed look around his apartment; it shamed him that he could not disagree with her. "There's barely room for one."

"We don't require much. The girls and I are perfectly content sharing a pallet," Em said. But he caught the way his sister's eyes flitted about the room.

"It will only be temporary," he said firmly, "until I figure out a better plan."

"Why wait? I have one already." Opening the small, pearl-encrusted bag on her lap, Marianne pulled out a card and handed it to Em.

"What is this?" His sister's brow furrowed.

"The address to my townhouse. I have so much room I won't even notice you're there," Marianne said airily.

Emma's eyes grew bigger. "Oh, but we couldn't ..."

"Of course we can't." Recovering from his shock, Ambrose drew himself up. "Though it is an undoubtedly generous offer, we Kents cannot impose upon you in such a way."

Marianne rose, her deep red skirts swirling regally around her. "Don't think of it as an imposition, then. Consider it an exchange."

"An exchange? For what?" he said, frowning.

"You've refused payment for the matter you are investigating for me. The least I can do is play hostess to your family. Do come along, Emma dear." Marianne headed to the door, clearly expecting to be followed. "You will help me make the necessary arrangements at home. Kent can fetch your family and deliver them to us."

Emma's gaze swung to him. "Ambrose ...?"

He studied Marianne's haughty expression. Not so long ago he would have been fooled by that façade of indifference. Now he knew her better, and a feeling broke inside him, so strong and foreign that he could only say thickly, "Go on, then. But mind you be a good girl and don't pester her ladyship."

Eyes shining with a dazed relief that mirrored his own, his sister stood on tiptoe to kiss his cheek. As she did so, his gaze went to Marianne. Her mask had slipped a fraction, a faint curve edging her perfect lips. Reckless words began thumping in his heart, and he retained just enough sense to hold them back.

Instead, over his sister's head, he mouthed, *Thank you.*

Marianne smiled, and her brilliance warmed him to his very marrow. To depths he hadn't known existed within him. Then she inclined her head and led his sister out.

Chapter Twenty-Six

"**Y**ou've *what*?" Helena stared at her as if she'd grown two heads.

Sitting across from her friend in the drawing room, Marianne lifted her brows. "As you're the one who's been promoting Kent, one would think you'd be more approving." She returned her gaze to the menu, scanning it before handing it back to the waiting housekeeper. "That looks fine, Mrs. Winston. From what Miss Kent tells me, there's not a picky palate amongst the bunch. Just keep things simple—and tell Monsieur Arnauld to dispense with his more adventurous dishes."

"Be an improvement, if you ask me. Nothing wrong with good, decent English cooking," Mrs. Winston muttered as she departed.

"*Miss* Kent?" Helena said, her hazel eyes wide.

"That would be Emma, Kent's younger sister. I finally convinced the thing to have a lie-down upstairs. She's got more energy than all the maids combined. Do you know she hasn't had a nap since she was in leading strings?" Marianne shuddered. "We'll have to set *that* to rights. Now I don't wish to be rude, Helena, but

I do wish you had sent word ahead of your visit. I'm expecting the rest of the Kents at any moment."

"I'm sorry to inconvenience you," the marchioness replied tartly, "but *why* are the Kents moving into your house?"

"It's a long story, dearest. Much too long for the time we have."

Which was only part of the truth. Marianne wasn't ready to discuss the other part with her friend. She had no wish to sound like a green girl, and she surely would if she blathered on about how noble she found Ambrose. How utterly attractive she found his devotion toward his family. Like germinating seeds, her emotions quivered with the desire to break the surface, yet they were too tender to expose to the rays of scrutiny. And what of her other secret? The one that kept pushing closer and closer to the light.

By the by, Helena, you also have a niece. A beautiful little girl ... who was sold to a bawd because of me. Because of my mistakes—my selfish, wicked desires.

Marianne's throat thickened. She had no right to think of her own happiness when Primrose's future remained so uncertain. She'd already failed her daughter once; she could not do so again. Finding Rosie took precedence over everything—including her feelings for Ambrose. Though she could no longer deny her physical attraction to him, she could not afford to lose her head or her focus.

The door bell rang, and she was glad for the interruption.

"Ah, here the Kents are now." She rose. "Come along if you'd like to meet them."

With Helena at her heels, Marianne arrived to see Lugo ushering her houseguests inside. The four children entered in haphazard progression, all of them dressed in ill-fitting garments cut from the same revolting grey material. It appeared that Kents came in all shapes and sizes. Hair color ranged from light brown to nearly black, and their gazes likewise spanned a range of hues. The main characteristic that linked the motley bunch was the aura of alertness and energy that crackled in their wake. None of them had spotted her yet: they were too busy talking, excitedly and at once.

"It's crying tears." The littlest girl, who Marianne saw with a pang might be Rosie's age, removed her thumb from her mouth and pointed at the chandelier. "Poor light—it's sad even though it's pretty."

"It's called a chandelier. And those aren't tears, Polly," the lanky brown-haired boy said, "they're crystals made of glass. They're cut with facets to reflect light. In point of fact, a simple equation describes how the angle of the facet determines the overall brilliance—"

"Oh, spare us the lecture, Professor." Accompanied by the rolling of caramel-colored eyes, this statement was delivered by a tomboyish girl who almost rivaled the boy in height. "We've heard it all before."

The boy glanced at her down the length of his nose. "If that were the case, Vi, why couldn't you solve that simple maths problem I posed on the way over?"

"There is more to life than maths problems, drat you," Vi said, her hands planting on her slim hips. "Let's see which of us can climb Mr. McGregor's tree the fastest—"

"Stop it, you two." A petite sister with oak-colored hair came between them. "We're guests, remember? We're supposed to be on our best ..." she broke off, coughing.

The bickering stopped. "Are you alright, Thea?" the battling pair said as one.

"Fine," their sister said between wheezing breaths. "'Twas the dust ... of the journey ..."

"You're here! I've been waiting for you all day." A beaming Emma flew down the stairs, her dark hair streaming behind her. "Vi, do help Thea with her cloak. Harry, help Polly with hers. And Polly you know better than to have your thumb in your mouth. Now where are Father and Ambrose?"

Marianne watched with amusement—and not a little amazement—as the siblings fell in line. To a certain extent, that was.

"Father doesn't want to get out of the hackney. You know how he gets about anything new. Ambrose is trying to coax him." Harry's forehead creased as he worked on the strings of his little sister's garment. "Christ's blood, Polly, a sailor couldn't tie knots like you."

"You oughtn't use the Lord's name in vain," Violet said.

"Bloody hell, then."

"Harry," Thea said with mild reproof.

Emma sighed. "Perhaps I should go help Ambrose."

"I'll do it," Marianne said.

Five pairs of eyes turned to her. If she hadn't already been used to Ambrose's intense regard, the impact of those bright, inquisitive gazes would have been rather unsettling.

"Oh, Lady Draven! I didn't see you there. Good afternoon," Emma said, dropping a curtsy. "If I may present my sisters Dorothea, Violet, and Polly, and my brother Harry?"

Emma shot a look at her siblings, who took the hint. The girls bent their knees, and Harry presented a surprisingly proper leg.

"Welcome, all of you," Marianne said. "This is my friend, the Marchioness of Harteford."

"How lovely to meet you, children," Helena said, smiling. "Is this your first visit to London?"

They all nodded. Polly's thumb crept back toward her mouth.

"I am sure you will enjoy yourselves thoroughly. Perhaps you'd care to freshen up and have some refreshment?" Ever the mother hen, Helena raised her brows at Marianne.

"I'm positively starved. There hasn't been much food late —*oof.*" Violet grunted, rubbing her side where Emma had discreetly elbowed her. "What did you do that for?"

"Mind your manners. We have already inconvenienced Baroness Draven enough as it is," Emma said between her teeth.

"I assure you, 'tis no inconvenience. And let us dispense with the formalities—it will be entirely tiresome to keep all the Miss Kents and Mr. Kents straight. In return, call me Marianne." She turned to her waiting manservant. "Lugo, please see to it that our guests have what they need. In the meantime, I shall see what I can do about the two outside."

She headed to the door. As she passed by the line of children, she felt a tug on her skirts. Polly was gazing shyly up at her.

Marianne's heart melted a little. "Yes, poppet?"

In an otherwise plain face, the little girl's aquamarine eyes glowed with startling acuity. "You're even prettier than the *shandy-leer*," she said.

"Why, thank you, dear."

Polly tipped her head to the side. "But why are you just as sad?"

Marianne's smile faded.

"I'm ever so sorry, Lady—I mean, Marianne." Emma's hands clamped onto her sister's shoulders. "I should have warned you about Polly. She can say the most outrageous things, but she doesn't mean anything by them." She turned to her youngest sibling, whose bottom lip had begun to quiver. "Now you apologize to her ladyship straightaway."

"No need for that." Crouching, Marianne met the little girl's gaze straight on. With a gentle hand, she removed the thumb that had found its way back into Polly's mouth. "You are right, dear. I *am* sad. But I do believe that will change, now that you are all here."

Polly's slow grin lit up her small face, and Marianne's breath stuttered. Heavens, did all the Kents have such heart-stopping smiles?

"I think so too," the little girl confided. "Actually, I *knew* it the moment I saw your—"

"Let's not hold her ladyship up," Emma interrupted in an oddly nervous manner. "She has to help Ambrose pry Father out of the carriage."

Harry strode over, taking Polly's hand. "Come on, sis. I'll bet they have some milk for you ... er, don't you, Mr. Lugo?"

Lugo inclined his head gravely. "I think we can find some, sir."

"I'll help with the children," Helena chimed in. "You go on ahead, Marianne."

Bemused, Marianne went outside to see what surprises awaited her next.

"Time is money, guv, and mine don't come cheap." The hackney driver's boot tapped against the perch. "Either get the old man out or I will."

"Just give us a minute." Ambrose fought his mounting frustration. Bending his head back through the carriage door, he said, "Father, you cannot stay in there. All the children are inside. You want to join them, don't you?"

His father scowled at him from the depths of the carriage, yet Ambrose could see fear in the faded eyes. Until recent years, Samuel Kent had been fearless in mind and spirit—to see him now, confused and clinging to the carriage strap like a drowning man to a piece of driftwood ...

"Didn't want to leave Chudleigh Crest. Why did you make me?" Samuel shouted.

For devil's sake. His patience fraying, Ambrose tried again to explain. "We had no choice, Father. After you nearly burned the cottage down, no one in the village would take you all in. Now come on, we haven't time to waste—"

"Perhaps I can be of assistance?"

Ambrose twisted his neck to see Marianne standing behind him. At the mere sight of her, something eased in his chest. With her platinum hair cascading from a loose topknot and a coral column skimming her elegant figure, she looked too damned lovely to be real. But it was more than her beauty that bolstered him: it was her unflappable expression. As if she didn't find this latest calamity with his family the least bit unusual or distasteful. As if she wouldn't turn away from him because of it—the way Jane had.

Yearnings crept over him. Irrational desires that he was having more and more difficulty keeping at bay. Christ, he wanted Marianne—and not just for a tumble or two. He wanted her by his side and in his bed, wanted hers to be the face that took him into his dreams at night, the first he saw when he awoke ...

But what the bloody hell do you have to offer her? You're a policeman who cannot support his own family. And you can't even give her the truth, for God's sake.

His hand clenched on the carriage door.

"Are we gettin' on with things or not?" the driver grumbled.

Marianne tossed the cantankerous fellow a coin, the glinting arc landing precisely in the driver's black glove. "That should cover your time—and your mouth, I should hope."

The man scowled, then turned his gaze forward and fell silent.

"One thing taken care of," Marianne said. "Now, Kent, if you'll hand me up?"

After a brief hesitation, Ambrose did as she asked. She took a seat next to his father.

"Good afternoon, Mr. Kent." The timbre of her voice was gentle, lulling, with none of her usual acerbity. By Jove, what man could resist that siren's call?

Not his father, apparently. Samuel peered at her with interest. "Who are you?"

"Marianne Sedgwick," she said, omitting her title. "I have the pleasure of hosting you and your family in London."

Samuel's expression darkened. "Don't want to be in London. Never wanted to leave the village and damn my boy for making us leave our home!"

Ambrose gripped the doorframe in frustration. He understood his father's anxiety, but when Samuel got into this state of mind, there was no bloody reasoning with him ...

"Your son only wants what is best," Marianne said in the same, soothing tone, "and that means coming into the house. The children are already inside. Emma has arranged a room for you. One that overlooks the garden—I'm told you like roses."

"Roses were Marjorie's favorite. Did you know her?"

The leap in logic squeezed Ambrose's chest. Before he'd gotten ill, Samuel Kent's mind and power of reasoning had been unparalleled.

"I'm afraid not. But I do have roses, and their scent is quite lovely. Do you want to come and see for yourself?"

His father's grip on the carriage strap loosened slightly, but his eyes widened. "I don't want to leave. It's safe in here."

Marianne wrinkled her nose. "It is as smelly and dingy as a cave in here. Wouldn't you rather have tea in the garden? I'll arrange for that: cakes and sandwiches next to the roses."

"Do you have plum pudding?" Samuel asked with the painful eagerness of a child. "I like plum pudding."

"If you like it, we shall have it. Come along, sir." Marianne held out a hand.

To Ambrose's relief, his father grasped her slim fingers. He helped Marianne and his sire alight, and he noticed that Samuel did not release her hand even when the old man stood upon the pavement. The hackney shot off, and Samuel squinted at Marianne.

"You're a looker, aren't you? Remind me a bit of my own Marjorie."

Ambrose choked back a laugh. He'd loved his stepmother to no end. But Marjorie, bless her heart, had been a short, robust lady with comfortable features.

Marianne dimpled. "A fine compliment indeed. Thank you, sir. Now shall we?"

Her gaze traveled from his father to him, and at that moment he knew his emotions hung upon his sleeve. For once, he was powerless to hide them. Whatever she saw in his face caused her to blush, duck her head in a distinctly un-Marianne-like fashion. And hope blossomed where it oughtn't, the petals catching in the thorns of his dilemma.

"Well, are we going to have pudding or not?"

Samuel's impatient demand broke the spell. Clearing his throat, Ambrose took his father's other arm. Together, the three of them climbed up the steps into the townhouse.

Chapter Twenty-Seven

C lad in a smoking jacket of maroon velvet, the gentleman made his way to his study. He'd decided to spend the evening in; he had much to contemplate, and he wanted no distractions. Locking the door to his private sanctuary behind him, he went to his desk. He clicked the hidden mechanism beneath the ledge; an instant later, there was a soft whir, and the panel of the adjacent wall slid open.

He stepped into his inner sanctum. No one but he knew of the existence of this chamber. As he gazed upon the gilt-framed portraits on the walls, some of the tension drained from him. He brushed a finger against one of the canvases, and he could almost feel a downy cheek instead of oil and cloth.

"Do you miss me, my sweet flower?" he murmured. "Never fear. We shall be together soon."

He walked from painting to painting, perusing each with proprietary delight. There were four in all: one to mark each of Primrose's birthdays since she'd entered his life. His child bride— almost ripe enough to claim. Almost, but not quite.

That hunted feeling returned, quivering in his midsection. His mama had always berated him for his delicate stomach. Then again, she'd been an overbearing termagant who made everyone around her miserable, including his father. The gentleman didn't blame the man for escaping to an early grave; death was preferable to being shackled to a shrew.

Well, the gentleman had learned his lesson. Unlike his sire, he was in a position to make a marital choice to improve his happiness rather than to replenish the family coffers. He'd invested his dead mother's fortune so that he wouldn't have to wed for any reason other than desire. Even if those desires came from traditions too noble for modern society.

He'd first come across the depictions of medieval child brides in the library books at Eton. His stomach churned anew at the memory of that godforsaken hellhole. The bullies. Their taunts and fists. Perspiration sprouted on his brow as the room closed around him, turned into the suffocating cellar of a village tavern. Fumes of stale ale and sex choked him. The boys' voices clamored in his head.

Prove you're a man. Stick your cock in her. Fuck her.

The old whore with her wrinkled breasts and rotted breath shouting back, *Wastin' your time an' mine, lads. This one's small eno' to toss back. 'E's limp as a baby eel!*

Face burning, the gentleman shut out the laughter, the jeering. Rage poured over him. He *was* a man—he'd show them all. While his old schoolmates were now dragged around Town by their prune-faced wives, *he* would have the most beautiful bride of all by his side.

His pulse calmed as he stared at the latest portrait of his love: at eight, Primrose had exceeded his expectations of her beauty. The purity of her corn-silk hair made a breathtaking pairing with eyes of translucent jade flecked with gold. His angel. His sweet-voiced, soft-skinned doll. She'd never gainsay him. Belittle him.

Sighing, he pressed his lips against her tiny pink slippers. Thank God he'd found her, a fresh blossom amongst the rubble of the stews. It had been Fate that led him to Kitty Barnes. The bawd had had a four-year-old orphan in her care: the by-product of an affair between an opera singer and a noble lover, she'd claimed. One glimpse of Primrose, her beauty and class, and the gentleman had known he had to rescue her.

He'd hired Leach to handle the transaction anonymously on his behalf. The thought of the blasted solicitor made his stomach pitch. With a shaking hand, he poured a drink and sat in the wingchair to nurse it. He assured himself that he'd carried out this last business with Leach perfectly: he'd tied a loose end ... and tossed in a few diversions as well. Enough to keep that Draven bitch busy whilst he figured out a way to rid himself of her once and for all.

The dirty slut thought to take what was his? His hand clenched the snifter as fury spiked.

I saved Primrose. Me. No one's taking her away.

Given the physical similarities between his sweet Primrose and the baroness, he couldn't deny the obvious conclusion. Kitty Barnes had lied about Primrose's origins; the Draven whore was the mother, and all that she'd done since arriving in Town—snooping around, hiring a Runner—had proved that she meant to have Primrose back.

Over my dead body. I've been cultivating my flower all these years. She's MINE.

The gentleman forced himself to take several calming breaths. Yes, Lady Marianne Draven was proving more of a nuisance than he'd first believed, but his secret was still safe. He had Primrose securely tucked away. He must not panic; he must stay on course and stick to the original plan.

In another three or four years, Primrose would ripen. At that time, when she was at the peak of her perfection, he'd pluck her once and for all. His loins stirred with anticipation. *See? I am a man! A man with rarefied taste.* Smiling dreamily, he imagined taking her abroad, marrying her some place free of nonsensical age of consent laws. After a few years, they'd return to Britannia with none the wiser.

Only one obstacle stood in his way: Lady Marianne Draven. The bitch had more lives than a feline. Somehow, she'd not only survived his efforts to have her killed but also his cleverly designed plan to have her framed for Leach's murder. His *coup d'état* would have killed two proverbial birds with the same stone. Yet she'd somehow escaped. *Goddamn her.*

For the inconvenience, she would have to suffer—she and that dull-witted policeman she'd managed to mesmerize. Anger hummed in the gentleman's ears. He'd taken a great risk in tapping Leach to engage the services of Bow Street, and all of it had come to naught because that *nobody*, that bloody River Charley, had failed to do his duty.

Agitated, the gentleman jumped to his feet. Paced before the portraits. Looking into Primrose's big green eyes, he saw her loving wisdom glimmering there.

"Only you understand me," he murmured. "Tell me, precious, how shall we get rid of them?"

The solution burst into his brain. *Divide et impera*—Caesar had the right of it. He chuckled with the sheer simplicity of the first step. A *fait accompli.* Nothing like betrayal to cause a schism. As for the second step ... For the sake of Primrose—and this *was* for her, to protect her and the love he would give her—he would show no mercy. Draven and Kent would have to die and in a clean manner, one untraceable to him.

Something in the order of ... an accident.

Yes, a tragic and public mishap would suit his purposes well.

The gentleman poured himself another brandy as the plan unfolded in his head.

Chapter Twenty-Eight

Kent made his way toward Marianne's suite, grateful for the thick carpeting that muffled the sound of his foot-steps. As he passed each closed door along the hallway, he feared that it would open to reveal one of his siblings. God knew what he would say if they asked him what he was doing skulking there in the middle of the night. Tactful by nature, Emma had not disclosed his relationship with their hostess, going along with his more circumspect assertion that he was being employed by Lady Draven and she had decided to act as a patron of sorts to his family.

He'd finessed the situation to protect Marianne's reputation; when she'd gotten wind of it over supper, she'd raised her brows and continued coaxing his father into eating the potato soup with a fancy French name. Nowadays, any change in routine roused his father's truculence, yet Marianne's unexpectedly patient and soothing manner had seemed to awaken Samuel's charm. Ambrose hadn't seen his sire so lively since before his stepmother's death.

Ambrose arrived at Marianne's door, which had been left ajar. Exhaling, he stepped inside and closed the door behind. His blood went hot at the sight of Marianne lounging on her bed. She looked up at him, and her welcoming smile made his cock jerk to attention.

"What took you so long?" She put down her book, her blush-colored robe fluttering languidly as she stretched her arms. "I almost fell asleep reading."

He had planned to first update her on the progress of his investigation. To demonstrate to her that he was committed to finding her daughter—and that her generosity to his family would be repaid in kind. Yet the invitation in her eyes dissolved his words. He found himself striding to the side of the bed. He sank his fingers in her hair and claimed her lips in a hard, demanding kiss. When it ended, both of them were breathing raggedly.

"I wanted to do that all night," he said, cupping her jaw. "All through supper, I thought of naught else."

She gave him a sultry look. "So that was why you looked so famished? And here I was thinking it was Monsieur Arnauld's excellent menu."

"The food was delicious." With each course that had appeared, his siblings' eyes had gotten bigger and bigger, and they'd piled more on their plates than politeness allowed. Knowing how little they'd had of late, he hadn't had the heart to chide them. "It was a treat for my family," he said gruffly. "Thank you."

"It was little enough."

"It was not little to them. Your generosity ..." He trailed off as the knots in his chest tightened. "A policeman's wages affords a simple life. My sisters and brother have known little in the way of luxury."

"They are delightful and unspoiled." With dexterous fingers, Marianne removed his cravat. "I shall enjoy rectifying the latter situation."

His throat grew dry as she moved onto his waistcoat. "Why are you doing all this?"

Rising on her knees, she kissed his jaw, murmuring, "I should think my intentions rather obvious."

"I don't mean this. I mean"—his voice went raspy as she investigated his ear with soft nibbles and licks—"why are you being so kind to my family?"

She drew back, smiled at him. "I like them."

"You do, truly?" he said.

"Why do you sound surprised?"

Because my ex-fiancée called them a raggedy, ill-bred lot. Shame crept over him to realize that Jane's words had somehow stuck in his memory. Shrugging, he searched for the right words.

"We aren't what one would call a conventional family. My siblings are spirited and bright—probably too much so for their own good. And my father isn't well. 'Twas the apoplexy that changed him. Before that he was the most intelligent man I knew."

"The physicians told you the changes were due to apoplexy?"

Ambrose frowned. "Do you doubt it?"

"I'm no medical expert. But Samuel seemed quite lucid over dinner."

"He had you to flirt with," Ambrose said wryly. "That'll get any man's attention right quick."

"Precisely. He reacted as any other man would in that situation. Ergo, he seems perfectly rational to me."

Ambrose considered that observation. "His confusion ... it comes and goes."

"Perhaps it comes on more when he is lonely and lessens when he has a distraction." Marianne paused. "I've seen grief masquerade as confusion. Your father's symptoms began after your stepmother's death, did they not?"

Ambrose blinked. "Aye."

"He loved her very much, I think. Such a loss could befuddle a sensitive man."

Why had this not occurred to him before? If Samuel's muddled state was due to grieving, then perhaps one day he would heal, return to his old self ... Feeling an odd pressure behind his eyes, Ambrose blinked and reached for Marianne's hand. He linked his fingers through hers.

"Thank you," he said, his tone husky. "It is good to talk—to hear another's advice."

"You are helping me," she replied softly. "Can I not return the favor?"

Guilt lanced him. The *last* thing he wished was for her to feel indebted to him. "I will help you no matter what. I'm making progress with the investigation. There is no obligation—"

Her lips silenced him. Stole his thoughts, his breath. He fell back with her against the satin sheets and, rolling atop, he kissed her neck, the supple dip above her collarbones. She tugged at his shirt, and he yanked the rough linen over his head. Fumbling with the tie of her robe, he pushed aside the gossamer panels. His heart stuttered; no matter how many times he saw those flawless curves, they would always stun him. Because she was beautiful—too damned beautiful for the likes of him. And because ...

Because he was falling in love with her.

The truth drummed in his chest, the rhythm one of panic. Beyond the fact that their relationship was built upon a lie, he could not ask the woman he loved to sacrifice a life of privilege for him. A temporary affair was all—more—than he had right to.

He tried to shut out the cold surge of desolation. To focus instead on the sweet heat of the enchantress in his arms. To take what the moment offered ... save it up for the long years ahead.

"What is it?" she asked.

"What do you mean?" Heat crept up his neck.

Her celadon eyes narrowed. "What are you thinking about, Ambrose? And before you say *nothing*, let me remind you that I am not a fool."

"Of course you aren't." He twirled one pale curl around his finger, buying himself time. Devil and damn, why couldn't he just take his pleasures like other men? For him, why did lust have to mingle with longings far more complicated? He was not ready to have this conversation. Unbridled lovemaking seemed a safer alternative.

"I was thinking ..." *Let it go, man.* The strand unraveled from his finger, and he heard himself say, "About the future."

"The future." A pause. "Between ... you and me?"

The incredulity of her tone provoked him. Was the notion so very absurd to her? Though he understood—and would never ask her to forgo her status and life of luxury for him—her astonishment nonetheless stung. He rolled off her, rising to sit at the edge of the bed.

"Forget it." He reached for his shirt. "I should go."

"What? Why? Look at me, Ambrose."

He was a man unused to making a fool of himself. To wanting what was beyond his means. Humiliation washed over him.

Meeting her vivid gaze, he said stiffly, "I can't risk my family seeing me in here. They are not accustomed to the workings of high society. We Kents lack such sophistication."

A shadow flickered in the clear depths of her eyes. Anger? Hurt? What did she have to be hurt about? He was the one so below her estimation that the mere idea of a relationship with him shocked her.

"Is that how you see me? Sophisticated and jaded? A dissolute widow out for a good fuck?"

Her sharp tone drew him back. Why was *she* attacking *him*?

"I never said that," he said tersely.

"You didn't have to. Your actions speak volumes." She crossed her arms beneath her breasts, and for a brief second, he was distracted by those heaving white globes, the taut rosy peaks. "Are you even listening to me?"

He snapped his eyes up. "Of course I am. But I have no idea what you're talking about. To what actions do you refer?" he said, matching his tone to hers.

"Oh, I don't know ... how about the fact that you *lied*?"

His stomach slammed into his throat. Had she somehow discovered the contract with Bow Street ...?

"Are you so ashamed of me, Ambrose"—her voice caught for a fraction of a second—"that you cannot tell your family the truth?"

He frowned. "I'm afraid you've lost me."

"You lied to your family about our relationship," she said succinctly, "and you've got Emma lying, too. I heard you both at supper telling everyone I'm providing a roof over their heads because I'm your patron. The altruistic widow who took pity on her employee's family."

He narrowed his eyes. "I don't believe I called you altruistic. Nor that we Kents were on the receiving end of pity. That aside, what would you have me tell my family?"

"How about the truth?" she shot back. "Unless, of course, it is too debased for your high moral standards."

He stared at her, stupefied. "You think I am misleading my family about the nature of our relationship because of *morality*?"

"Why else would you hide the fact that we are lovers?" Flags of color appeared on her high cheekbones. "I am not an idiot, Ambrose. I know what my reputation is." Despite the quaver in her voice, her chin angled upward. "I'd hoped that you saw me differently."

Understanding dawned. Incredible as it seemed, could this magnificent creature be insecure about ... *herself*? "You *are* an idiot," he said.

"How dare you—"

He didn't give her a chance to finish. Dodging her slap, he caged her against the mattress. Kissed her until she melted against him, her lips pliant against his once more.

"We're both idiots," he murmured, "you for thinking I could be ashamed of you. And me ... for being ashamed of myself."

"You?" She stared up at him from the pillows. "What have you to be ashamed about?"

He found it surprisingly difficult to meet her gaze. "You and I both know I'm not the kind of man you typically consort with."

"Typically *consort with*?" For some reason, that got her going again. She glared at him and pushed at his shoulders. "How many men do you think I've been with?"

He sensed a trap. "Er, I haven't ... that is ..."

"Two, Kent. And that *includes* you," she said acidly.

He hadn't thought he could smile at so perilous a moment. From their previous lovemaking, he'd guessed she was inexperienced. The fact that she'd known only one other lover filled him with primitive satisfaction. Less memories to compete with. More firsts to give her—

"Why must men be so asinine?" she sputtered, apparently catching wind of his thoughts. "Just get off me, you lummox. Get off—and get out."

He didn't budge. Instead, he blew out a breath and said, "I'm sorry. Forgive me, sweetheart?"

Her lashes formed lush crescents against her porcelain skin. "You're apologizing?"

"'Tis what one does when one is at wrong. I should not have assumed that you'd want to keep our affair a secret," he said. "That is why I kept it from my family: I wanted to protect your reputation."

"You did it for *me*?"

Her surprise struck a chord of tenderness this time. So strong yet so fragile, his *selkie*. He cupped her cheek. "It certainly wasn't for my own sake." Sobering, he forced himself to address the reality of their situation. "I haven't a reputation to lose, Marianne. I'm not rich or titled—no one gives a damn what I do or whom I sleep with. But you ... any man would count himself blessed to be your lover." Gruffly, he admitted, "I suppose I don't know why you've chosen me."

"You're right—you are an *idiot*." She tugged down on his head until his nose nearly touched hers. "Haven't you heard anything

I've said to you? I've never met another man like you, Ambrose. Not a single one."

He shook his head. "I'm a simple man. An ordinary one."

One with too many troubles. His ex-betrothed's voice played in his head: *I won't go down with a sinking ship.* Compared to Jane, Marianne had far more to lose in terms of status and opportunity. How could he ask such a sacrifice of her?

"I've told you before. You do know what your problem is, don't you?" she said.

His father's debts? His motherless siblings? Or perhaps the fact that in order to protect the woman he loved, he was lying to her like the veriest scoundrel?

"You've told me before: you think I'm a prig," he said dully. "A moralistic snob."

Hell, he agreed with her. His foolish pride had been his downfall. If only he could go back, do things differently …

"No, I think you're a man who takes too much on his shoulders." Her hand came to rest against his jaw, and her touch was tender, so very good. To his shame, he could not bring himself to part from it. "Why must you go at everything alone?"

She'd exposed it: the cold, solitary truth.

"Because," he said, his voice raw, "there's no one to go at it with."

Sea-green depths glimmered up at him. "I've long stopped trusting in the future. In making promises when I've yet to fulfill the one vow that matters most—the one that I made to Primrose the day she was taken." Her voice hitching, Marianne said, "I haven't much to offer. But what I have—this moment—I give gladly to you. Tonight I am yours, if you'll have me."

"It's more than I deserve," he said roughly.

So much more—but I can't let you go. God help me, I can't.

Before she could respond, he took her lips, drank in the cinnamon succor of her kiss. For however long this fantasy—this *now*—lasted, she was his. He'd be a fool to waste a single moment of it. Leveraging onto his side, he explored the delights before him. Her full, firm breasts, those lovely nipples which he had to taste again. He bent his head ... blinking when he suddenly found himself pushed onto his back.

Marianne climbed over him, straddling his hips. Her hair cascaded to her waist, offering peek-a-boo views of her creamy skin. When her dewy thatch brushed against his abdomen, his cock rose in an immediate salute beneath his smalls.

"I want to try something different tonight," she whispered. "Do you mind?"

"Not at all," he managed. "Just tell me what you want, and I'll —" He bit out a groan as she gently raked her nails over one of his nipples.

"I want you to lie there and let me explore as I wish. Could you do that?" His shaft turned harder than an iron pike, ready to tear through his trousers as she murmured, "Can you let me take charge, Ambrose?"

God Almighty, he'd never been asked such a thing. In the past, he'd always focused on his partner's needs. It had been a point of pride, in fact. He knew he was neither handsome nor rich, but he had the desire and the skill to see to his bedmate's satisfaction. Marianne's request, however, turned the tables. No woman had wanted to take the reins from him before. No woman had looked at him with such hunger in her eyes—with such sweet, wicked desire.

By Jove, what was Marianne capable of? Flames of anticipation licked his spine, made hotter by the spark of uncertainty. Could he relinquish control, put himself at the mercy of this naughty, unpredictable *selkie*? She wetted her lips, a small nervous motion, and he realized *she* was nervous too. Within that alluring skin lay vulnerability: this was about seduction, yes, but also something else. Something deeper she wanted to show him.

His reply emerged, thick and guttural. "Do as you wish, sweetheart."

Chapter Twenty-Nine

A thrill tingled over Marianne's skin. *He trusts me. He's letting me take control.*

She hadn't realized until that moment how very badly she wanted him to have faith in her. Perhaps it was her own sense of honor that demanded *quid pro quo*: after all, she had yielded more to him than she had to any man. Was it any surprise that she expected his trust in return? Yet this was about more than equality. Or even trust. What she truly wanted was to … ease his pain. To take away this proud, self-reliant man's solitude, if only for the night.

Recalling instructions he'd once given her, she said, "Put your hands on the headboard, then. And don't move them until I say so."

His amber eyes watchful, he reached behind his head, his long fingers curling around two wooden spindles. Eyeing the lean, delicious stretch of him, she felt a warm flutter in her belly.

"Like that?" he said gravely.

"Precisely." Her voice sounded throaty to her own ears. "And for following orders, you shall receive a reward."

Leaning down, she kissed his jaw. The first bristles of a night beard had already sprouted. She liked the faint rasp of his skin and his scent of soap and leather, honest and masculine just like him. Her mouth pooled with the need to taste every inch of him.

Moving on, she sampled the hard underside of his chin. His throat bobbed as she licked and nuzzled, making her way down the hard slope of his shoulders to the strong, hair-whorled planes of his chest. She circled one flat nipple with her tongue. At his sharp intake of breath, she closed her lips, sucking gently until he groaned.

"You like that." She didn't bother to hide the smugness in her voice.

"Aye, love," he said, his voice gravelly, "almost as much as I like suckling your pretty breasts. May I?"

It wasn't an unreasonable request. Her pulse kicked up a notch at the fact that it *was* a request—one she had the power to grant or deny. She slid up along his body, sighing as her taut nipples dragged against the masculine mat of hair, feeding her excitement and his too, if the flames in his eyes were any indication. With her knees bracing his chest, she leaned forward and presented a breast to his lips.

"Suck," she whispered.

A guttural sound escaped him as he did as she bade. He took her nipple in a fierce kiss, one that blazed heat straight between her legs. When his teeth grazed the sensitive tip, she whimpered. Honey flooded her pussy as he flicked in a steady rhythm. She felt herself melting ... yet she was supposed to be in control. She drew back, panting.

Raw desire glowed in his eyes. "Give me your other tit. I want to lick and suck you all over."

"No. That is enough for now," she managed. "I'm supposed to be doing the exploring, remember?"

His arms corded, the muscles flexing. He was so strong—he had only to let go of the headboard to take her. She was so aroused that a part of her wanted him to assume control. Wanted him to flip her onto her back, mount her, vanquish her emptiness with his rampant shaft ...

As if somehow sensing her ambivalence, his eyes crinkled at the corners. He kept his hands clenched on the wood. "Go on, then," he said.

She scooted back, trying to hide her ruffled state by resuming her perusal of his splendid form. He offered a wealth of distractions, and all of them ratcheted up her lust. Her breath puffed quick and hot between her lips as her fingers bumped over the taut ridges of his abdomen. Following the sensual trail of hair that bisected his belly, she made her way to his waistband. She slid her palm over the tented placket of his trousers, and molten heat gushed from her core.

He was so big, so hard—so much a man.

"You have this effect on me. A smile from you, a touch ..." He grimaced with pleasure as she squeezed. "God, Marianne, I lose my head where you're concerned."

She found the hidden buttons, unfastened them. With a swift yank, she freed him from the layers of wool and linen, the muscles of her sex quivering as she beheld his bold erection from the springy dark hair at the thick base, up the long, veined shaft, all the way to the proud dome. In the past, she'd never particularly appreciated this part of the male anatomy. With Thomas, she'd been too shy to look or touch. With Draven ... a remnant of the old humiliation surfaced, ugly ripples that distorted her desire.

"Sweetheart, do you want to stop?"

She met her lover's gaze and saw desire there, clean and pure. Nothing to be ashamed of. Nothing to fear. "No," she said softly, "not unless you want me to."

"Hardly. But ..."—the air hissed between his teeth as she curled her fingers around his girth—"I don't want you to do anything you don't want to."

Concerned for her, even at this juncture. It was so very *Ambrose* that it made her smile. Smile—and get aroused all over again. The heady surge of power swirled more potently than any aphrodisiac because it was tempered by trust. By the choice she was making to take pleasure at her will.

And what her will demanded was to give Ambrose Kent more bliss than he'd ever had. To have him remember this night forever, no matter what the future held in store. No matter if she didn't quite believe herself worthy of this magnificent male beast. Perhaps one day she could overcome the demons of her past. Tonight, it mattered naught.

Because tonight Ambrose was hers to pleasure.

She knelt between his thighs, continued to stroke him lightly. "Tell me what you like."

"I like what you're doing now." His heavy-lidded eyes told her it was the truth.

"Surely there is more. What have your other lovers done for you?" *Whatever they did, I'll do better.* "Tell me your desires," she said throatily.

"I like kissing you, tasting you," he murmured. "Especially between your legs."

Her sex grew damper at the memory of his skilled tongue, the voracious enjoyment he took in licking her there. Apparently, he was thinking the same thing for fluid leaked from the slit in his cockhead, slickening her grasp and making him groan.

"I like that too," she said, "but we're talking about you. Your pleasure."

A brief hesitation. "It's not a question I've been asked before."

"Never?" she said in surprise.

"I suppose my partner's satisfaction has come first in the past." When she continued to look at him, stupefied, he muttered, "It's not as if there have been dozens of women."

"Not dozens?" she said as casually as she could.

"More like four. And that includes you." He ground out the last word, probably because she'd taken her exploration to the root of his shaft. His stones fit snugly in her palms, supple yet with an intriguing heft. "Good God, woman, our play will soon end if you continue that."

But she couldn't help herself. Delight bubbled inside her. She *adored* the fact that he hadn't shared his bed indiscriminately. Knowing that sex wasn't a thing he took lightly made the intimacy between them even more profound. It made her want to do everything with him ... even the things she feared. Because with Ambrose, her impulses were not dirty or demeaning. Desire buzzed through her with a wild, empowering vitality.

She eyed his jutting manhood. "Have you been kissed there before?"

His hard-paved chest rose and fell. He shook his head. "I know what Draven made you do. And I don't want—"

He broke off with an oath because she'd leaned forward and touched the tip of her tongue to his cockhead. His essence teased her senses. Salty and clean. Virile, male ... delicious. Nothing to do with her experiences with Draven. The shadows receded as desire flowed over her, bright and cleansing. Here and now, basking in Ambrose's solid heat, his steady, reassuring gaze, only intimacy existed. She tasted him again, lingering this time, his harsh breaths driving her to fit her lips over the fat tip.

"Bloody fuck," he bit out.

Despite being occupied, her lips curved. Her earnest Ambrose —cursing? Hmm. What else could she make him do? She applied gentle suction, loving the way he growled her name. Loving that she was the first and only to give him this pleasure. Wrapping her fingers around his thick pole, she eased down the velvety skin, exposing the bulbous head. She rubbed her tongue against the underside, and he swore again, his hips jerking instinctively.

Gripping his shaft more firmly, she relaxed her muscles, taking him in deeper. Given his size, it wasn't the easiest task, but she was no shirker. The challenge excited her as did the thick, wicked slide of his cock filling her throat.

"God, sweetheart. It's so bloody good." His features taut with arousal, he watched her every movement. "You have *no idea* ..."

He broke off, groaning as she bobbed upon him. With each pass, her passion took her further, her excitement fueled by how she could undo this strong man, her steadfast lover. His wiry length vibrated, his hips lifting to get more of her kiss. All the while, his eyes never left her face, not even when he discovered her limit, nudging a barrier so deep that she swallowed instinctively. A feral sound tore from his chest.

"Enough," he gasped. "I'm not coming alone."

"I'm not stopping," she said, trying to catch her breath.

"I don't want you to stop. Just come here."

Before she knew what he was about, he sat up, his hands clamping onto her hips.

"Wait a minute, I never said you could let go. That's cheating —" She broke off, moaning, melting as he hauled her into a new position: her knees now straddled his head as she lay atop him. Her mouth hovered above his cock, her sex above his mouth. A cry left her as his tongue delved deeply. "*Ambrose,* dear God—"

"Yes, love," he said thickly, "give me your pussy, your sweet dew. Let me have all of you."

His guttural commands unleashed her wildness. With her hands planted on his thighs, she wriggled against his hot kiss. She let him take her with his tongue, riding wave after wave of sensation. When heat raged over her too quickly, she tried to withdraw, but he kept her in place. She gave a helpless whimper as his thick fingers stretched her opening.

"Push back against me, love. Take me deeper."

She could not help but obey his growling demand, her spine arching as she impaled herself on his touch. *So much pleasure.* Panting, she took him as deep as she could as he continued to eat her pussy. When his tongue circled her peak, searching out her nub, her vision blurred. The wet flicks made her fall forward with a moan ... and her cheek brushed his cock, causing a shudder to run through him.

"Let's not forget about you," she said with a dazed laugh.

She took him as wholly as she could with her mouth, her hands pumping what could not fit. His groan rumbled against her flesh, and she shuddered, stimulated beyond bearing. She rocked against him with reckless abandon as she gorged on his manhood. She rode toward the summit, needing to take him there as well.

"I'm close, love," he said in guttural warning.

She resisted his efforts to dislodge her.

"Come with me," she gasped, coming up for air. "I want to taste you, too."

His entire frame shook at her words. His touch roughened, the pace driving and relentless, and she returned his caresses measure for measure. She sucked and fisted him as his fingers rammed into her, his tongue stoking her wildness. When his teeth grazed her pearl, she screamed, the fever breaking, splintering her apart.

He shouted out at the same time, and she tasted his bliss, drank it in as the perfect accompaniment to her own. His pleasure warmed her inside out, melting her bones. For endless moments, she lay limp against his thighs, cocooned by the music of their labored breaths and the musky fragrance of their loving.

Somehow he found the energy to move. He gathered her to his chest, pressed a kiss against her forehead. His voice rumbled beneath her ear.

"A night with you, Marianne ... it's more than I expected of a lifetime."

Her heart too full to speak, she snuggled closer.

Chapter Thirty

L ater that week, Emma cast her eyes around Madame
Rousseau's changing room and whispered, "Are you
certain about this, Marianne? I don't need a French dressmaker; I can sew my own dresses. If you take me to the nearest
draper's—"

"When it comes to shopping, I am *always* certain." Marianne
cut off further protest with the wave of her hand. "Do not worry
about the cost, dear. Your job is to concentrate on cultivating your
style."

"My style?" The girl's smooth forehead lined as she looked
down at her patched and shapeless undergarments. "I am not sure
I have one."

"Precisely. 'Tis the problem we are here to remedy."

On cue, the modiste bustled back through the curtained doorway, bolts of fabric clasped in her thin arms. "*Je les ai trouvés!* The
muslins that I was telling you about." Setting the lot down on her
work table, she unrolled a length of white fabric patterned with
china blue stripes. "What do you think of this one?"

Emma's eyes widened. "It's the most beautiful thing I've ever
seen."

"Unfortunately, many agree with you. I've seen that print on everyone from milkmaids to dowagers," Marianne said. "We'll need something more unique."

Amelie gave a brisk nod. "*Alors*, here is another choice. A sprigged lilac: understated yet with a touch of sophistication."

"It's the most beautiful thing—" Emma began.

Marianne wrinkled her nose. "Rather dull, I should say."

"I have it somewhere—" Rummaging through the pile, Amelie pulled out a bolt. "*Voilà*. The perfect choice."

Marianne examined the selection. The eggshell muslin was simple, yet it had a subtle, glowing sheen to it. The effect was both pragmatic and spirited. In the week that she'd spent with Emma, she'd come to admire the girl for just those qualities.

"Not bad," she conceded. "What do you think, dear?"

"It's the most beautiful thing ... er, isn't it?" Emma said.

Marianne exchanged rueful looks with the modiste.

"*Charmant*." The modiste's lips twitched. "The girl suits the frock, *n'est-ce pas?*"

"We'll start with this one, then. What do you have in mind for the passimeterie, Amelie?"

"The what?" Emma interjected.

"The trimmings, dear," Marianne said. "Madame Rousseau is renowned for her cleverness in ornamentation."

Amelie preened. "We keep it simple, *non?* Rosettes, composed from the same muslin ... perhaps with a few amethyst beads sewn in the center. And vines embroidered along the hem."

"Fresh and delightful. Just like Emma," Marianne said, smiling.

Emma flushed. "'Tis terribly generous of you, my lady. But the expense—"

"Is not your concern," Marianne said firmly. "Now do hold still for Madame to take your measurements."

After the fitting, Marianne and Emma left the boutique. They decided to walk the few elm-lined blocks to Gunter's Tea Shop, where they were to meet up with the others. Helena and Percy had volunteered to act as guides for the other Kents whilst Marianne took Emma on the much-needed shopping expedition.

One thing I can take off my list. Pleased with the results of the morning, Marianne flicked open her parasol. Now that Emma's countrified facade was on its way to becoming a thing of the past, Marianne planned to tackle Harry next. With his fit figure and intelligent wit, the lad had the makings of a proper gentleman—if only he would stop blowing things up. Harry was the scientist of the family, and, as Polly had confided, he went by the philosophy that "every failure is a step toward success."

Clearly, Harry was taking the long road to triumph when it came to his experiments. Marianne hoped the sacrifice of her Dresden pitcher had been worth it. In truth, she couldn't feel anything but warm amusement toward Harry; his earnest charm reminded her too much of his older brother. Just thinking of Ambrose made her chest go soft like the center of a perfectly boiled egg.

Her skin prickled as she recalled being awakened by Ambrose's kiss this morning, by the slow, filling thrust of his body. His patience had driven her wild, and nothing she'd done—her pleas, her kisses—had dissuaded him from taking her in the manner of his choice. With a raffish grin, he'd turned her over, and her cheeks heated even now as she recalled how she'd sung her release into the pillow.

"Are you getting overheated, Marianne? You look flushed."

Emma's concerned voice reeled her back. Made her face burn even more.

"'Tis the heat," she said, clearing her throat. "An ice at Gunter's will be most refreshing. Your siblings will enjoy it, I think."

"I'm certain they will. As will I." A line appeared between Emma's sable brows.

"You don't look happy about the fact," Marianne observed.

"Oh, but I am! Please don't think me ungrateful." Beneath the brim of her well-worn bonnet, Emma's lashes flew upward. "It's just that, well, I feel ... guilty."

"About?"

The girl chewed her lip. "You've gone to such expense for us. How shall we ever repay—"

"Emma, dear, do not concern yourself over money," Marianne said. "Your brother is assisting me with a matter, and I assure you if there is any debt involved, it is mine."

"May I ask what Ambrose is helping you with?"

"That is private."

Emma's gaze fell to the paved walk, and Marianne silently cursed herself for her cutting tone, which had emerged on instinct. When would she get over this tendency to push others away? Would she one day be able to remove the walls she'd erected around herself?

She struggled to find a way to apologize—another skill she lacked.

Emma spoke first. "I need to ask you a question, my lady. It's impertinent, I'm afraid."

Seeing the resolute set of the other's shoulders, Marianne said, "I gather you are not asking my permission."

"If I may be frank, it's about Ambrose," Emma said in that dogged Kent manner, "and your ... er, relationship with him." Gathering a deep breath, the girl looked Marianne straight in the eye. "Which we both know is not entirely one of employer and employee."

"You are concerned that Ambrose and I are lovers?" Marianne said with equal bluntness.

Emma's terse nod caused a deflating sensation in Marianne's stomach. Even this snippet of a girl questioned such a liaison. Well, Marianne could not fault her. From what she'd observed over the past week, the younger Kents idolized their older brother. No doubt they'd want him to be paired with a different sort of woman —one as steady and good as he.

Not some notorious widow, certainly.

"What are your intentions toward him?" Emma said.

"That is between him and me," Marianne replied tightly.

"Not when it involves the rest of us. We're staying with you, depending on your generosity," Emma said, her voice quivering, "and it isn't right. Not unless ..."

"Unless?" Marianne cocked a brow.

"Do you mean to do the honorable thing by him?"

A choked sound escaped Marianne. "Haven't you got things turned around?"

"Obviously, you don't know my brother as well as I do. He is a gentleman to the core. He wouldn't dream of asking you to marry him because you're rich and we're ... not." Emma shrugged, and Marianne had to give the other points for directness. "Personally, I couldn't give a care about the money. We Kents don't need much to be happy." Emma drew to a halt on the walk, her young face fiercely set. "But I cannot stand by and watch Ambrose get hurt again."

Aware of the curious gazes of passersby, Marianne took Emma's arm and guided her along. Quietly, she said, "Has he been hurt before?"

"He hasn't told you about Jane?" Emma blurted.

"We haven't talked much about his past," Marianne said with a twinge of guilt. *We've been too focused on mine.*

"Perhaps I oughtn't have mentioned—"

"'Tis too late now. One cannot be candid halfway," Marianne said dryly.

"You do have a point." Sighing, Emma said, "Jane Harrow was the baker's widow. She was only twenty-four when her husband died and very pretty. All the men in our village sniffed at her heels, but she set her sights on Ambrose."

Jealousy knifed Marianne in the chest. Ridiculous ... but there it was. "He returned Mrs. Harrow's interest?"

Emma nodded. "Jane would come by our cottage on the weekends when Ambrose came to visit. She'd bring baked goods—she made the most marvelous cakes—and flirt with him. Soon, my brother started courting her. After a year, they became engaged. I think Ambrose quite fancied the notion of being married. He was saving up to buy a cottage for him and Jane."

A cottage and a pretty country wife who cooked. Of course that is what Ambrose wanted.

"What happened?" Marianne said grimly.

"*We* did. One tragedy after another struck our family. First Mother died and then Father developed apoplexy and couldn't work any longer. It fell on Ambrose to care for all of us. Truthfully, he'd been supporting us all along, but now he had to use all his earnings just to keep us afloat. He had to put off getting married." With a dark glance, Emma added, "That made Jane angry."

"But his situation—surely she understood his loyalty to his family."

"She wanted to have her own comforts," Emma said in flat tones, "and she was tired of waiting. Besides, I don't think she liked us very much."

"Why ever not?" Marianne said, surprised. Though she'd spent only a week with them, she found the Kents altogether charming. They were undeniably a ragtag bunch, yet there was an innocence to the family, a fierce devotion to one another that made her want to shelter them from the ugliness of the world. For one wistful moment, she let herself imagine what it would be like to belong ... to be a part of such unconditional love.

"In Chudleigh Crest we were considered a bit ... odd." A look flashed across Emma's face, and she quickly shrugged. "Not that it mattered to us. At any rate, Jane found herself another beau—a wealthy merchant passing through the village. She ran off with him."

"Dear God."

Emma nodded grimly. "When Ambrose found out, he went after them. He felt responsible, I think, because he had made Jane wait for him. He caught up with them in Brighton."

"And?"

"Jane was living under the merchant's protection. Apparently, he had a wife in London." With a look of disgust, Emma said, "Ambrose offered to take Jane back, to marry her—but she refused. Said it was better to be a rich man's mistress than a poor man's wife."

Anger smoldered beneath Marianne's breastbone. *The heartless bitch.*

"My brother has sacrificed too much for us. I hope you understand why I don't wish for him to be hurt again," Emma said.

"I'm not planning on hurting him." Yet guilt needled Marianne. She'd offered Ambrose so very little—nothing more than the moment. Whilst he ... he was helping her find her very heart again.

"Would you consider marrying him?" Emma asked.

"That has not come up." Discomfited by that inquiring brown gaze, Marianne said with a touch of defensiveness, "He hasn't brought it up, you know."

"And if he did?"

"That is between him and me." Thank God they had arrived at Berkeley Square. Marianne spotted Helena's open-air carriage beneath the waving maples, the Kents' heads gleaming in the sunlight as they ate their ices. "Ah, there is your family now. Let us rejoin them."

Emma chuffed out a breath. "If I may say just one more thing?"

Marianne raised a brow.

"I like you," the girl said, her eyes earnest, "and I hope you will consider marrying my brother. He's a good sort—loyal and loving." Her gaze lowered to the scuffed tips of her boots. "And I give you my word, my lady, that I shall do my best to care for my family. We shan't get in your way."

Marianne's throat thickened. Who knew the power of sincerity? The Kents seem to have it in spades. She tipped the other's chin up.

"Dearest girl," she said, "no matter how things unfold between Ambrose and me, you and your family are never the problem, do you understand?"

Emma blinked, her nod uncertain.

"Now let us join the others—" Marianne began when an urchin dressed in grimy rags came jogging up.

"Are you Lady Draven?" the boy said.

"I am," Marianne said, frowning.

The urchin held out a note. "For you, yer ladyship."

Marianne exchanged a coin for the sealed note. The urchin scampered off. A feeling of foreboding stole over her as she saw her name written in an unfamiliar hand.

"Who is that from?" Emma said.

Marianne forced a smile. "I'm not sure. Run along to Lady Harteford's carriage. I shall join you in a minute."

Brow furrowed, Emma did as she was told.

Marianne broke the wax seal. She scanned the single line, and her insides turned to ice.

Has Kent told you he's being paid by Sir Coyner of Bow Street to investigate you?

"You're to wait for Sir Coyner in here, my lady." Blushing to the roots of his fair hair, the clerk led Marianne into a well-appointed office and hurried to pull out one of the chairs facing the desk. "If there's anything I can get you—"

"That won't be necessary," Marianne said calmly as she sat.

Inside, her emotions roiled like a tempest. "Don't let me keep you from your work."

Bowing, the clerk left the room. The moment the door clicked shut, Marianne rose and circled to the other side of the desk. She wasn't sure what she was looking for—a clue, any reason at all why Bow Street might have an interest in her. She went through the neat stacks and found nothing. At the sound of footsteps, her eyes flitted to the door ... but whoever it was passed by the office. She returned her attention to the desk, eyeing the drawers. Dare she?

She pulled open the top one.

Her heart shot into her throat. *Bloody hell.*

With a trembling hand, she lifted the gilded invitation from the drawer. A hunting party, this weekend at the Earl of Pendleton's estate. The coincidence sent her thoughts spiraling, the connections ricocheting in her head. The invitation indicated that the magistrate knew Pendleton. And Leach had worked for Pendleton. Had Pendleton hired Bow Street to monitor her—was the earl the one who had Primrose?

Her head snapped up at the approaching footsteps. She shoved the invitation inside her reticule and closed the drawer. She made it to the window by the desk just before the door opened. Pulse racing, she turned to face the magistrate. The moment she saw Sir Coyner's overly pleasant expression, her heart froze.

He knows something. He's involved—does that mean Kent is too?

The notion made her want to weep. Instead she said in cordial tones, "What a lovely view you have, Sir Coyner."

"Thank you, my lady." There was no hint of deference in the magistrate's educated accents; she had a faint recollection that he was connected to titles and worked out of fancy rather than necessity. A true believer in justice. The irony made her sick.

"What do I owe the honor of this visit?" Beneath his neat mustache, his forced smile resembled more of a grimace.

She'd thought through her strategy on the carriage ride over.

She needed answers: the time for dissembling had passed, and the element of surprise would be her greatest ally.

"Why are you having me followed?" she said.

Coyner's throat worked, his Adam's apple surfacing over the top of his silk cravat. He recovered quickly. "I don't know what you mean," he said heartily.

"I think you do," she said, approaching him, "and I want the name of your client. Who hired you to have me watched?"

The magistrate drew himself up. "Bow Street is a respected institution, my lady. Unlike some,"—Coyner shot her a scathing look—"we at this office believe in law and order. And we uphold client confidentiality to the highest standards."

"So someone did hire you," she said coldly.

"I will neither confirm nor deny—"

"*You flaming bastard, did you order Ambrose Kent to monitor me?*"

Coyner blinked rapidly, his eyes shifting. He moistened his lips. Without saying a blessed thing, the magistrate had given her the answer. The last embers of hope snuffed out. Ambrose had betrayed her. From the very start, he'd been lying to her.

Everything was a sham ... he's no different from the rest. From Draven or Skinner or any other man. And like the veriest fool, I let myself be taken again.

Her heart began crumbling in her chest. Relentlessly, she held it together—caged it in a wall of ice. Cold and impenetrable, the only way to survive.

"How much did you pay him for the job?" she said with frosty derision. "Did you give him extra for seducing the suspect to get the truth?"

"Christ, he *bedded* you—" As if realizing what he'd admitted, the magistrate cut himself off. He pressed his lips together. "Any compensation we provide to our employees is solely for ethical purposes."

Ambrose betrayed me ... for coin. Everything that happened between us was a lie.

She realized she was shaking. With rage—with other emotions that might annihilate her composure if she didn't leave that very instant.

"Involve me in any other *ethical* endeavor, and I vow you'll answer for defamation," she spat.

She left the office. With each step, her emotions receded. No anger, no pain—only numbness that seemed to well from her soul. That had merely been biding its time, waiting for her foolish happiness to wither and die.

Lugo met her at the carriage. He must have read her expression, for lines of concern carved into his broad features as he handed her up. "My lady, what will you do?"

"What I should have been doing all along. I'm going to find Rosie on my own." The truth echoed hollowly in the cabin. "Make haste, Lugo, for we have a journey ahead of us."

Chapter Thirty-One

I t was nearing midnight by the time Ambrose jogged up the steps to Marianne's townhouse. He let himself in with the key she'd given him. As he strode into the dark foyer, anticipation simmered in his veins: this evening, Willy Trout had delivered Marquess Boyer's secret. As it turned out, Leach *had* helped the marquess to cover up a scandal; it did not involve Primrose, however, but a pair of twin footmen.

Which narrowed the field of suspects down to one: Pendleton.

Like any investigator, Ambrose had a sixth sense that told him when a development showed promise, and his instincts told him they were turning a corner with the case. He could not wait to tell Marianne, to see the hope light her eyes. After all she had survived, she deserved happiness. Such was his optimism that he allowed himself hope as well. When he returned Primrose to her and he could finally tell her the truth, might she forgive his deception?

Could there be some sort of future for them after all?

In his haste toward the stairwell, he nearly bumped into one of the maids.

"Dear me, you gave me a fright!" The girl's hands flew to her chest.

He remembered to remove his hat. Raking his hand through his fog-dampened hair, he said with an apologetic smile, "Alice, isn't it? I do apologize. I have an important matter to discuss with Lady Draven."

"Her ladyship is not in, sir."

Ambrose frowned. Though he knew Marianne's reputation for carousing, as far as he knew she'd curtailed late night activities to spend time with his family. In truth, it had touched him to see her rub along so well with his brother and sisters. Who'd have thought that the haughty Baroness Draven would enjoy games of charades and hide-the-slipper? Seeing her smiles, genuine and unguarded, had only fueled his reckless dreams.

"When do you expect her back?" he said.

"I'm not sure, sir. It might be days," the maid said.

"*Days?*"

He had not even realized that he'd raised his voice until steps came down the hallway.

"Is that you, Ambrose?" Emma rushed into the anteroom. She wore an old flannel robe, her hair hanging in a braid over her shoulder. Their father hobbled behind her on a cane.

"Is something amiss?" Ambrose said. "Why are the two of you still up? Where is Marianne?"

"Father and I were just discussing the situation over hot milk. Come, Ambrose," Emma said quietly, "or you'll wake the others. It took quite some coaxing to get Polly to bed this eve."

Growing more uneasy by the moment, Ambrose followed her to the drawing room. The instant the door closed, he said, "Tell me what is going on."

Emma and his father exchanged glances.

"Marianne left this evening. She wouldn't say where." Emma tugged nervously on her braid. "But she took an awful lot of luggage, and Lugo and Tilda went with her."

Ambrose stared at his sister, his mind reeling. "She said *nothing* to you at all about where she was headed and when she would be back?"

"She said she was ... bored," Emma admitted in a small voice. "And in need of diversion."

"I don't understand." Ambrose rubbed his neck, trying to think over the mangled morass in his head. In his chest.

Bored? In need of diversion? What the bloody fuck is that supposed to mean?

"She didn't send you word, my boy?" His father peered up at him from one of the wingchairs.

"No." Ambrose's fists clenched at his sides.

Though his relationship with Marianne was far from settled, he'd believed that a degree of intimacy had grown between them. That even without promises to one another, they had a certain ... understanding. One that, at the very least, involved her telling him when she planned to take off on a bleeding trip.

"Perhaps she sent a message and it got lost?" Emma suggested.

Ambrose didn't think so. From the looks on the others' faces, they didn't think so either. He braced an arm against the mantle, brooded into the flames for he didn't know what else to do. His emotions veered dangerously, volatile and beyond his control. He *hated* the feeling.

"Did the two of you have a lover's spat, my boy?"

Ambrose slid his father a startled glance. Behind Samuel's chair, Emma stood, her gaze widening. She shook her head, mouthing the words, *I didn't say anything.*

"Er, I don't know what you mean," Ambrose said.

Samuel snorted. "I may be old, but I'm not a fool. I was young once."

Despite his own turmoil, Ambrose was relieved to see the sharp-witted look behind his father's spectacles. Marianne had been right after all. Then again, she often was ... the ache in his chest grew.

"I know love when I see it," Samuel went on. "Didn't think I saw it with you and that other chit, and turns out I was right, wasn't I? But this one, she's different. You'd be a fool to let her go."

"It's not that simple."

"Young folk always complicate things," Samuel sighed. "It's exceedingly simple, actually. Either you love her or you don't. Which is it?"

I love her. Arse over elbows, like a sodding fool.

"She's a baroness," he said gruffly, "and I'm ... nobody."

"You're a damn fool if you believe that. A damn fool." Rapping his cane against the floor for emphasis, Samuel declared, "*Happiness depends upon ourselves.* How many times have I told you that?"

Ambrose raked a hand through his hair. "Enough for me to know that comes from Aristotle."

"Then you'll recognize this as well: *Love is composed of a single soul inhabiting two bodies.* Now is that or isn't that the case with you and Marianne?"

It *was* for him. When he and Marianne were apart, his thoughts returned constantly to her. And with her gone, he felt half-whole. Half-alive, devil take it.

"I don't know how she feels about it," he said in hoarse tones.

"Why? Because she is rich? Beautiful?" Samuel gave him a keen look. "She's proud and independent, no doubt about it. But so are you, son. Never saw two people more alike in that regard. Far as I can tell, the pair of you need each other."

Could his father be right? Ambrose could certainly see where he needed Marianne—but did she need him? Beyond his promise to find her daughter? He struggled to believe that Fortune would smile upon him in that manner.

Besides, if that were true, why in blazes had Marianne gone in search of *diversion*?

His gut knotted, but anger began to edge out despair. Damn it, he would not let her go without an explanation. Without a fight. He had to search her out—but where should he begin?

You're a bleeding investigator, aren't you? Think, man.

"I'll question her staff in the morning," he said. "For now, I'll search her bedchamber for any clues to her whereabouts."

He headed to the door, but his sister's quivering voice halted him. "Ambrose?"

"What is it, Em?" he said, turning.

To his surprise, her eyes filled with tears. "I think I know why Marianne left. All of this is my fault!"

"*Your* fault?"

Emma drew a shuddery breath. "Earlier today, I poked my nose where I oughtn't have. I ... I asked Marianne about the nature of your relationship."

Ambrose frowned.

"I know, I know, everyone is always telling me I'm too managing," his sister wailed, "and here I've gone and done it again."

"Tell me what transpired during the conversation," he said.

"I asked Marianne if she planned to ... to ..."

"Spit it out, child," Samuel said.

"I asked her if she planned to marry Ambrose." Biting her lip, Emma looked up at Ambrose through her lashes. "I *am* sorry. I was only trying to help."

Ambrose's throat felt like sandpaper. "How did Marianne respond?"

"She said it was a private matter. Between the two of you." Em hung her head. "I know I oughtn't have pried in your affairs, but I was worried for you. After what happened with Jane ... oh, Ambrose, I just want you to be happy."

Numbly, he realized why Marianne had left. She was spooked about a future with him; he'd been right about her reaction the last time. To have his sister bring it up a second time ... that must have prompted Marianne to bolt. *You're a sinking ship, man—did you honestly expect a woman like her to stay? To take you on?*

"You have always taken care of us—but who is to care for you?" Emma said in a small voice. "I wanted her ladyship to know that she would not be getting a bad bargain. That we would not interfere with your marital bliss."

Ambrose rubbed his temples, which had begun to throb. "Of course you wouldn't," he said distractedly. "It isn't about you, is it now?"

"It was with Jane. You had to give her up for us."

Despite his own disappointment, Ambrose saw his sister's chin wobble. Sighing, he said in a gentler voice, "Jane wasn't mine in the first place. Father was right. I have no regrets over what happened."

"And Marianne?" Emma hesitated. "If things ... do not work out, will you have regrets about her?"

For the rest of my days.

He gave a weary shrug. "Don't worry your head over it, Em. When Marianne returns, she and I will sort matters out." His chest tight, he said roughly, "More change for all of you, I'm afraid."

Though he'd never intended for his family to get used to living in the present circumstances, his search for a more permanent place for them had thus far yielded options he'd rather not consider. But he'd figure something out. The Kents would not stay where they were not wanted.

Emma came to him and took his hand in hers. "As long as we're together, everything will be fine," she said earnestly.

"Hear, hear," their father said.

Ambrose wished he shared their optimism.

Marianne peered out the curtain as the carriage rolled past the gates and along the paved drive. Immaculate lawns lined both sides, beyond which spread woods reputed to be the finest hunting grounds in all of Berkshire. The main house came into view, a stately Georgian residence with sprawling wings and a spectacular dome above the entrance.

Across from her, Tilda let out a light snore. They'd traveled all through the night to arrive mid-morning. As the carriage came to a stop, she heard one of the footmen outside query Lugo about their business, and a minute later Lugo appeared at the door.

In a low, urgent voice, he said, "I beg you to reconsider, my lady. It is not too late. We can turn back."

"Nonsense. We are close to finding Rosie." Marianne adjusted her décolletage and smoothed her gloves. For the next step in her plan, it was critical that she look her very best. "We are certainly not going to turn back now."

Lugo glanced behind him before whispering, "If Pendleton is the villain as you suspect, then he is dangerous, and we are entering his territory unprepared. I cannot take on all his men alone. Please, my lady, let us go back and speak to Mr. Kent. He's a decent sort. Perhaps there's been a misunderstanding—"

Pain pierced her armor, sharper than any blade. It took everything in her to stuff her emotions back into their old box. To remain numb, focused on the only goal that mattered.

"There's no misunderstanding," she said flatly. "We've been over it. Sir Coyner as much as told me that Kent was working for him. Kent betrayed me, Lugo—I'll never trust him again."

I never should have trusted him in the first place. Fool me once, shame on you. Fool me twice ... shame on me.

Her throat swelled. There was only one road left to redemption. She had to get Rosie back on her own.

"But what about the urchin? Who sent him? You aren't thinking clearly—"

"Who's not thinking? About what?" Tilda sat up, rubbed her eyes. "Are we there yet?"

At the sound of crunching gravel, Marianne hissed, "Hush, both of you. Here he comes."

"Ah, Lady Draven. What an ... unexpected pleasure."

She took the smooth, manicured hand and stepped down from the carriage. "Lord Pendleton," she murmured, bending in an elegant curtsy, "the pleasure is all mine."

In his early fifties, the earl wore his age well. His iron-grey hair was coiffed above a noble forehead and his tall, thickening figure shown to advantage in a tweed hunting jacket. He studied her with a dark, reptilian gaze—trying to recall, no doubt, when he'd issued her an invitation. Pendleton's exclusive guest list would typically not include the widow of a mere baron. Being a gentleman, however, he could not openly accuse her of crashing his house party.

"I was not certain you would make it," he said in ironic tones.

"To be honest, neither was I," she said with a light laugh. "But then my plans got cancelled, and I recalled your lovely invitation," —she removed the gilt card from her reticule, waving it strategically above her bosom—"and I simply could not resist the opportunity to further our acquaintance."

His eyes caught for a moment on her décolletage. He said only, "Indeed."

Dash it, Pendleton was living up to his reputation as a strait-laced snob. She brightened her smile and tried a different tactic. "I believe you are acquainted with my dear friend, the Marchioness of Harteford. The Earl of Northgate's daughter? When I told her I was coming here, she said to send you her best regards."

Pendleton's posture relaxed somewhat at the mention of Helena's distinguished bloodline. "Fine family, the Northgates. Haven't seen the earl for ages—meant to give him my condolences." Pendleton's mouth edged into a smirk. "But a title's a title, I suppose."

Marianne knew he was referring to Helena's marriage to Harteford, who'd once been a pariah amongst the *ton* due to his open engagement in trade and his humble beginnings. Owing to Harteford's enormous power and wealth, most of the scandal had faded in the past years. Yet snobbery apparently died hard amongst a select few.

Biting her tongue, Marianne gave a false yawn. "Do excuse

me," she said prettily, "but I'm afraid the journey was quite wearying. Travel does so affect my sensibilities."

"As it would any lady's." After a slight hesitation, Pendleton said, "You must come in and refresh yourself. I'll have your luggage sent to your rooms."

"You are too kind, my lord," Marianne murmured.

As she took his arm, a shiver stirred her nape. *The game begins.*

Chapter Thirty-Two

L ater that afternoon, Ambrose stomped up the stairs of Wapping Street Station to his office. He was in a foul mood. Owing to Marianne's abrupt departure, he'd gotten no sleep the night before. He'd combed through her chambers and found no clue to her whereabouts, and the servants had not proved any more helpful. *Perhaps a house party, sir?* one of the maids had suggested. *My lady receives invitations all the time. She is ever so popular.*

His jaw clenched. Had Marianne gone off to cavort at some party? If so, she'd made it clear that he had no right to interfere with her plans ... no right even to know of them. Hadn't she told him time and again that she could only offer him the moment?

You're a bloody, bloody fool, man.

He tossed his hat on his desk, his mood darkening further at the sight of the report he'd yet to complete. He'd spent the day trying to find the captain who'd slipped by the excise officers without paying the duties, but the bastard had proved as slippery as an eel. Ambrose had followed one lead after another today, and all had come to naught.

Devil take it, he needed some good news for a change.

Johnno's curly head emerged through the doorway. One look at his subordinate's somber face, and Ambrose knew that none was forthcoming.

"What is it, Johnno?" he said wearily.

In a low, urgent voice, the waterman said, "Dalrymple's been looking for you. He had a visitor while you were out. A magistrate from Bow Street—"

The hairs on Ambrose's neck rose at the same time that Johnno's head whipped around.

"G-good afternoon, Sir Dalrymple," he heard Johnno stammer.

The magistrate nudged the lad aside, his girth filling the doorway. "There you are, Kent." The smug look on his superior's face fostered Ambrose's sense of foreboding. "I've been looking all over for you."

Ambrose came to his feet. "I've been out on an investigation, sir. The excise case—"

"Never mind that now. I need to have a few words with you. Follow me to my office," Dalrymple said in peremptory tones.

Ambrose saw no choice but to obey. As he passed by Johnno, the waterman gave him a sympathetic nod. Ambrose followed his supervisor, preparing for things to go from bad to worse.

"I hope you are not finding us dull, Lady Draven. Perhaps it is just that our company is ... different from what you are accustomed to?"

Marianne's attention snapped back to the drawing room. To the circle of ladies sitting on the little gilt-backed chairs, their expressions tinged with scorn. For the past hour, she'd been subjected to relentless condescension; fortunately, she'd been too busy plotting her next move with Pendleton to pay them much mind. Faced with a direct question, however, she needed to reply.

"Different? In what way do you mean, Lady Castlebaugh?" she said with feigned innocence.

The middle-aged duchess gave a brittle laugh. "I merely meant to say that you must be unused to being surrounded by the gentler sex. 'Tis well known that you are popular amongst the gentlemen, my dear."

Coy looks spread around the circle, and one of the ladies, a petite, newlywed countess, turned bright pink.

Marianne returned the duchess' smile. "'Tis a problem, I'm afraid." She gave a flick to her skirts, noting the envious way several ladies eyed Amelie Rousseau's latest creation: the color of tender leaves, the airy muslin fitted sleekly to Marianne's upper torso before cascading into an unexpected celebration of tiered flounces. "Then again," she drawled, "I'd say 'tis a better problem than the opposite ... but for that I must solicit your opinion, *dear* Lady Castlebaugh."

Several of the ladies tittered. The little countess fanned the air with rapid strokes.

"I certainly *cannot* speak to that," Lady Castlebaugh snapped. Despite her distinctly horse-like features, Her Grace's vanity was well known. "Any time *I* spend in the company of gentlemen, however, falls within the bounds of propriety and good taste."

"Of course, my lady. Would I suggest any different?" Marianne waited a heartbeat. "And speaking of good taste, I've heard it said that your newest groom is rather ... delicious."

Lady Castlebaugh's narrow cheeks turned scarlet as gazes flew to her. Marianne smiled placidly. It always paid to know the *on-dit*; in this case, the duchess' penchant for bedding servants followed a tiresomely predictable pattern.

Truly, Marianne had no use for this meaningless drama; she had important matters to attend to. She got languidly to her feet. "I declare, all this talk of gentlemen makes me want to search them out. I wonder where they have gone?"

Strained silence filled the room. Then the young countess

spoke up. "I think they are in the billiards room," she volunteered shyly. Marianne was surprised to note the sparkle of admiration in the other's gaze.

"Put a bunch of gentlemen in a room, and they must knock their balls together," Marianne said with a sigh. "I suppose I will go interrupt their manly endeavors."

She gave a mock curtsy before departing the group. Behind her, she heard the countess' gurgled laughter, which was quickly stifled by a reprimand by Castlebaugh, the old bat.

Alone in the corridor, Marianne made her way towards the billiards room. She paused outside the doors, listening to the rumble of masculine conversation. Satisfied that they sounded sufficiently occupied, she moved on. She turned right and headed unerringly to Pendleton's study. Her heart galloped as she looked this way and that. No guests or servants were nearby: a rare opportunity.

She tried the beaded knob, but it did not turn. Plucking a jeweled hair pin from her coiffure, she set to work on the lock. The hair pin had dual purposes: it would serve as a tool for entry and an alibi. Pendleton had given her a tour of the house earlier. If he happened upon her in the study, she'd simply say that she'd lost her hair ornament and had returned to look for it.

The lock clicked, and, with another quick glance around, she slipped inside. Her eyes traveled over the baroque grandeur of Pendleton's private sanctuary. Wealth and influence saturated the gilt and velvet, the antique furnishings that had been used to entertain visiting monarchs over the centuries. Goose pimples dotted her skin. The man who owned this room had power at his disposal ... and was not one to cross lightly.

But if Pendleton had Rosie, then woe be it to him.

With determined steps, Marianne made her way to the imposing desk. The globe atlas on the blotter rattled as she yanked on the top drawer. To her surprise, it slid open. A quick rummage through each of the drawers revealed why: there was nothing out of the ordinary within.

Blowing out a breath, she surveyed the room. *If I were Pendleton, where would I hide my secrets?* She went to the pair of large portraits hanging on the wall opposite the desk. The elegant, fashionable poses suggested the work of the popular society painter, Sir Thomas Lawrence. One frame portrayed her host posed with his arm upon a Greek column; the other showed his mama, a stern-faced dowager, sitting beneath a weeping willow. Running her hands along the edges of the heavy frames, Marianne found no obvious mechanisms, no hidden cache behind the paintings.

Dash it all, there has to be a clue in the study. Something hiding in plain sight ...

Her gaze returned to the globe on the desk; she suddenly recalled one that a shopkeeper had tried to sell her. *Inside is a hidden compartment, my lady, a safe for your fine jewels.* Going over, she crouched so that she was eye level with the sphere. She examined the markings on the papered surface, her fingers tracing over the lines. Her pulse sped up as she encountered a faint, nearly imperceptible groove along the Tropic of Cancer. She continued rotating the globe until her index finger landed against a notch. A locking mechanism of some sort.

She inserted her hair pin ... and the door opened behind her.

"What are you doing in here?"

She jerked away from the globe, spinning around to see Pendleton in the doorway, staring at her with cold eyes. Her heart gave a panicked lurch as he shut the door behind him and came toward her, his features carved with menace.

"M-my lord," she stammered.

"What in blazes are you doing in my study?"

She scrambled to gather her wits. She held up the hair pin, managed to keep her hand and her voice steady. "I came looking for this. It must have fallen when you showed me your study earlier." With a light laugh, she shook out her skirts. "Silly to go to all the trouble, I know, but it happens to be my favorite."

Pendleton's black gaze did not waver. "How did you get in here?"

"The door was unlocked," she lied glibly, "and I didn't want to disturb anyone over so trifling a matter, so I thought I'd take a quick peek myself. Oh dear, I hope I haven't caused any alarm, my lord?"

"That depends on whether you are telling the truth."

A tremor passed over her at her host's blunt words. *Stay calm. You've brazened your way through worse situations.* She licked her lips, gave him a look from beneath her lashes. "The truth, my lord? How very droll of you. " She managed a teasing tone. "Why ever would I lie?"

"I don't know. Then again, I don't know you well at all, do I?"

His cool consideration sent a warning chill over her skin. He took another step toward her, and she backed away, the desk's edge jamming into her spine. He raised a hand, and when she flinched, pleasure lines flickered around his mouth.

Sadistic blighter. I know your sort. I won't give you the satisfaction.

Trapped, she forced herself to remain still as his finger traced the edge of her bodice with insolent familiarity. Her skin crawled, yet she said lightly, "'Tis an oversight I am sure we can correct during this visit."

"Why not now?" Pendleton's smile was contemptuous, hard as the part of his anatomy jutting rudely against her. "That's why you're here, isn't it? For a little amusement."

"Diverting as that sounds, my lord, we could be seen. The risk to my reputation—"

"Your reputation? No need to close that barn door—the horses have long bolted." He gave a scathing laugh, and for an instant his finger dipped beneath her décolletage, causing her hands to ball. She would not blow her chances unless she had to, but if Pendleton pushed her any further ... "Little schemer, we both know why you're here." As her throat cinched, he said with a smirk, "Your charming cunt is the only reason I've allowed you to stay. My hospitality doesn't come for free: one must sing for one's supper, after all."

The reptile had crept from beneath his well-bred shell, showing his slimy self. Typical man. She suddenly flashed to Kent, and pain knifed between her ribs. *I thought you were different ...*

Resolutely, she focused on her dilemma. Her fist trembled; she wanted so badly to knock the smirk off the earl's face. But Pendleton was hiding something, she was sure of it. It behooved her to play along, to get close to him.

She flipped through her options. She'd sworn to do whatever was required to find Rosie, yet now the notion of touching a man, of letting a man other than Kent touch her ...

Damn Ambrose Kent. He's made me weak, stupid—when I vowed never to be taken in again. I must stand on my own two feet, depend on no one.

"Well? I haven't got all day," Pendleton said.

Her fist unfurled. She raised a hand to his lapel—and a knock sounded on the door.

Pendleton swore. "Keep quiet," he said. "They'll go away."

The door swung open.

"Lugo." Marianne's voice almost broke with relief as she snatched her hand away. *Thank you, old friend.* "Is something amiss?"

"A message arrived for you, my lady." Lugo met Pendleton's furious gaze with an unblinking one of his own. "It is most urgent and requires your immediate attention."

"Of course. If you'll excuse me, my lord?"

Pendleton's eyes slid from her to the imposing figure of her manservant. His lips thinned as he stepped back. "It seems we must continue this conversation at another time. Though make no mistake, my lady,"—he grabbed her arm just as she tried to slip by,

squeezing it hard enough so that she had to bite back a wince—
"we *will* settle it."

She pulled free. Though her pulse was racing, she executed a
cool curtsy. "Good afternoon, my lord."

With Lugo at her back, she exited the room.

Chapter Thirty-Three

Ambrose left Wapping Station, his heart as leaden as his steps. He told himself he shouldn't be surprised; it had only been a matter of time before Dalrymple found a way to get rid of him. His superior's smug face flashed in his head:

Had a visit from my old friend, Sir Coyner of Bow Street, and he had quite a few things to say about you, Kent. Nothing that surprised me, of course—always knew you were too big for your own boots. But bedding a suspect? Dalrymple's beady eyes had gleamed with malicious glee. *Well, that tops it all, doesn't it? Can't have such despicable behavior tainting the honor of the Thames River Police, sirrah. Pack your things, Kent—'tis the end of your time here ... and your career. By the time I spread the word, you won't be able to find a job blacking boots.*

With dusk bleeding overhead, Ambrose trudged along, his mind and heart a fracas. At least now he knew why Marianne had bolted. Somehow she'd discovered his one-time assignment with Bow Street. She'd gone to confront Sir Coyner, and the magistrate must have confirmed Ambrose's involvement.

Devil take it, how had Ambrose made such a shambles of

things? His good intentions—his desire to safeguard both Marianne and his family—had proved the old adage. He'd landed himself in hell. Because of his pride, his arrogance in believing that he could take responsibility for everything, he'd ended up hurting everyone he cared about.

He tried to reason it out: he had to find Marianne, to somehow explain that he hadn't told her the truth because he'd known how she would react. He didn't want her to push him away because he wanted to protect her, to find her daughter. In other words ... he'd lied to her for her own good.

He cringed. *Bleeding hell.*

How on earth had he convinced himself that this was a good idea?

Given all that Marianne had suffered at the hands of men, he couldn't blame her for hating him, for wanting nothing to do with him. Hell, he knew he didn't deserve her trust.

He shoved his hands into his pockets. Perhaps he'd do better to visit Coyner first and try to make amends there. Because if he didn't, his livelihood was lost. The tide he'd kept at bay battered at his defenses. He could practically feel the cold, black water closing over his head.

If you don't, the family will suffer. Em, Father, all the little ones —they'll be on the streets. All because of your failings.

"Mr. Kent! Hold up!"

The low, chuffing voice cut into his bleak thoughts. He turned to see a short, scruffy man in a weather-beaten hat hurrying toward him.

"Trout?" Ambrose said, frowning. "What can I do for you?"

"'Tis what *I* can do for *you*." Looking this way and that, Willy Trout said, "Found that cove you're lookin' for."

Ambrose stiffened. Trout had located Skinner, the Runner who had accosted Marianne?

"Where is he?" he said tersely.

"Like you said, a man never strays far from 'is 'abits. 'E's got a friend wot owns a flash house near Bottom's End. Close to all 'is vices—whores an' gin 'ouses." Shaking his head, Trout wiped his tattered sleeve under his nose. "'E's 'iding from something, that's for certain."

"Why do you say that?"

"Changed 'is name. Goes by Tanner now." Trout rolled his eyes. "An' what from I 'ear, 'e's more skittish than a virgin on 'er weddin' night. Best 'ave a care if you mean to pay 'im a visit."

Skinner was the one who needed to watch out.

Even if Ambrose's relationship with Marianne was beyond repair, this was one thing he could do for her. The only thing within his power to do that would protect her. He'd failed her once—he'd not do so again.

His hands flexed, bunching at his sides.

"Take me to the bastard," he said.

Aptly named, Bottom's End occupied one of the most wretched corners of the stews. Though the cloak of night had not completely fallen, vice already flourished in the fetid streets. Pimps occupied every corner, their expressions calculating as their whores cooed out invitations to all passersby. Drunkards stumbled in and out of the taverns, and the stench of spirits and detritus mingled sickly in the dank, stifling mist. Nothing clean or fresh penetrated the maze of narrow streets.

From an alleyway, Ambrose and Trout monitored the back of the flash house.

"Skinner should be comin' out any minute. Keeps a regular schedule, that one," Trout said.

Like clockwork, a figure staggered from the flash house. He glanced around, and apparently detecting no threats, steadied himself against the wall with one hand and unfastened his trousers with the other. Grunting, he began to relieve himself.

"That him?" Ambrose said in disgust.

Trout squinted into the darkness. Gave an affirmative.

Silently, Ambrose handed Trout a bag of coins.

Instead of taking the money, Trout tipped his hat. "This one's on the 'ouse, sir. Consider it a return for lookin' out for my brother," he said in a low voice.

"'Twas my duty—"

But Trout had melted into the darkness. Bemused, Ambrose re-pocketed the money and returned his attention fully to Skinner, who was still going strong. Devil take it, how much had the sot had to drink? After a few more shakes and grunts, Skinner tucked himself in and teetered north. Ambrose took pursuit.

Skinner wove down a lane crowded with barrows and people. The throng gave Ambrose easy cover; whenever Skinner paused, casting a bleary and furtive gaze behind him, Ambrose simply turned to inspect a display of goods or bent his head as if speaking to another in the melee. People were too half-seas over to even question a stranger talking to them, and Ambrose received several friendly slaps on the back. Finally, Skinner turned right, disappearing between two narrow tenements.

Counting to ten, Ambrose followed.

The air was choked by smoke from open grates attended by figures pickled in misery. Ambrose blinked, trying to see through the haze. He caught a movement—the tail end of Skinner's greatcoat disappearing down steps. Ambrose navigated past the homeless wretches to the place where he'd seen his suspect go. A basement tenement—a place for the lowest of the low.

Muscles coiling, Ambrose descended into deeper darkness. His grip tightened on his wooden truncheon as he found the rotting door ajar, pushed it open. Pitch coated his vision. His other senses flashed alive, the pressure in his veins building—he felt the movement before he saw it. He dodged on instinct, going low and kicking out.

He heard Skinner curse, the heavy thud of a body hitting the ground. The next instant Ambrose was atop his assailant. The other man struggled, grappling with considerable strength. A violent blow connected with Ambrose's shoulder, sending his truncheon flying. Ambrose held on, pinning the other by the neck. Panting, he raised a fist and plowed it into his opponent's jaw.

Skinner groaned, and Ambrose did it again. And again.

When the fight finally left the bastard, Ambrose reached for the pistol in his boot. He cocked it, the deadly click letting the other know he meant business. Rising, he kept his weapon aimed at the moaning figure whilst he found a lamp on the nearby table and lit it.

Shadows licked the walls of the squalid den, and Ambrose got a clear look at Skinner for the first time. With heavy jowls and a balding head, the rotter resembled a monstrous babe as he lay curled on his side, whimpering. A dark trail trickled from his nose. Rage boiled in Ambrose's veins at the thought of Skinner threatening Marianne, propositioning her. His grip on the pistol tightened.

Skinner's beady gaze widened at the sight of the weapon.

"Don't hurt me, please," the bastard gasped. "Whatever he's paying you, I'll give you double. Just don't hurt me."

Ambrose narrowed his eyes. "What the bloody hell are you talking about?"

"I know *he* sent you."

Skinner licked his lips, smearing the blood that had dripped there. He rose on his knees, and Ambrose took aim at the other's heart.

"Move another inch, and I'll shoot," Ambrose warned.

A pleading look crossed Skinner's features, his posture one of supplication rather than threat. "I won't tell a soul, I swear it on my mother's grave. Tell him I won't. His secret is safe with me."

A sudden premonition snaked down Ambrose's spine. "Tell me his name."

Skinner trembled, his gaze flitting left and right. "Are you testing me? If anyone asks, I won't breathe a word, I swear. About him and Leach. Tell him his name will never leave my lips. Just please don't kill me," he sobbed.

Ambrose brought the pistol between Skinner's eyes.

"For the last time, give me his bleeding name," he said.

Chapter Thirty-Four

Two days later, Marianne took the note from the footman and closed the door to the guest bedchamber. She scanned the brief lines.

"What does it say, my lady?" Tilda asked.

Marianne crumpled the paper. "Pendleton wants to meet me. At a clearing just beyond the woods."

Standing next to Tilda, Lugo shook his dark head. "'Tis a trap, my lady. Far too dangerous. Look what almost happened in his study—"

"I must go," Marianne said, though her heart thumped. "Hiding from Pendleton is not going to get me Rosie back. I came here to find her—and find her I will."

"Perhaps you ought to think twice, my lady." In an unusual move, Tilda cast her vote with Lugo. "There must be another way. Maybe we can get into the earl's study again ..."

Marianne shook her head. "Pendleton now has a footman stationed there around the clock. And I am certain that whatever he had hidden in that globe is long gone. No, time is running out. I must confront him before he grows too suspicious and tosses me out."

From the cold glances he'd given her over supper last night, she was certain that if she continued to avoid him, he was not going to allow her to remain much longer. The summons to the meadow was his move. She knew she would either have to play ... or go home.

Resolve bolstered her spine. Like hell she would back down. But she wasn't a fool either. Since the near disaster in the study, she'd revised her strategy. In retrospect, she'd realized that she hadn't been in her most rational mindset coming to Pendleton's—and she put the fault for that squarely on Ambrose Kent's shoulders. His betrayal had unmoored her, driven her to act recklessly. Though she could now see the danger inherent in her situation, there was no turning back.

The time for seductive wiles was over. She had to confront Pendleton and back it up with a show of force. She'd give him no choice but to admit the truth.

"You cannot meet Pendleton alone," Lugo insisted.

"I won't go unaccompanied." Going to the armoire, she removed the wooden carrying case tucked beneath her undergarments. She flipped the lid and removed the pearl-handled pistol. "I'll be bringing a companion."

Lugo shook his dark head. "And if the earl doesn't tell you what you want to know? Will you use it, then? Shoot a peer of the realm?"

"I'll do what needs to be done," she said evenly.

"Oh, my lady," Tilda said, wringing her hands, "you could hang for that!"

"I have no choice." Marianne slid the pistol into the hidden pocket of her cerise skirts. Seven years she'd spent grieving, and she couldn't stand a minute more. Her life wasn't worth ashes without Primrose ...

And Ambrose.

The unbidden addition perforated her defenses, released a hot, raw feeling beneath her breastbone. *Do not go there. Do. Not.*

"Actually, you do, my lady. Have a choice, I mean." Shifting on his feet, Lugo coughed into his fist. "There is something I should tell you."

She had a feeling she wasn't going to like it, whatever it was. She raised a brow, waited.

The manservant blew out a breath. "You could wait for Mr. Kent. He will help you."

"We've been through this before. I cannot trust—" Something in Lugo's shifting stance cut her off. A pounding started in her ears. "What do you mean *wait* for Kent?"

"I sent him word," Lugo muttered.

"You did *what*?"

"After the incident in Pendleton's study, I saw no choice. You are not yourself—not of a clear mind." He crossed his burly arms. "You need assistance, my lady, whether you like it or not. I sent the message two days ago. Mr. Kent should be arriving at any moment."

Bloody hell. Et tu, Lugo?

"And how exactly does your disloyalty serve me?" she said with furious disbelief.

"Lugo was only trying to help—" Tilda began.

"I serve you to the best of my ability," Lugo said, his gaze narrowed, "and that is why I contacted Mr. Kent. In my eyes, the man has proved himself. Whatever your current misunderstanding, he has protected you time and again. Yet you swear him off so easily."

That stung. "He was the one who betrayed *me*, the one who was lying—"

"Mr. Kent does not seem to me a man to lie without reason. Why do you not stop to think why he might have done so?"

Despite the faithless flutter in her chest, she steeled herself. She had an excellent reason not to mull over Kent's myriad possible defenses: she did not trust herself. The humiliating, reprehensible truth was that her judgment concerning men had proven her downfall. She'd been lied to, betrayed by the opposite sex too many times to count, and she had no one to blame but herself. 'Twas her weakness, her Achilles' heel—the very failing that had cost her Primrose.

And it would be so easy to succumb to Kent once again. To listen to his explanations, to open her weak and traitorous heart to him ...

"There is no excuse for deception," she said, her jaw clenching.

Lugo's gaze remained steady. "Because you have been burned before, you run at any sign of smoke. Your fear threatens your judgment in this instance. You do not ask who sent you the note about Kent's connection to Bow Street, nor do you stop to wonder why. What motive—"

"Whoever sent that note did me a favor! The fact is Kent *was* spying on me for Bow Street. Sir Coyner confirmed it."

How could she have let herself trust again? Shame clawed at her, her head throbbing with the effort to keep her failures caged. To keep the beasts of the past at bay. Yet their talons sliced into her anyway, the truth trickling darkly through.

You stupid doxy! Her father's florid face, his heavy fist. *You've made your bed, and you will damn well sleep in it* ... Draven's sneering features, his fingernails digging into her scalp. *You're nothing but a worthless whore. Your daughter is paying for your sins.* And the deal with the devil himself, Bartholomew Black: *One day soon I'll come lookin' for my due* ... Her head whirled as Skinner's, other male faces bled into one ... *Stupid cunt, you'll do as I say— submit to me* ...

Never. Her breath serrated her lungs. *Never again.*

It will be my way—or no way at all.

"My lady—"

"I'm getting Rosie back, and I'm doing it now," she bit out. "Nothing is going to stop me."

She pushed blindly past Tilda and Lugo to the door. As she strode down the hallway, she knew hell was waiting. It was no more than she deserved, and this time she would confront it or perish trying.

Ambrose sprinted through the woods, his alert gaze scanning the leafy trees and tall grasses for any sign of Marianne. Lugo caught up with him, panting.

"Where the devil is she?" Ambrose snarled.

The manservant shook his dark head, his expression mirroring Ambrose's anxiety.

Ambrose had arrived at Pendleton's estate less than a quarter hour ago, running into a panicked Lugo. Apparently, Ambrose had just missed Marianne's departure. She was supposed to be heading to the meadow to confront Pendleton. But there was no sign of her. His chest palpitated with panic.

She's in danger. Have to get to her.

"We split up." Ambrose could see light up ahead, the smooth sweep of the clearing that provided prime hunting ground. "I'll go west—you take the eastern edge. We have to find her, man."

Lugo jerked his chin, and they split off without another word.

Fear for Marianne pumped Ambrose's blood, fueled his pounding steps over the mossy forest floor. It was too quiet here— too secluded. The perfect setting for an attack. His instincts sharpened, his senses on high alert. Through the blur of the passing trees, he saw deer in the meadow, their ears pricking as he raced by.

Where the bloody hell are you, Marianne?

Then he saw her. Up ahead, her berry frock a bright splash against the greenery. She stood at the edge of the forest, at the perimeter between dark and light, and panic gave him another surge of power he didn't know he possessed. Sprinting toward her, he shouted her name. She turned, her eyes a vivid flash in her pale face.

"Stand down, Kent," she said.

He halted, paces away from her. His gaze fell on the pistol she aimed at his chest. Lungs working harshly, he said, "Marianne, come to me. Let me explain—"

"I said, *back off.* I don't want to hear any more of your lies. Now get the hell away, or so help me God I *will* shoot you again," she hissed.

He took a step closer. "Shoot me, then. But you have to listen, you're in danger—"

"No thanks to you." She cocked the pistol, her color high. "I know you were following me, I know everything between us was a lie!"

There was no time to argue with her. He made his move, lunging to capture her arm. He gave her wrist a quick but gentle twist—sufficient to make her drop her weapon, which thudded to the ground. She swore, struggling against his hold.

He kept his grip firm, growling, "'Tis Coyner who has Rosie. The bloody magistrate has your little girl, do you hear me?"

Marianne stilled, her eyes widening. "What?"

"I'll explain everything, but let us get out of here first—"

A movement flickered at the corner of his eye. His head whipped toward the meadow; his gaze honed in on a movement in the trees across the clearing. Sunlight glinted off leaves and a patch of brown hair ...

"Coyner!" he roared.

A puff of smoke erupted from the trees. Ambrose shoved Marianne to the ground, sheltering her with his body as a blast tore through birdsong—

An unholy force punched into him, throwing him backward. He landed, blinking up at the perforated canopy, blinded by the dancing light. Ringing erupted in his ears, yet above it he thought he heard his name, streams of light cascading across his face. Silken sunshine, the scent of summer rain. The leaves blurred into emeralds, and he closed his eyes, smiling, before the pain swept him up in a violent rush.

Chapter Thirty-Five

With Lugo's help, Marianne managed to get Ambrose back to the main house. Entering the foyer, she ignored the shocked exclamations from the guests, her heart thumping as she saw Ambrose's pallor, the blood soaking through his shirt.

"What in blazes is going on?" Pendleton came toward them, his voice imperious.

"A man has been shot," Marianne said through her cinched throat. "We need a room and a physician summoned immediately."

Pendleton flicked a glance over Ambrose, who lay slung over Lugo's shoulders. "The devil you say. Why should I concern myself with—"

"He was shot on your property. By Gerald Coyner—an acquaintance of yours, I believe?" she said in a quiet yet steely voice.

Color ebbed from the earl's face. He recovered the next instant, barking to one of his waiting footmen, "Get the man to a room. And send for the village doctor."

The physician arrived soon thereafter, and Marianne kept vigil by the bedside as the old man dug around Ambrose's wounded arm like a zealous miner searching for ore. She gripped Ambrose's good hand, feeling the silent shudders that wracked his body and wishing helplessly that she could somehow absorb his pain. After removing the shot and dousing the wound with spirits, the doctor produced a needle and thread. In the end, Ambrose lost consciousness—which, the medical man assured her, was a good thing.

Now, in the dark hours before dawn, Marianne didn't share the man's confidence. The candle's glow revealed the clammy cast of Ambrose's skin, and the moan that left his lips made her eyes well with heat. Not knowing what else to do, she whispered soothingly to him and reached to change the damp washcloth on his forehead. She bit her lip: the linen steamed, burning to the touch.

"Why isn't he getting any better?" she said, her voice cracking.

"The doctor said to expect a bit of fever," Tilda said from the other side of the bed. "God was watching over Mr. Kent, I reckon. The bullet would've done a good deal more damage if it'd hit anything other than flesh."

Guilt permeated every fiber of Marianne's being. As she reapplied a cooling compress, her fingers lingered against Ambrose's bristly cheek.

This was her fault. He lay there injured and in pain because of her. Once again, he'd protected her—oh God, he'd taken a *bullet* meant for her. Why hadn't she given him a chance to explain the business with Bow Street? Why had she run away rather than face the truth of her emotions? She'd feared opening her heart; now, with that organ torn wide open, she could see what lay inside. A sob hitched in her throat.

Forgive me, my love. Forgive me for being the biggest fool. You pull through this, you pull through or else—

"Why don't you take a break, my lady?" Tilda said softly. "You've been by Mr. Kent's side day and night now."

Marianne shook her head. "I'm not leaving him." *Never again.*

Tilda sighed. "I hope Lugo returns soon."

After seeing Ambrose settled, Lugo had departed for London. Marianne had sent him to gather reinforcements in the form of the Kents and Hartefords; she didn't trust Pendleton or that his reluctant hosting would last. Her fear for Ambrose led her to do what she'd never done before: she'd written Helena, begging for help. In her note, she'd exposed her secrets—her affair with Thomas, Rosie, everything. She prayed her friend would understand the urgency of the situation and not let her down.

Hearing Ambrose mumble, she leaned over anxiously.

"Yes, darling? I'm here," she said, squeezing his hand.

His thick lashes lifted, his gaze unfocused. "Coyner ... Coyner has Primrose ... must find him ..."

"Shh, my love, rest easy." Even in this state, Ambrose was worried for her daughter's safety. God, how could she have doubted him? Her throat thick with remorse, she said, "We'll find Coyner. The bastard won't get far." She pressed a kiss to his knuckles. "But for now, I want you to rest. You must get well, darling."

Lines bracketed his mouth in a harsh grimace. His enlarged pupils dimmed the brightness of his gaze, and she couldn't be sure that he saw her at all.

"Idiot for lying," he said in a thick, guttural voice. "Afraid you'd shut me out ... wanted to protect you, find your girl ..."

She'd thought she couldn't feel any more remorse than she did already. Her vision misting, she said, "Shh, love. It's alright. I understand."

"Quit ... five days. After first time together." His lashes shut, a grimace passing over his face. "Lost *everything*. Can't take care of you, my family. Sorry—"

She pressed a finger to his lips. "You have nothing to be sorry about. I'm the one who has made a mess of things. But we'll talk later, when you're well. And you must get well. Your family isn't the only one who needs you, you know." Her voice broke a little. "I need you too."

His head made an agitated movement against the pillow, and she knew he was lost to the effects of the laudanum and pain.

"Rest, darling," she whispered, "don't strain yourself any longer."

His lashes formed dark crescents against his pale skin. Though raspy, his breathing seemed to ease a little. Still clutching his hand, Marianne continued to watch over him. To watch and to pray.

"London and make haste!" the gentleman barked as he ascended his carriage.

"Yes, Sir Coyner. Straightway." With a word to the horses, the driver cracked the whip, and the conveyance lurched forward.

Only when the vehicle cleared the vicinity of Pendleton's property did Gerald Coyner release a breath. He reached for the handkerchief in his pocket, his hand shaking. He mopped his damp face and tried to calm his disordered thoughts.

Damn Kent. He's ruined everything. But he shan't have Primrose—she's mine!

How could this have happened? He'd chosen Kent because the fellow was an order-following nobody—a man whose respect for law and authority should have made him the perfect tool to be used. A soldier, stalwart and expendable. Instead of providing the evidence to frame that brazen Draven bitch, however, Kent had *saved* her time and again—and for what purpose? To lie between those well-used thighs?

Coyner shuddered with disgust. He'd make sure that the apple —the sweet, nearly ripened fruit of his eye—fell far from the tree. Primrose was the embodiment of purity, innocence. His hands grew clammier at the thought of losing her.

Not after all I've worked for, how long I've waited. Primrose is mine by right.

Rage cleared away some of the fear. He'd never give up his treasure. Did he regret that he'd now have to leave his old life behind? Perhaps. Yet he was an adaptable fellow; if he could survive Eton and his mother, he could survive this.

Thinking of the past agitated his stomach. Life was blasted unfair. Pendleton, Ashcroft, and Boyer got away with everything, whilst *he* had to toil and live in fear. Those three bastards had carried out heinous acts; they'd committed rape and buggery, had profited from the misery of others. Coyner's idea of altering the dates on Leach's receipts had been brilliant: let that Draven whore expose the men's sins, bring scandal down on their heads. Red herrings *and* justice, how perfect was that?

Yet his ploy had come to naught.

Instead, *he* was the one being persecuted and for what? All he wanted was to care for his Primrose. *Sweet flower, only you understand me. I will protect you, let nothing come between us.* When the time came, Primrose would transition from being his ward to his dutiful, loving wife. He grew hard, imagining her small body next to his. Ah, he was looking forward to a new beginning. A new life where he would be ruled by no desires but his own.

To achieve that, he'd have to make his next moves with care. He figured he had a small window of time—a day, two at most— to make his escape. At present, Lady Draven would have her hands full tending to her injured lover ... irritation nettled Coyner once more. He might have finished her and Kent off, if that giant African hadn't come running to the rescue. His stomach knotted, and he forced himself to take a breath. At the very least, mayhap he'd managed to end Kent with that bullet.

Comforted by the possibility, Coyner reviewed his plans. He'd make a quick stop in London to pick up his emergency belongings. Then he'd go pluck his pretty flower from the secret garden where he'd kept her all these years. Together, they would head to new shores and leave this cursed uncivilized place behind.

Calm settled over him as he envisioned his future with his child-bride at his side.

Chapter Thirty-Six

The world slowly came into focus. Groggily, Ambrose registered that he was lying in a strange bed. Posh furnishings, pale light seeping through a crack in the curtains, and dozing on the chair next to him ...

"Marianne?" His voice came out hoarse, slurred.

Her head snapped up. She blinked at him, her hair an untidy tumble over her shoulders. Her face blurred in and out of focus, and he tried to shake off the buffle-headedness. He felt a squeeze on his hand, her touch grounding him.

"How are you feeling?" she said softly.

"Like the devil." He grimaced as the words dragged against his dry throat. His head throbbed as if he'd consumed pints of ruin, and when he moved, fire lanced through his right arm. Breathing harshly, he looked down and saw the bandage wrapped around his bicep. It all came back to him.

Chasing Marianne down in the woods. Coyner. *The shooting.*

Fear jolted him upright. "Are you hurt?" he said tersely.

"I'm fine. After you saved me, Lugo arrived and scared Coyner off." Gently, Marianne pushed him back to the pillows. Her soft palm settled against his forehead. "The fever's only just gone down, darling, so have a care. Here, take a sip of this, and mind you drink it slowly."

Perching on the bed next to him, she held a glass to his lips. The cool water slid down his parched throat, and he couldn't help but drink greedily. When he was done, Marianne blotted his lips with a napkin.

"We've got to find Coyner—" he began.

"Easy, my love. You must rest."

"Coyner has your daughter." Urgency cleared his head. "He hired Leach to purchase Primrose from Mrs. Barnes."

"How do you know this?" she asked.

"I found Skinner, and he told me everything," Ambrose said. "When you hired him to investigate, he picked up the trail to Leach early on. He followed the solicitor around for weeks. Eventually, he stumbled upon a meeting between Leach and Coyner. He overheard the solicitor trying to extort Coyner for more money to keep the transaction for Rosie a secret."

Marianne turned pale. "Why didn't Skinner tell me?"

"Having done contract work for Coyner, Skinner knew that he was dealing with a powerful and ruthless man. That's why Skinner disappeared: he was afraid of Coyner. Of what Coyner might do to preserve his secret. Coyner killed the solicitor, and that was him in the woods." Ambrose's jaw tautened. "He's tying up loose ends."

"You hunted Skinner down ... for me?" Marianne said.

Ambrose jerked his chin. "You don't have to worry about him any longer. Now to catch Coyner, we must act—"

"Ambrose, can you ever forgive me?" He was startled to hear the hitch in her words, to see the sheen of moisture upon her cheeks. Her gaze lowered to his chest, she said, "I—I've treated you monstrously. I've been horrid to you when I should have trusted you. When all you've ever done is help me."

"No, sweetheart," he said thickly, cupping her cheek with his good hand, "I should have told you the truth from the start. That I'd been hired by Bow Street to follow you."

"Why didn't you?" she whispered.

"When I took on the assignment, I didn't know the suspect would be you. After our first time together, I went to resign, but Coyner put an end to the assignment on his own. He swore me to confidentiality, said he'd see to it that I'd never work again if I spoke of the case to anyone."

"I understand. You needed your livelihood to take care of your family. They come first and well they should," she said tremulously.

He let out a breath. "That was only part of the reason—and a smaller part than I'd like to admit. In truth, I didn't tell you because ... I was a coward."

Her brow pleated.

"I wanted to tell you about Bow Street. But I feared you'd shut me out." Shaking his head at his own folly, he said, "I wanted to protect you, to help you find Primrose, and I knew that you wouldn't trust me to do so if you learned the truth."

"Because I blew up at you?" she said, biting her lip. "For questioning Leach's clerk without telling me?"

"And because you told me how you'd been betrayed in the past. How could I expect you to trust me after all that you'd been through?" He drew another breath. "I told myself that one deception did not matter because I'd cut my ties to Bow Street and would keep you safe from that moment on. But a lie is a lie. And I beg your forgiveness, Marianne."

"I forgive you," she said quietly, "if only because my sins are far greater than yours. I should not have reacted so foolishly—going to Coyner when I should have gone to ask you directly."

"You're not to blame. If I'd told you the truth, you'd have had no cause to seek out that blackguard. He's played us all."

"What excuse did he give for having me followed?"

"Coyner claimed that an anonymous client had retained Bow Street to monitor a suspected anarchist. In truth, there was no client—Coyner had fabricated the whole story."

"Why?" Marianne whispered.

"I think he wanted to keep tabs on you. To have information that could be used to ruin your character, discredit any accusations you might level against him if you discovered his identity. I also think he meant to have you framed for Leach's murder and thus to rid himself of two problems at once."

"Did you believe him ... that I was an anarchist? I suppose given my actions, after I shot you and you found me at Leach's ..." Her gaze fell to his chest.

"After I got to know you, I knew you were no anarchist," he said.

"How can you say that? I've done such wicked things." Her throat rippled. "I've had a daughter out of wedlock, degraded myself, and committed deeds no decent woman would do."

"Always out of love." With his thumb, he edged away the tears tracking silently down her face. "Marianne, you are the bravest woman I know. You've survived, through your cleverness and wit and pure strength of will. How can I but admire you and your devotion to your daughter?"

"I don't deserve that you should be so good to me," she said, cradling his hand against her damp cheek. The expression in her eyes was so penitent and tender that his breath left him. "You are too fine a man for me, Ambrose."

"'Tis the opposite that's true. Marianne, I—"

He was cut off by voices and what sounded like a stampede from the hallway. A moment later, the door flung open, and his family flooded the chamber.

"Ambrose!" Polly dashed toward him first, and Marianne stepped aside to let her through.

"Mind you don't jolt his wound, Polly," Emma chided, following close behind.

"I am fine," Ambrose assured her.

Rising on her toes, Polly brushed a careful kiss against his cheek. "I was so scared for you," she confessed. "Lugo said you'd been shot and—"

"How are you feeling?" Violet said, trying to peer from behind the other two. "Do you need anything? We packed some food—"

"He's not going to be hungry, you silly chit. When one loses blood, the most important thing is adequate hydration. I read it in a medical book." Giving him a man-to-man look from the foot of the bed, his younger brother added, "The girls have been quite worried. But I told them you'd be alright."

Seeing the anxious line between the lad's brows, Ambrose said gently, "You were correct, Harry. I am quite well, and there is nothing to concern yourselves over."

"Now that we are here, we will take care of you," Emma said.

"Perhaps what our brother truly needs is time to rest." This came from Thea, who entered the room with their father. She smiled her gentle smile. "You must be tired, Ambrose."

Ambrose began to shake his head—and the room suddenly wavered.

"We best leave him be." Leaning on his cane, Samuel came forward and peered down at the bed. Gruffly, he said, "Do you have everything you need, son?"

"Yes. Marianne's been tending to me," Ambrose said.

Six pairs of eyes turned to Marianne, who'd retreated silently to a corner.

"Well, then. Nice to know the boy's in good hands," Samuel said.

Marianne blushed, a rare sight indeed.

"Thank you, my lady," Emma said. "You look like you could use some rest yourself. If you'll tell me what needs to be done, I'll—"

"I'm staying." Marianne's gaze met his, and he basked in her verdant warmth, his pain subsiding. "I'm not leaving him."

"Perhaps, Marianne, you might take Miss Kent up on her offer for a few minutes?"

The cultured feminine tones came from the doorway. Surprised, Ambrose looked over to see the Marquess and Marchioness of Harteford standing there. What were they doing here?

Typically the epitome of politeness, Lady Harteford ignored him and said, "I believe you and I have a matter to discuss, Marianne. In private."

Behind his petite wife, the marquess took in the scene with an impassive gaze. "I trust that you are well, Kent?" he said gravely.

"Thank you for your concern, my lord," Ambrose said, still confused. "I hope you have not come all this way on my behalf?"

"We came at Lady Draven's behest, and we've brought along Dr. Farraday as well," Harteford said.

At the mention of the famed Scottish physician, Ambrose winced. Though undoubtedly skilled—Farraday had attended to the great Wellington himself—the doctor did not possess a soft touch.

"Now that Mr. Kent is attended to," Lady Harteford said with that strange steel in her voice, "shall we find some place to talk, Marianne?"

Marianne's cheeks had lost their color. Squaring her shoulders as if preparing for battle, she said to her friend, "We'll find privacy in the garden."

Pendleton's rose garden was a formal affair. Marianne led the way to the gazebo in the far corner, away from prying eyes. From beneath the sloped, gabled roof, she had an unimpeded view of the house as well as the precise, colorful rows of rose bushes. Currently, the only movements in the garden came from butterflies and buzzing insects—the non-human kind. The houseguests were still abed at this hour.

Helena remained standing, her gloved hands curling around

the gazebo's railing. Beneath the graceful brim of her straw bonnet, her hazel eyes shone with accusation.

"Is it true what you wrote in the letter?" Helena said in a tight voice.

Shame and fear mingled sickly. For so long, Marianne had kept her secrets—even from this woman, her closest friend. Now there was no longer any place to hide.

"Yes," she said in a low voice. "I have a daughter, Helena."

"And she ... she is Thomas' child?"

Marianne swallowed. "Yes. Your brother and I ... we were together. In the months before the carriage accident."

The marchioness looked away. Marianne knew how much the loss of Thomas had affected Helena, who'd been a girl back then. An innocent who'd idolized her older brother—who'd had no idea what he and her bosom friend had been up to behind her back.

"How could you have kept this from me?" The brim of the bonnet shielded Helena's profile, yet Marianne could see the rigidity of the other's spine, could hear the anger trembling in her voice. "All these years, how could you have not said a word?"

"Because I ..."—Marianne was mortified to hear her voice crack, to feel the heat rise behind her eyes—"I just couldn't," she said helplessly.

"Do you trust me so very little then?" Helena faced her. Spots of color blazed on the marchioness' cheeks. "All my life, I have come to you. I have confided *everything*—even when it came to my marriage. Yet you ... you have kept everything to yourself! Do you think yourself so above me that I am not worthy of your trust? Not worthy of knowing that I have a *niece*, for heaven's sake?"

Remorse pounded at Marianne's temples. She shook her head. "No, Helena, it's not you. It was never you. Don't you see?" Her throat clogged. "I was ... ashamed."

"You might have come to me! I would have helped."

"How?" Marianne said thickly. "You were but a girl when Thomas died."

"But my father, surely he would have—"

"Your father knew about Thomas and me. We had approached him to ask permission to wed." Humiliation washed over Marianne anew at the memory of the tense interview. "The earl said it would be over his dead body before he allowed his heir to marry a country trollop."

Helena stared at her. "Papa said that?"

The Earl of Northgate had said a good deal more. None of which Marianne could bear to repeat to her friend. "You can ask your father, if you don't believe me." Dashing at her eyes, she forced herself to go on. "On the day Thomas died, he'd gone to see about a special license. I never knew if he'd been successful. But the way he'd tried to come home in the rain ... how fast they said he'd been driving when he lost control of the carriage—"

Marianne was startled to hear a sob. To feel her body shake with the force of it. But she made herself continue, no longer caring about the tears trickling down her face. "Thomas never knew about the babe. I didn't know myself until weeks after his funeral—the funeral that your father forbade me to attend."

"So that is why you were not there. I—I always wondered," Helena whispered.

"How could I go to your father then? He thought me a whore; he'd never believe that the child was Thomas'," Marianne said bitterly. "And he didn't even know that I was in part responsible for Thomas' death—"

Suddenly, soft arms came around her. Words offering comfort instead of blame, hatred. And Marianne felt herself dissolving, losing herself in the terrifying tumult she'd held back all these years. The emotions swept through her, and she clung to her friend like a drowning woman to a piece of driftwood.

"Oh, Marianne," Helena said in hushed tones, "how could you blame yourself for Thomas' death? 'Twas an accident. Thomas was always a dear, reckless boy, and you know it."

Fresh tears welled in Marianne's eyes. Speaking the words

aloud and hearing Helena's response let her see the truth. Yet she'd held the pain so closely and for so long that it now felt like a part of her.

Her friend sighed. "At least now I understand why you married Draven and disappeared without a word. But why did you not tell me this after Draven's death, when we reconnected in London?"

"I couldn't bear it. To speak of my shame. With Thomas ... and what I had allowed Draven to d-do ... to my Primrose ..." Marianne's voice broke again.

When her tears subsided, the marchioness drew back to look at her, and Marianne saw the moisture spiking her friend's lashes. The hazel eyes—so like Thomas'—flickered with hurt yet also warmth. Something eased in Marianne's chest, the releasing of a breath she hadn't known she'd been holding all these years. Despite what she had done, the fire of friendship had not been extinguished. Somehow it persisted, strong and true.

"I don't deserve to have you as a friend," she said, sniffling.

"Fustian. I have relied upon you more than I can say; I only wish you might have felt free to do the same." Helena sighed. "That is water under the bridge, however. What we must focus on now is getting your daughter and my niece back."

Marianne clasped the other's hand with gratitude beyond words.

"Tell me the rest, my dear. And this time," Helena said sternly, "don't leave anything out."

Chapter Thirty-Seven

A mbrose hissed out a breath as the physician secured the fresh bandage.

"That should do it," Farraday said in his thick brogue. "Right as rain now, aren't you, lad?"

Upon examining his patient's bicep, the physician had let out a string of curses. His Scottish accent had made most of it unintelligible, but Ambrose got the general gist of it. Farraday had insisted on cutting free the stitches—*Even a wee bairn knows to let such a wound heal from inside out*, he'd muttered—and irrigating the gash with a solution of salt water.

The repeated cleansings had not been pretty. Though he'd seen gruesome business in his line of work, the memory of all that blood gave Ambrose a queasy feeling; glancing at Harteford, Ambrose saw he was not the only one thus affected. The marquess stood at the window, his face pale beneath his swarthy complexion.

"Anything else you require, Kent?" the physician said, his grey brows raised.

"Thank you, Dr. Farraday," Ambrose said, "you've done quite enough."

At that moment, Marianne reentered the chamber with Lady

Harteford at her side. Ambrose noticed that both women had blotchy cheeks and red smudges beneath their eyes. The marchioness, however, came toward him with her usual warm smile.

"How are you feeling, Mr. Kent? I must apologize; in my haste earlier, I did not even inquire into your health," she said.

"Kent here has a stronger constitution than most," Farraday intervened. "I daresay all that running along the Thames does a man good. A few days abed and he'll be as good as before."

"Thank you, doctor." Marianne bestowed a dazzling smile upon the Scotsman.

The hapless man turned red beneath his sideburns. He made a precise leg, and muttering something about cleaning up, he departed.

Marianne approached the bed and, to Ambrose's astonishment, took his hand and held it, right there, in front of her friends. Yearning spun out inside him, and though he knew he had no right to want what she was giving, he grasped on tightly.

The marquess came to put his arm around his wife's waist. Oddly enough, the two did not look shocked or put off by the fact that their well-born friend was currently holding hands with a policeman. Instead, Lady Harteford beamed at him.

"Marianne has told me everything," she said, "and you are to be commended, Mr. Kent, for your efforts in locating Primrose."

"We haven't found her yet," Ambrose said grimly. "We must start the hunt for Gerald Coyner straightaway."

"Sir Gerald Coyner, the Bow Street magistrate? He has Lady Draven's daughter?" Harteford said, frowning.

"We'll fill you in," the marchioness told her husband, "but first we need to interview our host. Pendleton was previously a suspect in Primrose's kidnapping, and Marianne believes he is hiding something."

"I came to Pendleton's party because of an invitation I found in Coyner's desk. Pendleton has some connection to the magistrate," Marianne said.

"Pendleton may be able to tell us something important about Coyner," Ambrose agreed. "In the meanwhile, Lord Harteford, could you send word to London to have Coyner arrested? Your influence will hasten the process."

"I'll contact the magistrates immediately," the marquess said.

Removing her bonnet, the marchioness patted her brown curls and smoothed her pink gown. Despite her delicate appearance, her hazel eyes shone with a fierce light.

"Now we have an earl to interrogate," she said. "Wait for me here—I shall return with Pendleton directly."

When Pendleton entered the chamber a quarter hour later with Helena on his arm—or, more accurately, with his limb within the lady's firm grip—he ignored Marianne completely.

"Harteford, I just ran into your wife. Well met," Pendleton said with a stiff nod, "though, of course, one regrets the circumstances."

Expression aloof, the marquess inclined his head.

"Now Mr. Kendrick, is it?" the earl said.

"It's Kent," Ambrose said flatly.

"Whatever. I do hope you are feeling more the thing." The earl's thin lips curled into what was possibly supposed to be a smile. "Would have come by earlier—but duties as a host and all that. This is, after all, my largest hunting party of the year."

"I'm sorry my getting shot inconvenienced you." Marianne could see the muscle ticking along Ambrose's jaw.

Pendleton frowned. "No need to get testy, sir. Need I remind you that you were trespassing on my property? Not my fault you got in the line of fire—the meadow is prime hunting ground. You should have watched where you were going."

"'Twas no hunter who took a shot at me," Marianne intervened coolly. "Mr. Kent saved my life and in doing so risked his own. We intend to bring the shooter to justice—so you may as well cooperate and tell us all you know."

"*Me?* Involved in some sort of crime?" Pendleton shot her an affronted look. "What the devil are you talking about, you ill-bred jade?"

"I believe Lady Draven is referring to the fact that you know a man by the name of Sir Gerald Coyner," Helena said.

"So what if I do? The upstart's made a name for himself these days," Pendleton said in a nasty tone. "Self-important magistrate of something or another."

"We are investigating Sir Coyner for kidnapping and a possible murder attempt. In the course of our investigation, your name has cropped up time and again," Ambrose said.

In contrast to Pendleton's blustering anger, Ambrose exuded calm and control. Even abed, wearing a loose shirt and a bandage, he possessed far more dignity than the earl. Marianne felt a rush of pride and gratitude that he was on her side. Despite all her mistakes, her efforts to push him away, he'd remained steadfast.

Her heart squeezed. How could she be deserving of such a man?

"Apparently, you have a secret to hide, my lord," Ambrose continued. "You can either talk to us or the magistrates—'tis up to you."

"Are you threatening me, you insolent *nobody*? By God, I'll have you tossed out on your arse—"

"You had dealings with Reginald Leach. The solicitor kept files on his clients," Ambrose said.

The color drained from Pendleton's face.

"'Tis a matter of time before we discover what Leach did for you." Harteford spoke up, his voice cold. "If you cooperate with us now, your secret can remain in this room. If not ..." The marquess did not finish.

He didn't need to.

"You're *blackmailing* me?"

"We're giving you a choice," Ambrose corrected. "Whether you wish to keep your activities free from public consumption is up to you."

The earl's checkered waistcoat rose and fell with furious breaths.

"Come, my lord, your secret will be safe with us," Helena said in an impatient tone. "Much safer than, say ... with Duchess Castlebaugh? I believe she is a current guest of yours, and no one brews scandal broth like Her Grace does. Why, if she were to catch wind of your possible involvement with Mr. Kent's shooting—"

"Alright! Devil take it, I'll tell you." Pendleton glared at them all. "Though I don't know what my involvement with Leach has to do with catching Coyner."

"Leave that to us to piece together," Ambrose said. "Now your business with the solicitor, my lord?"

Silence tautened in the room. Then Pendleton snarled, "He helped me with transactions related to several properties of mine."

Marianne narrowed her eyes. "What sort of properties?"

"I have holdings in Covent Garden. And north of that," the earl said curtly.

Understanding dawned.

"You bloody hypocrite," Marianne breathed. "You sneer at trade, hold your nose at such high altitudes that it's a wonder it doesn't bleed. And all this time your wealth has come from the lowest of the low. What do you own, my lord? Brothels? Gin shops?" By the earl's florid color, she knew she'd hit the nail on the head. "Why, you're nothing more than a pimp and barkeep."

Pendleton's lips pressed in a mean line.

"And Sir Coyner? What is your relationship to him?" Ambrose said.

With clear reluctance, the earl replied, "He found out about my holdings and threatened to expose me if I didn't help him gain entrée into the *ton*. Even back at Eton, he was a pathetic little climber. We called him *Jericho*—Gerry Co., get it?—which was where we wished him." Pendleton smirked at his own cruel wit.

"You knew him at Eton?" Harteford said.

"I wouldn't say I *knew* him. My society has always been several spheres above his. He's got but a questionable speck of blue in his blood."

"I believe his paternal grandmama was the youngest daughter of the Comte Valois," Helena put in.

Marianne had to marvel at her friend's facility with titles, foreign and domestic.

"A penniless French aristocrat. And Jericho's mother was a merchant's daughter." The earl directed a hostile glance at Harteford, who returned his stare impassively. Sneering, Pendleton continued, "Little Jericho used to try to rub shoulders with my cronies and me. He was willing to do anything to fit in, which provided us with hours of entertainment."

Marianne recoiled at the earl's sadistic glee. Coyner had undoubtedly suffered at the hands of Pendleton and his ilk. Was that why he'd planted evidence on the earl?

"One time, we brought him with us to the village. There was an old tavern slattern who'd tumble anyone for a shilling. We locked Jericho in a room with her," Pendleton said with a nasty laugh, "and wouldn't let him out until he'd done the deed."

"That's despicable." Marianne's fists curled.

"It was amusing. Especially since he failed to perform. According to the old hag, his little soldier wouldn't stand to attention."

Was this humiliating episode the seed of Coyner's sickness? Or had his peers' abuses merely shaped an existing perversion? Marianne's insides wrenched with fear for Primrose.

"Were Boyer and Ashcroft part of your pack?" she asked.

"How did you know?"

"Call it a good guess." Marianne exchanged grim glances with

Ambrose. Pieces were falling into place. "Is there anything else you can tell us?" she pressed. "If Coyner kidnapped a child, where would he take her?"

"How the devil am I supposed to know? As I've said, he's no friend of mine." Bristling, Pendleton drew himself up. "I've told you what you wanted to know—I trust I can rely on your discretion."

It took everything Marianne had not to spit at the blighter. At this point, it'd do no good.

"If you'll excuse me then, I have guests to see to." His composure regained, the earl exited the room with his nose held high—though, perhaps, not as high as before.

Harteford spoke first. "Pendleton's a sick bugger. But he gave us useful information."

"We have a motive for why Coyner framed the others," Ambrose said, his eyes narrowed, "and why he led Marianne here. He planned to kill her and make it look like a hunting accident on Pendleton's property."

"We must find Coyner straightaway," Helena said with a shudder.

"Let us leave for London immediately," Ambrose said.

"You cannot travel in your condition." Looking at her lover, Marianne bit her lip. "You have done too much for me already. I cannot allow you to compromise your health further."

"I'm fine," he said stubbornly. "There's no time to waste—"

"Marianne is right," Helena chimed in. "You cannot be moved, Mr. Kent, at least for a few days. Harteford, you'll take Marianne back to London and begin the search, won't you?"

"What about you, love?" the marquess said, frowning.

"I shall keep Mr. Kent and his family company until he is ready to make the journey back. And I will ensure that Pendleton continues to extend his hospitality to us all."

"I am ready to leave—"

Marianne quieted Ambrose's protest with a finger to his lips.

Looking into his mutinous eyes, she murmured, "Please, do this for me. I couldn't bear it if anything happened to you, my darling."

He stilled at her words, his breaths turning shallow. In that silent exchange, she willed him to know what was in her heart— even if she couldn't yet say it aloud. She flashed to her bargain with Black, and her insides constricted. The future lay so uncertain before her ... she must focus first on Rosie and deal with all else later. In the interim, she would not make promises to Ambrose that she could not keep. It was the least she could do ... for the man she loved.

To Helena, she said softly, "You'll take good care of him?"

"Of course," her friend said with a smile.

As Harteford put his arms around his wife, murmuring his goodbyes, Marianne bent toward Ambrose.

"I'll miss you," she said tremulously.

"And I you, *selkie*. Don't do anything reckless, you hear?" Though his tone was stern, his eyes were warm. "I'll come as soon as I'm able."

His good hand closed on her nape, pulling her down for a kiss. The contact of their lips was searing and filled with a sustaining sweetness. For those few moments, she basked in his strength, knowing she would need it to see her through the days ahead.

Chapter Thirty-Eight

Marianne paced the length of her drawing room, waiting for Harteford's arrival. He'd dropped her off at her townhouse the night before, promising to return in the morning with news. Seeing the carriage pull up, she raced into the foyer. Lugo opened the door, and the marquess entered, looking more severe than usual.

"Have you any news from the magistrates?" Marianne said. "Where is Coyner?"

"No one's seen hide or hair of Coyner," Harteford said. "He hasn't gone into the Bow Street office. The magistrates interviewed the servants at his home. They say they last saw him two days ago, when he showed up briefly and left again without a word."

"But where is he now? Where is my daughter?" Marianne's voice rose in desperation.

"Kent gave me the name of a contact—we'll have a list of Coyner's properties by the end of the day. Do not fret, we'll find him."

"I cannot just sit on my thumbs and *wait*."

"As a matter of fact, we're not going to wait. We're going to

Coyner's townhouse," the marquess said. "I've arranged for Sir Richard Birnie to meet us there."

Sir Birnie, the Chief Magistrate of Bow Street and an influential figure in law and politics, had a reputation for being impartial to the point of ruthlessness when it came to upholding the law. Last year, he'd been instrumental in foiling the so-called Cato Street Conspiracy. Birnie's investigation had resulted in death sentences for some of the anarchists and transfer to penal colonies for the others.

Birnie detested those he viewed as anti-establishment. Recalling Coyner's ploy to label her as an anarchist, Marianne experienced a stab of worry. Her reputation was not the most sterling to begin with; garnering Birnie's support would be no easy task.

"Are you certain he's willing to hunt down one of his own?" she said.

"Birnie will not allow Bow Street's reputation to be tarnished. If he believes Coyner to be guilty, he will help us," Harteford said.

When they arrived at Coyner's snug Kensington residence, the butler informed them that Sir Birnie had already arrived. They were led to the parlor, where the Chief Magistrate sat at an oval dining table, questioning a young maid who stood before him. At their entry, Sir Birnie rose. Though short and stocky, he wore a mantle of importance. His dark hair was pomaded into precise waves, his ensemble as somber as, well, a judge's. Marianne put him in his mid-thirties, yet his grave manner made him appear older.

"Good morning, Lord Harteford. Lady Draven." Birnie bowed, a gesture more impatient than refined.

"'Tis a pleasure to meet you, Sir Birnie. Thank you for taking time out of your busy schedule to assist in this matter," Marianne replied.

"When a matter involves Bow Street's reputation, I make time."

Birnie's assessing glance spoke volumes. He was willing to do what it took to clear his agency's name of wrong-doing, yet he remained suspicious of her. Or perhaps he held her responsible for causing her own misfortune. Marianne steeled herself; it didn't matter what Birnie thought of her, as long as he helped in the search for Primrose.

"As I arrived early, I have begun the interrogations. This is Lucinda, Sir Coyner's housemaid." Birnie sent the girl a disgruntled look from beneath his straight brows. "She can't seem to recall anything of use whatsoever."

Given that the girl was trembling like a willow, Marianne wasn't surprised. "Lord Harteford, wasn't there something you wished to discuss with Sir Birnie? Perhaps while you gentlemen talk, Lucinda and I might have a word to ourselves."

The Chief Magistrate frowned, but Harteford caught on and gestured toward the doorway. "I'd hoped to review a few details. After you, Sir Birnie?"

Left with the maid, Marianne pulled a chair out from the table. "Perhaps you'd care to have a seat, Lucinda?"

"Yes, m'lady," the girl mumbled.

Marianne took the seat next to her and reached for the tea pot. "Tea?"

The maid gave a hesitant nod.

Pouring out two cups, Marianne passed one to Lucinda, who looked scarcely older than sixteen. She waited until the girl had taken several gulps of tea, then she pushed over the plate of biscuits as well. After a moment's pause, the maid took one and polished it off.

"Have you been working for Sir Coyner long, Lucinda?" Marianne asked.

The girl's ginger curls wobbled beneath her cap as she shook her head. "No, m'lady. I wouldn't say so. Less than a year, it's been."

"Do you like your job, Lucinda?"

"I'm glad to 'ave a position, m'lady."

Glad but not particularly thrilled, Marianne guessed. It would help that the maid didn't harbor undying devotion to Coyner. "When did you last see your employer?"

"Two days ago. But I didn't see 'im,"—the maid's forehead scrunched—"only 'eard from the butler that the master was back. Before I could bring up the tea, 'e was off again and without a word as to when 'e'd be back."

Marianne's hands clenched in her lap. By the sound of things, Coyner had been in a rush—picking up a few things for the flit, no doubt. She had to learn more about him: his patterns, where he might go.

"During your time here, what have you noticed about your master's comings and goings?"

Eyeing the biscuits, Lucinda shrugged. "'E's like any other gent, I suppose. Comes and goes as 'e pleases."

The maid's fingers crept toward another biscuit, and Marianne gave her an encouraging smile. "Was there any particular pattern to his activities?"

"Mostly 'e stayed in London. But ev'ry month 'e took off for a few days," Lucinda said as she chewed. Marianne's heart thudded faster. "Ne'er said where 'e was goin', o' course."

"You haven't any idea where he went?" Marianne persisted.

Lucinda dusted the crumbs from her fingers. "None o' my business. None o' the servants knew much 'bout the master— except maybe the groom. 'Is lips are sewn tighter than a seam, seein' as 'e's been with the master for years."

The groom was currently chauffeuring Coyner's getaway, so no help there. Thinking quickly, Marianne switched to a different tactic.

"What about when Sir Coyner was here at home? What was he wont to do?"

"Not much. The gent's not the carousin' type. Mostly 'e spent time in 'is study—sometimes I think 'e slept in there."

"What makes you say that?"

Lucinda gave her a wry look. "The sheets on 'is bed weren't touched when I went to change 'em in the mornin'."

Interesting. Marianne would have to investigate Coyner's study next. "What about visitors? Who came to call upon your master?"

"'E was a private sort. Didn't 'ave much in the way o' friends. Once in a while, one o' the Runners might drop by, but 'twas always for work." Lucinda's tone drifted into a wistful range. "Those Runners are a dashing lot, ain't they?"

Marianne stifled a sigh. She wouldn't get much more from the maid. "Thank you, Lucinda," she said. "Could you show me the way to the study?"

Out in the hallway, Marianne met up with Harteford and Sir Birnie, and the trio followed Lucinda to Coyner's study. Cramped and furnished in a Spartan fashion, the square chamber was no more than fifteen feet across. It housed only a desk and a single wingchair by a small grate. Bookshelves covered one wall of the room, making it seem even smaller.

Marianne surveyed the close quarters. "According to Lucinda, Coyner spent most of his time in here. Doing what, I wonder?"

"Working? Reading?" Birnie grunted as he looked over the desk. "Can't fault a man for that, can we?"

Joining him, Marianne saw nothing out of the ordinary on the blotter: a small brass statue of a horse stood on its surface next to a folded newspaper and an inkwell. She opened the single drawer and found a few pieces of parchment and an assortment of writing instruments. Seeing a crumpled ball in the back corner, she fished it out and smoothed it flat.

She read the two sentences aloud. "*Endeavor to show indefatigable courage. The implacable receive their just rewards.*" She paused. "What in blazes does that mean?"

"The words of an ambitious man," Birnie said, shrugging.

Leaving the paper on the desk, Marianne circled her gaze

around the chamber once again. Something felt wrong about the stifling space. It was too small, too neat—too perfect for a man who had as much to hide as Gerald Coyner.

"The maid said he oft *slept* in here," Marianne said slowly. "Where would he do that? There's not even a sofa."

Harteford paced the length of the room, and she could tell he had hit upon the same notion as she had. He stopped in front of the bookshelves. Clearing a few volumes, he reached in and knocked against the wood. A hollow sound emerged, and Marianne's pulse sped up.

"Could be an antechamber behind the shelves," he said.

Marianne rushed over, running her hands along the book spines. "How do we get inside?"

Together, they began to remove the volumes. When the books lay in heaps upon the floor, they examined the seams where the shelves met the wall. Neither found a hidden latch or anything that would provide a way to get inside.

"There's something behind here, I know it," she said with mounting frustration. "We need to get the proper tools, a saw or a—"

A creaking noise cut off her words. To her astonishment, an entire section of the shelves parted, swinging inward like a door. Her gaze shot to the Chief Magistrate, whose hand rested on the brass horse statue on the desk. He twisted it another quarter turn and the gap in the wall widened further.

"An ingenious design. Seen a few in my time," Birnie said by way of explanation.

Taking a breath, Marianne entered the hidden chamber. The space was dark, the air heavy. A light floral perfume tickled her nose, and she squinted in the gloom, making out vague shapes on the walls. A match rasped behind her. She blinked in the flaring brightness ... and the air rushed from her lungs.

Pain, shock, longing. Feelings exploded from the locked box within her as she regarded the portraits of her daughter. For 'twas undeniably her girl—her own blond tresses and green eyes glowed in the swirling oils. Within the four gilded frames, her little girl, captured at various ages, beamed down at her.

"Primrose," she said in a broken whisper.

"My God." Sir Birnie's choked exclamation came from behind her.

Marianne walked over to the closest portrait—which showed Rosie at the age of five or so—and ran trembling fingers over the smooth ripples of paint. Her lashes grew damp. Her intuition—her maternal knowledge—had always been right.

Her babe was alive; her babe needed her.

She faced the Chief Magistrate. "You believe me now?" she said in suffocated tones. "Coyner has my daughter—has had her all these years. We must find him."

Shock edged Birnie's features. Clearing his throat, he said, "Dear lady, if I had known, had suspected that Coyner was capable of ..." He broke off, shaking his head. "Rest assured I will do everything in my power to see your girl returned to you. You have Bow Street at your disposal. And I will personally offer a substantial reward for the capture of this nefarious criminal."

"We'll get the Thames River Police on this as well," Harteford said. "I'm acquainted with the Chief Magistrate at Wapping, and I'm sure he will want to join the effort, especially since one of his finest was shot by Coyner."

How she wished Ambrose was here at the moment. Marianne gave a tearful nod.

"In the meantime, we'll go through Coyner's personal effects and search for clues as to his whereabouts," Birnie said.

"Thank you both," Marianne whispered.

She went to the last painting in the line. Judging by Rosie's age in the portrait, it could not have been done long ago. Seeing the small gold placard affixed to the bottom edge of the frame, she leaned closer.

Her blood turned to ice as the words beneath her daughter's image became clear.

Lady Gerald Coyner.

Chapter Thirty-Nine

Three days later, Ambrose arrived in London. It was past nine in the evening when he and his family entered the townhouse. They were met at the door by Lugo, who informed them that Marianne was currently out but would be returning soon. Seeing his family's yawns and drowsy faces, Ambrose sent them all off to bed. He lingered in the foyer with the manservant.

"I'm surprised you made it back so soon," Lugo remarked. "Is your injury healed?"

"Healed enough." In truth, Ambrose's arm throbbed like the devil after the jostling carriage ride, but he didn't give a damn about the pain. "How is she, Lugo?"

Lugo filled him in on the progress that had been made. Some of Ambrose's worry eased when he learned that Bow Street and the River Police were now involved in the search for Coyner. A question remained in his mind, however.

"There's something I wanted to ask you, Lugo."

"Sir?"

Ambrose eyed Marianne's loyal servant, who stood tall and

staunch—a soldier no different from himself. He cleared his throat. "Why did you send me the note telling me that she had gone to Pendleton's?"

"I've known my lady for a while now," Lugo said. "I know when she is in over her head."

"And you trusted me to help her?"

"Took a bullet for her, didn't you?"

Ambrose grimaced. "Wasn't the first time, either." And not the last, if it came to that. He'd protect Marianne to his dying breath.

"Not my place to say, but she could do worse than you." A quicksilver smile flashed across the other man's ebony features. "Had a guest chamber set up for you. The one next to my lady's."

Heat crept over Ambrose's jaw. "Yes. Well."

He was saved from saying more by the sound of footsteps. He reached the door in several strides and yanked it open. Marianne's startled gaze met his.

"You're back," she said tremulously. Her eyes fell to the bandage bulging beneath his sleeve. "Oh, Ambrose—"

He pulled her inside. Pulled her close. Her hair smelled like jasmine and sunshine, and he hadn't realized until that instant how much he'd missed her. *Everything* about her—her unique scent, how soft she was, how perfectly she fit against him.

Letting out a quivery breath, she rested her head against his good shoulder, her arms circling his waist. For several long moments, they simply held onto one other. Out of the corner of his eye, Ambrose saw Lugo begin a quiet retreat.

Marianne lifted her head. "Lugo?"

The African paused. Turned. "Yes, my lady?"

"I wanted to say ... thank you." She smiled at him. "For your wisdom, dear friend. For making the right choice when I was too blind and stubborn to do so."

"You have my gratitude as well, sir, for keeping your mistress safe." Ambrose gave the other man a wry grin. "'Tis a monumental task not many would have been up to."

Lugo scratched his head. Shifted his boots. Then, with a quick nod, he continued on his way.

"It felt like weeks being apart from you, Ambrose," Marianne said, tipping her head back to look at him. "There's so much I have to tell you. Where is your family?"

"They wanted to wait up for you, but they could scarcely keep their eyelids open so I sent them to bed." Ambrose pressed a kiss to her forehead. "Lugo provided a summary of the last three days, but I'd like to hear it from you."

"Let's talk upstairs." The husky timbre of her voice heated his insides.

He cleared his throat. "My room or yours?"

"I'll have my bath and come to you," she murmured. "Wait for me?"

Wait? Only forever.

Silently, he held out his hand, and fingers linked, they mounted the steps.

A little while later, Marianne entered the adjoining suite where Lugo had conveniently placed Ambrose. Wryly, she reflected that for the African, this gesture was tantamount to giving Ambrose a hearty male slap on the back. Lugo approved of Ambrose—and the manservant did not approve of many. Men of a taciturn feather, she supposed.

Her humor evaporated at the sight of Ambrose sprawled on the divan before the fire. Despite his injured arm, he'd managed to get his clothes off and donned the black silk dressing robe she'd left out for him. His hair was damp and curling from the bath he'd taken as well.

At her approach, he rose immediately, and her heart fluttered as readily as a debutante's. Dash it all, he was so *fine*. She adored his lean toughness and his long, loose-limbed stride as he came toward her. She couldn't help but allow her gaze to linger at the V of his robe, which offered a tantalizing view of his chest. Beneath her peach dressing gown, her nipples budded at the memory of the exquisite scrape of that hair-roughened skin.

He cupped her jaw, and she rubbed her cheek against his callused palm, feeling the strength of his touch. The honesty and gentleness.

"You look tired," he murmured.

Honest to a fault, her policeman. Smiling, she said, "We haven't seen each other for days, and that's the best compliment you could come up with?"

"It was meant to be an observation, not a compliment." His eyes crinkled at the corners in the way she loved. "Vanity, thy name is woman. But if you must,"—with a swiftness that stole her breath, he yanked her against him—"*here* is your compliment."

"Oh," she sighed. His unmistakable tribute pressed against her belly like an iron bar; her thighs trembled. "I do believe that is the *largest* compliment I have ever received."

"I plan to flatter you all night long." His gaze reflected the intimate warmth of the candlelight, and his mouth crooked up at the edges. "But first we should talk."

She blew out a breath, her blood humming. "Yes, we should."

They went to the divan. He settled her on his lap, and in a precise manner, she reviewed the events of their time apart, including what she'd discovered in Coyner's secret antechamber. She told Ambrose that his contact, Willy Trout, had provided a list of Coyner's holdings: three of the properties were within two to three days' travel from London. Runners and River Police had been sent to investigate each estate, and Marianne expected to hear from the scouts on the morrow.

"You're certain that Coyner left London?" Ambrose said.

Marianne nodded. "If he were here in town, Gavin Hunt's men would have found him. Hunt runs half the stews, and Percy volunteered his services to us."

Ambrose's lips twitched. "The bigger they are, the harder they fall," he said. His arms tightened around her. "It seems we must wait to make our next move. How are you holding up, sweetheart?"

"Seeing those portraits of Primrose ..." Marianne's throat clogged. Every night since, she'd dreamed of her daughter. Saw herself following the sound of Primrose's sweet laughter down a shadowy corridor, knives of panic twisting in her chest as the laughter turned to screams and all she could do was shout, *I'm coming. Wait for me ...*

She blinked away the despair. "I can't fail her again, Ambrose. I can't."

"We're getting close to Coyner. We'll find him." With his thumbs, Ambrose wiped away her tears. "I won't stop until we do."

Shaking her head, she said, "Why are you so good to me?"

He touched her cheek. "You deserve to be happy."

His sincerity made her go softer than the center of Monsieur Arnauld's soufflés. Desires trembled inside her, yet so many obstacles stood in her path. First and foremost, she had to regain Primrose. She could not even think of her own selfish needs until her daughter was safe once more. God willing, that would be soon—but after that there was still the business with Bartholomew Black. The bargain she'd signed with her soul. Her skin crawled at the memory of the instruments of degradation he'd had mounted on his wall.

No matter what she desired, she couldn't escape the darkness of her past. She hadn't the freedom to offer fidelity or commitment. Her future remained uncertain, her ability to give anything beyond the moment curtailed. Yet she needed Ambrose, needed his strength and his warmth though she had no right to ask for any of those things.

So instead, she showed him with a kiss. Cupping his jaw, she poured all she could not say into that hungry meeting of lips. Her heart's yearnings broke free as his tongue stroked hers, his hand closing fiercely in her hair. The kiss turned ravaging as if he, too, sensed the tenuousness of this moment and wished to lay claim to it. Moaning, she shifted onto her knees, straddling him. She kissed his jaw, nipped the tough tendon of his neck, her hands wandering feverishly—

He jolted against her, an oath hissing between his lips.

"Lud, I'm sorry!" Her hand flew from his wounded arm where she'd unthinkingly gripped him. Dash it, how could she have been so careless? "Are you alright? Did I hurt you—"

"'Tis nothing. Carry on," he said.

Yet she could see the raggedness of his breath. Remorse flooded her, streams from past and present. She tried to wriggle off his lap, but his hand clamped on her waist.

"Let me go. I don't want to injure you further," she said in a suffocated voice.

"You're not injuring me. But you will if you don't stop moving about."

She stilled instantly. "I'm hurting you?"

"Absolutely." His eyes gleamed like molten amber. "My cock aches like the devil."

The truth of his words poked through her panic ... literally. She became aware of his manhood, rigid as a steel pike, thrusting against her lower belly; only thin silk separated her flesh and his. Lust shivered over her. Yet she could not quell her anxiety—or her guilt over how she'd treated him.

Ambrose deserved more. He deserved a woman who didn't have a wicked past and an uncertain future. He deserved a good woman who could love him with a heart that was pure and whole.

"I'm sure you are fatigued from your journey." She dropped her gaze. "You shouldn't overtax yourself when you are still healing."

His grip on her loosened. She took the opportunity to slide off him, getting to her feet. He watched her with hooded eyes.

"You're right," he said finally. "I am tired."

She fumbled as she tried to tie the belt of her robe. "Yes, well, it's hardly a surprise—"

"I'm tired of you hiding from me. Of seeing you ruled by the past. Why do you castigate yourself when you are the most courageous woman I know?"

Her vision shimmered. How did he always read her so well?

"Old habits die hard," she said, her throat constricting.

He studied her. "There's a cure for that."

"Really," she said skeptically.

"There is. But you'll have to listen to me for a change," he said. "Take my instruction."

Her brows rose. *Instruction?*

"Take off your robe," he said.

The calm command sent a delicious shiver over her. Everything female in her responded to the authority, the hunger in his eyes. When her steady, principled Mr. Kent shed his civilized skin, she could never resist him. Wistfully, she realized that she didn't want to. Her fingers slipped into the knot. Untying it. The silk slid off her shoulders and pooled at her feet.

"You're beautiful, *selkie*," he said, "all the way through. You know that, don't you?"

When he looked at her that way, she *felt* beautiful. Not just on the outside—but inside, where the ugliness festered. The shame, guilt. So much regret. Yet he had seen that part of her, and he still thought her deserving of happiness.

"Come to me," he said.

She chose to obey his order, her nerves sparking. Who knew it would be so exciting to let a man take charge? To trust him enough to submit to his command? With each step, her anxiety about the future abated as the warm approval in his eyes enveloped her. As she let herself sink into the certainty of the moment, the now that was everything. She stopped an inch away from his large, bare feet.

He untied the belt of his robe. The black silk parted, and she licked her lips at the sight of his cock. It was big, thick and heavy. So turgid that it curved upward, the broad crown brushing just below his navel. Her intimate muscles quivered as he gripped himself, his long fingers barely circling the girth.

"See how hard you make me? How badly I want to be inside you?"

His bluntness made her cheeks flame and her sex grow wetter.

"I want you inside me," she said.

His nostrils flared, and she saw his cock jerk in his fist. "Are you wet enough for me? I'm quite large at the moment, and I don't want to hurt your sweet little pussy."

Her breathing quickened as she realized what he was telling her to do. She loved this side of him—the challenging, wicked gleam that replaced his usual sensible gaze. With deliberate slowness, she brought her hand to her belly. She traced a path down the soft slope and saw how this made his cockhead bulge in his grasp. At her sex, she paused before running her middle finger through the damp curls.

"I'm wet," she said throatily, "drenched for you."

He watched her, his chest heaving, his hand stroking up and down his straining cock. "Just to be sure, I want you to touch yourself for me. Yes, sweetheart, just like that. You know just how to pet your pussy, don't you?"

She moaned as her fingers swirled against her own wet flesh, finding the lovely peak where her pleasure gathered.

"Have you done it before? Touched yourself thinking of me?"

"Yes," she sighed, "oh Ambrose, yes."

"Good. I want you to be pleasured, thinking of me." Removing a French letter from his robe, he sheathed himself slowly, letting her see the pleasure that awaited her. "When I frig myself, I think only of you—of how sweet and brave you are. How I die every time we fuck."

His words drove her over the edge. The orgasm hit her, her

knees buckling. He caught her, pulling her astride him. Before she had time to regain her breath, she was spread across his hard thighs, his cockhead stretching her still quivering entrance.

Oh God. He was big. So hard.

"You're beautiful, inside and out." His eyes burned with a dark flame. "Say it, Marianne."

"I ... I'm beautiful."

"You're worthy of happiness," he said sternly.

Her throat worked. "I am. I know I am."

"And you're mine."

A wistful breath left her. "Yours ... for tonight."

He regarded her intently. Small lines fanned from his eyes.

"I love you," he said.

Shock and joy ricocheted inside her. Before she could react, he gripped her hips. He thrust upward at the same time that he pulled her down with ruthless force. She screamed with pleasure at the bold impalement.

"Ride me. Move on my cock, sweetheart," he ground out.

She obeyed. Her pussy rippled as she adjusted to his thickness. To the bliss pounding in her heart. *I love you.* A gift he'd given to her freely, no strings attached. How she yearned for the freedom to reciprocate. Her chest throbbing with emotion, she rose on her knees, then sank fully down upon his prick. He groaned as she took every inch of him, showing with her body what she could not give in words.

"Somehow I knew you'd like being on top." Though his voice was ragged, his lips quirked. "Lean forward, love ... you'll like that even better."

Placing her palms on the divan's edge behind his shoulders, she rocked on him again, and she gasped as sparks showered through her sex. She repeated the motion, moaning as with each rise and fall his shaft rubbed against her pearl. His lips closed over a nipple, licking, sucking, and the sensations shot straight to her womb, adding to the clenching delight. She thought it couldn't get any better until suddenly his hips surged upward, his cock butting an exquisite spot.

Lights danced before her eyes. "*Ambrose, my God—*"

"Goddamn, you're gripping me like a vise," he groaned. "I can't last much longer. Come for me, sweetheart."

His hands gripped her bottom, holding her prisoner to his ravaging cock. He slammed into her again and again. Her spine turned molten, and she dissolved in a hot rush of sensation. Pulse after pulse of pleasure traveled through her groin, catching fire in her belly, and she exploded, flew apart in sparkling, white-hot shards.

Strong hands lifted her, tossed her onto the cushions. Breathless, she lay on her back as Ambrose stood over her. His neck corded, he tore off the French letter and fisted his cock.

"Do you want to feel me?" he rasped.

Floating in the aftermath as she was, she nonetheless felt a primitive quiver. Because she knew the answer. She *craved* his heat —wanted to absorb his essence into her very soul. His nostrils flared when she cupped her breasts, creating a valley between them.

"Here," she whispered. "Come to me here."

He was magnificent in his pleasure, all lean, quivering muscle, his eyes piercing and locked on hers. His passion brimmed as keenly as her own, and it was a bright, beautiful thing. One, two, three strokes and his spine bowed. His face tightened in a harsh grimace. He shouted out as his release arced from his cock and rained upon her skin.

A spatter landed on her right nipple, coating the sensitive peak. She touched the creamy essence and brought her finger to her lips, humming as his musky taste warmed her senses.

Groaning her name, he collapsed next to her and pulled her into his arms. "You'll be the death of me, woman."

"Perhaps the reverse is true. Here I was thinking you were a nice man, Mr. Kent," she murmured.

"Not *too* nice, I hope." She felt the shape of his smile against her cheek. "After all, my lady, I wouldn't want to bore you with my dull Johnny ways."

Chapter Forty

The following morning, Ambrose looked at the group assembled in the breakfast room. The Hartefords occupied one end of the table whilst Miss Percy Fines and Gavin Hunt perused the sideboard together. Percy's mother occupied a chair next to Ambrose's father; the two appeared to be hitting it off. Samuel fed biscuits to the fat pug in Mrs. Fines' lap whilst the good lady went on about the details of her daughter's upcoming nuptials.

Despite the jovial chatter, an air of anticipation hung over the room. Marianne's friends had come to offer support and assistance; the scouts who'd gone to investigate Coyner's estates were due to return today. For purposes of minimizing the mayhem, Ambrose had asked Emma to keep their siblings occupied elsewhere.

Marianne sat next him, picking at her plate. He placed his hand over hers on the table, squeezing it, and she glanced up at him. Anxiety darkened her eyes.

"It'll be alright," he said. "One way or another, we'll find Coyner, love."

Her chin trembled, and she nodded, her hand clinging to his.

"Magistrates have scoured the city, so at least we know Coyner isn't here," Harteford said over his coffee cup.

Hunt snorted as he held out a chair for his betrothed. "Bunch of Charleys, what do they know? But Harteford's right. Coyner's done the flit. My men have combed London, and there's no sign of the bug—"

Mrs. Fines coughed loudly.

Hunt's scarred face reddened as he darted a glance at his future mama-in-law. "Er, I mean we haven't seen any trace of Coyner," he muttered, sitting down.

"If Mr. Hunt says Coyner's not here, then we'd best look elsewhere," Miss Percy said. "Mr. Hunt is ever so clever, and he knows practically every inch of London, don't you, sir?"

If possible, Hunt turned redder at his intended's praise. He gave a gruff nod.

"Let us hope that one of the scouts brings us good news. I have been thinking," Lady Harteford said, her hazel eyes narrowed, "that if I were the villain, surely I would not feel safe remaining in the country."

Ambrose had been working on the same hypothesis. "You mentioned, my lady, that Coyner has French relatives?"

"The Valois, on his grandmama's side," she replied. "I did a little digging on my own."

"Do you think he'd take my daughter to France? How would he explain her presence to his family?" Marianne said.

Silence deepened in the room as they all contemplated the possible alibis Coyner could give ... and the reality of what he intended to do to Primrose. Ambrose's hands curled into fists; he couldn't wait to get his hands on the bastard. From the grim looks on the other men's faces, they shared in that desire.

A knock resonated. Marianne spun in her chair as Lugo opened the door.

"A member of the River Police has arrived, my lady," he said.

Johnno entered the breakfast room, his cap jammed atop his

auburn mop. The tense lines on the waterman's face eased when he spotted Ambrose.

"Mr. Kent, well met." Johnno came forward eagerly. "Me and the fellows at Wapping have been wondering about you. Heard about the shooting and—"

"I'm fine as you can see." Standing, Ambrose exchanged hand-shakes. "Tell us your news, Johnno."

The waterman's gaze darted to Marianne, who remained seated with an outward air of calm. Yet Ambrose could read the anxiety in her pallor, in the way her hands clenched in her lap, and he prayed the waterman had good news to share.

"Coyner was keeping the girl up at 'is place in Northampton," Johnno blurted.

A collective breath was released into the room.

"Do you have them?" Marianne's voice quivered with tension.

The waterman shook his head. "No, milady. 'Fraid not."

Ambrose put an arm around Marianne's shoulders as Lady Harteford said sharply, "Where are they, then?"

"On the run." Johnno tore his cap off in disgust, twisting it in his hands. "The suspect must've caught wind o' trouble. I inter-viewed the servants, and they said 'e left with the little miss and 'er governess the day before we arrived." Clearing his throat, he said, "From what I was told, Coyner treated the girl like a princess. The staff believed she was 'is ward, and apparently there was nothing ... untoward 'appening. At least, nothing that the servants knew of."

A shuddering breath left Marianne. Her shoulders sagged as if she could no longer support herself. Ambrose held her tighter, willed her strength.

"It'll be alright," he said in a low voice. "We'll have her back soon." Turning to Johnno, he said, "Where is Coyner now?"

"Squirrely bastard went by a different name up in Northamp-ton, and 'e's stayed one step ahead o' us, dodgin' this way an' that," Johnno said, scowling. "Last I knew 'e was bound south through Hertfordshire. Caster's still on their tail."

"Caster is one of my men. He excels at tracking," Ambrose told the group.

"We decided I should come and tell you the news. And to see if you've any idea of where Coyner might be 'eaded. Best to 'ead 'im off at the pass," Johnno said.

Ambrose frowned. "France seems most likely. But we haven't proof." He looked to Marianne. "There was nothing in Coyner's study to indicate his intentions?"

Her celadon gaze glimmered with frustration. "We didn't find anything."

"The three of us searched thoroughly," Harteford said. "Lady Draven, you had Coyner's personal effects from his desk brought here, did you not?"

"I've gone through it all with a fine-toothed comb," Marianne said.

"I'll take a look. Fresh eyes," Ambrose said.

Marianne led the way to the drawing room. The group formed a ring around the open box on the coffee table. Rummaging through the contents, Ambrose found the sort of paraphernalia one would find in any office desk.

"That's the sum of it," Marianne said.

Ambrose continued to rifle through the objects: assorted quills, an inkwell, and sheets of blank parchment. Picking up a leather-bound notebook, he flipped through the pages and found them blank. He tossed that aside and lifted a crumpled sheet from the bottom of the box. His blood pumped with sudden ferocity.

"You found this in Coyner's desk?" he said.

"*Endeavor to show indefatigable courage. The implacable receive their just rewards.*" Marianne recited the words, her voice dull with despair.

"Well, lad?" Ambrose said to his waterman.

A grin split across Johnno's face. "Bloody hell, Coyner's headed to *Dover*."

"My thoughts exactly." Satisfaction surged through Ambrose.

"Alert the men at Wapping and let Sir Birnie at Bow Street know as well. We'll nab Coyner at the port."

"Aye, sir." Johnno ran off.

"I don't understand," Marianne burst out from behind him. "How do you know from that note that he's headed to Dover?"

Ambrose turned to her. "Because I'm a River Policeman, sweetheart." And, damn, if he wasn't grateful for his extensive knowledge of water travel in this instance. "The *Endeavor*, *Courage*, *Indefatigable*, and *Implacable* are all passenger barges. Coyner must have written this reminder when he researched his possible escape routes and then forgotten it in his haste."

"These ships, they dock at Dover?" Marianne said, sounding dazed.

Ambrose nodded. "Lady Harteford's hunch was right. Coyner is headed to France—the port at Calais, to be precise. We must stop him before he leaves our shores."

"We can take my carriage. From Johnno's information, Coyner is still at least two days' drive from Dover. If we leave straightaway, we'll get there before he does," Harteford said.

Ambrose looked to Marianne. "Can you be ready to leave in an hour?"

"Give me fifteen minutes," she said.

"We'll need to go home and arrange for the children—" Lady Harteford began, but her husband put his finger to her lips.

"'Tis too dangerous. Not to mention too strenuous for your condition," he said firmly.

The marchioness bit her lip. "But Primrose is my niece. And Marianne will need all the help she can get."

"Don't worry about that, Helena," Miss Percy chimed in. "Marianne will have plenty of assistance with Nick, Mr. Kent, and Mr. Hunt going along."

"*I'm* going?" Gavin Hunt raised his tawny brows.

"Of course you are. How else would you repay Marianne?"

"For what?" Hunt said.

His fiancée looked at him with guileless blue eyes. "If it weren't for her guidance, it might have taken me a great deal longer to realize that I'd fallen in love with you." She touched his jaw, smiling at him. "Then where would we be?"

Even fierce fellows had their weaknesses.

Hunt muttered, "I'll take my own carriage. Be faster that way."

Lady Harteford went over to Marianne and gave her a quick hug. Ambrose saw the latter cling to her friend for an instant, blond curls trembling against brown ones.

"You'll be careful, won't you, Marianne?" the marchioness said tearfully. "Know that you're not alone in this."

Marianne nodded. Her eyes met Ambrose's.

"I know I'm not alone any longer." Her gaze shifted to include her circle of friends, and she said in a tremulous voice, "With your help, I know we'll bring my daughter home."

Chapter Forty-One

With a gloved hand shading her eyes, Marianne surveyed the bustling docks of Dover at dawn. The sounds of gulls and lapping waves filled the air. The silvery fog of the night before had lifted, revealing that the ghostly behemoths along the pier were in fact sturdy ships set to sail. Dazzling white chalk cliffs guarded the calm waters. Atop the precipices, military battlements stood at the ready to ward off hostile invasions.

Ironically, the present enemy was hidden within the harbor, and the task was to prevent his escape. Frustration knotted Marianne's stomach: there was no sign of Coyner or her daughter in the busy flow of people and baggage.

"Could we have missed them?" she said anxiously.

"They're here." Beside her, Ambrose was monitoring the situation, and she took a measure of comfort in knowing that nothing would escape his vigilant gaze. "The River Police are standing by the ships, with an eye on the manifests. And the Runners are guarding all roads out of Dover. Coyner can't escape—we'll find him and Primrose."

They'd arrived yesterday afternoon and contacted the captains of the four ships. Only the *Courage* and *Implacable* made outbound voyages today, narrowing the field. They'd run over the passenger manifests of the two vessels; of course, no Gerald Coyner had been found. That would have been too easy, and Marianne expected nothing to be simple where the squirrely blackguard was concerned.

Reviewing the voyager lists of the two ships, she and Ambrose had identified the likely suspects. Amongst those were father-daughter pairs and—thanks to Johnno's information about the governess—trios that included a female companion as well. They'd given the names of those passengers to the policemen, who were supervising the boarding.

Harteford and Hunt strode toward them.

"Hunt and I checked with the businesses along the harbor and in town," the marquess said. "No one recalls seeing a little girl of Primrose's description."

"Knowing Coyner, he stayed away from public areas. He knows we're after him," Ambrose said grimly.

"He might spook when he sees the Charleys by the ships," Hunt said.

"My men are disguised as sailors," Ambrose replied.

Hunt's gaze rolled upward. "If Coyner can't spot a Charley from a mile away, he isn't half as clever as you make him out to be."

Apprehension gripped Marianne; she could see Hunt's point.

"Coyner will make a go for it," Ambrose reassured her. "At this point, he has no choice—he can't outrun us forever on British soil. His best and only chance is to head for France."

Marianne gave a shaky nod. She lowered the veil on her bonnet, and the filmy white material drifted over her face to obscure her identity. She'd dressed in a nondescript putty bombazine to blend in with the masses.

"Let's go find my daughter," she said.

They split into pairs as they'd planned. Each had with them a whistle to sound the alarm if Coyner was sighted. Harteford and Hunt went to circle the pier by the *Implacable*, and Marianne and Ambrose headed for the *Courage* at the western edge of the docks. As they neared the gleaming row of ships, Ambrose pulled her off to the side, using a stack of steamer trunks for cover.

"I can see Johnno and the lads up ahead at the *Courage*," he said in a low voice. "If you spot Coyner, you raise the alarm, do you hear? I won't be far away, sweetheart."

Because Ambrose would be too easily recognized, he'd arranged to keep watch from the deck of an adjacent ship. He'd be there, protecting her. As he'd done from the moment they'd met. Her eyes prickled with heat. He'd given her everything and asked for naught in return. Not even three simple words: ones he'd offered without condition and which she secretly clung to like some fretful child to a doll.

Her throat thickened. "Ambrose?"

His eyes continued their unceasing scan of the pier. "Yes?"

"I ..." She swallowed. "Thank you."

Before he could say anything, she lifted the veil and kissed him. Then she turned and walked steadily toward the ship. His presence anchored her every step, bolstering her strength as she went forward to claim her daughter.

Passengers had gathered near the gangway. Dozens of people—men, women, and children—milled about, their voices and the summoning bells rising in a confusing cacophony. Marianne lingered at the fringe, trying to scan the faces one by one. With the wide-brimmed hats and bonnets currently in fashion, this proved a harder task than she'd anticipated. Children, due to their shorter stature, were swallowed up in the sea of moving bodies.

She craned her neck to see the head of the line, where Johnno and another Thames River Policeman stood in seamen's garb. They had posted themselves by the roped entryway leading to the *Courage*. As boarding commenced, she saw that they were studying each passenger's face as he or she presented their ticket.

An idea struck Marianne. She loosened her grip on her reticule, letting it thud to the planks. Bending to her knees as if to retrieve it, she found a less fettered view. She focused on the shoes —on finding a pair of footwear suitable for an eight-year-old girl. Seeing a pair of tan half-boots in the right size, she rose and plunged heedlessly into the crowd. Indignant cries greeted her.

"Well, I never!"

"I'll thank you to mind your manners, miss!"

Ignoring the comments, she elbowed her way through. Her heart stopped at the sight of the little straw poke bonnet. The girl's profile was obscured by thick golden curls.

"Primrose?" she said in a shaking voice.

The girl turned, looking up with quizzical brown eyes. "Beg pardon, missus?" she said.

"Hush, Hattie." The gentleman next to the girl twisted his neck around, his weather-beaten face creased with suspicion as he looked Marianne up and down. "Haven't I told you never to speak with strangers?"

"My apologies. I made a mistake," Marianne said.

She tried to move back, but the wave of eager passengers carried her forward. She fought against the tide, trying to get a glimpse of the other children in the crowd. Through a gap, she saw a mop of blond hair ... dash it, belonging to a boy. A plain silk bonnet trimmed with daisies flashed in the distance, but auburn ringlets peeped out.

Desperation climbed; she was never going to get a clear view this way, and there was no escaping the throng. She'd have to hold on and trust Johnno and his partner to perform their duties. When she reached the head of the line, Johnno pulled her aside.

"Haven't seen 'er yet, my lady," he whispered. "The families o' three on the list are all boarded. Got a few father-daughter pairs left —'ere's one comin' up behind you."

Panic clawed at Marianne's insides. *Please be Primrose.*

She faced the pair. Her heart plummeted. The brown-haired

girl chattered happily on as her Papa—not Coyner—held out the tickets.

"Don't worry. Plenty more to go," Johnno said.

But when the last identified duo—a Mr. Yardsmith and his daughter Sally—was crossed off the manifest, worried lines fanned from Johnno's eyes.

"They're o'er at the *Implacable*. That must be it," he said stoutly.

Marianne tried to resist the despair. The fear that spilled over her insides, swamping her.

Where are you, Rosie? Please ... give me a sign. Help me find you.

"Stay here and keep an eye on the rest o' the passengers," she heard Johnno instruct his partner. "I'll take milady o'er to the other ship so we can sort this out."

Numbly, she took the waterman's arm. They navigated around the remaining crowd vying to get on board. Sunny tones caught Marianne's attention.

"*Mademoiselle,* have you ever seen a boat this large?"

Marianne's skin prickled. She halted, looking wildly into the throng. Not seeing the source of that dulcet voice, she craned her neck, her senses straining. Another voice, with a heavy French accent, drifted toward her.

"Hush, *ma petite.* We are almost there."

Heart palpitating, Marianne pushed her way into the horde. She heard Johnno call out, but she ignored him, intent on finding the origin of those voices.

Where are you, darling? Talk to me, Primrose. Talk to me ...

"I'm hungry, *mademoiselle.* Will they serve us tea on the boat?"

Marianne shoved her way toward the melodic tones. Paces away, she saw the pair. A straight-backed woman held the hand of a small girl whose head was obscured by a large straw bonnet. Marianne pushed forward, reaching out to grab the girl's arm.

The girl started and spun around, clutching a doll to her small chest. Dark brown curls kissed her forehead ... but Marianne would know those eyes anywhere. Green as spring and flecked with gold. Eyes as bright as hope itself.

"Primrose," she whispered.

The girl's gaze widened further, her rosebud lips parting in surprise. "How do you know my name?"

"Let her go!"

The heavily accented words tore into Marianne's reverie, and Primrose was suddenly torn from her grasp. The Frenchwoman inserted herself as a barrier between Primrose and Marianne. Drawn to the unfolding drama, the remaining passengers formed a circle around them.

"You leave her be." Beneath the dark brim of her bonnet, the woman's eyes snapped at Marianne. "Haven't you done enough?"

"She's my daughter. My little girl. Give her back to me," Marianne said, her voice breaking.

"Enough of this nonsense! I know what you did, you strumpet. *Monsieur*, he told me all about you." The woman's eyes were slits in her bony face. "*Putain*. You ought to be ashamed, showing your face in public."

Marianne swallowed, but she refused to be cowed by shame any longer.

Her gaze locked on her daughter's small face, she said softly, "I am your mama, and I have been searching for you for a long time. Please, come to me."

The woman turned to Primrose, saying sharply, "Do not listen to her! You and I, we are getting on that boat as your guardian instructed."

Primrose blinked, looking back and forth between her governess and Marianne. "But ... he said my mama was dead." The uncertain quaver in her voice stabbed at Marianne's heart. "That I became his ward after he rescued me from Mrs. Barnes."

"He is right. This is a madwoman, and you must ignore her falsehoods," the Frenchwoman insisted.

Marianne's mind raced. How much should she tell Primrose? She wanted to protect her daughter's innocence, for—miracle of miracles—Primrose did indeed appear innocent. Naïve, unsullied. Her eyes traveled over her daughter's healthy, glowing disposition, and she knew that whatever nefarious deeds Coyner had planned, he'd not yet put them into action.

Relief filled her like sunshine, dissolving some of the shadows.

"I'm not dead, my darling," she said huskily. "A bad man took you away from me, but I am your mama. Your hair, underneath that dye, it's golden like mine, isn't it?"

Clinging to her doll, Primrose gave a tentative nod.

"And your eyes,"—Marianne crouched so that she and Primrose were at eye level—"they're green like mine, aren't they?"

Primrose let out a shuddery breath. "Yes."

"You have a small birthmark. It's shaped like a flower. On your left knee."

"H-how do you know that?" Primrose stammered.

"Because," Marianne said in a suffocated voice, "for the first year of your life, I spent every minute with you. Before you were taken, you were my world. And even after ..."—her voice trembled as she fought to maintain her composure—"oh, my darling, there hasn't been a moment in the last seven years when I haven't yearned to have you back in my arms."

"She's telling you the truth, little miss." Marianne turned her neck to see Ambrose standing behind her. In calm, reassuring tones, he said, "I am a member of the Thames River Police. And we have been helping your mama look for you."

Primrose's lashes lifted, her chin wobbling. A single tear spilled down her cheek, and Marianne's heart wrenched. It was asking too much for her baby to understand, too much—

"Mama?" Primrose whispered.

A sob lodged in Marianne's throat. "Yes, my precious girl. *Yes*." She opened her arms.

The Frenchwoman stepped between them. "*N'attendez pas*," she said to Primrose. "These are all lies—"

Ambrose gripped the governess' arm, pulled her out of the way. "Lady Draven tells the truth. It is you who has been told the lies. Unless you want to be charged as an accomplice to kidnapping, you will tell me where your employer is."

"I will say nothing," the Frenchwoman spat.

Marianne's gaze stayed on her daughter. Her entire being shook with the need to seize Primrose up, gather her close. Yet she feared that she would frighten Rosie further.

So Marianne remained where she was, her heart and her arms wide open.

Heartbeats passed.

Then, like a miracle, her daughter ran to her.

Chapter Forty-Two

The return to London took two days. Throughout the journey, Ambrose kept close watch over Marianne and Primrose. Coyner, damn his eyes, had somehow managed to escape. Ambrose had questioned the governess, and she'd admitted that Coyner had planned to meet her and Primrose at a hotel in Calais. Sir Birnie had sent Runners to the French port to hunt Coyner down. In the interim, Ambrose remained on high alert; his instincts told him Coyner was an obsessed lunatic, one who would not easily give up on the object of his fixation.

Looking at Primrose and Marianne now, Ambrose felt a fierce surge of protectiveness. Mother and daughter sat next to one another on the carriage cushions, and with the dye removed from the latter's hair, their heads resembled two bright blooms bent together. Marianne spoke in gentle tones, answering Primrose's questions. Over and again, her hand smoothed the girl's hair as if to reassure herself that her daughter was safe in her arms at last.

Ambrose's throat thickened. By God, he'd do whatever it took to give Marianne the sense of security she deserved. To ensure that nothing and no one threatened her and Primrose again.

"Are we almost there, Mama?" Primrose asked for the umpteenth time.

"Nearly, my darling." Over her daughter's head, Marianne sent him a smile.

A sweet, sharp longing struck Ambrose. Though he had no right to hope, he nonetheless did. He told himself to focus on the future one day at a time. First things first, he had to see Coyner captured and behind bars. Then, and only then, could he broach the topic of the future with Marianne. To convince her that he could be a worthy husband for her ... and father to her little girl.

In the short time he'd spent in Primrose's company, he'd come to adore the little imp, who shared her mother's beauty and charm ... and strength of will as well. He listened with a faint smile as Marianne asked what Rosie would like to do in London, and the child rattled off a list that included everything from visiting Astley's Amphitheatre to acquiring a pretty bonnet to match her Mama's. Praise God, it appeared that Coyner's main sin—beyond kidnapping the girl—had been in overindulging her. Without a firm and steadying influence, Primrose would no doubt turn into a hoyden.

"And will Mr. Kent be staying with us too?" Primrose said.

Ambrose waited for Marianne's answer. In tacit agreement, he and she had been entirely circumspect in their behavior since finding Primrose. At the inn where they'd stayed last night, Marianne and Primrose had shared a room whilst he'd taken an adjacent one. Things were confusing enough for the little girl without her having to wonder about the state of affairs between her mother and the policeman who was guarding them.

"Would you like him to stay with us?" Marianne asked.

Primrose's nod warmed Ambrose's chest.

"Then he will, won't you, Mr. Kent?" Marianne said to him.

"If it pleases Miss Primrose," he said, inclining his head.

"And her mother," Marianne murmured.

Desire curled in Ambrose's gut.

"Mr. Kent's family is staying with us as well," she continued. "He has a sister named Polly the same age as you, and I think you two will get along famously."

"I've never had a friend. Or been around other children." Primrose's voice lost some of its cheery confidence, and her small hands clutched her ever present doll.

"You'll like Polly and my other siblings," Ambrose assured her even as he saw Marianne's lips form a tight line.

In order to spare her daughter from further trauma, she hadn't revealed the full extent of Coyner's nefarious plan. She'd said that Coyner had stolen Primrose because he wanted a child of his own. At Ambrose's urging, Marianne had warned her daughter that Coyner was a dangerous man—that whilst he might seem kind on the outside, he was not to be trusted and under no circumstances should Primrose have any contact with him. Though Primrose's brow had furrowed, she'd agreed.

Arriving at the townhouse, Ambrose disembarked first, and when he found no sign of threat, he escorted Marianne and Primrose into the house where his family was waiting. They were greeted with shrieks of welcome and the usual pandemonium. By the time the dust settled, Primrose stood sandwiched between Polly and Violet, her arms linked with the other girls'.

"May we show Primrose her room?" Polly said.

"We decorated it," Violet added. "Emma cut yellow roses from the garden, and Harry and I helped put up the new bed-hangings."

Marianne smiled. "How lovely of you all. Would you like to go with them, Rosie?"

"Yes, please," her daughter said with shining eyes.

"I'll be along in a minute," Marianne promised.

After everyone left, she turned to Ambrose.

"What is it, love?" he said.

"I don't know. Having Primrose here, at last, it's like a dream ..." She trailed off, shadows darkening her gaze. "Oh, Ambrose, she's safe now, isn't she?"

He cupped Marianne's face in his palms.

"We'll keep her safe," he said. "You have my word on that."

The next few days passed in a blur of activity. Ambrose insisted that until Coyner was caught, Marianne and Primrose remain in the house. Marianne agreed ... and, to his exasperation, proceeded to bring the world into her townhouse instead. Day after day, he and Lugo scrutinized a parade of dressmakers, shoemakers, and haberdashers as they tromped their way to the drawing room. Not only did Marianne outfit Primrose to the nines, but she insisted the Kents have the same royal treatment as well.

Indeed, his family's future was looking as bright as their new buttons. Yesterday, Magistrate Simpson from Wapping Station had come to offer Ambrose reinstatement as Principle Surveyor. Apparently, his old superior Dalrymple had been investigated and sacked for malfeasance, and Ambrose and his team would now be working under Simpson. Simpson had given Ambrose a raise and assigned him as liaison to Bow Street during the ongoing hunt for Coyner. Shaking hands with his new magistrate, Ambrose had been reassured by the other's forthright grip.

Then, at week's end, more good news arrived, delivered this time by a Runner named George Smythe. Ambrose had met Smythe before at the Bow Street offices; something about the fellow's pomaded curls and flashy waistcoat set his teeth on edge. It didn't help matters that Smythe was making eyes at Marianne as she opened the missive bearing Sir Birnie's official seal.

"Have you been with Bow Street long, Mr. Smythe?" Ambrose said curtly.

"A few months, give or take. Made my reputation as a thief-taker before that." Smythe winked. "But the ladies—they prefer a Runner, eh?"

Ambrose scowled at the same time that Marianne said, "My God."

"What is it?" he asked.

"They've got Coyner." She raised glimmering eyes. "They found him in France, and they're bringing him back to face justice."

Knots loosened in Ambrose's chest. He opened his arms, and Marianne walked into them, burying her face against his chest.

"Welcome news indeed," he said hoarsely. "When did they find Coyner?"

"Three days ago," Smythe said. "Accounting for the travel time, they expect to have him back in London by early next week."

A shudder traveled through Marianne, and Ambrose held her closer.

"Sir Birnie asked me to bring Lady Draven in to take an official statement. He wants everything in order so that the magistrates can try Coyner as soon as he arrives," the Runner added.

Marianne drew a breath and straightened. "I can go right now."

"I'll come with you," Ambrose said.

She shook her head. "I want you to stay here with Primrose."

When he tried to argue, she placed a finger to his lips. "Please, Ambrose. Even with Coyner in custody, I'd feel better knowing that you are here with my daughter."

Ambrose frowned. "What about you?"

"I'll take Lugo," she said. "We shan't be more than an hour or two."

Ambrose hesitated. Reluctantly, he said, "Mind you go straight to Bow Street and back."

She nodded.

The Runner offered his arm. "Shall we, my lady?"

An hour later, Ambrose stood on the terrace next to his father. His siblings and Primrose were present as well, and they all watched as Harry prepared to show off his latest experiment. On the outside, the invention looked innocuous enough: white paper tubes were strung together and suspended from a hat rack.

"Behold the Chinese Firecracker," Harry said.

As the others applauded, Ambrose said beneath his breath, "Are you certain this is safe, Father?"

"Harry's been experimenting for weeks. I'm sure he has it down," Samuel whispered back. In a louder voice, he said, "Go on and give us a show, lad."

As Harry reached for the matches, the door bell rang. Relief washed over Ambrose. Marianne was back.

"Wait up," he said with a grin. "I'm sure our hostess won't want to miss this."

He strode to the foyer, where Tilda was opening the door. The maid let out a gasp at the same time that a roar filled Ambrose's ears.

Lugo stood there, disheveled, his face swollen almost beyond recognition. Blood dripped from the large gash on his cheekbone.

"It was a trap," the African said hoarsely. "The note was forged. Smythe's working for Coyner—"

"Where is she?" Ambrose snarled.

"Coyner has her." Lugo held out a note. "Says to follow these instructions ... or my lady dies."

Chapter Forty-Three

Marianne blinked, the world coming into focus in bits. Darkening sky. Lapping waves. A cutter anchored next to the pier where she was lying on her side, her cheek pressed against the rickety planks. She tried to move, but her hands and feet were tied. Everything returned to her. The ambush in the carriage. Coyner and Smythe holding Lugo at gunpoint whilst they beat him to a pulp. Her throat clenched. *God, Lugo.* She'd tried to scream for help, but Coyner had smothered her with a handkerchief, and the noxious fumes had sent her into oblivion.

She fought the panic. Tried to think. Where was she ... where was Coyner?

"Awake, are you?"

A boot pushed her shoulder, rolling her onto her back. She stared up at the man who'd imprisoned her daughter for nearly four years—who'd meant to do unspeakable harm to her little girl. Hatred poured through her veins, dissolving her fear.

"You won't get away with this," she said. "Kent will hunt you down."

"That's the plan. I even gave him the directions." The maniacal edge of Coyner's laugh raised the hairs on her skin. "You're the bait, you see. He'd do anything for you. Because of that, he'll bring my treasure straight to me."

"She's not yours, you perverted bastard," Marianne hissed. "She's eight years old—a *girl*."

"*Primrose is mine, you worthless slut.*"

Coyner grasped her by the hair and yanked her up. Tears of pain welled behind her eyelids, but she refused to cower, kept her gaze steady on her enemy's face. Coyner's eyes had a wild, glazed look. Spittle clung to his lower lip, dripped down the spotty stubble on his jaw. He looked and smelled as if he hadn't bathed in days. A lunatic on the edge.

Could she push him over, gain the upper hand? Pendleton's revelations about Coyner rang in her head. "Why do you want my daughter, *Jericho*?" she said.

His pupils dilated. "Don't call me that. My name's Coyner. Sir Coyner."

"Do you want a girl ... because you can't get it up with a woman?"

"Shut up! Shut up, you whore!"

His hands closed around her throat, yet she gasped out, "Couldn't fuck the tavern wench, could you? Everyone at Eton laughed about it. Everyone knows you're an impotent—"

His grip choked her. Dots danced before her eyes.

"They're here, sir!"

The shout caused Coyner to release her. She fell to her knees, her lungs pulling for air. Through the strands of hair that had fallen over her face, she saw an approaching rowboat. Ambrose was rowing it with only one other boatman, and between them was a small blond head ...

"No!" she shouted. "Keep her away, Ambrose—"

Coyner backhanded her. The taste of pain flooded her mouth, and black waves split her vision.

"Gag her," Coyner snarled.

Smythe appeared and, though she struggled, he held her down and wound a length of filthy linen around her mouth. He hauled her back up, and panic clutched her heart: the rowboat had docked at the other end of the pier. Her daughter was within Coyner's grasp.

She prayed that whatever Ambrose had planned would work.

Because she'd die before she let Coyner get hold of Primrose again.

As the boat bumped against the dock, fear and frustration scalded Ambrose's gut. *This is my fault. I let Marianne go. If anything happens to her—* Yet his self-directed anger was of no use at the moment. Later, he could berate himself further for his failure to protect Marianne. Right now he had to ensure her and Primrose's safety and to take care of Coyner once and for all.

Coyner had planned this meeting with crazed, desperate genius. The bastard had named this abandoned pier east of London, which had nothing but derelict factories to bear witness to the exchange. His note had been succinct: *Bring no authorities, no more than a single boatman, or the bitch dies.*

His throat raw, Ambrose looked at Primrose. "You're certain you wish to go through with this, little one?"

"Yes, Mr. Kent." In the light of the boat's lamp, the girl's lips trembled, but she lifted her chin. "I want my mama back."

Her mother's daughter.

"Brave girl." Ambrose cupped her cheek gently. "You remember the plan, then?"

"Yes," she said and hugged her doll to her chest.

Ambrose turned to his waiting waterman. "Johnno?"

"Aye, sir. At your signal," Johnno replied.

Ambrose rapped his knuckles against the boat. "Wait here. I'll go up first."

He stepped onto the planks. His heart pounded at the sight of Marianne standing at the end of the pier. Her hair glowed against the violet sky and the dark waters just beyond. He counted Coyner and six brutes surrounding her. A well-built cutter was anchored behind them. No doubt Coyner meant to make a swift escape through the Thames Estuary once he had his prize. It gave Ambrose a measure of comfort to know that the River Police would be waiting for the villain there—though he had no intention of allowing the blighter to make it that far. Or to lay hands on Primrose. Ambrose clenched his pistol.

"Let Lady Draven go, Coyner." His voice rose above the sound of the waves. "I've come as you asked."

"Show me Primrose," Coyner shouted back.

Ambrose jerked his chin, and Johnno helped the little girl onto the pier. She clutched her doll in one hand, the lamp in the other. The glow illuminated her face.

"Primrose, *my angel*. Have you missed me? Come to me, sweet flower."

Though the shadowy dusk obscured Coyner's expression, Ambrose heard the fevered passion in the bastard's voice, and his hold tightened instinctively on Primrose's shoulder.

Have to let her go. Just for a few moments.

"We'll release them together, Coyner," he forced himself to call out. "They walk at the same time."

Swearing, Coyner hissed an order to one of his lackeys. The man untied the rope that bound Marianne's ankles, but did not free her arms or remove her gag. She was shaking her head, her voice desperate and muffled. Coyner kept a pistol trained on her back.

"Move forward," he barked.

With a quick prayer, Ambrose let go of Primrose—the hardest thing he'd ever done.

"I'm right behind you," he whispered. "Don't forget that, poppet."

She nodded and started forward. Ambrose's gut wrenched as step by step the girl moved beyond his reach. As he'd instructed her, she matched her pace to Marianne's. His muscles coiled in readiness as the two came closer and closer, nearing the middle of the pier. Then Primrose stopped, directly next to Marianne.

Now, little one. Do it now.

As if hearing his thoughts, Primrose brought her doll closer to her chest. Though her movement was subtle, Ambrose saw that she had positioned the doll over the lamp she held in her other hand.

And set the hidden fuse beneath the doll's skirt into the flame.

The next second, Primrose flung the doll toward Coyner. Ambrose heard her cry out, "Jump, Mama!" and the sound of splashes before Harry's firecrackers exploded into the night. Coyner gave a cry of alarm, but Ambrose was already racing forward, firing his pistol through the screen of smoke and chaotic explosions. He heard footsteps pounding behind him, more shots fired. Hunt and Harteford—who'd been hiding in the smuggling boat's false bottom—had joined his offensive.

Going low, he could only spare a glance to ensure that Primrose and Marianne were safe in the shallow water next to the pier. He reached for the fresh pistols at his belt, continuing to fire into the haze of smoke. He heard cries of pain, and then the other two caught up to him.

"Bloody hell, Kent, leave some for me," Hunt said.

The smoke cleared, revealing the bodies upon the planks. Ambrose spotted Coyner and two others scrambling toward the cutter. His gaze returned to the water; Johnno had arrived and was helping Marianne and Primrose into the rowboat.

"We're fine, Ambrose," Marianne shouted up at him. "Get Coyner!"

"Stay with them," Ambrose said to Harteford, who jerked his chin in assent. "Hunt, let's get that bastard."

A feral smile crossed Hunt's face.

They raced forward, dodging bullets and returning the fire. With his last shot, Ambrose took aim, and the brute at the helm of the cutter gave a cry as he crumpled, bleeding from the chest. Two enemies left to go. Hunt jumped on board first, tackling Smythe with a roar. Coyner stood by the mainsail, struggling to reload his pistol. Ambrose dove for him, wrestling the bastard onto the deck. They grappled, then Coyner kneed him in the solar plexus. In that instant, Ambrose lost the upper hand, and a blade materialized in Coyner's grip, swinging down in a vicious arc.

Ambrose rolled to evade it, but the blade caught him, fire lancing through his arm. With a maddened howl, Coyner pinned him, and the knife swiped downward again. Ambrose caught Coyner's weapon arm with his good hand, his muscles straining to keep the glinting steel tip from sinking into his throat.

"Primrose is mine!" Coyner screamed. "I'm going to kill you then get her bitch of a mother!"

Like hell you will.

With a surge of power, Ambrose brought his injured arm into play. Just as Coyner bore down with murderous intent, Ambrose gripped his opponent's wrist with both hands. He snapped it upward, reversing the momentum of the knife. Coyner cried out in pain, and Ambrose took that instant to roll free. On his feet in the next breath, he stood ready to finish the fight.

Coyner remained lying face down on the deck.

After a few heartbeats, Ambrose nudged the man with his foot. His boot came away stained with a dark liquid. Skin prickling, he rolled his foe over. The hilt of the blade protruded from Coyner's chest, crimson blossoming from the fatal wound.

Blood gurgled from Coyner's lips. "My sweet flower ..." he gasped. Then the crazed light faded from his eyes, and his head fell to the side.

Seconds later, Hunt arrived and peered down at the still body. "Done?"

Ambrose's gaze honed in on Marianne and Primrose upon the pier. They sat huddled beneath blankets, sodden and no doubt exhausted. But they were safe.

"Yes," he said with quiet relief. "It's finished at last."

Chapter Forty-Four

"Have something for you, son," Samuel said a week later.

"What is it?" Ambrose paused in the act of packing his father's books into a trunk.

On the morrow, he would take his family back to Chudleigh Crest. With the reward Ambrose had earned from Bow Street for taking down Coyner, he'd had enough to pay off his father's debts and purchase his family a comfortable new cottage. He planned to settle them in, then return to London and carry on his job with the Thames River Police.

Everything had fallen neatly into place. Everything ... but his relationship with Marianne.

Since Coyner's death, Marianne had been thoroughly occupied in her role as a mother. She spent every moment with her daughter. During the day, she entertained Primrose and Ambrose's siblings; at night, she slept in the governess' bed in Primrose's room. Her anxiety was slow to fade, and Ambrose could not blame her. When he thought of her and Primrose on that pier ... his jaw tautened. He hadn't forgiven himself for his failure. Henceforth, he swore to do a better job of protecting them both.

Yet was he deluding himself, thinking about a future with

them? Did Marianne want him to have a role in her life? In her daughter's? The truth was she'd never promised more than the moment. And given the trauma of recent events, he hadn't felt right pressuring her to think of other matters.

He blew out a breath. *Be patient. Give her the space with her daughter that she needs and deserves. Take care of matters with your own family first—then bring up the future with Marianne.*

Samuel finished rummaging through one of the bags. "Ah, here it is. Come have a look."

Ambrose went over and took the small wooden box from his father. Opening the lid, he found himself looking at a ring. A small emerald winked at the center of the delicate gold band, which was otherwise smooth and burnished by time. He experienced a fleeting memory: this ring upon a gentle hand, a loving touch that took away fear and pain.

"This ... this was my mother's."

"Yes. I gave it to her on our wedding day," Samuel said with a misty smile. "It brought us much joy—it brought us you."

Ambrose didn't know what to say.

"When you were engaged to that flit-wit Jane, I knew you weren't ready for this ring. But now you are. Give it to the woman you love and who will love you wholeheartedly in return."

Ambrose's hand closed around the box. God, he wanted to.

"Marianne's been through too much of late," he heard himself say. "I can't ask her to consider other life-altering changes as well."

"You can't ... or you're afraid to?"

Damn. Schoolmaster Kent was indeed back in full possession of his faculties. Marianne had been right about his father's grief masquerading as illness.

"Both," Ambrose admitted. "If the circumstances were different, if she were not so high above me—"

"I thought we already covered this nonsense. Because that's what this excuse is—nonsense. What has class to do with love?"

He couldn't expect his father to understand. After all, Samuel had wisely given his heart to women who occupied the same world as he did. He'd never put his lovers in the situation where they'd have to choose between being a titled lady and plain Mrs. Kent. A policeman's wife.

"She'd be giving up much for me," Ambrose said, his jaw taut.

"And gaining much more in return. Do you love her so little, son?"

"I love her with all that I am," Ambrose said fiercely.

"Then why are you afraid to let her make her choice?"

Because ... what if she doesn't choose me?

His deepest fear crystallized in his mind. Though he believed that she cared for him, she'd never told him she loved him. Their relationship had developed amidst chaos and turbulence; now that the storm had passed, would she regret her involvement with a man like him? Now that she no longer needed his assistance in finding her daughter, did she want him still? Even after he'd nearly bungled his role as her protector?

"It's not just the money." His shoulders hunched. "I failed to keep her and her girl out of harm's way. If Coyner had—"

"No one's perfect, boy, and the sooner you accept that the better. In the end, you rescued Marianne and Primrose: that's what matters." His father sighed. "If you insist on taking responsibility for everything, you'll wind up no better than a stick-in-the-mud."

A moralistic snob, God help him.

"All you can do is your best. The rest?" Samuel shrugged. "You live with it."

Ambrose knew he had little to recommend his suit. Could he present himself to Marianne, knowing his own faults? Could he hope that she'd accept him as he was, flaws and all?

"Didn't raise you to be namby-pamby," his father commented.

Ambrose rubbed his neck. Devil take it, he *was* being an idiot. He wanted Marianne—in his bed, by his side forever. So why was he making excuses, prolonging the torment? Either she wanted him ... or she didn't. If she didn't know by now, waiting wasn't going to make a lick of difference.

He tucked the ring box into his pocket. "I'll go talk to her. Wish me luck."

"Good luck, boy." Smiling, his father patted him on the shoulder. "Though somehow I don't think you'll need it."

Heading down the stairs, Ambrose encountered Violet and Polly on the landing. His sisters had Primrose in tow.

"Good morning, Mr. Kent," Primrose said, dimpling.

He couldn't help but smile at the pretty picture the three girls made with their hair in ringlets and tied with satin bows. "And to you, little one. Where are you all dashing off to?"

"We're going upstairs to play Spillikins." Violet rolled her eyes. "Can you *believe* Primrose has never played before?"

"Picking up sticks is not the only way to pass one's time. I'm sure Primrose has enjoyed other leisure," Ambrose chided his sister.

"Actually, I haven't," Primrose blurted, her face falling. "My life before ... it was ever so boring."

Ambrose's chest constricted. For a young girl, Primrose had been through so many changes; the harrowing episode at the pier hadn't helped matters. Marianne had fretfully told him that Primrose sometimes suffered terror dreams at night.

As Ambrose searched for the right words to comfort the girl, to assure her that from now on everything would be alright, Polly slipped her hand into Primrose's.

With a child's simple ease, his youngest sister said, "You've got us now, Rosie."

"And we're *never* boring," Vi added.

"I wish you didn't have to leave tomorrow." Primrose's bottom lip trembled. "I shall miss you all dreadfully."

Three hopeful pairs of eyes turned to Ambrose.

"Run along now," he said gruffly. "We'll talk later."

The girls went off to enjoy their game, and he continued down the stairs. He headed to the drawing room, the place Marianne was most likely to be this time of day. As he approached, he heard the sound of female voices. Marianne's ... and Lady Harteford's. The door was ajar; though he couldn't see into the room, snippets of their conversation drifted through.

" ... I'm glad to have a moment alone with you, Marianne." The marchioness's voice was low, serious. "How is Primrose faring?"

"Considering all that she has been through, I should say quite marvelously. She's a resilient little thing." Despite the obvious pride in Marianne's tone, there was a quiver, too. "I still have nightmares of what might have happened if Coyner had succeeded in ..."

"He didn't, and he's dead. That is justice," Lady Harteford said firmly. "Now we must focus on doing everything we can for Primrose. Have you given thought to when you will introduce her to Society?"

Though Ambrose knew he should leave the ladies to their private talk, the anxiety in Marianne's tone held him captive outside the door.

"It is too soon. She is a bastard, Helena, and I do not wish her to be harmed by my mistakes."

"Fustian. There are plenty of by-blows running amok in the *ton*. Primrose is the granddaughter of an earl and niece to a marchioness, and she has as much right to be in Society as any of them. And anyone else, for that matter."

"I don't want her exposed to ugliness," Marianne insisted. "You know how cruel the so-called 'polite world' can be."

"Indeed. That is why we must have a plan."

"You sound like you already have one." Ambrose could imagine Marianne's leveraged brow.

"I do. In these situations, one must rally the troops. You, my dear, must make a point of courting those with social influence."

Ambrose tensed, his gaze dropping to his worn boots.

"You know I detest the snobs," Marianne protested.

"You don't detest me or Harteford, surely. We will throw a party for Primrose and make sure my father is present. If you are comfortable, we will make our connection to her and support of her indisputable."

"Thank you," Marianne said.

"But we will not be enough. You will have to reform your reputation, my dear. No more scandal and running with the fast crowd. From here on in, you must gain acceptance from the sticklers. Only then will you be able to help Primrose gain entrée into the best drawing rooms."

As Marianne again murmured her assent, Ambrose's jaw clenched. He could not argue with Lady Harteford's reasoning. Because of the circumstances of her birth, Primrose faced disadvantages—and possible rejection by society if she did not have the protection of a good name. One associated with wealth, privilege. A title.

Primrose Kent would have none of those things.

"Which brings me to the matter of the Kents," the marchioness said in a hesitant manner.

Ambrose knew he should go. He leaned closer.

"You know I adore them. And Mr. Kent has done so much for you and Primrose. But what do you intend for the future?"

Ambrose waited, his heart thumping. He knew he should relinquish his selfish desires. Knew it would be best for Primrose. Yet if Marianne gave him even the slightest reason to hope—

"I can't speak of it now," Marianne said.

"Why not?"

"I just can't." Marianne sighed—in disgust? Frustration? "It's complicated, Helena. But I've never lied to Ambrose. I haven't made promises to him because the truth is ..."

She paused, and every fiber of his being tensed, his breath held, his soul waiting.

"The truth is, I can't keep them," she said flatly.

The words struck him like a direct blow to the gut. Before he could recover, Ambrose heard Lugo's rumbling voice coming down the corridor. He came to his senses and walked away from the drawing room. The ring box bumped heavily in his pocket. As he mounted the steps, he cursed himself for being an idiot. For letting his heart rule his head so completely. For believing, even for an instant, that dreams had anything to do with reality.

Chapter Forty-Five

The morning light imbued the soft green drawing room with tranquility, an emotion far removed from Marianne's own state as she sat with her bosom friend.

"*Why* can't you keep a promise to Mr. Kent?" Helena said. "You care for him, I know you do. And it's obvious he returns your affection. Harteford and I both agree that you two make the perfect pair."

Marianne bit her lip. "I will tell you, Helena. But you must promise me not to tell Ambrose. Not yet, anyway."

Though Helena's brows lifted, she gave a quick nod.

Blowing out a breath, Marianne confided her debt to Bartholomew Black. When she was finished, Helena stared at her with rounded eyes.

"Heavens, you agreed to *anything* Black wanted?"

"What choice had I? He was my only hope of finding Primrose. I don't regret it," Marianne said, though her palms grew clammy, "and given the same choice, I'd make it again."

"No one doubts your devotion to Primrose, dear. But what of your own happiness?" Helena's hazel eyes reflected her concern. "You do deserve it, you know."

Marianne blinked away sudden moisture; Ambrose had said the same thing. "Oh, Helena, do I? Do I deserve a man as good as Ambrose Kent?"

"Why, of course you do! Why would you even ask such a thing?"

"Because ..."

Marianne had to clamp down on her lower lip again to stop it from trembling. Lud, what was happening to her? She was *never* a watering pot, and yet the events of the past days had eroded her famed self-composure. Hidden floodgates opened inside her. She felt things she was not accustomed to feeling. She yearned for things she was afraid to want.

"You can tell me, Marianne. After all, you saw me through my troubles with Harteford." Her friend reached for her hand. "Can I not offer you the same comfort when it comes to matters of the heart?"

Marianne returned the squeeze. "Of course you can, Helena. The truth of it is ... I am most wretchedly in love with Ambrose." Saying the words aloud was like pulling on a loose thread. Her emotions unraveled with stunning speed. "He's everything I could hope for. He's loyal and steady, strong yet tender. And after everything he's done for me ..."

Her cheeks flushed as she realized how much she'd taken Ambrose for granted. He'd been there when she needed him, saving her and her daughter and vanquishing Coyner once and for all. In the week since the villain's demise, Ambrose had provided a shoulder for her and a calm, kind presence for her daughter. Yet he had made no demands of her. At night, he'd retired to the guest bedchamber, and given her preoccupation with Rosie, she'd given little thought to his needs.

It wasn't until he'd quietly announced his intention to return his family to Chudleigh Crest that she realized the unsettled nature of their relationship. Feelings came crashing over her, intense and confusing. She wanted him so badly, and she was ... terrified.

"It's clear that Mr. Kent loves you," Helena said. "I don't see what the problem is."

"What have I to offer him in return? I've made so many mistakes ..." Swallowing, Marianne forced herself to speak her fears. "How can I expect him to take on ... damaged goods?"

Helena stared at her. "I cannot believe you just referred to yourself in those terms."

"It's true, isn't it?" Marianne lifted her chin. "I've always called a spade a spade. I have a bastard, I've done things no lady should have done. And then there's my debt to Black, what he may want ..." Shuddering, she couldn't make herself give voice to the vile possibilities. "Can you in all honesty say that I am the sort of woman a decent man would want for a wife—to bring home to his family, to be the mother of his children?"

"I begin to think I do not know you as well as I believed." Blinking, Helena said, "All these years, I thought you were the one with the confidence."

"Self-possession is an excellent mask for insecurity," Marianne said wryly.

"Be that as it may, how can you doubt Mr. Kent's devotion to you? You yourself have said that he's protected you time and again. And the way he looks at you ..." Helena gave a heartfelt sigh. "As for the Kents, they adore both you and Primrose. When I see all of you together, I see no mismatch. No inequality. What I see is ..."

"Yes?"

"A family," Helena said gently.

Dash it, there were those blasted tears again.

"Truly?" Marianne dabbed at her eyes. "You aren't saying these things just to make me feel better?"

"Not at all. But I do agree that a significant barrier remains to your happiness."

"Black." Shivering, Marianne said, "I have to go to him, Helena. I have to discharge myself from his debt before I am free to go to Ambrose."

"You are certain you cannot tell Mr. Kent about this?" Helena frowned.

Marianne shook her head adamantly. "Black hates the law and Charleys in particular. I can't endanger Ambrose in that fashion. Besides, there's nothing he can do in this situation, and if he tries to challenge Black ..." She refused to have Ambrose hurt again because of her. "I gave Black my pledge, and I must honor it."

"You have a point. Male bravado can unnecessarily complicate things." Helena chewed on her lip. "Let us go together, then, and find out what this Mr. Black wants."

"You'll come with me?"

"Of course. After all," the marchioness said with a glint of mischief in her eyes, "it wouldn't be the first time you and I shared an adventure together, would it?"

With Helena at her side, Marianne entered Black's domain. This time, he was waiting for them in a sumptuous breakfast room.

He rose from the end of the long table, wiping his mouth on a napkin. Today his stout figure was swathed in an old-fashioned banyan made of green silk; in lieu of his usual periwig, a small yellow turban was perched on his shorn head.

His eyes narrowed. "Wasn't expecting company this early else I'd 'ave dressed for the occasion."

"I am sorry to intrude, Mr. Black," Marianne said, "but I have an urgent matter to discuss with you."

"That's a familiar tune, ain't it?" Snorting, Black shifted his gaze to Helena. "Who's she?"

"Forgive my manners. This is my friend, the Marchioness of Harteford."

Helena inclined her head. "Good day, Mr. Black."

"Harteford, eh? Met your husband once. Not a bad sort for a

nob," their host said. "Well, since you're both 'ere, pull up a seat. Plenty o' food to go around."

Perching upon a chair, Helena began, "Thank you, we have breakfasted—"

"Woman in your condition ought to keep 'er energy up." Black forked up some eggs. "Eatin' for two, ain't you?"

Helena's jaw dropped. Cheeks pink, she looked helplessly at Marianne.

"Thank you for your hospitality, Mr. Black. We shan't be staying long. I have come with only one purpose in mind," Marianne said. "The matter of my debt to you."

Black slurped from his cup. "What about it?"

"I've come to discuss the terms."

"The terms are for me to decide, not the other way around."

Taking a breath for courage, Marianne sat up very straight. "I will not share your bed, sir."

Black choked on a mouthful of food. Bits sprayed out as he thundered, "You won't share *my bed*, you say?"

"No." Though she trembled inside, she said firmly, "Circumstances have changed for me, Mr. Black. I cannot betray the man I love. You will have to think of some other way that I may repay you."

"What the bloody 'ell gave you the idea I wanted to tup you in the first place?" Glaring at her, Black swiped his mouth with the sleeve of his banyan.

"Oh. Well. I just assumed ... that is, most men ..." Marianne faltered.

"Got a 'igh opinion o' yourself, don't you? Little hussy!" Pushing from the table, Black stalked to the sideboard, muttering to himself as he filled another plate. "Me—a cradle-robbin' lecher! Imagine that!"

Marianne exchanged an uneasy glance with Helena.

"Sir," Helena said, "if an, ahem, intimate favor doesn't interest you, what *would* you like?"

Black's plate thumped onto the table. He scowled at them both. "I ne'er said I didn't want an intimate favor."

Marianne swallowed. "I already said, I will not—"

"Oh, get your guts out o' the gutter. I'm not talkin' 'bout bed sport." Black's eyes rolled toward his turban. "Is that all you fillies can think about?"

Marianne blushed. "Then by *intimate* you're referring to ...?"

"My daughter Mavis is gettin' hitched. After all she went through with 'er last 'usband—may the bastard rot in 'ell—I want to send 'er off in style. A weddin' fit for a princess."

Marianne looked at him blankly. "And how can I help?"

"Well, look at you." Black gestured at her with his fork. "Got style in spades, don't you? Practically drippin' from your pores. You know where to get the best—and that's what I want for my Mavis. The best."

"You want me to ... to take your daughter *shopping*?"

Black frowned. "Bit more involved than that. I want you to plan the whole bloody thing from top to bottom. Got to 'ave the best food, best guests, best music—I want it to be the best damn weddin' this town 'as ever laid eyes on."

Relief and joy bubbled through Marianne. Giddily, she got to her feet and crossed to Black. "It'll be the most stylish affair of the Season, I can promise you that." Impulsively, she leaned down and kissed him on the cheek. "Thank you, sir!"

"There'll be none o' that—told you I weren't no lecher." Though Black shooed her away, his jowls reddened. "My Mavis, she's a good girl. Could use some females o' quality in 'er circle."

"We'll be pleased to make her acquaintance," Helena said, smiling.

Black nodded. "Good. It's settled then."

Marianne laughed ... because it was.

And she was finally *free*.

Chapter Forty-Six

After the meeting with Black, Marianne returned home, brimming with excitement. She was eager to see Ambrose, to confess her heart. But he wasn't there. According to Emma, he'd stepped out and hadn't left direction. Marianne bided her time, allowing the girls to gleefully trounce her at Spillikins and Fox and Geese. When Ambrose did not return by supper, however, she began to worry. After the meal, she tucked Primrose in bed, left her in Tilda's care, and went in search of him.

She began at Wapping Station; no one had seen him there all day. Johnno suggested a nearby pub—but Ambrose wasn't there either. Finally, she headed to his apartment. She rapped on the peeling door, her belly twisting.

What if he's not here? What if something's happened to him?

On the fifth knock, the door opened.

Ambrose's lean frame filled the doorway. His hair was scruffy and his jaw stubbly with the beginnings of a night beard. His collar lay unlaced, revealing his strong throat and a glimpse of his hair-dusted chest. His trousers had seen better days, and his large, masculine feet were bare.

Lord, he was beautiful. Her pulse thumped harder.

"What are you doing here, Marianne?" he said.

She blinked at his curt tone. Not exactly the passionate welcome she'd been hoping for. Her confidence dimmed a little, but she said lightly, "You aren't in the middle of a rendezvous, are you? I know all your sisters now, so you shan't be able to use that excuse this time around."

"There's no one here but me."

"May I come in?" she said.

His lashes veiled his gaze. "If you like."

She followed him into the cramped space with mounting nervousness. Ambrose's manner was ... different. He'd oft called her a *selkie*, but now it seemed that he was the one who'd shed his skin. His usual steady warmth was missing; in its place was that smoldering intensity that never failed to arouse her ... and alarm her, just a little.

But she'd never seen Ambrose quite in this state. When he'd allowed his dominant side to show at other times, it had still been controlled, honed. Tonight, it was as if his self-restraint and patience had reached their limits. He was a male on the edge, and she had the fretful thought that she'd finally pushed him beyond reason. Worse yet, had he given up on her? Having suffered so much at her hands, had he decided she wasn't worth the trouble?

Her insides chilled. Licking her lips, she glanced blindly around the Spartan room. It remained unchanged from her last visit, with the exception of the pallet he'd moved next to the fire. A bottle of whiskey and a book lay on the floor beside it. Fighting nerves, she peered down at the title.

"Dante. Cheerful choice," she said.

"It suited my mood."

When he didn't elaborate, she said awkwardly, "We missed you at supper. Monsieur Arnauld made your favorite, *boeuf bourginon.*"

"I wasn't fit for company." His thumbs hitched behind his braces, and his brooding gaze bored into hers. "Why have you come, Marianne?"

"I ... I thought we should talk. Before you leave for Chudleigh Crest."

What was going on behind that amber gaze? She'd gotten accustomed to interpreting his expressions, yet at the moment she couldn't read him at all.

"Go ahead and talk," he said.

Her pulse a furious staccato, she said, "We haven't been alone this past week. And there are things we should discuss. About our relationship."

His mouth compressed. "You're right. Let's finish it, then."

Finish it? What did he mean by *that*?

She swallowed. "How much have you had to drink tonight?"

"Not nearly enough." The bitterness in his smile—so foreign —caused her heart to squeeze. "Now what was it you came here to say? Or should I say it for you?"

"You *know* what I wish to say?" That made her lift her brows.

He returned her look with a sardonic one of his own. "First, you want to thank me for all I have done for you and Primrose."

"True," she allowed.

"You want to tell me you've enjoyed our time together. The pleasure we've shared."

His bright gaze dared her to disagree, but why would she when he spoke the truth?

"A great deal of pleasure, I should think," she said softly.

He flinched, as if her words had caused him physical pain. He straightened his shoulders, met her eyes. "Be that as it may, you have responsibilities. A daughter to think of." His lashes grazed his cheek. "And you want to remind me that we've never made promises to one another."

Her throat thickened. "Haven't we?"

His gaze snapped back to hers. "Don't play games with me, Marianne. It doesn't suit you," he said tersely. "You and I both know you've committed nothing to me."

She ached fiercely for the hurt she saw in his beautiful eyes. And his courage and innate heroism struck her once more: he'd given her so much—her daughter, her very life back—with no expectation of receiving anything in return. On a flash of insight, she realized that she was dealing with a wounded male. Her skin tingled with remorse and love ... so much love.

"But *you* have," she said, her voice tremulous. "You have committed something to me. You said you loved me, Ambrose."

A weaker man might have taken back those words. Excused them as a moment's folly, meaningless sentiment uttered in the heat of passion.

Ambrose only shook his head. "I cannot do this anymore. I can't live for the moment. The mistake was mine in thinking that I could." His hands balled at his sides. "I'm a simple man, Marianne, with simple wants. And I see now that what I want is not possible with you."

"Why not?" she whispered, reaching for him.

He took a step back. "No ... don't. This ends now. You and I both know that is what is best for Primrose. For you."

"*You're* best for us," she said softly. "I want you, Ambrose."

A spasm crossed his features. "You can't have me, Marianne. I'll not be content to share your bed as the moment suits. I want—nay, I *deserve*—more."

"You deserve everything," she agreed. "Everything and more. If you give me a chance, I vow I'll do my utmost to give it to you."

He stared at her. "What are you saying?"

"I love you." Strange how she'd held on to those words with such trepidation; now they left her lips with no hesitation at all. With nothing but a rush of liberation and joy.

"I love you so very much, Ambrose," she said steadily, "and if you will have me, I promise to spend the rest of my days proving that to you. I'll never give you cause for regret. I'll make myself worthy of your name, if you bestow it upon me."

She saw the fire kindling in his eyes, the sudden flare of hope. Yet his hands stayed clenched at his sides.

"You cannot mean that," he said. "You have Primrose to think of. Lady Harteford was right: your daughter needs the protection of wealth, a title."

"You heard our conversation?" she said, frowning.

Though he flushed, his gaze did not waver. "Enough of it to know that you spoke nothing but the truth. I—I can't give you and Primrose a position in society. I can't provide for you, not in the style you are accustomed to."

"I don't need you to provide for us. I have plenty of money," she said. "As for Primrose, I've decided that her happiness is more important than what the *ton* thinks. We'll have our friends and our detractors, and that is the way of life. Primrose will do well to learn that lesson early on." She gave him a wistful smile. "What she needs is a father—a good, decent man to protect and love her."

"I failed to keep you safe. I exposed Primrose to harm."

At his stark words, she looked at him in surprise. "How can you say that? Thanks to your ingenuity, you saved us both. You freed us from Coyner once and for all."

His throat worked, and she saw how much he was struggling between his principles and his desires. Between what he thought was right and his own happiness. Silly man, didn't he realize they were one and the same? Shamelessly, she played her trump card.

"My daughter needs you, but *I* need you even more," she said, her voice breaking just a little. "I need to fall asleep in your arms each night and to wake with you beside me. I need your advice, even though I won't always heed it. I need to share your laughter and your woes and to be a part of the family we will create together." Blinking away sudden moisture, she said, "Most of all, Ambrose, I need you to love me as much as I love you."

Her breath came fitfully as silence followed her declaration. She'd exposed her heart: stripped away the layers, left herself vulnerable and without defense. If he didn't want her, if he no longer loved her—

A sound left him, and suddenly she was in his arms. In heaven. His lips claimed hers in a kiss of pure possession, and she almost sobbed with relief. She clung to him, meeting his hunger with her own, wrapping her arms around his neck, needing to be as close to him in body as she was in heart.

"I love you," he said against her lips. "So bloody much, Marianne."

Wonder suffused her. Its warmth spread like sunshine through her soul, melting away the wasteland of the past and sowing bright, beautiful blossoms in its wake.

Nuzzling his chest, she said, "You won't regret me, I promise. I'll be so good to you from now on—the kind of wife you've dreamed of."

"Christ, never mind that. Just be mine."

"I can't wait to be Mrs. Kent," she said tremulously.

"Are you absolutely certain, sweetheart?" The familiar line worked between his brows. Her stubborn, honorable Ambrose— how she adored him. "Because it will change things for you. Even with your money, you'll lose much—"

"And gain more in return." With sly furtiveness, she found the buttons hidden inside the placket of his trousers and popped them free. His breath grew harsh as she raked her nails lightly along his impressive length. "*Much* more, I should say. You'll give me everything I want, darling, of that I have no doubt."

His eyes gleamed down at her. "So I'm to spoil you, is that it?"

"If the shoe—or in this case, the *cock*—fits ..."

Her laughter spilled over as he caught her up in his arms and carried her to the hearth. He lay her on the pallet, the expression in his eyes as he undressed her making her feel like a queen. He shed his clothes, and then she knew she *was* the richest woman in the world. Firelight licked his lean physique, and she could scarce believe that this delicious male, this noble, loving man was all hers.

Yet as he stretched next to her, she saw the question lingering in his eyes.

"What is it, my love?" she said.

"When I overheard you and Lady Harteford earlier today, you said you couldn't make me any promises." He brushed his knuckles along her cheekbone. "What has changed?"

Lud. She'd forgotten all about Black.

Sliding Ambrose a look beneath her lashes, she said, "Promise you won't get angry."

"The fact that you're asking for that promise is not reassuring. Tell me, Marianne."

Reminding herself to begin as she meant to go on, she told him the truth of her bargain with Bartholomew Black.

"You *what*?" He stared at her in disbelief.

"There's no need to get overwrought," she said quickly. "All's well that ends well, as they say. My only obligation is to plan a wedding—a task so simple I could do it in my sleep."

He sat up, his features carved in granite. "That's not the point. Black could have demanded anything. How could you have been so reckless, so utterly irresponsible—"

She really wasn't in the mood for a lecture. So she rose on her knees and began to press kisses against his hard jaw, noting with interest how the muscle ticked there.

"Don't think you can distract me," he said, frowning.

"I love it when you get stern." She licked the hard bump of his throat.

"Your wiles aren't going to work this time. When I think of the danger you put yourself in, what might have happened—" His voice hitched. "*Christ*, woman, what are you doing?"

"Answering your challenge," she murmured. "Now are you certain this won't distract you ... or this?"

He groaned.

And the lecture was put off ... at least until the next time.

Epilogue

Protected from the chilly winter wind by his new greatcoat, Ambrose returned from visiting his family down the lane. He pushed open the garden gate to his own cottage; the creaking hinges reminded him that he'd have to oil them soon, and he smiled ruefully as a long list of other repairs ran through his mind. When Marianne had presented him with his wedding present—a cottage close to his family's in Chudleigh Crest—she'd given him the authentic thing, tumble-down charm and all.

He approached the snug abode he occupied with his wife and daughter during their frequent visits from the city. After the wedding, he'd adopted Primrose, and he loved her as he would his own flesh and blood. His family adored her as well, and tonight she was staying with them so she and his siblings could watch the constellations through Harry's new telescope.

Much as he loved Rosie, anticipation stirred in Ambrose's blood at the thought of having his wife to himself for the evening. Today marked the half-year anniversary of their marriage, and he couldn't recall a happier time in his life. There had been conflicts, of course—both of them being of strong will and independent mind—yet he and Marianne had managed to learn the art of compromise. In retrospect, their quarrels had led to growth and deepening intimacy between them. And the lovemaking after their rows?

Ambrose got hard just thinking about it.

To celebrate their months together, Marianne was planning a private supper. In and of itself, that was not cause for alarm. When she'd informed him, however, that she planned to *cook* the food herself, he hadn't been able to conceal his reaction.

"You needn't look so surprised," his wife had said in her adorably haughty way. "If I can shoot a man and rule the *beau monde*, surely I can toss a few things in a pot."

"But why would you wish to?" He'd been genuinely perplexed. The Marianne he knew was not acquainted with ordinary tasks. Her legion of servants served that purpose far better.

Her gaze had dropped in a distinctly un-Marianne-like way. Then she'd lifted her chin. "I daresay I can take care of you as well as any country wife."

Realization had dawned, then, that she wished to ... *please* him. Love and lust had surged over him, and he hadn't been able to resist gathering her in his arms and tossing her onto the bed. Her shrieks of laughter had turned into moans of pleasure as he'd showed her how utterly perfect a mate he found her.

To his secret amusement, she'd nonetheless spent the week cloistered in the kitchen with Emma. He'd been expressly forbidden to set foot inside the cottage during those meetings. Now, spotting the grey smoke wafting from the front door, he steeled himself. Whatever Marianne had prepared, he made a silent vow to eat it and say that it was the best he'd ever had. Ignoring the acrid scent tickling his nostrils, he stepped gamely inside.

God Almighty. A haze of smoke shrouded the front parlor.

Coughing slightly, he called out her name. When no response came, he set down the basket he'd been carrying and went to look for her. She wasn't in the kitchen, which looked like a small hurricane had blown through it. He winced; the cook maid would not be pleased on the morrow. He crossed the small dining room, where a table had been beautifully laid out with crystal and linens. Silver domes covered various dishes. He lifted one—and hastily placed it back.

Passing two cozy bedchambers, he reached the master suite. He paused at the closed door. Was Marianne upset? His *selkie* liked things to go her way; failure was not an option she was particularly fond of. His lips twitched. If she was put out by the supper fiasco, he knew just how to soothe her ruffled pride.

He knocked lightly.

Dulcet tones bade him to enter.

He stepped into the bedchamber, and his mind emptied. Most likely because the blood had plummeted from his head and landed straight in his groin.

"You're back earlier than I expected," his wife said from the bed.

He stood there, riveted. Backlit by the hearth's roaring flames, Marianne lay on her side on red satin sheets, her head propped up by one hand and her hair flowing in gleaming waves over her bare shoulders. She wore a prim maid's apron and, Christ's blood, nothing else. Her creamy curves played peek-a-boo along the edges of the starched white cloth; the hem of the apron reached just below one of his favorite places on her body and showcased her long, shapely legs.

In his entire life, he'd never seen anything more erotic. His vision wavered, darkening with lust. He began to shed his clothes.

She smiled at him, so beautiful that the beast in him clawed to get closer. "I hope you're not hungry. As you may have surmised, the menu didn't go quite as planned."

"To hell with food." He tossed his boots aside. "Right now I've an appetite for something else."

She rolled onto her back, settling against the pillows in a provocative posture that made him yank so hard at his waistband that buttons skittered onto the floor. "Do you know what I've decided?" she said sultrily.

He mounted the bed, fully aroused, his cock straining toward her. "What, love?"

"It's too much trouble to be good at everything."

Despite the lust clouding his brain, he grinned. "Find it tiresome, do you?"

"I mean, one has to have priorities, doesn't one?" She twirled one tress around her finger. "So I've given some thought to mine."

"Have you now?" He crawled over her, their bodies not quite touching. Heat gathered and crackled in that sliver of space. He pressed one soft kiss to the curve of her neck, savoring her shiver of excitement. Drawing back, prolonging the desire while he had any control left, he said huskily, "What have you decided?"

"That I should focus my wifely energies on one room at a time. So what will it be? The kitchen, the drawing room, or"—her vibrant eyes held a knowing, loving sparkle—"the bedchamber?"

He lowered himself onto her, grounding his hips in answer.

She purred, and he sucked that sweet sound into his mouth. God, he loved the taste of her. He took his time kissing her, sipping on her sighs of pleasure. Then other delights called to him, and he tore himself from her lips to sample her neck, the smell of her perfumed skin igniting his senses. Desire pulsed in his blood, building with every breath, and when he couldn't reach the knot to remove the bloody apron, he rose on his knees and flipped her over in a smooth motion.

Christ. His nostrils flared at the sight of his wife's pretty backside.

Rubbing her cheek against the silk coverlet, she said throatily, "Is this how you fancy me tonight, Mr. Kent?"

"I'll have you anyway I can get you."

He made quick work of the apron strings and tossed the fabric aside. Reverently, he ran his palm along the smooth length of her spine, past the elegant dip, and over her sweetly rounded bottom. Would he ever stop marveling at all the grace notes on her person? Without a doubt, he was one lucky bastard.

"Mrs. Kent," he said gravely, "have I told you lately how much I adore your ass?"

She sent him a coy look. "Aren't you afraid of offending my delicate sensibilities with such language, sir?"

"If you're offended by that, I shudder to think what you'll think of this." Reaching for a pair of pillows, he tucked them under her hips. Elevating her thus gave him delightful access. He fingered her delicate pink crease, a growl rising in his throat. "I love how wet you get for me, sweetheart."

She hummed with bliss. "Mmm. That feels so nice." When he continued to gently pet her, however, she grew impatient. Cheeks flushed, she said, "Oh, do stop playing now. I'm awash already —*hurry.*"

"You know I'm a patient man," he chided her, "and never one to rush my pleasures. And you are mine, aren't you, love?"

"*Ambrose.*"

At his wife's threatening tone, he hid a grin and bent to taste her honey. His name left her lips again, only this time it was a keening cry. He licked her slit up and down, her addictive flavor making him want more. Spreading her with his thumbs, he entered her with his tongue. Moaning, she began to wriggle, pushing back against him, craving even that small penetration. As he stabbed his tongue in a steady rhythm, he reached beneath, plucking and rolling her swollen pearl.

She came apart against his mouth, and he almost came, too, from the joy of seeing his wife go over. Breathing harshly, he moved onto his knees between her quivering thighs and notched his cock to her opening. He loved to watch her pussy spread for him, the primal delight of seeing her flesh blossom around his veined beast. Flames licked his spine as he sank in, seating himself to the last inch. With her snug heat pulsing around him, the angle impossibly deep, it took everything he had to hold still.

"Alright, love?" he rasped.

"I'm not certain." The languid twitch of her hips nearly undid him. "You'll have to fuck me so I can decide."

With a laughing groan, he acquiesced to her demand. He withdrew and pushed inside, each thrust building his hunger. Her sighs urged him on as he began pounding into her, his mate, his love. His vision blurred, his body melting in her fire. There was nothing like this in the world—nothing to compare with the heat, need, the unending desire.

"I love you." The words tore from his chest, his soul. "With all that I am, Marianne."

She twisted to look at him, and her glowing eyes affirmed all that was in his heart. He lost himself in their hot intimacy, in the wet, rhythmic slap of his bollocks against her sex. He played with her knot as he fucked her, and when her moans soared in a sweet, familiar crescendo, his dew-slickened finger searched out her shy, puckered hole, sliding in deep and true, in the way that never failed to summon his wife's bliss.

She cried out instantly. She pulsed around his cock, his finger, and shuddering, he crammed himself as deeply inside her as he could before her contractions overtook him. Her release milked him, suctioning the seed from his cock with violent, ecstatic force. Panting, he collapsed onto the bed and pulled her close.

He didn't know how long they dozed, but he was awakened some time later by the unladylike growling of his wife's stomach. Smiling, he ran a possessive hand over her hip.

"Hungry, love? Emma packed a basket for us."

"Thank goodness for the dear," Marianne said ruefully. "I'm starved."

Ambrose went to fetch the basket, and they had a midnight picnic upon the bed. Feasting on roasted chicken, pickled garden vegetables, and fresh baked bread, they reminisced about the past and talked of the future. Earlier this month, Ambrose had given his notice at Wapping. To his surprise, he'd grown tired of being a soldier—he now wanted to march to his own drum. With Marianne's encouragement, he'd decided to open a private investigation agency.

"By the by," Marianne said, "I have something for you."

"I thought we agreed on no gifts for our anniversary," he said with faint alarm.

It was one of the few sticking points between them. Marianne enjoyed showering him with *things*. While he appreciated the thought, he felt wholly inadequate at returning the favor. When it came to trinkets, his wife had expensive tastes, and since he refused to touch her money, he was left with few options. He'd stuck with poesies and the like and though Marianne always had stars in her eyes when he bought her anything, privately he wished he might give her more.

Thank God for his mother's ring. It was one thing he'd given Marianne that he knew she adored, for she never took it off. The emerald winked at him now as she handed him a box the size of a pack of cards.

"It's not a gift for our anniversary," she said. "Open it."

Resigned, he untied the ribbon and lifted the lid. An elegant silver calling card case gleamed in a nest of tissue. He took the case out, his thumb brushing over his engraved initials.

"It's very fine," he said. "Thank you."

"Look inside," she said.

The case contained thick ivory calling cards, with his name, the direction to his new office, and the words "Enquiries Welcome" embossed in black.

"I hope I had enough made. You're going to be such a smashing success," she said confidently.

Emotion tightened his chest. He didn't know what he'd done in his life to deserve such a woman. Putting the box down, he leaned over and kissed her with everything he had been, was, and hoped to become.

"You're very welcome," she said breathlessly, moments later.

He caressed her cheek. "You've given me so much, Marianne. It shames me to say that I haven't anything to offer in return."

"As a matter of fact, that is untrue."

"I mean any material thing," he clarified. "You must know that my heart and my soul are yours."

"That's comforting to know, of course," his wife replied, "but in addition you have recently given me a rather substantial and undoubtedly material gift."

He gave her a puzzled look. "My mother's ring? I gave that to you months ago."

"Guess again, darling."

"That volume of poetry I gave you last week was hardly substantial," he muttered.

She peered at him from beneath her lashes. "Do you need a hint, Mr. Kent?"

Perplexed, he nodded.

"Now this gift has not yet arrived, but I believe you made an initial deposit during our stay with the Hartefords. In the solarium?"

His mind raced back two months. They'd spent Christmas at the Hartefords' country estate, where Marianne had orchestrated the wedding of Black's daughter. And alone in the solarium one midnight, beneath the twinkling stars, they'd—

His jaw dropped. "You're ... *increasing*?"

"Bull's-eye, Mr. Kent." Her eyes lit with laughter. "On all accounts."

With hands that shook slightly, he framed her face. "How are you feeling, love? Is there anything you need? Anything I should do—"

"Just love me, Ambrose," she said simply. "Love our family. That's all I need."

"To the end of my days," he said.

To seal his vow, he kissed her. She kissed him back. The wealth of their love flowed through him, and he knew that whatever their future held, it would be rich indeed.

From Grace's Desk

Dear Reader,

Thank you for reading *Her Protector's Pleasure*! Marianne and Ambrose stole my heart with their opposites-attract romance, and I hope you loved them too. You'll see more of this fan-favorite couple in the Heart of Enquiry series, which tells the stories of Ambrose's siblings finding love and adventure.

And for the final book in this series: *Her Prodigal Passion,* which features the romance between Charity Sparkler and her long-time infatuation Paul Fines. What's a wallflower to do when she has an unrequited passion for her best friend's brother? Find out in this steamy Cinderella story...which also has a marriage of convenience AND a prizefighter!

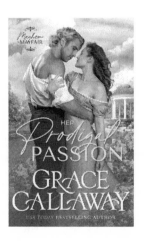

"I thoroughly enjoyed this story. Grace Callaway is a remarkable writer."
-Love Romance Passion

Until the next time...hugs and happy reading,

Grace Callaway

Acknowledgments

To my readers and fans: a huge THANK YOU for all your support! I'm so grateful to be able to share the world in my head with you. Like that first cup of coffee in the morning, your lovely emails and reviews get me up and going at my keyboard.

My appreciation also goes out to Rob Jeffries and Joz Joslin at the Thames River Police Museum. Thank you both for taking the time to share your extensive knowledge with me. Any historical inaccuracies in the work are entirely mine.

To my writing posse: Tina Folsom, you're an endless fount of energy, wisdom, and inspiration. Thanks for being there through thick and thin. Love you, girl. Virna De Paul, thank you for your insights on my work and for being a companion on this wild ride. And Diane Pershing: you always find the weaknesses and know exactly how to fix them. Bravo!

To my family, who puts up with a scribbling maniac: hugs and kisses to you all. To my husband, Brian: thank you for providing the real-life inspiration for my romances. And for copyediting until the wee hours of the night. And for cleaning the kitchen, doing laundry ... the list goes on. Smooches! And to our l'il buddy: you are our guiding star. Love you forever.

Last, but not least, this book is dedicated to my sister, who recognized the potential between Marianne and Kent before I did.

About the Author

USA Today & International Bestselling Author Grace Callaway writes hot and heart-melting historical romance filled with mystery and adventure. Her debut novel was a Romance Writers of America Golden Heart® Finalist and a #1 National Regency Bestseller, and her subsequent novels have topped national and international bestselling lists. She has won the Daphne du Maurier Award for Excellence in Mystery and Suspense, the Maggie Award for Excellence, the Golden Leaf, and the Passionate Plume Award, and her books have been shortlisted for numerous other honors. She holds a doctorate in clinical psychology from the University of Michigan and lives with her family in a valley by the ocean. When she's not writing, she enjoys dancing, dining in hole-in-the-wall restaurants, and going on adapted adventures with her special son.

Keep up with Grace's latest news!

Newsletter: gracecallaway.com/newsletter

facebook.com/GraceCallawayBooks

bookbub.com/authors/grace-callaway

instagram.com/gracecallawaybooks

amazon.com/author/gracecallaway

57368034R00229